The
OTHER SIDE *Of* VISIBLE

♛ ♛ ♛ ♛

A Novel By

JANET KELLER RICHARDS

Author's Website:
    www.janetkellerrichards.com
Facebook Page:
    Janet Keller Richards, username **@othersideofvisible**
(This information is correct at the time of printing.)

The Other Side Of Visible is copyright © 2017 Janet Keller Richards. All rights reserved. No part of this book may be used or reproduced in any manner whatsoever, including electronically or in printed form, without prior written permission from the author, except in the case of brief quotations embodied in articles or reviews.

Cover photograph ID 32418970 © Lonely11 | Dreamstime.com
Cover design by Endless Press, www.endlesspress.org

This novel is a work of fiction. Names, characters, places, and incidents either are the product of the author's imagination or are used fictitiously. Any resemblance to actual events, locales, organizations, agencies, or to persons living or dead is entirely coincidental and beyond the intent of the author.

ISBN Paperback: 978-0-9857450-2-8
ISBN Ebook: 978-0-9857450-3-5

Printed in the United States of America

23 22 21 20 19 18 17
7   6   5   4   3   2   1

DEDICATION

To my true Prince with all my love. For the sake of our great big family scattered all over the world.

To my earthly prince, my husband. You have profoundly enriched my life with your treasures of love, encouragement, and so much more.

CHAPTER ONE

Shin shot up out of a sound sleep. Her heart was pounding hard against her ribcage, her lungs were inhaling air so fast they were making her dizzy, and every hair on the top of her head was tingling from fright. Clamping a hand over her own mouth to silence her gasping, she listened through the darkness to locate the source of the crashing noise.

Nothing. Not one unordinary sound. Only the usual night shift machine racket coming from Cutter's Garage next door.

Petrified to reveal her presence in the alleyway, Shin leaned silently to her left and groped for the steel pipe she kept next to her sleeping bag. Her fingers found its cold metal. She pulled it toward her and tightened her grip around it until her wrist ached.

Sitting as still as the pavement underneath her, Shin waited. But after several minutes with no more unexpected noises, she laid the pipe down and mentally scolded herself for being such a sissified wimp. Exhaling hard to push away thoughts of danger, she wondered if it was possible to dream such an ear-splitting sound.

She glanced up at the sky and noticed the night was still solid, with no sign of morning's thinning. Porky, her calico cat, appeared through the darkness and pressed against her side as though he wanted to be seen as important. Giving him a couple of strokes, she cleared her groggy throat. "It was nothing, Porky. Go back to sleep."

Yanking her sleeping bag against her neck to squeeze out the cold night air, Shin grabbed the one possession she still carried from when she'd lived with her mom—her stuffed toy dog, Herbie. Pulling him against her chest, she nestled back down into the warmth of her makeshift street home.

But no sooner had she shut her eyes to drift off to sleep than a booming clang let loose nearby. Metal slammed loudly against metal, too close to be a car wreck out on the street. Something or someone was bumping and ramming the low-tech alarm system of junk she'd set up around her alleyway cave!

As quickly as it had begun the sound ended, but by that time Shin was already crouching with the pipe in her hand. She mentally scoured her street home for an escape route and much to her horror, realized there was none. With a brick wall at her back, she'd unknowingly penned herself in by her own metal maze. There was only one way out, and that was to head straight toward the noise.

The tin door of her cave shook thunderously. Quivers of fear shot down Shin's spine and she panicked. Wildly flailing her pipe as a weapon, she barreled full steam ahead through the door and charged directly into a large body. Her pipe clubbed the shadowed figure hard enough that a gravelly male voice cursed loudly.

Kicking and shoving, she blindly tried to force her way past the intruder. But he was bigger and stronger, and her frenzied thrashing was no match for his hulking form. He wrenched the pipe from her hand, tossed it aside, and wrapped his arms around her torso. His iron grip tightened until Shin felt her stomach squeezing against her spine.

"Ya' little creep! You ain't goin' nowhere tonig—"

But just as the man started spitting out venomous threats,

Shin leaned down and found his arm with her mouth. Landing a bite, she sank her teeth in fiercely, as though her future on planet Earth depended upon it. Her attacker's voice bellowed and he loosened his hold.

In the few seconds he took to recoil from the pain she managed to break free. Taking off down the pathway her feet had tramped countless times, Shin instinctively navigated every turn and pothole and jutting chunk of metal. She rounded the corner at the end of the alley.

He was swearing and giving chase through the darkness. A wave of terror pursuing her, every muscle in Shin's body throbbed with the force of escape. She ran wildly, refusing to be overtaken.

While Shin darted as fast as her legs would carry her, surging all around her in the invisible realms there was a tremendous clash of claws, wings, laser-swords and otherworldly muscle. An unseen light-being called a dazzle pulled out his laser-sword and thrust it at a hideous charging drab. The vile creature instantly flew backward to avoid being pierced and then circled around to try and get at Shin from another direction.

The dazzle, whose name was Rahzell, called over to his partner. "Ahnah! The larger drab! It's heading straight for the girl!"

Ahnah jerked her head around just in time to catch a glimpse of the drab's dark form flying fast in her direction. "Take this, you foul beast!" she said under her breath, and swung her light-sword violently in a wide arc behind her. Surprising her enemy, Ahnah landed a hefty blow directly on its left shoulder. It reeled away and crumpled to the surface, crying out in agony and grabbing the wound with its claw.

The injured drab lay writhing in pain. Ahnah could see fresh puss oozing out of its cut. She started toward it to unleash one more powerful, incapacitating stroke, but before she got close enough, somehow the thing managed to rouse itself. Flapping its wings madly, it limped away until it was able to take off in erratic flight and disappear into the black of night.

Normally, she would've chased after it and given it the kind of thrashing it would remember for epochs to come. But the child's protection was priority. She called back to Rahzell, "I'll stay with the girl," and flew off to catch up to their charge.

♛

Shin careened through the tangle of city streets, desperately trying to shake off the human assailant still hot on her trail.

Near the charging earthman flew a second unseen drab, flapping its wings alongside and giving the man an earful. "Gaw, the little monster bit you! Don't let her escape! Catch her and pay her back for—" and in a sickening way, the drab became strangely excited and started trembling and wriggling. Its voice grew raspy, and it salivated large drops of yellow liquid that dripped from its fangs. "And pay her back for what she did. Get even! You deserve vengeance!"

Now, the running man couldn't actually hear the repulsive words the drab was spewing into his ear. Humans rarely comprehend directly what drabs or dazzles say. Naturally then, this earthling didn't audibly understand the suggestions being made by his malicious tag-along. Rather, the drab's vile talk registered inside the man as a sensation, like a thought, an emotion, an impression. And right away, he began thinking of all the ways he was going to hurt the girl when he caught her. And his hateful mug started to resemble the detestable leer of the beastly thing floating invisibly by his side.

While the drab was engrossed in all its deplorable trash-talk, Rahzell snuck up behind it and said to himself, "This is going be fun." Then, to catch the brute's attention he made one little sound. "Psst!" When the drab turned its beady eyes in his direction, he leaped forward and yelled, "BOO!"

The critter was so startled it accidentally released a cloud of putrid gas, shot straight up into the atmosphere, and quickly vanished from sight.

"Whooh, did you have to?" Rahzell waved his wings to dispel the fetid odor, flew sideways to get some fresh air, and then promptly turned his attention to the earthman. Pulling alongside, the dazzle laid a light-hand on his shoulder and expressed words like they were medicine. "My friend, you don't want to harm this child. There are better ways to spend your time. She's noble after all, a young woman to be treated with dignity."

The truth of Rahzell's words entered into the man's being as a healthy dose of guilt. He slowed his pace, yet stubbornly chose to continue chasing after Shin.

"Sir, you weren't created for this kind of violence. Remember your real color. Think of your true self."

Though with a little less conviction, in spite of Rahzell's counsel the mortal continued to run.

"All right, I will help you make a proper choice." And with that, the dazzle held his light-saber in front of the man's moving feet.

At that exact moment the runner's large form fell headlong onto the pavement. He smacked his face against the macadam and something in his nose crunched loudly.

"Ouaawch!"

"Oh." Rahzell grimaced. "That's going to hurt."

Stunned by the impact of his fall and tired from the chase, the man didn't move.

"But you'll be glad you stopped." Rahzell pulled closer and placed his unseen hand on top of the earthling's head. "I've spared you some future regrets, and if you'll sober up, eventually you'll understand what I'm saying is true."

Sitting up, the pained man groaned and quickly searched in his jacket for a handkerchief to stay the blood gushing from his nose.

Rahzell touched his nose and instantly the bleeding stopped. "I'd get to a hospital if I were you. That thing's going to swell like a new star." He smiled at the misguided man. "Farewell sir," he said, and lifted up and away to join his partner.

♛

Ahnah was keeping pace with Shin as she crossed streets, ran by an apartment building, a strip mall, a gas station, and finally circled around Everington Bank to cut through the opening in the fence at the back of the bank's parking lot.

Her lungs burned but Shin wouldn't stop. She raced to save her life, flying in and out of the neighborhood the way a bird flies in and out of shrubs. Before long she'd covered the whole distance to one of her secondary hiding places—a low archway between two storefronts, seven blocks away from her own alleyway cave.

By now the only sounds she was aware of were the slapping of her worn sneakers on the pavement and the inhaling and exhaling of her throbbing lungs. She slowed, and for the first time since exploding into a full throttle run, Shin came to a standstill and took a split second to glance behind her.

There was no sign of anyone nearby.

She ducked into the passageway and moved quickly toward its dark center. Hunkering down under the arch, she leaned against the old stones of the curved wall and sat on the cold cement floor.

Not a sound, you jerk! Shin silently commanded herself. Slowing her breathing, she locked her back, legs, and arms in place and sat completely, absolutely still. She didn't want to give that creep a clue as to her position, not by movement, nor by scent, not by one single, careless noise in the dark.

While she sat as motionless as the windless night, Ahnah hovered around her with all the vigilance of a trained Watcher. Like every other dazzle, she was composed of their realm's light, so it was normal for her to simultaneously share space with the physical matter of the archway. Now, as she circled around her statue-like human, she passed invisibly through stone and mud and mortar.

At the moment a completely different group of drabs floated in a nervous huddle off to Ahnah's left. She kept her eye on their activity. They didn't seem interested in attacking and stayed at a distance, but by their movements she could tell her closeness to the child was agitating them infernally. Sensing what their twisted little minds were thinking, she said, "Hear me, savages, this child doesn't belong to you. Even if she has given some assent to your conniving words, you don't own her. She's a Light-Seeker, and it's only a matter of time before your influence in her life will be finished."

Upon hearing Ahnah's honest words the three lingering drabs got all stirred up. Their gnarled bodies shook with fury, their dark wings trembled, and they flew toward her in a rage.

Ahnah unfurled her light-sword and stood at the ready.

It was true, since these drabs had influenced the child's life for quite some time, they felt she belonged to them. They wanted this human. But the pain and suffering that could be inflicted by a dazzle's light-sword posed a greater threat than being separated from their earthling.

Seeing the light-sword, the angry cluster of drabs hissed and spit but came no closer. Backing off to regroup, they soon began arguing among themselves, as each member of the threesome commanded the other two drabs to attack the dazzle. And when no one moved they loudly accused one another of cowardice.

The disagreement quickly escalated into a skyward brawl, and they forgot their present focus on Shin. Flying erratically in a clump, they smacked and pulled and clawed and scratched each other, their flurry of infighting continuing as they traveled upward. Finally, they flew so high, their whole lot disappeared from view.

Ahnah shook her head and sheathed her light-sword.

Even after countless encounters with drabs, she never failed to be amazed at their absolute depravity.

Turning her attention back to the earth child, she noticed that for the first time in more than ten earth minutes, the girl was stirring.

Now that Shin was no longer in immediate danger, she allowed herself to feel. Waves of relief and anger rippled through her body in a latent adrenaline rush, and she collapsed onto the pavement under the archway. Shivering violently, not so much from cold but from shock, her muscles wobbled and shook until her physical reactions ran their course and her trembling gradually subsided.

She sat up in the empty silence under the span of the archway. During three years of living on the streets she'd never once been attacked with that kind of violence. Even when people stole stuff, they hadn't been vicious or savage. *Whoever that guy was,* she thought, *I don't EVER wanna' meet him again!*

Shin glanced toward the arch's entrance and pulled her coat tighter around her waist. Wearing only a thin hoodie sweatshirt and jeans, she was starting to feel the chilly night temperatures in her bones. The fact that the stones around her dripped and oozed dampness made the cold even worse. Why had she thought this stupid place would work for hiding?

Pressing her hand on the pavement to shift her weight, Shin squished a pile of wet muck. *Ewww, gross!* Making a face, she held her hand to her nose and took a hesitant whiff. Fortunately, it was only mud.

Scraping as much of it as she could from her hand onto the wall to her right, Shin sighed miserably. Even if the place weren't a five-star hotel, she would stay put. The city after dark was way too risky for wandering around, especially in the projects where she'd set up camp. During the night hours her scruffy hoodie was enough to make her a target for roaming thieves. That lesson had been learned the hard way, by once losing a pair of good sneakers to some louse of a guy. She would just have to endure until morning.

Leaning back against the wall, Shin tried to push the attack out of her mind, but it kept creeping back as if it had squatter's rights. *Was that guy looking for food, or goods, or was it ME he was after?*

She closed her eyes and mentally retraced her steps to every place she'd gone that day: the zoo, the library, Fourth Street, Penn Avenue, Orange Street, and Southside park. *Did I do something that could have gotten somebody mad at me? Did I look anybody in the eye?* Always careful to scan her surroundings, she couldn't recall anyone studying her.

In the end, Shin made a decision to work much harder at staying unnoticed whenever she went out in public.

Ahnah sensed the girl's unsettledness and gently stroked her head with a light-hand. "There, there, child. Rest yourself. You're safe. The drabs have been dealt with. Those un-creatures won't bother you anymore tonight."

When Ahnah placed an invisible hand on her head, Shin experienced an immediate sense of being out of harm's way. Though she didn't physically feel the dazzle's touch, her whole body relaxed at once. And feeling tremendously tired, she lay down on the pavement to get some sleep.

CHAPTER TWO

Being invisible was the one thing in life Shin thought she did well. She could slink around with her eyes lowered, avoiding all bodily contact, and pretty much manage to be ignored by the whole world. On crowded city streets, in grocery stores, at the zoo or the library, most people didn't even know she was alive.

She called it being cloaked. And ninety percent of the time it worked, which was exactly what she wanted. There was no way she was going to let herself be caught and hauled back into that dreadful foster care system. One of the main reasons she'd worked so hard to master the art of cloaking was to stay out of sight from truant officers and other official snoops who could sabotage her quiet little life on the streets.

Of course, Shin had no idea how thoroughly and utterly visible she was, or that all her daily routines were under twenty-four hour surveillance. She knew nothing of the dazzles who followed her wherever she went, all around her alleyway, all around her daily begging territory, all around the city.

She was convinced she was invisible.

And when she crawled out of the small archway next to

Lou's Wash N' Dry Laundromat looking like she desperately needed Lou's professional help, Shin was unaware of the two watcher dazzles hovering by her side. She was also unaware that for the moment, there were no drabs in the vicinity.

Yawning, she stretched to un-kink cramped muscles that for too many hours had been contorted into the warmest possible sleeping positions. Under normal circumstances Shin wasn't a morning person, but on this day she couldn't have been happier to see dawn rising above the city rooftops.

She moved closer to the entrance of the laundromat and quietly peered inside. No one was washing clothes at the moment. Opening the door, Shin sneaked inside and disappeared into the ladies' room.

Thanks to Lou's unknowing generosity, five minutes later she stepped outside a little more awake, and with the remains of the archway's mud washed away. While considering what to do next, images of Herbie and Porky walked across her mind and stopped her in her tracks. *Blast! What if that creep took them?*

As her first pet, Porky was great company. He was a safe friend who purred whenever she fed him, and then roamed and reappeared like a homeless wanderer. They understood each other perfectly.

And as for Herbie, it didn't matter that she was twelve years old. Shin needed that stuffed dog. He was her only tie to the days before foster care, when she had still lived with her own family. That is, if a drunk mom and her live-in boyfriends could be called family. Herbie saw all the craziness then, as well as later, in each foster home. That was why, without ever saying a word, he could comfort her as good as a mama cat wrapping itself around its kittens.

He was older now but every bit as supportive, even if too much squashing had caused his Fox Terrier ears to fray, thinned his plaid dog suit, and put some bald spots in his fur. And somewhere along the line his right eye decided to look around the neighborhood all by itself.

But Shin didn't mind Herbie's abnormalities. They made him fit right in with her odd little family of three. She and Porky and Herbie got along just fine together.

Until that cruel thug turned their lives upside down. *Ugh! What a stupid beast of a man!* As a second unnerving thought shot through her brain, she smacked her thighs in disgust. *Oh no! What if he tries to take over MY alleyway?*

Losing Herbie and Porky was unthinkable. But equally as terrible was the idea that she could lose her home. She'd managed to camp tucked away in that alley for six and a half months, her longest time in a hideaway since taking to the streets three years earlier.

And now if that guy had a mind to, he could decide to stake a claim to her territory.

"You have no right to MY stuff or MY place!" she said out loud at the man as she gave the pavement an exasperated stomp. But she wasn't stupid. A skinny girl was no match for the kind of muscle that had attacked her. She could get as hot as a summer sidewalk about what he'd done, but in reality that thug could help himself to whatever he wanted. He could get away with the whole shebang.

"Ugh!" Shin punched the brick wall of the laundromat with her fist and then leaned against the building and rubbed her stinging hand. *Now what do I do?* Closing her eyes, she tried to come up with a plan. But the injustice of it all kept pulling her brain sideways into a rut of irritation and worry.

Being so preoccupied, Shin forgot all about scanning her surroundings. Chalk it up to not sleeping very well, or to worrying about Porky and Herbie, or to the fear of losing her alleyway. But whatever the cause, less than eight hours after resolving to be more careful, she mistakenly allowed herself to be uncloaked. To be un-invisible. And in the wrong place, at the wrong time.

Ahnah and Rahzell both noticed the slew of drabs

swarming around a group of approaching humans. They pulled closer to the girl.

"Company's paying a visit." Rahzell shook his head and added, "Man, there sure is a whole lot of ugly in that crowd!"

Being a leader and a warrior, Ahnah was by nature the more serious of the two dazzles. Even so, she couldn't help grinning at Rahzell's choice of words. He loved playing around with human expressions. She agreed with his assessment though: the drabs circulating around the earthlings were their usual hideous selves.

Both dazzles drew their weapons.

"Let's stand back-to-back and cover the girl with our wings," Ahnah said.

"Done." Rahzell took his place on one side of the girl and faced outward. Ahnah did the same on the other side, and they both unfurled their large wings, enclosing their human in light.

At the exact moment the dazzles' invisible wings covered her, Shin heard the sound of voices. Opening her eyes, she saw a group of male teenagers heading in her direction. They looked as if they were begging for trouble the way she begged for money. She lowered her head, shrank into her jacket, and turned away to slip into the laundromat before they took notice of her.

But it was too late.

"Hey chickenhead, where you goin'?"

Shin heard the teen's question and shot a glance up and down the street to look for other people. No one was in sight—a bad omen for her immediate future. *If I go inside they might follow me. Better to stay outside if there's trouble.*

The teenage bullies pulled around her in a semi-circle, each wearing an attitude. With their baseball caps on backward and their oversized pants drooping toward their kneecaps, the peach fuzz on their faces revealed they weren't quite men, but neither were they boys. Some were white-skinned and some were ebony, and all were heady to strut their power.

Pinned against the bricks in the middle of their gang, Shin reminded herself, *Don't look them in the eye and don't let them see I'm afraid.* Her hands in fists and her muscles taut, she lowered her head.

"Hey, check out the grubbies. She be homeless," one of them said.

Shin considered trying to break through their ranks to make a dash for it, but they were six and she was one. Instead, she decided it was the perfect time to disappear and go somewhere safe. Anywhere but in their circle.

Closing her eyes, she imagined Africa, one of the many lands she'd read about in her library books. In her mind she was soon on a faraway safari, watching a pride of lions off in the distance. The adult lions were stretched out for sleep as their cubs playfully tumbled over one another in the tall Serengeti grass.

While Shin pretended to be absent from city streets and impending trouble, eight drabs buzzed angrily above the teenage hoodlums. The girl child, the object of this particular strike, was hidden from their view under the wings of two dazzles. That agitated the drabs to no end, but none of them was foolish enough to move in any closer. They would stay well clear of their foes and focus their energies on inciting their male earthlings.

One drab flew straight into a teen and shrieked, "Don't just stand there, you mama's boy! Prove you're a man! Prove you've got guts and go after her!"

Like Rahzell, drabs also copied human language. But unlike the dazzle's fun-loving nature, they only imitated for the purposes of taunting, provoking, and tormenting earthlings.

The teen lunged and grabbed Shin's shirt, twisted it into his fist, and pulled her close. "Yo, Shorty, what's the verdict?" Inches from her own body, he sneered into her face, until a whiff of stench filled his nostrils. "Oh, man! She stanky!" Releasing his grip on her shirt, he backed off in disgust.

Another voice spoke from across the circle. "Yeah, well, I ain't interested. She spoiled goods, you know whut I'm sayin'?"

As the drabs throbbed back and forth, Ahnah motioned to Rahzell to surround the girl with his own wings and then promptly flew off through the wall of the laundromat.

Rahzell repositioned himself in front of the child and wrapped his wings around her human body.

A large drab flew over several of the kids and shouted at them. "Come, on, you namby-pamby cowards! Don't be such weaklings!"

A different drab landed on the head of the tallest teen and sank a claw into one of his shoulders. "She's an easy target! At least rough her up, you weasel!"

Shin was in and out of the circle, traveling back and forth in her imagination between the brick and cement of the city and the plains of Kenya. In Africa, evening was falling, the winds were blowing, and the lion pride was standing to move on from the shade of a large tree.

The sound of mucus being coaxed into a throat drew her back to the city sidewalk. A second later spit sprayed across Shin's face in tiny droplets. Another throat cleared. Wetness struck again, but this time a large, single glob landed squarely on her nose and dribbled down into her mouth.

Her body stood still.

The rain had come to the African plains and the lions were lying down to wait it out. It was a strong rain, a monsoon rain.

Soon, with laughter and husky, self-congratulating remarks, saliva was flying at Shin from all the around the half circle. Her face was the main target, but also her hair. Shirt. Jacket. Jeans. Shoes.

But just like when she'd been a young child, and the sounds of angry voices and flying fists had filled the atmosphere of their home—Shin was elsewhere. She'd vanished.

"Hey! You kids! What are you doing?"

Ahnah flew beside a man who had exited the laundromat and was walking toward the circle of teens.

Rahzell saw her next to the approaching human and put two and two together. "Way to go, Ahnah! Good move."

"Thank you, my friend. I thought so too." Smiling, Ahnah rejoined Rahzell in covering the girl.

In response to the voice hollering from beyond their circle, the teens stopped spitting momentarily.

The man shouted again, "You get out of here, you hear me? Go on, get to school and leave that girl alone!"

As the circle opened up and the teens reluctantly spread out, another wad of spittle hit Shin's neck.

"Sleazebag," one kid slurred her way.

"Cow," another said as he swaggered off in his hundred dollar sneakers.

The last one to pass by Shin lobbed a final loogie in her direction, but it missed and landed on the cement.

"NOW!" the commanding voice yelled.

The air became quiet.

"You okay?"

Her rescuer was beside her. From her downward view of the sidewalk she could see a pair of shiny black shoes. They were tramping on two wet circles of spit.

"Good thing I came outside for some fresh air."

His voice sounded nice, even kind, but Shin kept her head lowered. She didn't want him to see what a sleazebag cow looked like. Especially one that had hot tears rolling down her cheeks.

"Here. You can use this." The gentle voice offered her a small towel. "And if you want to, there's a bathroom in my laundromat where you can wash up."

Shin released her fists enough to take the towel from his extended hand.

"Sorry about those bullies. Have they caused you trouble

The Other Side Of Visible 17

before today?"

She shook her head and with the towel, slowly pushed at the slime on her face. It slid around and didn't come off so easily. But at least it camouflaged her crying.

"Are you Lou?" She was breaking her own rule of invisibility by speaking to him, but she wanted to move the conversation away from herself.

"Huh?"

"Lou of the laundromat."

"Oh. Roland. Lou was my grandfather. We never changed the name."

Shin wiped her face and neck. The shaking inside of her settled slightly.

"Listen, I have to get back to work. Before you head to school, if you want to use our bathroom to clean up, you feel free, okay kid?"

He patted her on the back. As he walked away, Shin raised her eyes enough to catch a quick glimpse of Roland, grandson of Lou. Dark hair, medium build, looked harmless. He thought she was normal: not spoiled goods, but a kid that went to school.

"Thank you," she called after him too quietly to be heard.

He disappeared into the wash n' dry and Shin finished wiping everything that was covered in spit. Still sticky, she decided, this time with the owner's full permission, to go inside and get rid of the remaining saliva. And while she was at it she would try to lessen her body odor. And maybe scrub off the mortification of being . . . of being . . . well, just of being.

A little while later, Shin emerged cleaner than she'd been in days, at least on the outside. She didn't know how to get rid of the awful stain on the inside.

Rahzell and Ahnah waited to put away their swords until the crowd of drabs had tagged along after their human posse and were long gone. When their young earthling exited the laundromat they floated along at her side and talked about the good things that were coming, about times when the child's present struggles would hold no more pain. At some point, they surmised she would discover the realm of OtherSide, a future prospective for which they were both particularly and immortally thankful.

CHAPTER THREE

A block away from Lou's Laundromat, Shin's stomach grumbled a desperate plea for coffee. Ever since someone offered her a sugary swig at the age of ten, a cup of java in the morning had become a daily essential. She needed coffee. Coffee would jumpstart her brain so she could figure out what to do about Herbie and Porky and her alleyway. Coffee would make her normal; less like homeless trash, and more like all the city people who drink it on their way to work.

She would go to the zoo.

One of her favorite places to hang out, the zoo took her far away from the city, to places she'd read about in books. Around the wild animals Shin could pretend she was in other lands—where monkeys or zebras or kangaroos lived—and imagine other, happier existences.

The best animals were the big cats. She often sat on the benches in front of the tigers or lions or leopards or cheetahs, watching them glide in and out of the trees on their large, padded feet. In their spotted or striped coats or their impressive manes, they were as regal as kings. It was as if they knew they were important, and no one could convince them otherwise.

She envied their self-confidence.

And thanks to some big honcho donor there was no admission charge for school-age kids, which meant she could come and go as often as she wished.

The zoo also happened to be her preferred begging area. In the morning before the day warmed up, little old men and women sat on benches along its tree-lined pathways, wasting hours together as if their lives would go on forever.

Now as she rounded the corner at the entrance gate and walked up to the first bench, her empty stomach rumbled a second time. Holding out her hand toward two gray-topped, prune-like faces, she focused on her own fingers and avoided their eyes. "Please, may I have a dollar for breakfast?"

They shook their heads and she moved on.

For a second or two Shin considered staging a hunger strike. With all that had happened during the last twelve hours, begging for food felt about as pleasant as a splinter. But she had to get coffee in order to think more clearly about her present predicament.

Another plump zoogoer sat to her right feeding pigeons. This lady was one of the regulars at the zoo and could always be relied on for some coins. But she was far too talkative, and since Shin's goal was to be entirely cloaked, all that chatter was plain nerve-racking.

Under normal circumstances Shin only begged from her as a last resort. But today, the sooner she could get food money, the better. For a quick buck she'd tolerate the old biddy. *There's gotta' be a better way*, she thought honestly, and walked in her direction.

The woman was leaning forward and chatting in a singsongy voice to a pigeon darting back and forth on the ground. The bird flew away as Shin pulled up and faced the lady. Averting her eyes, she stared at the paisley design on the woman's skirt. Forcing a polite tone, she said, "Good morning, could you spare some change, or maybe a dollar or two for coffee and a muffin?"

She could feel the elderly woman gazing at her, as if searching for something in her face.

After a brief inspection the lady answered with all sincerity, in a warbled voice that belied her age. "Thank you so much for coming again, dear one. I do appreciate your asking me!"

Shin's eyeballs bored a hole into the pattern on the woman's skirt. She shifted back and forth from one foot to the other. *Why is she thanking me for begging from her?*

There were loads of compartments in the lady's purse. Slowly, she fumbled through each one in search of some coins. But in the end she looked up at Shin apologetically. "Oh dear, I can't seem to find my change just now." At once, she sat up taller and clapped her hands together. "But I have a brilliant idea! Shall we go to breakfast together? It'll be my treat. You can have bacon and eggs, toast, or oatmeal. You can eat whatever your little tummy is hungry for. How does that sound to you?"

Blinking, Shin pulled her eyes over to the nearby bushes. She certainly was hungry enough for all that food, but this wasn't her usual interaction with the woman. Her suspicious brain quickly turned the white-haired grandma into a foster agency spy whose all-too-eager smile was concealing a sinister plan to capture her and drag her straight back into the system. Glancing to her left, she searched the bushes for hidden accomplices. Even though she didn't see anyone, it didn't mean they weren't there. After all, spies were good at disguising themselves.

For fear of being lured into a trap, Shin justified passing up a huge breakfast. *I mean, who would wanna' sit with such an old geezer for a whole meal, anyway?* "No thanks," she answered minimally, and backed away from the bench to head toward the zoo's exit.

The woman called after her. "Well, dear one, I do understand. After all, who would want to sit with such an old geezer for a whole meal?"

Shin stopped and jerked her head around. *She just repeated my exact thought!* Quite by accident, she caught sight of the woman's face, and for a few seconds their eyes met. Gazing back at her were two round, dark pupils that were swimming with kindness. She yanked her eyes away and fixed them on the arm of the bench.

Piping up with another suggestion, the woman said, "Well then, why don't I give you a bill so you can go eat breakfast? And when you're finished, just return the leftover change to me." The lady's wrinkled hand promptly reached into her purse, produced a one hundred dollar bill, and held it out for the taking.

Shin had never laid eyes on such a large bill, and having it waved in front of her face threw her completely off balance. She pulled her eyes downward and honed in on the weeds under the bench. *This lady is bonkers! Totally crazy!*

Images of all the stuff one hundred smackers would buy flashed through her mind. She could get a new rain poncho, a flashlight, some jeans and shirts at the thrift store, and maybe even a coat. Plus, she could eat real meals for a couple of days!

"Okay, I can bring it back," she answered with all the genuineness of a pack rat. Grabbing the bill out of the woman's hand, Shin started off in the direction of The Hungry Appaloosa Diner.

The wobbly elderly voice called after her, "I'll be here until ten o'clock this morning, dear one. Otherwise, you'll have to give me the change tomorrow."

"Uh, okay." Waving a response, Shin kept walking as though the money would disintegrate if she didn't use it real soon.

Priscilla, the kind woman Shin had pegged as "Bonkers,"

happened to be intimately acquainted with OtherSide. She was also keenly aware that valiant dazzles and contemptible drabs flew just beyond the veneer that separated Earth's realm from the invisible realms.

Her morning routine of going to the zoo had nothing to do with feeding pigeons or frittering away time. And though she did thoroughly enjoy watching the big cats, her true reason for sitting in front of their habitats each day was none other than to help recolor the life of the young runaway who panhandled from her more or less regularly.

This little old lady knew about the realm of UnderSide and about its strategy to uncolor Earth by ruining one human at a time. In fact, Priscilla understood that for his entire despicable existence as the leader of UnderSide, the Light Stealer had existed for one single, solitary passion. He was determined to replace every bit of light on planet Earth with heinous blackness.

This horrid chief had decided long ago that absolutely no light or color—since light is the embodiment of all the colors mingled together—should be allowed to exist anywhere in the sphere of mankind.

He constantly barked sinister commands to his drab supervisors. "Get rid of every putrid ray! Annihilate every beam! Remove every tint or dye! Eradicate them! Don't even speak those obnoxious words in my presence, unless it's to tell me the repulsive stuff has been eliminated from planet Earth!" And then he stamped his beastly feet, twisted the wrinkles of his hideous face into hard lines, and threatened everyone with painful torture if they didn't meet his demands.

But in spite of all his bellowing the Light Stealer had a problem. And it was this: the commander of UnderSide hadn't created the sun, which meant he couldn't uncreate the sun. Neither had he created color, so he certainly couldn't uncreate it. He wasn't that powerful. His utter inability to uncreate anything made it necessary to search for another way to destroy light and color on planet Earth.

Light Stealer stewed and paced and murmured and cogitated about how he could effectively stop light. Then one day, deep in the bowels of his demented little brain, he hit upon a plan to systematically eradicate both light and color from Earth. A real plan. One he was certain would succeed. When he got it, the ruler of UnderSide was so pleased with himself, he cackled a great disturbing laugh and danced a perversely happy jig. His officer drabs didn't know what to do, since they'd never seen their leader dance, even if it was a terribly villainous dance.

"Aha! Why didn't I see it before? Of course! Of course, that's IT!" Light Stealer slapped the ranking officer to his left with a painful whack on the shoulder. He tittered, snickered, and then burst into a deviant guffaw, laughing so hard he almost fell off the step next to his grandiose, black throne. When at last he gathered his dark wits about him, Light Stealer calmly sat down and casually slouched his spiny back against his throne. Propping his angular feet on a footstool, he placed his sharp elbow on the armrest and rested his pointy chin on his claw. From this relaxed position he proudly announced the plan.

"My fiends"—*my fiends* was how the Light Stealer addressed his officers when he was pleased with himself—"I have concluded that we cannot remove"—and here Light Stealer, who, for obvious reasons loathed even his own name, cringed and could not bring himself to say the word *light*. "My fiends, we cannot remove that ghastly substance from planet Earth. No, we cannot. Nor can we remove col—" He was trying to say the word *color*, but that too, was painfully impossible for him to speak. "Nor can we remove pigment from Earth." He managed to say *pigment*, because the chief's favorite earth animal was the pig, and by adding *-ment* he could spit it out with some force.

The ruler of UnderSide sat up and narrowed his eyes until

they were hard slits. "But the answer, lamebrains, the answer has been right in front of you, as plain as the snouts on your beastly little heads!"

He stood and began to pace with excitement, stopping directly in front of an officer drab. The drab saluted his master and stood nervously at attention. Light Stealer leaned in until they were nose-to-nose and eye-to-eye and then roared at the top of his lungs. "WE CANNOT REMOVE THAT GHASTLY SUBSTANCE, BUT WE CAN BLIND HUMANS FROM BEING ABLE TO SEE IT!"

Sputum and spittle from the Light Stealer's mouth showered the ranking drab with sticky globs. The officer blinked, but to preserve his own hide he didn't flinch even one hardened sinew. And to his relief, the commander-in-chief turned away and shouted up toward the ceiling, like a mad emperor.

"WE WILL MAKE THEM PIGMENTBLIND!"

While the Light Stealer expounded on his plan the whole company of officer drabs leaned in and hung on every nuance of every syllable of every word. Like it or not, they and their underling drabs would be expected to carry out his strategy with absolute success. And wherever they failed, there would be swift and dreaded reprisals. In the realm of UnderSide, even the smallest defeat resulted in cruel punishments.

Here was their ruler's strategy: from that moment on, the whole of UnderSide was to focus on making the lives of human beings wretched, insufferable, and miserable. In this way, they could be made to lose hope. And eventually, with time and sorrow, people would begin to perceive the world as dull and gray, as dark and colorless, and without possibility or promise. As humans forgot about goodness, their internal eyesight would grow dim and their light would fade, since everyone knows—and even Light Stealer is fully aware of this—that goodness and color and light are inseparable.

This is exactly how it came to be that color was systematically and gradually removed from the human world. A gloomy pall was all that remained during the day, giving way to inky blackness at the deepest part of night.

Of course, scientifically speaking, color on Earth hadn't disappeared. And light still arrived every morning in the planet's cycle of nighttime and daytime. But humans could no longer see their world in its full reality. They were no longer aware the atmosphere was brilliantly crystal clear, or that its surface exploded with crimson reds, sapphire blues, royal purples, vibrant yellows, and a host of other colors. Instead, they became accustomed to living in murky grayness. They were pigmentblind and no longer remembered or believed that color existed.

But Ambassador Priscilla Conrad, who watched as Shin retreated from her bench, could see the beautiful colors of the green trees and the bright orange flowers and the deep blue sky. She was well acquainted with the invisible light that pierced through the veneer from OtherSide, the light that was the source of every orb of light in the universe.

Quietly, the distinguished grandma held out her hand to unleash a shining. Flaring out from her palm, the powerful beam of OtherSide light hit Shin squarely in the back, flowed through her body, and circled firmly around her heart.

Shin paused. Though unaware of the shining, out of the gray she started to feel terribly guilty for stealing the woman's money. And then she remembered. *Wait. The lady GAVE me the money to use for breakfast.* She was allowed to treat herself before returning the rest of the money! A warm feeling spread through her chest and she continued on her way, salivating at the thought of the lip-smacking meal she was about to inhale.

CHAPTER FOUR

On those rare occasions when begging brought in five or ten dollars, Shin usually took the cash and headed to her favorite diner, The Hungry Appaloosa. Always busier than a beehive, the restaurant had a seat-yourself policy and waitresses who never asked questions. Plus, the portions were large enough to feed a whole herd of wildebeests. It was the perfect place to stay cloaked while stuffing her face.

Sitting near the rear entrance with a one hundred dollar bill in her pocket, stuffing was exactly what she did. After three and a half gargantuan, trucker-sized flapjacks, a side of bacon, and two cups of coffee, Shin was so full she could hardly move. She downed a last bite of pancake, wiped her mouth with a napkin, and gulped the rest of the coffee in her mug.

Getting up slowly, she waddled to the cash register to pay for the meal. Handing over her diner bill and the money, she held onto the take out bag that contained half a pancake for Porky's breakfast. She always saved some food for her cat and hoped she'd be able to find him later in the day.

"Hmmmm." The register man scowled. "Young lady, this seems like a lot of money for you to be carrying." He held the one hundred dollar bill up to the light to search for the

Federal Mint's hidden identity stripe.

Shin hadn't seen this guy before and didn't think about the fact that someone could question a larger bill. Fixing her eyes intently on a goober-like stain in the middle of his tie, she said, "It was lent to me by a lady in the park. I'm gonna' take the rest of it back to her."

The man leaned down close to her face and waved his crooked finger. She was forced to shift her stare to the tip of his nose.

He squinted and his nose hardened to resemble the beak of a hawk. "You be sure to return all of it, you hear?" Straightening his stance, the man put the bill in his register and handed her the change.

"I will, I promise!" She locked her gaze on the money being put in her hand and tried to sound as convincing as possible.

Once outside, Shin stuffed the cash into the pocket of her jeans and started walking down the sidewalk. Tossing the receipt on the ground, she also threw away her promise to the register guy.

During breakfast her mind had begun spinning with all the things the leftover money could buy. Before long she was pushing down guilt that poked at her insides. And by the time she took her last bite of pancake, she'd managed to justify spending the entire remaining wad.

Her fingers played with the crinkled bills in her pocket. Giddy at the idea of being able to buy stuff, Shin considered her options. Her first stop would be new duds at the thrift store on Second Street. That way, at least for a while she could look just like everybody else. Living on the streets, clothing inevitably got dirty and smelly, but until her new purchases became soiled, she would appear normal.

As she pulled up to the corner and waited for the walk signal to cross the street, a realization burst into her mind. *Wait! If I don't return the old lady's change, I'll never be able to beg from her again!* Cheating the woman would mean finding a whole new place to panhandle, and that was no small thing. The last time she'd tried to change begging areas, Shin had gone hungry for days. Besides, she liked the zoo too much to give up going there regularly.

Aw, man. A good begging connection is worth more than a hundred dollars! Well, ninety dollars, with breakfast and the tip. She tipped whenever she could, because if she were a waitress she'd want to be tipped.

But what if my stuff is gone from my cave? I could really use this cash! Frowning, Shin's shopping mood fizzled and she knew what she had to do.

She turned back and headed toward the zoo, and before long she was approaching the woman. With her eyes trained on the money in her hand, she stopped in front of the lady's bench. "Brought your change."

Caught dozing, a flustered Priscilla sat up quickly. "Oh, thank you! Perfect!"

"I gave a tip too, but the rest is all there. You can count it if you want to." Shin handed her the crinkled bills from her pocket and all the coins.

"Oh, that won't be necessary. I trust you, dear one." The woman put the money back in her purse, leaned in closer, and whispered as though revealing a secret. "I can see you're a Light-Seeker."

"Yeah, well, thanks a lot." Shin had no idea what it meant to be a Light-Seeker, and she wasn't about to ask. She turned to leave.

"Don't you want to know what a Light-Seeker is?"

Lady, I just wanna' get out of here, was what she thought. But she'd just scored a generous hit from the old coot. Even if she didn't want to stay, Shin knew it would be stupid to blow her off. Turning back, she shrugged reluctantly and stared down at the scuffs on her sneakers. "I guess so."

The woman glanced at her watch and clucked her tongue.

Standing up, she changed her mind. "Well I can't tell you today, dear one. I don't have enough time. Come back tomorrow and we'll have breakfast together. And then I'll tell you all about the Light-Seekers."

That's when the lady's whole plan became glaringly obvious. *THAT'S what she's up to! She's baiting me today so she can turn me over to the authorities tomorrow!*

"And I promise, I'm not baiting you and I have no intentions of turning you over to the authorities tomorrow. Or any other day, for that matter. That's as certain as the sky is blue, dear one!"

Shin gasped. This woman was either clairvoyant or certifiably nuts! Clairvoyant, because that was the second time she'd repeated her exact thought. And nuts, because everybody on Earth knew the sky was a dull gray and not *blue*, whatever blue was supposed to be.

"Uh, I gotta' go. Thanks again for breakfast." Shin took off at a trot toward the zoo's exit. She was in a hurry to get away from such a wacky encounter. And she wished the loony old woman would stop calling her *dear one*.

"See you tomorrow, dear one!" Priscilla called out affectionately, and waved goodbye. Standing up to leave the zoo, she released another shining in Shin's direction.

Across the veneer, Ahnah and Rahzell followed their girl child, smiling gratefully. Priscilla's shining had surrounded them with the glow of OtherSide, and they were both feeling quite refreshed and invigorated.

Rahzell tilted his head toward his partner. "What do you think our Little Streak is up to now?"

"Little Streak?"

"It's my new name for the girl. She doesn't quite run with the speed of a dazzle, but for a human she can keep a good pace."

Ahnah enjoyed working alongside this amusing one. He sure made things interesting. Now he was imitating human beings by creating nicknames.

"Ah. I say she'll want to check on her Earth home."

"And I think you'll be right about that."

Ahnah sighed ardently. "I hope her time is coming soon."

"To meet them, you mean."

"Yes. Nothing will thrill me more than to see her with them."

They both understood by *them,* Ahnah was referring to OtherSide's benevolent sovereigns, the royal Original Family.

Little Streak, as Rahzell had named Shin, decided for the sake of Porky and Herbie and her stuff, she had no choice but to check on the condition of her cave.

Absorbed by the thought of temporarily having a one hundred dollar bill in her hands, Shin jogged toward her alleyway. She regretted having to give the money back. Yet without question, the zoo was one of her best sources for food money. She felt she'd made a wise decision. *But, what a WEIRDO!* She sniggered and made up her mind to give that odd woman a nickname. From now on she would call her "Crazy Lady."

Approaching the north end of the alleyway where her cave was situated, Shin slowed her pace and tiptoed so she could be especially cloaked. For all she knew, her attacker was lurking right around the corner, waiting to pounce on her a second time. Her armpits leaking sweat, she moved cautiously along the front of the abandoned store adjacent to her alley. Sidling up to the corner and peering carefully around the edge, she scanned her cave and the surrounding junk.

He was not there.

But she wasn't about to risk exposing herself to danger, so just to be sure, Shin inspected every piece of metal and every scrap of clutter, back and forth, up and down. Then she studied it all a second time. And finally, though still leery that someone could appear from out of nowhere, she took a couple of uneven strides into the alleyway and walked toward her cave.

Standing over her things, she was amazed nothing was missing.

"Herbie!" With a relieved sigh, Shin picked up her stuffed dog and gave him an eye-threatening squeeze.

Everything else was in its place: her sleeping bag, two library books, her ratty second pair of pants, her second shirt with holes in both arms, her plastic garbage bag that she used as a makeshift rain poncho, and her meager toiletries. All of her belongings were right where she'd left them.

Shin was as confused as ever. *So, who WAS that guy, if he wasn't out to take my stuff?* Thinking of his possible motives gave her the willies. A cold shiver ran down her spine and into her legs, so that she involuntarily jerked and looked like she was doing a little jig. But as she glanced around, dancing was the farthest thing from her mind.

Just then the Pit Bull over at Cutter's junkyard started barking savagely. Though chained to a doghouse, its vicious yelping was enough to make Shin jump with fright. She twisted around to search for whoever or whatever had caused it to bark so wildly. But she was alone. It was barking at her. "Be quiet! It's just me!" With her hands on her hips she demanded, "Why didn't you bark that way last night? You could've warned me that creep was around. Where was your ferocious barking then?"

The dog got distracted and stopped yelping.

"Fine watchdog you are. Stupid mutt."

After recovering from being scared out of her wits, Shin turned her attention back to her alley. An old car fender lay in the middle of the pathway. Picking it up, she shoved it back in its place near her cave's entrance. *Maybe he tripped and fell over this.* She was grateful the metal stuff she'd placed all around had done its job of warning her of danger. But one thing was certain. An escape route would definitely be in place before nightfall.

That is, IF she decided to stay.

Because now she had a problem. Her alleyway was the perfect place for her to hide away from annoying people on crowded city streets. But as a result of last night's attack, a malicious bully knew where she lived. And just to be mean, he could return whenever he felt like it and strong-arm her world into oblivion.

While Shin considered her options, Ahnah and Rahzell floated nearby. Ahnah saw movement out on the street. "Uh oh. We've got a situation."

"We certainly do." Rahzell noticed the two earthmen at the same moment. They were walking toward the alleyway. One wore a uniform the dazzles recognized as a symbol of law-keeping authority in the realm of humans.

"They have none of our light." Ahnah was scanning the two men, searching for any trace of OtherSide. She found nothing whatsoever.

"That could explain why there are three seriously repulsive drabs trailing them."

"This is not her time, Rahzell. She's not to be caught in this way."

"My thoughts exactly." He flew next to the girl. Leaning in, he said affectionately, "Little Streak, this is not the correct time for you to be taken into custody. That will come later. Right now, you need to run away."

"I'll handle the drabs," Ahnah said.

Rahzell smiled. "And I'll go with Little Streak when she takes off."

"Stellar. See you on the other side." Ahnah pulled out her sword and flew straight at the approaching humans. The drabs behind the two men saw her light-saber and backed off in the opposite direction. She pursued them to be certain they wouldn't circle around and make trouble for the girl child.

As Ahnah chased after the drabs, the two men appeared at the south end of Shin's alleyway.

A police officer walked beside Mr. Cutter, the owner of the salvage yard next door. As Cutter spoke to the cop he lifted his tattered baseball cap to scratch his balding head. Glancing casually in Shin's direction, he did a double take, put the cap back on his head, raised his voice, and pointed. "Hey! She's the one who lives here! That's her stuff!"

Lost in contemplation about whether to stay in the alley or move her things to another location, Shin heard a voice. Looking up, she saw Cutter and a policeman heading her way. At the sight of a law officer all systems hit panic mode, and while the cop was still registering in her brain, her leg muscles were already reflexively bolting toward the north end of the alleyway.

"Stop! We only want to ask you some questions!" the police officer shouted.

Ignoring the voice, Shin kicked into an escape plan she'd worked out soon after setting up her cave in the alleyway. She shot across the street, dangerously dodging a car whose driver was forced to slam on his brakes. Continuing to run, she vaguely heard the chain reaction of blaring horns from other vehicles behind the first car.

Down the next street, she split right into another alley, and then left through an old cellar door. She crossed out into a third alleyway. Taking another right turn, she could hear someone was pursuing her. Her friend Dibs had once told her that in a race even a single backward glance wasted precious seconds. So she ran without looking back, faintly hearing the thick cellar door open and then close some distance behind her.

"Stop, and you won't be harmed!"

Shin heard the command in the distance and kept running. She turned onto Newberry Street, tearing up the sidewalk like her feet were on fire. There was an opening in the traffic and she sprinted across, aiming for Penn Avenue. If she could reach its corner several seconds ahead of her pursuer, she planned to lose him by a series of switchbacks.

Penn Avenue was a very short block and it had a public restroom right around the corner. She darted into the ladies' room and stood behind the cement wall at the opening, breathing as quietly as possible for someone who had been charging at full speed.

Perhaps seven seconds later Shin heard the sound of footsteps running by the restroom. Counting five seconds after they passed, she emerged cautiously to see if her pursuer had cleared the end of the block.

He was nowhere in sight.

Doubling back onto Newberry Street, she turned left, sprinted to the end of the fourth building, and turned left again into a small passageway.

The passage fed into a grassy patch between the back yards of two lines of city row homes. Not wanting to draw attention, Shin slowed her pace to a fast walk. She reached the end of the block and glanced all around to make sure she was alone. Seeing the coast was clear, she quickly entered through a rickety gate in the high wooden fence that surrounded the last row home on the right.

Closing the gate behind her, she stood in the back yard of an abandoned property. A tall, outdoor cabinet sat to one side of the yard. Opening it, she stepped inside its empty frame. Here she'd visited twice before, and here she would stay, hidden from the police until danger passed.

She looked down. Herbie was still in her left hand. Hugging her stuffed dog close to her chest, she leaned against the wall of the cabinet and slowly slid down to a sitting position.

Panic subsided. In its wake was a jumbled mess of thoughts about Cutter, the cop, her alleyway, and last night's thug. Shin sighed and slouched down even farther. Propping her elbows on her knees, she grabbed her head in her hands and willed her mind to go somewhere else. Picturing herself standing on the grassy knoll of a photo in a familiar library book, she watched as a small band of gorillas ambled down a well-worn pathway in the Congo. Rich scents of the forest floor were all around her. She inhaled deeply. The gorillas started feeding on low-hanging fruit from several large trees.

Shin yawned and opened her eyes. Her mind had quieted. Being tired from lack of sleep the night before, and with syrup and pancakes sitting heavily in her stomach, she became drowsy. Before long, in the privacy of the backyard hideaway, she was dozing soundly.

CHAPTER FIVE

Rahzell stood by while the child rested inside the large wooden box. He was vigilant and ever mindful of three drabs hanging around in the vicinity, the same cluster that often bothered the girl because they wanted her. He rankled with disgust at the idea that drabs used unknowing humans to express themselves.

"Good thing there are shinings being released into her little life," he said to no one in particular.

The girl began to move.

"Well, good day, child!" Rahzell knew Little Streak wouldn't hear his indomitable cheer, but he couldn't help himself.

Shin woke up with a start and caught her breath. She'd been dreaming, standing inside a brilliant light that engulfed the whole atmosphere with a glare stronger than fire. In the brightness of its blazing intensity, all her personal flaws had been completely visible. She had nowhere to hide.

Groaning, she sat up and pushed the nightmare out of her mind. Drool ran down her chin. As she wiped it with a sleeve, neck muscles pulled that had become stiff from sleeping awkwardly against the side cabinet. Stretching slowly, she took a peek outside and saw dusk was approaching, which meant she'd sacked out for a long time.

Her stomach gurgled. She remembered the huge pancakes she'd eaten that morning and thought of her bizarre encounter with Crazy Lady. From there, her mind wandered to Mr. Cutter and the policeman, and the reality of her present situation hit her like an unexpected smack on the face. *Aw, man! I have no sleeping bag, no extra clothing, no rain gear, and no toilet paper!* She slammed her fist against the sidewall of the cabinet. *And what about my library books?*

In addition to the zoo, Shin loved to visit the library. Although Falisha, a pretty library worker in her mid-twenties and an adult she sort of trusted, had made it very clear to her that absolutely no begging was allowed on library property.

Shin was positive the lady had figured out she didn't live in a real home. For one thing, in order to borrow stuff from the library, people first needed to fill out a form giving their address and phone number. But the first time she'd worked up the courage to ask about checking out books, Falisha hadn't asked her for any information. Instead, she'd typed a generic code into the computer, one workers used when they needed to access the library's electronic catalog of information.

Thanks to the young woman's generosity, from that time on Shin had borrowed three or four books each week. Then, during the middle of each day, when the gray sky hung close to the ground and the air molecules refused to move, she'd hide away from the world and devour pages and chapters and stories and a plethora of information.

Until her present dilemma, she'd always been careful to keep the library's books dry, and to return them on time. For a fact, she knew the two books at her cave were due in three days. But with a cop in the picture, going back to get them was out of the question.

Now what do I do? Shin punched her thigh in frustration and bit her lip. Tears tried in the worst way to come up and spill out of her eyes. She angrily wiped them away and told herself to stop blubbering. No one was going to come to her rescue. It was up to her to work things out. Either she stayed in the cramped cabinet to shiver out the night, or she came up with another solution.

But she was having trouble thinking clearly about what to do because she really had to go to the bathroom. And she wasn't about to do it in that backyard.

An idea flickered inside her head. *Dibs! I haven't seen him for a few days! Maybe I could stay at his place tonight.* He was the closest thing she had to a friend. Solo even longer than her and two years older, he understood all about life on the streets.

She shifted her position and leaned against the rear wall. If she was going to choose that option it had to be fast, before night arrived.

Climbing out of the wooden box, she peered through the cracks in the fence around the yard. No one was in sight. She opened the rickety gate and stepped out onto the grass. If she jogged part way, there would still be enough time before dark for a fast bathroom stop to wash her face, drink some water, and use the toilet.

As she broke into a run Rahzell trailed closely, followed at a distance by three annoyed drabs. Unwilling to yield their territory so easily, the drabs seemed determined to wait for the next opportunity to rejoin their human.

Six city blocks later, Shin stood safely in front of a tall, dented metal door that was covered in graffiti and grime. She rapped on the door using the code they had established for those rare occasions when she came into Dibs' domain: one single tap, three rapid knocks, and ending with another single tap.

Ten seconds later the door opened far enough that she could see Dibs peering out at her.

"Shinny! Visiting me!" He caught the miserable look on her face. "Wait a second." Going away briefly, he returned with a key and unlocked a padlock that held together two links of a chain. Removing the lock and pulling the chain off, he opened the door and backed away so she could step into his abandoned warehouse. "You must be in trouble."

Shin pushed past him and entered the place he called home. Far nicer than her alley cave, he had a sofa, a little table, an office chair, and even an oil lamp. True, they were all shabby, and the sofa smelled of rat urine, but when it rained he was dry and relatively warm in his hideaway. She envied him and felt sorry for herself.

"I lost everything! Again! A cop chased me like I'm some sort of criminal, and I can't go back or he'll nab me!" In exasperation Shin slapped the support beam next to her, and a hollow metal thud reverberated throughout the room. "How many times do I have to start over and find new stuff? Ugh!" She sat down on the sofa, put Herbie beside her, and rubbed the sting of the slap from her hand. "And my library books are there!" She let out another groan.

Dibs, being generally in a good mood, sat down beside her. "Tell you what, Shinny. You can stay here tonight, no worries. And tomorrow we'll look for a place that'll be way better than your cave. Guaranteed." Like a fourteen-year-old big brother would do, he reached over and playfully gave her head a knuckle rub. "How's that sound, huh?"

Shame, one of the three drabs floating nearby, watched the hovering dazzle and carefully moved in a little closer. "You don't deserve this, bad girl! You can't accept his help, because you're nothing but street trash!"

"Stand back, scoundrel." Rahzell moved toward the drab, but not so far away from Shin as to allow the other two drabs access.

Shame backed off at the dazzle's movement but continued to shout accusations toward his target. "You're a user, little brat! You don't care about him at all! Selfish, that's what you are! You should be ashamed! You only came here to get a place to stay!"

"Uh huh, and you're going to rue the day your twisted little mouth yammered so incessantly." Urielle, the watcher dazzle assigned to the young earth man, answered the drab's accusations and moved closer to help protect the girl human. A good friend to Rahzell and Ahnah, she wanted nothing more than to muzzle the creature's blathering tongue. But unless humans stopped them, drabs could continue to rant and spew their poisonous garbage as much as they liked.

Shin jerked her head away from Dibs' hand. Heat filled her chest and crept up into her neck and face. She'd come to his digs hoping for a place to crash for the night, so why did his invitation make her feel so uncomfortable? It was the same sensation that squeezed against her ribcage whenever passersby made fun of her, or when store clerks accused her of stealing, or people in restaurants scowled and moved further away from her tattered appearance. His attention made her break out into a sweat.

He probably thinks I'm such a pain. She zeroed in on a stain on the floor and wished she'd never come to his warehouse.

"Well? I said, how's that sound?" Dibs was waiting for an answer.

At the sight of Shame's success, the other two drabs flying close by grew brash. They circled behind the dazzle to come at the girl from another direction.

Rahzell repositioned his grip on the handle of his light-saber, and Urielle unsheathed her sword.

The second drab, Fear, flew as near to Shin as he dared. "Stay here little wretch, and you'll lose your independence! But if you go outside you'll get attacked again! You're not safe here or there! You'll never be safe!"

Shame jumped up and down with sick glee and simpered ghoulishly. "Yes, and if you stay here, he'll hate you for bothering him!"

Control, the third drab, flew in alongside Fear and was

The Other Side Of Visible 43

about to spew his own detestable tirade. But just then he saw a laser-sword swinging toward him. Though he moved back instantly he wasn't quick enough, and the light-sword nicked him on the forearm.

"Aauuw!"

His panicked cry was enough to set the other drabs on edge, so that by the time Rahzell pulled up his sword for another strike, the whole lot had turned tail and cleared out.

Urielle watched the trio fade into the distance. "Those beasts sure like to swagger, don't they?" Sheathing her sword, she put her hands on her hips. "But stand up to them and their cowardice shows up real fast."

Rahzell threw his friend a knowing smile and put his own light-saber away. "We shouldn't be seeing their ornery faces for a while."

"And that makes me happy!" Urielle was a dazzle with irrepressible energy. The thought of being drab-free for awhile set her to gently flapping her wings and hovering up and down out of sheer happiness.

As far as dazzles went, she was shorter than most and slightly plump around her middle. A lustrous braid of golden hair hung down her back and nestled between her wings. She had an adorable little nose and freckles that sparkled with OtherSide colors. But her best feature by far was a pair of twinkling eyes. Like her jolly disposition, they were full of playfulness.

Amused, Rahzell folded his arms across his chest and grinned widely. As he watched her finish her little dance, a motion from the human world caught his attention. He nodded toward the girl child and both dazzles turned their attention earthward.

Shin stood. Though desperate to sleep in the comfort of the warehouse, she was hesitant to take Dibs up on his offer. Glancing at the door, she debated. It was already dark and getting colder by the minute. *But who would choose to spend the night freezing outside, without a sleeping bag?*

Everything in her felt so awkward. Finally, she blushed and heard herself giving into his niceness. "I don't wanna' be a pain, but if you're sure it's okay, I guess I can stay here."

And then Shin remembered Porky. Her cat gave her a reason to change the subject to something other than being a freeloader. "Oh no! What about my cat? Who will take care of Porky now?" Somewhere along the route of her escape she'd dropped the diner's to-go bag with his half of a pancake. "I never had a pet when I got chased out of my other places. He could starve!"

Dibs sat down beside her on the sofa and threw her a big brother, *you-gotta'-be-kidding* look. "Shinny, cats are predators. They're made to take care a' themselves." He leaned into her face and formed menacing claws with both hands. "They got long, sharp nails. And with old man Cutter's junkyard right there, where the mice and rats party all night, Porky will be just fine." He slapped her leg. "Don't you worry 'bout him. He'll be fat in no time."

"Oh." She picked up Herbie for comfort. "But I liked him. He kept me company." Changing the topic of conversation helped Shin feel less self conscious about mooching off of Dibs. Still, she honestly missed her feline friend.

Dibs wouldn't let her sulk. "I know, I know. I feel the same way 'bout the rats in the warehouse here. They keep me company too."

"I hate rats!" Shin rapped him on the arm and shot up out of her seat, shuddering at the thought of beady eyes lurking in the corners, watching their conversation.

"Sit down, scaredy-pants. If you keep your place clean, with no food layin' around, you're gonna' be okay. You only gotta' keep yourself covered up at night so they don't munch on your toes."

"Eww!" She made a face. Even if what he'd said was true, it grossed her out.

He pulled on her shirt so she would take a load off and quit her worrying. "I ain't seen a rat for months. You don't gotta' worry 'bout 'em showin' up here. I promise."

She sank back down into the couch, glad to hear that bit of news.

"How long you been at the alleyway, anyway? Two, three months?"

"Six and a half months! Longer than I lived in any other street home." She frowned. "That little cave I made was the best hideaway ever."

"Got any clue why the cops were after you?"

Shin threw her hands into the air. "Who knows? Maybe Cutter saw all my junk in the alley and thought I stole it from him." After a few seconds of contemplation, the real reason for the cop's visit crystallized in her mind and turned into solid irritation. Her face muscles tensed as she stood and paced. "I know exactly why they showed up today. Some moron attacked me last night. Cutter probably heard all the noise, and this morning he and that cop came snooping to see what was going on. That's got to be the reason!" Shin exhaled. She was beginning to despise that creepy attacker for how he'd ruined her life.

"You okay, Shinny? Did he hurt you?"

"Nah. I got away. I think he fell over some of the stuff around my cave." She sat down again and stared at the faded fabric of the sofa, surprised that Dibs seemed to genuinely care.

Dibs got up and walked over to an old wooden box near the table. "So, you eaten today? I scored a huge sub this evening and I only ate half. You can have the rest of it." He opened the lid and pulled out a bag containing half a sandwich. "And I refilled a water bottle from the drinking fountain. You can have that, too."

"I don't wanna' take your food." Shin knew the value of a hard-begged meal. Plus, she was feeling a little bit of that pressure in her chest again. "I can wait until I go out tomorrow."

"Okay, it's your call. But like I said, I already ate. And I don't wanna' attract any rats that might come lookin' for grub. So maybe you should eat it, just in case."

He was staring at her, trying to convince her. She sat silently, torn between hunger and the embarrassment of taking his food.

"C'mon Shinny. I also had an apple and some chips they'll never miss off the market shelf. And thanks to a nice guy on Second Street who decided I wasn't a lazy bum and laid a fiver in my hand, I pigged out on half of this sandwich. That's plenty for me." He held the bag out toward her. "I promise."

Shin didn't like taking his food, but he had already eaten, and she was hungry. And since the sandwich was sort of extra, maybe just this once she would indulge. She took the bag and the water. "Thanks, Dibs."

Biting off a chunk, she chewed a few times and swallowed the first mouthful. "I haven't eaten anything since this morning, when an old lady at the zoo"—she stopped and looked Dibs' way—"oh yeah, you'll love this! An old woman at the zoo, she handed me a hundred dollar bill and told me to bring her the change after I ate breakfast at a restaurant. I had three and a half huge pancakes this morning, and bacon!"

Dibs' eyes got almost as large as those pancakes. "A hundred dollars! Where's the rest of it?"

"I gave it back to her." Shin looked at him guiltily and took another bite.

"Shinny! You coulda' used that for tons of stuff!"

She knew to Dibs, money in the hand was always a serious subject. Swallowing, she shot back a defense. "Hey, the lady's a good begging connection. I figured if I didn't return it to her I'd never be able to beg from her again. You know how great it is to have people you can count on. Besides, she's a nice lady." She added the last comment to justify her actions, but it was also true. Even if the woman seemed kind of crazy, she was an agreeable person.

"Too bad you don't have it now. You could buy a sleeping bag and all that other stuff you lost."

She took another bite of the sandwich and answered through a mouthful of Provolone cheese and Italian lunchmeat. "I dibn'th know I'b be chathed oudda my home, or I mydda' keppth thuh money." Downing that mouthful, she added, "That lady, I'm pretty sure she's harmless, but she's definitely strange. Like, she kept reading my mind. A couple of times, I thought something in my head, and a second later she said the exact same words."

Remembering the last part of her conversation with the eccentric woman, Shin chomped more of her sandwich and said, "She callb me a Light-theeker."

Dibs came and sat down on the sofa beside her. "What did you say?"

Shin swallowed. "She called me a Light-Seeker."

"Hey, that's what the guy who gave me the money today said about me! He called me a Light-Seeker, too!"

They stared at each other and both said at the same time, "Weird."

Shin took another bite. A piece of sandwich fell out of her mouth onto the floor. So the rats wouldn't find it, she quickly picked it up and stuffed it back in her mouth. "You're seriouth? He callb you a Lighth-theeker?"

"I swear! He seemed friendly, and five bucks, well, that's pretty generous compared to the usual amounts people give."

They both sat and quietly considered the strange coincidence.

Shin popped the last bite of her sandwich into her mouth and took a swig of water. She chewed, swallowed, and wiped her lips with the back of her hand. "What do you think they mean?"

Dibs leaned back and twiddled his thumbs. Almost

without thinking he said, "No clue. Maybe Light-Seekers are tired of the way things are and they want a normal life."

Shin tried to imagine what a normal life looked like. "It'd be nice to be in a family. In my family." *Without the hitting or drinking.* She kept the last thought to herself.

Dibs stopped twiddling. "Yeah. One that shows you what it's like to be a man."

Shin glanced at him. *Melancholy,* the new word she'd learned from her most recent library book, described the expression on his face. She understood. Thinking about her family was what melancholy felt like.

Neither of them said anything for a few seconds.

Dibs stood up and nodded toward a raised area in the room that had once served as a loading dock. "You take the sofa. I'll sleep on the ledge."

It looked cold and hard. "Dibs, I don't wanna' take your couch. I'll sleep up there."

"Quit it, Shin. I'm tryin' to be nice, okay? I'll use the sleeping bag and I'll be fine. Blankets are over there for you." He pointed to the corner where two old blankets sat neatly folded.

Shin went and got them. Even if she did feel guilty for invading his space, she was glad for a dry, safe place to stay for the night. At the moment she was also grateful for a friend. "Thanks, Dibs. You're the best. Like the brother I never had."

Dibs grinned and blushed. "We're in it together, Shinny. You an' me." He laid out the sleeping bag on the cement. "G'night, sleep tight. Don't let the bed bugs bite."

Shin shuddered at that thought and plopped onto the soft sofa. Pulling the blankets up around her chin, she tucked them in tightly to prevent rat invasions.

Blowing out the flame of his oil lamp, Dibs stumbled over to the ledge and did the same rat prevention technique as Shin. He sighed loudly, pushing out the old day's worries to make room for what a new day would bring.

As their eyelids grew heavy and their thoughts sluggish, both Light-Seekers slipped into dreams of white shafts piercing their gray like lightning, but without the sting; white shafts piercing through from another place, to wake up desires long ago forgotten and discarded.

CHAPTER SIX

Much to Shin's displeasure, she and Dibs were entering the gates on the south side of the zoo, near the big cat habitats. She had planned to avoid Crazy Lady for a few days in hopes that her stupid idea about going out to breakfast together would be forgotten. But Dibs had nagged and pushed to meet the nosy old woman, and finally, his insistence won out. As nice as he'd been about letting her crash at his digs, she felt she had no choice.

But she detested begging as a twosome. It took much longer to get enough change for both people to eat. And it drew too much attention to the fact that they were both young and homeless. If the wrong person noticed, they could end up back in foster care to get chewed up, regurgitated, and spit out in worse condition than if they'd been left alone to fend for themselves.

Approaching the bench where the woman usually sat, Shin stuffed down annoyance about going against her better judgment. She glanced up at the figure sitting there and realized it wasn't a lady. It was an old man. Similar to Crazy Lady's daily habit, the man was feeding a flock of gray, fluttering pigeons.

Relieved, Shin came to a standstill.

"What's the matter?" Dibs pulled up next to her.

"It's not her. It's a man. Let's go." She turned and started back toward the zoo's entrance. This was her perfect excuse to split up and beg separately.

"Hold on, Shinny!" Dibs whispered loudly. "Maybe it's her husband or somethin'. You ever seen him before?"

"Never." Shin kept moving.

"C'mon!" He pulled on her sleeve. "We should at least walk by the bench and check him out. It can't hurt to do that much."

Shin huffed impatiently. "Oh, all right! We'll walk by him, but that's all. Nothing else." Turning back, she blew by Dibs so fast, he had to trot to catch up to her.

As the earthlings hustled along the pathway, Ahnah and Urielle sped up to stay with them. Looking ahead, they were both pleasantly surprised to see one of their own kind hovering directly above where the older human being sat. The dazzle was almost a head higher than Ahnah, which meant he was quite a bit taller than Urielle.

"Eleah is my name." He bowed in the usual greeting of honor between dazzles.

"I'm Urielle." She bowed in return.

"And I'm Ahnah." Also bowing, she nodded in the direction of the older earthling. "You're with the ambassador."

"Yes."

It was quite easy for Ahnah to recognize the man sitting on the bench as a human ambassador of OtherSide. Since they spent so much time visiting with the Original Family, ambassadors radiated sizeable amounts of that realm's light.

Their dazzles also reflected a deep golden glow of resilient strength, the very reason Eleah shone brightly from within.

By way of introduction, Urielle placed a light-hand on her human's head, leaned down, and smiled directly into his face. "I'm with this spunky young man. He's a fun one to watch."

Seeing her manner with the boy, Eleah's face lit up. "It

seems to me you would find anyone fun to watch."

With one hand on a hip Urielle straightened up, stared into space reflectively, and then nodded in Eleah's direction. "You know, come to think of it, I can't recall one earthling I haven't thoroughly enjoyed watching. And I will say, I've watched a few uncommon ones."

Eleah laughed as though he'd experienced a few of his own uncommon assignments. "Thanks to the Original Family's artistry, no human being is common." He turned to Ahnah, who was quietly enjoying the conversation. "And I assume the earth girl is your watch."

She nodded. "I share this assignment with my compatriot Rahzell, but at the moment he's assisting another dazzle."

Studying her thoughtfully for a few seconds, Eleah broke into a wide grin. "Isn't he the one who likes to scare drabs instead of skewering them?"

She smiled. "I see his renown is spreading. But be assured, he'll run them through as quickly as the rest of us."

The activity of a flock of flying birds drew the attention of the dazzles back toward Earth's realm. Their humans were about to interact. In unison, the trio turned and gave their focus to watching.

Pigeons rose and scattered as Shin and Dibs neared the bench. Once more, Dibs pulled hard on her sleeve to slow her down. Squaring off to face the bench-sitter, he said cheerfully, "Good morning, sir!"

Shin groused inwardly and stopped next to him. Dibs hadn't planned to just walk by the bench: he had every intention of begging from the man!

Looking up from his bag of pigeon feed, the elderly man's eyes grew wide with surprise. "Well, it's about time. I thought you weren't coming!"

"Aw, well, we're here now." Dibs had no idea what the man was talking about, but he played along anyway.

Shin took a sideways glance at the old codger. He looked

real distinguished, like at one time he'd been an undertaker, or maybe a spy. He wore the kind of overcoat a secret agent would wear, with a flat sort of English snapped-to-the-brim cap to match. Underneath the cap he had a full head of neatly cropped white hair, complemented by a thick white mustache. He seemed to be about the same age as Crazy Lady. She wondered if he was her husband, like Dibs had suggested.

"Come sit down, both of you!"

The man was seated smack in the middle of the bench. Gesturing to either side of him, he invited them to join him. But sitting down wasn't part of their plan, so neither Shin nor Dibs moved.

"I'm safe, mind you. Couldn't hurt a flea. Come now, have a seat." He patted the bench several times.

To Dibs, the man seemed completely harmless, and he thought sitting down might be part of the bargain to get some money. So he gave in, walked over, and perched himself on the right side of the bench. A whiff of sweet, musky cologne wafted his way. It was pleasant, in the same way smelling coffee in the morning always made him think good thoughts.

"You too, young lady."

The gentleman patted the bench on his left side.

Since stupid Dibs was already sitting next to the old guy, Shin felt weird just walking away. Hesitating for a few seconds, she tried to come up with another option. In the end, she sat. Grudgingly. And at the far end of the bench, in case she had to make a run for it.

She turned her eyes downward and focused on the patch of grass in front of her feet.

Immediately, the wizened gentleman introduced himself. "My name is Oscar and I'm sixty-nine years old."

Shin snickered under her breath. *He's a fossil!*

"You probably think that makes me a fossil, don't you?"

The man looked at Shin as she accidentally sucked spit into her esophagus and had to cough hard. She stared straight ahead to avoid his gaze. *He's doing it too! How in the world do they know what I'm thinking?* She started to ask, "Are you Crazy Lad—" but catching herself midsentence, she backpedaled. "I mean, are you the husband of the woman who was here yesterday?"

"Good heavens, no!" He slapped his knee and rocked forward with several rollicking hoots. "You're thinking of Priscilla, the ambassador who was assigned to this territory until yesterday. I'm her replacement, and I knew her, mind you, but she was never married. My own dear wife Veronica passed through the veneer to OtherSide several years ago, after forty-seven years of courtship." He leaned over and nudged Dibs. "We liked to pretend our marriage was one long date."

Dibs smiled politely. What kind of mess had he gotten himself into this time? This kooky old guy was talking complete nonsense.

"Now where were we? Oh yes! As I said, I'm Oscar. And you are the Light-Seekers I am to meet today."

Shin jerked her head around and she and Dibs locked eyes. For the second time in less than twenty-four hours, a stranger had called them Light-Seekers!

"Yes, well, do you have any questions for me? I'll be glad to answer every inquiry, no matter how curious."

The old man winked at Dibs on his right. And then, though Shin was staring hard at a grass patch beneath her feet, he smiled in her direction.

"Well, go ahead, ask me something."

Both kids sat tongue-tied.

As Shin scraped the dirt under the bench with her worn sneakers, it occurred to her that even if they were quite old and definitely odd, Crazy Lady and this Oscar guy were sincere. There was nothing fake about them. Suddenly she wanted to ask what a Light-Seeker was, but it sounded too good for the likes of her. She sat quietly, not saying anything.

"What's a Light-Seeker?" Fortunately, inquisitive Dibs wasn't so timid.

"Oh good question, my young man. You're a bright one, I can see that."

As the old man patted his knee with a sort of fatherly approval, Dibs felt tingly warmth spread all over his insides. It was the same sensation he'd felt when Shin had praised him the night before.

"A Light-Seeker is someone who has gotten tired of the way things are, and they want a better life. Light-Seekers know there's more out there somewhere, but they don't know how to get there, and they don't know what it looks like."

It seemed to Shin that Oscar might be a real spy who had listened in on their discussion at the warehouse the night before, and now he was repeating it back to them.

"And though at the present time you can't see into the realm of OtherSide,"—and here, the man leaned over and tapped Dibs on the chest—"on the inside of both of you are star-eyes just waiting to be opened. And when they're opened, you can visit the Light Prince, and your lives will change for the better!"

Oscar's conversation with the earth children was quite enthralling to Eleah, Ahnah, and Urielle. Listening to an ambassador speak of OtherSide and of the Original Family was a true power surge. The light around the ambassador's words energized them, and they swelled and beamed.

But the reactions of the human children were much more down-to-earth. While Dibs was giggling, Shin wasn't at all amused by the foolish talk she was hearing. All sorts of uncomfortable emotions were bubbling up inside, things she hadn't felt for a long time. She'd always wanted there to be more to life, but everything in her young experience told her that possibility was an outright lie. Why then, was there a big ache pushing against her chest and a lump in her throat that was making it hard to swallow?

Her head began swimming, her stomach reeled with nausea, and she thought she might hurl in front of everybody. She desperately needed to get away.

Oscar's smile disappeared into seriousness and his mustache turned downward. He reached out and touched her arm gently. "I'm sorry. I may have said too much, too fast. Forgive me if I made you uncomfortable, dear one."

Shin stood and withdrew her arm from the old man's touch. *Dear one. Who ARE these weird people?* Her skin was clammy. It was hard to breathe. She had to leave pronto.

Ahnah smelled a familiar odor and swirled around to see the drab regulars that claimed the girl child as their own. "They're not happy."

"They're never happy."

All three dazzles smiled at Urielle's obvious statement.

Shame shouted loudly from a safe distance. "Little scumbag, you know none of the things he says could ever be true for you!"

Fear flew in next to Shame. "Don't trust the old geezer! Look at him. He's perverted and dangerous! Get out of here, before he does something harmful to you!"

With a look as foul as UnderSide and his arm still bandaged from the nick of a light-sword, Control cowered behind the other drabs to yell his accusations. "Run away, child! Run from thisss old man! He'sss evil! The man'ss evil!"

"Enough!" Ahnah's wings turned the color of hot gold and she shot after the three drabs. Nodding her head toward the young earthlings, she called back to Urielle and Eleah, "Watch them!"

"I'm on it!" Urielle said enthusiastically.

Ahnah moved with such blazing speed, the drabs had to flap their wings violently to stay ahead of her and avoid a collision with her light-sword.

While she gave chase, the other two dazzles discussed the human activity below. In particular, Eleah was struck by his ambassador's manner. "He certainly loves these earth children."

"And it's a good thing he does. Sometimes I think the earth girl is frightened of her own shadow. Just look at the distress on her face." Urielle flew over and laid her light-hand on the girl's head.

Shin turned and stared at Dibs. "I have to go find a sleeping bag. Are you coming with me?"

But before Dibs could answer the old man gasped loudly. "Oh my! Where are my manners? You two haven't eaten, have you?" Reaching into an inside coat pocket, he removed his wallet. "Here. This should give you a nice breakfast." He held out a twenty-dollar bill.

Dibs stood up and eagerly grabbed the money. "Thanks, Mister! I mean, Oscar. This'll do great for breakfast!"

Oscar touched Shin's arm. "And after breakfast there is a place over on James Street, a private home, where you'll find a brand new, free sleeping bag waiting for you. The address is 127 James."

"Wow, thanks! Right, Shinny?" Dibs poked her with his elbow.

The queasiness in her stomach was subsiding. She took a glimpse at the man, and for a moment their eyes met. Kindness stared back at her, the same kindness she'd seen in the face of Crazy Lady.

She looked away. "Yeah. Thanks, Mister."

Oscar stood and gathered up his bag of pigeon food. As Dibs and Shin walked away he said, "You'll find me right here most mornings if you need me, dear ones. Bye!" He waved and then quietly released two shinings in their direction.

The powerful beams shot out from his hands and swirled around their heads like a warm massage.

Any remaining confusion in Shin's mind quieted down, and a calm settled into her stomach.

Dibs sighed with satisfaction. Life had just taken a serious turn for the better; he was about to pig out on breakfast.

The three humans exited the zoo. The young ones were bound for The Hungry Appaloosa Diner. The old man was headed to a sporting goods store to buy a sleeping bag for one very special young lady, whose whole existence had turned topsy-turvy at just the right time.

CHAPTER SEVEN

Tall Eddy answered his ringing cell phone. "Hey, what's up?" The caller was Adam Fox, a cop who worked the twelfth precinct. Adam also happened to be one of Eddy's indispensible partners in the chop shop theft ring that based itself out of Joe Cutter's garage.

Two men in the police department knew about the illegal operation's business of stealing cars and reselling their parts: Adam, and Paul Monson, Chief of Police. Both took secret cuts from the profits of the precinct's shadier businesses—including Cutter's garage—in exchange for a look-the-other-way policy.

Eddy listened to Adam's inquiry while fidgeting to turn up his phone's volume control. "Yeah, I know exactly who you're talkin' about. I even met the kid a couple a' times. She's Dibs Colby's little buddy. He calls her Shin."

Eddy listened as Adam explained the reason for his call. Cutter had heard a ruckus outside his garage around midnight and thought it probably came from the local homeless kid camping in the alley next to the junkyard. In his opinion she was living far too close to their chop shop operation. He was insisting they track her down to find out how much she knew about their nightly goings-on. At the very least, he wanted her out of the alley for good.

That was why, if for no other reason than to calm Joe Cutter's overactive imagination about the whole situation, Adam wanted to use her runaway status as a reason to bring her in for questioning.

But the girl had gone missing ever since they surprised her in the alleyway, which was where Eddy came into the picture.

"No problem, I got the skills. It'll be easy to use my connections to find her." Tall Eddy nodded instinctively. "I can lean on Dibs. He owes me big time for keepin' him outta' juvenile hall a couple a' months ago."

After a few more comments from Adam's end of the line Eddy finished with, "I'll check it out and give you the low down." He nodded once more. "Later," he said, and ended the call.

At six feet, four inches, Eddy was almost as thin as he was tall. With jet-black hair, he had a spiny nose that pointed toward a U-shaped chin and several pimples that sat like tiny volcanoes on his right cheek and neck. He wore a gray T-shirt tucked into tight jeans, and black sneakers that had seen a lot of wear.

Good attire wasn't out of his price range, since he made a decent amount of money as the chop shop's Operations Manager. But Eddy preferred to keep a low profile. A lavish condominium and partying on weekends were his extravagances, luxuries that could stay relatively hidden from the public eye. He wanted it that way to protect his reputation as an everyday, law-abiding citizen.

As Tall Eddy parked his car and cut through the back pathway to Dibs' warehouse, a skillful drab named Intrigue floated beside him. Invisible to his eyes, the drab was nonetheless as real as the man's dishonesty.

Eddy knocked on Dibs' door. Finding no one home, he

perched himself on a waist-high stone wall just around the corner from the warehouse entrance.

Intrigue followed after him. He'd been tracking this human for years, long enough that he felt the man was his property. After all, it was quite evident the mortal had taken on some of his own drab-like qualities. That fact alone made him cocky, and confident of possessing rightful ownership.

When his human stopped and sat, Intrigue settled down to hover nearby.

Eddy loved to catch people off guard because it threw the advantage his way. If he surprised Dibs from the shadows, the edge belonged to him. And since he had time to kill, waiting for his victim to show up wasn't a problem.

Pulling out his cell phone, he began to play his favorite game in hopes of beating his old record.

But thanks to Oscar's generosity, Tall Eddy and his tag-along drab would have to hang out for a while longer before the appearance of their quarry.

Dibs was on his third cup of coffee at The Hungry Appaloosa, and he was wired. Shifting in the booth where they sat waiting for breakfast to arrive, he jabbered away. "Y'know, I was thinkin' we could look for real jobs, you an' me. Might take a little risk at first, to find somebody who's willin' to pay us without askin' questions. But if we could save up money here and there, who knows? Maybe we could pay for a room somewhere that has a couple a' beds and running water and a fridge."

As their breakfasts arrived and Dibs picked up a fork, Shin looked at him, surprised he would even suggest the idea.

He stopped his forkful of eggs in midair to answer her frown. "Like family, Shin. I don't mean nothin' more than that. You said last night I was the brother you never had. And I thought about that, and well, it's kinda' true. We're like our own little family, seein' as we got nobody else out there. If you know what I mean."

She knew exactly what he meant. They both had living relatives, but neither his dad, who was serving a prison sentence for involuntary manslaughter, nor Shin's Mom, who had lost temporary parental rights as a result of neglect and rampant alcoholism, counted as true family.

"Everything okay here?" A waitress was passing by with a carafe to offer more coffee.

"Juth greath!" Dibs answered through a mouthful of food. He pointed toward the pastries in the showcase up at the register. "Uh, could I hab one of thoth bear claw pathtries?" He swallowed largely and added, "Shinny, you want one too?"

In the middle of a mouthful of home fries, she nodded.

"Make it two, please." Dibs smiled as the waitress left to pick out their sweet treats.

"So whatta' you think? About jobs, an' workin', an' savin' money t'get a room?"

Shin snorted. "You've never even saved up two bucks in all the time I've known you!"

Lowering his head, Dibs stared at his coffee cup and said quietly, "People change, y'know. I can learn t'save."

Shin tried to undo the damage of her sharp tongue. "Hey, don't get me wrong. Saving is a great idea, but looking for work is way too scary. I mean, we could get caught." She grinned. "And I'd miss you if you got hauled away."

Dibs looked up and caught her smile. He grinned back.

The waitress dropped off their pastries. Picking up his bear claw to take a bite, Dibs stopped and said, "Shinny, for awhile, if you wanna' crash on my sofa, I don't mind sleepin' on the ledge. Until we figure somethin' out."

While he dunked his gooey Danish pastry into sugary caffeine, Shin blushed at his kind proposal and shyly focused on licking off her sticky fingers.

They finished their sweets without conversation and slid into the aisle. While Dibs went to pay their bill with Oscar's charity, Shin made a bathroom stop.

Stepping outside, they ambled down the sidewalk. Coffee-hyper Dibs jumped high to pull down branches from three overhanging trees. Shin kept thinking about the idea of the two of them being family and of Dibs' nice offer to sleep on his sofa. It made her feel silly enough to jump up alongside him under the fourth tree.

He turned and gave her arm a soft whack. "Hey, we oughta' wait 'till later to pick up that sleeping bag. That way, if those James Street people are anything like Crazy Lady or Oscar, they might shell out money for supper. An' then we can eat real good twice in one day." Poking her with his elbow, he said, "Great idea, huh?"

They'd just eaten and Dibs was already thinking ahead to the next meal. Shin wanted to go get the sleeping bag right away, but he was being so pleasant, she shrugged and agreed to his timing. They turned and headed back toward the warehouse.

With so much coffee in his system Dibs gabbed the whole way home, amusing Shin with his non-stop chatter.

As they neared his grungy entrance he pulled out his key to put it in the padlock.

"DIBS! WHAT'S UP? Nice t'see you!"

Standing right behind them, Tall Eddy had practically shouted in their ears. Dibs let out a yelp and dropped the keychain into the weed patch in front of the door. Sandwiched in between them, Shin almost jumped out of her skin.

"Hello, Shin, great t'see you, too. How have you been?" Looking terribly pleased about something, Eddy flashed a wide, toothy grin.

Intrigue was in the middle of the humans as an unseen part of every double-dealing second. The drab was filling his human's mind with sinister advice and malevolent ideas. And since his earthling was already tuned in to UnderSide, he barely had to make a suggestion and the man quickly picked

The Other Side Of Visible

it up and made it happen.

After recovering from Eddy's loud greeting, Shin purposely ignored him. Even if he had once helped Dibs avoid being incarcerated, she despised the man. Being around him made the hair on the back of her neck stand up, like it did whenever lightning bolts crashed close during a storm. She didn't like him, trust him, or want to be near him. Ever.

Intrigue looked up from the earthlings and noticed one of his own kind lingering off to his right. The other drab seemed to be claiming the girl human as his property. That was fine with him, as long as his man was left alone.

Control eyed Intrigue with an equal amount of suspicion. "She'ss mine. You can have your human. Jusst don't ssscrew up my territory."

"You stay away from my man-property and I'll not touch your worthless little earthling." And just to prove he was superior, Intrigue added, "Let me have my way in these human interactions and you might learn a thing or two about laying out successful traps."

Control scowled. "Your pompousss sschemess can sstay intact. Jusst leave my planss alone. They're inssidiousssly better than yourss!"

Intrigue scoffed and spit but said nothing in response.

Through their interactions the two vying drabs understood each other perfectly. They could work side-by-side, as long as cooperating gave each of them their desired outcome.

Dibs picked up his keychain, fumbled to find the right key, unlocked the lock, and removed the chain. He didn't particularly like Tall Eddy. But a few months back when he'd gotten caught for swiping some food at the convenience store on Pine Street, Eddy pulled some strings to keep him from landing back in juvenile hall for another stay. Since he'd saved his hide, Dibs felt a duty to be nice.

Besides, Eddy was seven years older than him and sort of

a bully, and he didn't have the guts to stand up to him. Managing only a small protest, Dibs said, "Eddy, do you always gotta' scare the snot outta' me?"

As Dibs and Shin stepped into the dark warehouse, Eddy excused himself and walked away to make a quick phone call.

Adam Fox answered on the other end of the line.

"Hey, I got the homeless kid," Eddy said quietly. Listening for a response, he grinned. "Yeah, I told you I got the skills. She walked right into my trap."

After giving the address for the warehouse, he listened again and nodded. "No problem. I can hold her five minutes, easy. See you in a few." Ending the conversation, he slipped his cell phone into his pocket and stepped inside.

"Hey guys, whatcha' been up to? Fill me in!" Tall Eddy propped himself against the table and waited for somebody to answer.

Shin glanced at his eager face. He was acting as though he really cared, pouring extra grease into his sleaziness. Grabbing Herbie, she pulled him close. She was uncomfortable. As a matter of fact, if spooky Eddy was going to stay and visit, there was no way she was hanging around.

Control stood nearby. His two fellow conspirators, Fear and Shame, were nearby in case they were needed. But at the moment Control and the other man's drab clearly had the situation covered.

"Dibs, I have to go," Shin lied. "That guy with the sleeping bag is expecting me." Turning to Eddy, she lied again. "Sorry I can't stay and visit."

"Hey, what's your hurry, Shin?" Eddy leaned forward. "Haven't seen you for a long time. I'd like t'know how you're doin'. Find out what's new. How's your little home in the alleyway?"

"Got compromised, thanks to your boss." She knew Eddy worked at Cutter's Salvage Yard. That was another reason not to like him. Ever since showing up in her alleyway with a cop,

Cutter had been put on her Never-To-Be-Trusted list.

"No kiddin'. What happened?" Tall Eddy's eyes were filled with surprise.

"Almost got me nabbed by the cops and jerked back into the foster system. Lost all my stuff, too." Eddy was such a thuggy kind of guy. She was wasting her breath.

"Hey Shin, if I'd known, you can be sure I woulda' said somethin' to old man Cutter. You want me to explain to him and see if we can get your gear back?"

Shin thought of her library books, and for a second she considered accepting Eddy's help. But he was the type of person to call in a favor somewhere down the line. If he got involved, she'd pay for it sooner or later. "Nah. I have other plans now, so I don't need that stuff anymore." Maybe she'd talk to Falisha and tell her someone stole the books. Which was sort of true.

Having no desire to prolong the conversation with skunky Eddy, she walked toward the door.

"Hey, where you goin', Shin?" Tall Eddy got up, beat her to the doorway, and blocked the exit. "You okay? Anything I can do for you?"

Shin felt smothered. Why was he so antsy all of a sudden? She ducked under his arm, shoved the door open, and stepped out into the gray day. Ignoring Eddy, she called over her shoulder, "Gotta' go, Dibs. I'll see you later." Slamming the door shut, she began to quickly walk away. *Ugh, he's the creepiest! I can't stand him!*

The door shot open and Eddy followed on her heels.

Intrigue was close by his side.

Looking up, Shin saw a woman appear from around the corner of the warehouse, coming from the direction of the empty lot next door. She was beautiful, with ebony skin and crystal clear eyes. Her hair was neatly smoothed back into a ponytail, and she was wearing jeans and a tailored shirt.

The lady called out sincerely and urgently, "Oh, honey,

Shin, there you are! Sweetie, we are SO very late for our appointment! If we're going to make it in time we have got to leave right this very second." When she reached Shin the woman grabbed her arm and pulled hard in the direction of the street.

Shin had no idea how the stranger knew her name. But at the moment, going with her seemed like a better option than staying around ghastly Eddy. She played along. "Right! I forgot!" Looking at Eddy, she said, "See you."

His mouth hung open and he stared. The phony niceness in his face disappeared, and his eyes began to bulge with something ominous. Shin was glad to be getting away from him.

"But Shin, you can't go. We haven't finished our little chat. And I don't know when I'll see you again."

Though Tall Eddy's voice was full of plastic sweetness, his eyes were seething.

"NOW, Shin, or we'll miss our meeting!" The woman yanked on her arm a second time.

With threatening charm, Eddy quickly walked toward them. He held out his right hand and demanded of the lady, "I don't think we've met. I'm Eddy. And who are you?"

The woman ignored his outstretched hand and spoke once more to Shin. "We MUST leave."

Shin turned away from Eddy's chilling glare and said to the lady, "Let's go."

Thanks to a complete stranger entering the picture, Eddy could do nothing except watch while Shin got away. As the two females exited the driveway, he spit out a string of expletives, threw his hands up in the air, and stomped back into the warehouse.

Fear and Shame had joined Control, and the three drabs nervously followed after their human child. Though they couldn't identify what had changed, they all felt something in the atmosphere was different. The air was treacherous.

There was a noise behind them, and the threesome spun around to see the tip of a light-saber rushing at their faces. They scrambled to get away but it was too close. Catching Control in his midsection, the laser-sword plunged directly into his back and pierced him clean through. Coming out his front, it set his innards on fire. He howled in excruciating pain and tumbled helplessly backward through space.

Fear and Shame were terrified at the sight and roared away faster than two meteorites.

Ahnah lifted her saber. As the two drabs sped out of sight she called after them, "That's right! You should fly away, because if I ever have the opportunity, I'll do the same to both of you." Turning, she saw one drab still hanging around. Well out of range, it was quaking with fear. She intentionally positioned her body as a light shield between it and the girl. "Come any closer and I'll give you the same privilege I just gave to your crony."

"And if you were thinking of causing any more trouble, I'll take up where she leaves off." Urielle was hovering nearby and waving her own laser-sword at the drab.

Intrigue recoiled by ten paces, his wings and gnarled body trembling. "I have no quarrel with you and I have no interest in the child." He whimpered and backed away even farther, keeping his eyes firmly planted in the direction of the dazzles.

Ahnah and Urielle knew not to trust the word of a drab. They kept their swords drawn, just in case. Yet the beast did seem to be primarily interested in the adult male earthling standing nearby.

Armed with that bit of information, Ahnah sheathed her sword and bowed to Urielle. "I'll see you again soon, my friend."

"Sure will." Urielle's eyes were fastened on the motions of the drab, so instead of a bow she nodded her head and called over her shoulder, "I'll catch you on the flip side!"

Ahnah grinned. Such a great friend she had in Urielle,

who was as fun-loving as Rahzell. Grateful to the royal family for the privilege of working together with both of them, she lifted up and flew off to catch up to her partner and their earth child.

"NOW, Shin, or we'll miss our meeting!"

The ebony stranger pulled Shin firmly along, walking so fast she had to push herself to keep up with the woman's pace.

By the time they reached the end of the second block, Shin figured it was safe to stop pretending. She pulled her arm away from the mystery lady at her side and bent down to remove a stone in her shoe that had been bothering her for the entire hurried trek from the warehouse.

"Lady, I don't know who you are or how you knew my name, but this is all the farther—" Shin grabbed the pebble from her shoe, tossed it aside, and straightened up to finish her thought. "Lady, this is all the farth—" she stopped speaking and stared in every direction. Her rescuer was gone. Looking left, right, ahead and behind, she saw no one. *What in the . . . ?*

The woman just plain vanished! Moving off the sidewalk, Shin sat down on the grass. *Where did she go?* She happened to glance down. Herbie was still in her hand. Absentmindedly, she gave him a stroke while her mind replayed the last ten minutes. Amid a whirl of thoughts, the only one that made sense was that Tall Eddy was not a good person. She was glad to be away from him.

She looked around. The stranger was nowhere to be found. *So now what?* There was no going back to the warehouse while Eddy was still in the picture. *I suppose I could go over and see about the sleeping bag, like I said I would.*

She stood and searched again for the ebony woman. Baffled by her disappearance, Shin shook her head and began walking in the direction of James Street.

While she walked, Rahzell reappeared above her. He was back in his true dazzle light form. And like a dog shakes its fur after a bath, he shimmered hard to readjust whatever had gotten misshapen during his formation into humanness. He happened to be one of those dazzles who actually enjoyed temporarily impersonating a human being. To be convincing enough that the girl would agree to accompany a stranger, Rahzell had chosen to show up in the form of an intelligent, confident, well-spoken woman.

His choice had been impeccable and his plan worked masterfully. And once again, with his ingenuity and Ahnah's bravery, the two dazzles successfully prevented a second premature capture of their girl child.

Ahnah met Rahzell and they flew side by side. "Well done," they said simultaneously, and then laughed out loud at their synchrony.

Ahnah sheathed her sword. For the time being, it appeared their dramatic confrontations were over and they could stand down and take on a more relaxed posture.

CHAPTER EIGHT

Except for those she begged from, most of the people Shin knew lived in run-down apartments in the projects. Now she stood gazing at a real nice suburban home. Its lawn was evenly clipped, and a gorgeous flowerbed ran along the entire front of the house. Behind the flowerbed was a porch, and on the porch sat a painted wooden table and chair set, and a sizeable barbeque grill.

But what struck Shin more than anything was the neatness of the whole property. Everything was clean and tidy and ordered. Even the flowers in the flowerbed flowed together in a pretty rhythm of tall and wide shapes with dark and light hues.

In the yard was a swing set and on one of the swings was a girl.

"Hello," the girl called out while swinging back and forth.

Shin realized she must have been gawking. "Oh. Uh, hi. I came for a sleeping bag." She hoped she wouldn't have to explain the deal she and Oscar had made earlier that morning.

Bringing her swing to a standstill, the girl said, "Just a minute, I'll go ask my mom to come." She hopped off and disappeared inside.

A few seconds later, Oscar walked out of the front door

and straight toward Shin. "Hello, my dear," he said cheerfully. "Thanks for coming. I'm honored!"

She was surprised the old man had directed her to his own home. "You said there was a sleeping bag here," Shin said self-consciously.

"Yes, of course. But please come in for a visit, and meet my family." He glanced up and down the block. "Didn't your young friend come with you?"

Assuming he meant Dibs, Shin started to answer him but caught sight of a police car slowly rounding the corner at the end of the block. Kicking into survival mode, she chose the closest escape route available and hollered, "I'd love to visit, Mister Oscar!" Without waiting, she ran directly into his house and slammed the door behind her.

Half a minute later the police car pulled into the neighbor's driveway and an officer got out.

Though surprised by Shin's reaction, Oscar quickly put two and two together.

Adam Fox opened his car door and greeted the elderly gentleman. "Good morning, sir." His partner joined him and they walked over onto Oscar's sidewalk.

"Hello, officers." Oscar studied their eyes while quietly seeking the opinion of the Light Prince for wisdom on how to handle the situation. As a man of honor he always respected other human beings. But he was saddened that there didn't seem to be one bit of OtherSide light reflecting back to him from either of the policemen's faces.

"Sir, is this your property?" The officer gestured to Oscar's home.

"Yes, it certainly is," Oscar smiled. "I've lived here for forty-five years."

Nodding politely, the policeman continued, "We have reason to expect a runaway girl will be coming to this address for a sleeping bag. She goes by the name of Shin. She's thin and about so tall,"—he demonstrated with his hand—"with shoulder-length dark hair, wearing jeans and a white T-shirt, a dirty hooded jacket, and worn white sneakers. She's been living on the streets for a while, which means she's probably used to lying and cheating and stealing. And she's high-strung, you can be sure of that." With distain he added, "Be careful in your interactions with her. Homeless kids can be like a dog that's been backed into a corner, if you understand my point."

Oscar thought they weren't being very kind. But he knew how he was to respond. "Oh, a girl was here earlier that fits that description. But you're right, she was so frightened she ran away!"

The policeman scowled. "How long ago? Which way did she go?"

Truthfully, Oscar pointed straight toward the house. "I'm rather certain she went in that direction. Hasn't even been that long ago. Less than fifteen minutes. She's probably still in the neighborhood."

Adam Fox thanked him and nodded to his partner. "Let's go." They both hurried to their police cruiser.

As they backed out of the driveway and took off in pursuit of their runaway, Oscar politely waved goodbye.

Sheer reaction led Shin into a simple but beautifully decorated living room. Attractive furniture sat on light-hued area rugs overlaying wooden floors. Windows were decorated with soft, flowing curtains. Bright pictures hung on the walls. To her left in the dining area sat a table with place settings already arranged, waiting for the noon meal. Happy sounding music was playing softly in the background, quite the opposite of Shin's present state of mind.

She looked down at the worn out stuffed dog in her hand and felt completely out of place. They were both misfits around such squeaky cleanness.

Leaning against the door, she tried to think about what

to do next. But before she had time to consider her options, a woman walked around the corner from the kitchen area.

"Hello, may I help you?"

Shin hid Herbie behind her back and stood up straight. "Uh, Oscar said . . . he said I . . . uh . . . I came for a visit."

"Oh!" the woman said enthusiastically. "You're the young lady he met in the park this morning! Wonderful! My name is Maggie Owens and I'm Oscar's daughter-in-law. And this is my daughter, Madison." The lady pointed to the girl Shin had seen on the swing set, and then held out her hand in greeting.

Remembering her manners, Shin wiped her right hand on her pants and shook their hands. "I'm Shin," she said, staring awkwardly at the floor.

"Wow, that's a different name," the girl said.

"Shin, welcome to our home. Would you like a drink of iced tea, or lemonade?" Mrs. Owens asked.

She nodded, keeping her eyes fastened on the wood floor near her feet. "Lemonade," she said quietly. Even if she felt as comfortable as a worm on dry pavement, she *was* quite thirsty.

"How old are you?" Madison asked, while her mom went to the kitchen to pour Shin's drink.

"I'm fourteen." For some reason Shin wanted to appear older than her real age, so she lied and made sure Herbie was still hidden behind her back.

"I'm eleven. How did you get that name?"

Shin decided she wasn't so fond of this question-asking girl. "It's a nickname. I hit my shin and the name stuck." Not wanting to be more uncloaked than necessary, Shin purposely left out the fact that it had to do with daydreaming. She'd absentmindedly walked directly into a park bench, and the pain in her leg caused her to dance a little jig, which Dibs thought was hilarious. He'd laughed so hard, he ended up rolling around on the ground like a turtle on its back. Ever since, she'd been called "Shin."

"Well, I like that nickname. It's totally unique, and I like unique."

I don't like weird at all, Shin thought sarcastically, and looked away from the girl.

"But I don't like weird at all."

Shin frowned and glanced at the kid. *Not another one.*

"Weird is usually negative but unique is positive."

The girl was smiling and her voice was bouncy-nice.

How do they do that mind reading thing?

"Where is Dad?" Mrs. Owens came and handed the drink to Shin and then pulled back a curtain to look out the window. "Hmmm. There's a police car pulling out of the neighbor's driveway. I wonder what that was all about."

Shin's heart started beating faster. The cops were next door! She stepped farther away from the window to be sure she wouldn't be seen from outside.

Just then Oscar walked in the front door and said enthusiastically, "It's lunchtime!" He turned to Shin and smiled. "Have you met my daughter-in-law and my granddaughter?"

Shin nodded and nervously studied the zipper on her jacket.

"Dad, is everything all right? What did the police want?" asked Maggie Owens.

"Oh that! They were looking for someone. A runaway. But I told them she'd been scared away and had run toward the east. They left to search for her."

Shin's head shot up. The police were looking for *her*! She stared as a second realization sank into her brain. Oscar hadn't turned her in. He'd protected her from the authorities!

Oscar smiled at her and turned to walk into the dining room. He gestured to a chair. "Come, sit down, Shin."

She moved toward the table, trying to hide her astonishment.

It was barely lunchtime and she'd eaten a huge breakfast,

but they were offering free food. Besides, with the cops out there canvassing the neighborhood, she wasn't going anywhere, at least not for a little while.

When they were all seated Oscar looked at Shin and pointed at the food. "Dig in!"

Setting Herbie on her lap under the table, she watched Oscar and his family so she could imitate their way of doing things. She hadn't eaten in a home since foster care days. It was hard to remember how she was supposed to act.

These three people were being real polite. They offered the platters of food to her before taking stuff for themselves. And they weren't complaining or criticizing or saying any bad words at all about other people. They were probably putting on their best behavior for company.

With the same bouncy voice as before, Madison asked, "Do you have grandparents like I have Oscar?"

Shin didn't want to talk about her life. She already felt like an alien from Mars. Bringing up her past would only prove she didn't belong on their suburban planet.

"They're all dead. At least I think so." She didn't remember her birth father, and she hadn't seen her mom for eons. How was she supposed to know the status of her grandparents?

"Oh. That's too bad. My dad died when I was little. But I think Grandma and Grandpa were sent to live with us to help take his place." She smiled at Oscar and kept talking. "I miss my dad, and I miss Grandma, too. But I wouldn't expect them to come back. They're way too happy, now that they live in OtherSide."

Shin focused on her plate. The chatty kid was bringing up that imaginary world. Maybe they were the aliens.

"There's plenty of everything, so have as much as you like, dear one," Maggie Owens said.

She was beginning to get irritated. *Dear one. What is up with that?* This family was so sweet it almost made her want to barf. Like the time she downed an entire bag of candy bars.

After a serious case of nausea, the whole bag got hurled into a waste can.

She couldn't wait to leave. Just ten or fifteen more minutes. When she was positive the police were no longer in the area, she would shove off.

But first she needed that sleeping bag. Maybe if she brought up the subject it would jog their memory. She glanced in Oscar's direction. "Thanks for the sleeping bag. That was nice of you to offer."

Maggie Owens looked at Oscar and then at Shin. "This morning after Dad—after Oscar—came home, we all decided we want to give you some other things as well: a backpack, some new clothing, a good rain poncho, a flashlight, sneakers, and some toiletries."

The invisible atmosphere grew tense, to say the least. Ahnah, Eleah, and several other dazzles hovered around the humans. They were keeping their eyes on two foolish drabs. The things were hopping up and down, their soot-black wings shaking feverishly, and their mouths foaming with rage. It was obvious they dreaded the loss of their girl child and were making every frantic effort to prevent the inevitable.

From a distance they shouted their lies. "Look at yourself! See how disgusting you are? You're gross, sleazebag! That's why they want to clean you up!" Shame was screeching his words with fury. He knew the girl hated being called a sleazebag. When things got desperate, it was the first insult he pulled out of his arsenal of slurs. Being in the home of an OtherSide ambassador was one such occasion. He hoped it would be enough to make the child run.

Fear joined his accomplice. "Leave! This place looks just like foster homes! They're using you! They're tricking you! You're not safe! Run! Now!"

"How I would love to silence your dark, wagging tongues." Ahnah knew her human was in distress. And the drabs weren't helping matters. Moving closer, she placed a light-hand on Shin's shoulder. "Shhhhh, be still. You are safe here, more than you know."

The other dazzles gathered in closer and formed a light barrier to encircle the struggling girl.

At Maggie Owens' offer to give her free stuff, Shin felt her face turning hot with an all too familiar embarrassment. She lowered her eyes and noticed her clothing. Tugging at her soiled hoodie, she pulled it closed and hoped they hadn't seen the holes in her T-shirt.

Her mind flashed back to a day in kindergarten when a raggedy coat stole her away from the only family she'd known. She and her mom were poor, and Shin—known then as Amber—had thought it was normal to wear last year's coat, even though it was tight. It hadn't been washed at the end of the previous year's Head Start classes, and near the beginning of kindergarten her mom pulled it out of a cardboard box from their musty old basement. Putting it on her daughter, she sent her off to school.

Amber was late again that day and entered the classroom after the other children had already begun quietly working at their desks. As she walked to her seat at the back of the room, one pretty little girl named Darcy innocently announced to the teacher in front of the entire class, "Mrs. Wilson, she smells like garbage!"

That provoked Mrs. Wilson to talk to the principal. The principal promptly called Children's Welfare Services. And later in the day, one of their agency caseworkers stopped by Amber's house unannounced and found her mother in a drunken stupor, lying on the floor in mountains of dirty laundry. The kitchen was full of crusty, unwashed dishes. On the cluttered counter were boxes of cereal that had tipped over and spilled, their contents mixing with rat poison pellets scattered around the drain board of the sink.

Children's Welfare Services promptly removed Amber from her home. And for the next four years, until she escaped and took to the streets, her life became an endless cycle of being transferred from one foster home to another.

And it all happened because of one lousy, filthy coat.

Sitting in the middle of this perfect house and perfect family, Shin caught a whiff of her own odor. Keenly aware she probably smelled like garbage, humiliation pushed against her chest. She shoved her chair back from the table and stood up to leave. Herbie tumbled to the floor, forgotten for the moment under the table.

"That's right, run, scuzzball, run!" Fear cackled and shook feverishly with a perverted hope that the girl would get up and dash out of the house.

Ambassador Oscar quietly released a shining in Shin's direction. The beam hit her right in the heart.

One of the other dazzles blasted after the drab to chase it away. "You run away, foul brute! When a human agrees with you we're not permitted to quiet your voice. But in this case the odds are in our favor: the ambassador and his family stand with us, and we stand against you!"

Fear and Shame spread their wings and flew away.

The dazzles knew they would return at another time. Until the girl made them leave, the beasts would never give up taunting her.

Right then and there, Shin felt like bursting into tears. She focused on the floor and fought back emotions that were pushing hard to find a way out. "Look, I appreciate the food, but I don't get why you're doing this." Blood pounded in her head and she glanced up. Their eyes were watching her the way she watched animals in the zoo. Turning, she walked to the front door and reached for the doorknob, but stopped. Staying was almost unbearable. Getting hauled back into foster care by roving cops was even worse.

Oscar got up from the table and came closer.

Letting go of the knob, she turned away to avoid him and blurted out, "Why didn't you let me get turned in to the cops? Why are you being so nice to me? What do you want from me?"

The old man stood next to her. Like the grandpa she never had but always imagined, he began talking in reassuring tones.

"Shin, you're a beautiful young woman. You're creative and intelligent, and you've got all the potential in the world. And someday you'll be a discerning, influential ambassador. Dear one, exciting and wonderful adventures are waiting for you." His voice was full of kindness as Oscar paused and gently put his hand on her shoulder. "But above all, it's your great stature in OtherSide that we honor. The Original Family has loved you, and they can't wait to meet you face to face."

Like fuel added to fire, his words made her insides ache and burn even hotter. No one had ever spoken words like that about her. And even though she didn't understand all their meaning, Shin could no longer hold back the moisture that leaked hard through her eyes and nose. She wiped a sleeve across her wet face.

Mrs. Owens came from behind and handed her tissues.

Oscar turned toward the living room and gestured for her to follow him. "Come, sit down, Shin. I think it's time we talk."

She averted her eyes but tagged along and sat clumsily at the opposite end of the sofa from him.

Maggie and Madison Owens excused themselves to clear the lunch dishes from the table, leaving to Oscar the job of explaining everything.

"Shin dear," he made wide sweeping motions with his arms, "all around us there exists another realm that is invisible to our earth eyes. Maggie, Madison, and I go there regularly to visit with the Original Family."

There he was, bringing up that world again. Talking like a whacko interplanetary tour guide from one of her science fiction books. People in those stories were always traveling to other worlds that were sometimes fantastic and sometimes

times terrible. But it was all just *fiction*.

"The Original Family is your family too, Shin. And meeting them is as easy as having your star-eyes opened."

Sniffing, she wiped her nose with the tissues and glanced over at the old man. He looked pleased, as if he'd just shared the greatest secret of the universe. And that's when a wild, upside-down idea marched straight into her head that was as meaningful to her as Oscar's universe secret was to him. *What if all these kind people are NORMAL? What if my life is weird and I'm the abnormal one?*

She took mental inventory. The people in the projects all lived in apartments. She was one of the few homeless ones. Strike one against being normal. And the majority of those people either had a job or lived on welfare. Only a few begged for food money. Strike two against being normal.

But none of the people in her neighborhood ever talked about the existence of another world as though it were REAL. Well, except for a few nut cases roaming the streets who believed in aliens and spaceships. But they had good reason. There were too many screws loose in their brains.

The Owens family and Crazy Lady were definitely quirky, but she was pretty sure they still had all their nuts and bolts in the right places.

This is either the biggest piece of stupidity, or I'm clueless.

She gave Oscar a fast once-over. His eyes were closed and he was sitting quietly. Except for his universe secret, he looked perfectly ordinary.

Between the internal ache and the oddity of it all, Shin felt quite divided. Having spent her whole life trying to perfect her own invisibility, the idea of an invisible world was right up her alley. But it was all so incredibly outlandish.

A large sigh escaped her lips as Shin came to the conclusion there was only one way to find out whether or not Oscar's universe secret existed.

"So, how do my star-eyes get opened?"

"Ask." Oscar opened his eyes and smiled, as if everyone knew how.

"Ask what? Who?"

"Ask the Light Prince to open your star-eyes, so you can turn and see what's been there all along."

Slumping forward, Shin squirmed. Oscar may as well have said, "Ask a *cop* to open your star-eyes." Was he kidding? She could never meet a prince! As sure as rain makes mud, she'd make a fool of herself. Around sophisticated types she always managed to do something stupid and come across like a real dirtbag. And anyway, Light Prince was a silly name. It sounded like something right out of a fairy tale.

"You'll absolutely love him. He's just like you."

Well then he's not a real prince, that's for sure. IF he even exists.

"What I mean is, he's not stuffy or formal. He's comfortable and relaxed."

Shin sat silently.

Finally, Oscar offered, "I promise, you will like the Light Prince. But if you don't want to meet him today, I understand. It's your choice, dear one. You're not obligated."

She glanced at the door. In a few minutes the heat from the cops would lift and she'd be able to leave. So if this craziness didn't pan out there would be no harm done. *I suppose it can't hurt if I play along.*

"Okay, I'll meet him. Where is he?" She looked around.

Oscar laughed. "You can only see him with your star-eyes. Close your natural eyes, Shin, so your earth vision doesn't interfere with the unveiling."

Shin shot a wary glance toward the old man. She wouldn't dare close her eyes for even a second—not in the house of three almost-strangers! In a force of habit, her left leg started bobbing nervously, and her chest tensed with worry.

The old man's smile faded, and for a few seconds he sat quietly.

Shin watched his smile disappear. *I was right. Their sugary sweetness is just an act.* She started to get up and move away, when Oscar spoke.

"It's true," he motioned toward the kitchen where Maggie and Madison were loading dishes into the dishwasher, "you haven't known the three of us very long. In one sense we're almost strangers, so I can understand why you might think it's foolish to close your eyes while in our house." His smile returned and he waved a hand in the air. "But don't worry, the Light Prince can still meet you if your earth eyes are open. I only suggested it for your sake, to make it a bit easier."

Sinking back onto the sofa, Shin didn't know whether she should be upset that he'd read her mind again, or relieved to know they probably weren't dangerous psychopaths.

"And Shin, if you don't want to stay in OtherSide, you can come back to Earth whenever you choose."

She gave him another quick glance with a small nod attached.

They sat in awkward silence. She wondered why Oscar was just sitting there, until she remembered he was waiting for her to ask that prince guy about those star-eyes. And doing just that, Shin stumbled head-on into one of the most important decisions of her life. *Okay, uh, Mr. Light Prince . . . guy . . . sir . . . if you're real . . . I don't know how it works, but if there IS something I haven't seen . . . would you come and open my star-eyes?* She sat for about ten seconds. Nothing. Fidgeting, she uncrossed her legs and wanted to quit such a stupid game.

"Be patient, Shin," Oscar said quietly. "And don't think too hard. You can be sure he'll come."

Feeling ridiculous and weird and maybe the tiniest bit hopeful, she considered shutting her eyes to make it easier. Since Oscar and his family weren't psychopaths, Shin turned away from the old man so he couldn't see her face, and closed her earth eyes on the chance that there was something to his universe secret.

CHAPTER NINE

Eddy had pressured Dibs to fess up about where Shin was headed. He then gave the information to Adam Fox and his partner, and they hurried over to James Street.

After the police left the warehouse, Tall Eddy stepped inside the door. "Dibsy, it's time for us to have a man-to-man talk." He sauntered over to the sofa and sat down next to Dibs. Narrowing his eyes, he leaned front. "Y'know, if the cops hadn't been so intent on finding your little girlfriend, they probably would've interrogated you and hauled you in, seeing that you're a minor on the loose, just like her. I bailed you out today. Got them focused on the girlfriend instead." Tall Eddy held up two fingers close to Dibs' face. "That's twice in the last couple a' months I did you a big favor."

Intrigue was nearby. His panic had subsided, since there was only one dazzle hanging around. Still, a laser-sword was pointed in his direction, so he carefully preened his wings at a safe distance. One eye on the dazzle, he flicked away some loosened dirt, straightened out his clean wing, and pulled the other wing toward himself to continue grooming. There wasn't much else for him to do, because his human was well trained, and the present interactions were going smoothly. His earthling was representing UnderSide quite effectively, which made him look good. He raised his voice and called toward his earthling, "Keep it up, fool, and I might get a promotion."

Dibs frowned and leaned front to rest his elbows on his thighs. He didn't like the sound of the conversation. First of all, Shin wasn't his girlfriend, though he did worry about her being hunted. But mainly, he hated the idea of becoming even more obliged to Tall Eddy, who was more crooked than a bent nail.

Eddy slapped the side of Dibs' leg and changed subjects. "So, what's up? Are you still just makin' it day by day, or did you find real work so you don't have to be a freeloader on society?"

Uneasy, Dibs defended himself. "Eddy, just this mornin' I said I'm gonna' find work. But I gotta' be careful, 'cause if an employer is too nosy, I could get hauled in."

"Well," Eddy shot back, "it just so happens I have a proposition for you. And I can even give you somethin' for your work." He paused to reconsider. "Though, come to think of it, since you owe me paybacks I might have to wait for a while before I start handing you the green stuff." He leaned over and gave Dibs a punch on the arm. "But outta' the goodness of my heart I'll see that you get three square meals a day. And I'll make sure you stay outta' juvenile hall."

Dibs liked the idea of being fed, and finding work had been on his mind. Just not with this particular person, who was slimier than anyone he'd ever met. He was feeling pushed into a corner.

"So, what were you thinkin' of?"

"Glad you asked!" Tall Eddy flashed a smile. "How about if you come to work with our operation at Cutter's Salvage? We got a real good thing goin' there, but we need reliable lookouts to protect our guys." He pointed at Dibs. "That's where you come in. You already have street smarts, so all you gotta' do is be on site when they're snatching a car, to alert the crew if somebody gets too close. It's easy."

When Dibs had talked about getting a job, he'd meant more or less honest work. Stealing a little food here and there in order to be able to eat was one thing. But snatching cars, that was real stealing. "Eddy, thanks for thinkin' of me. But maybe I'll try a couple a' other options and let you know in a week or two."

Eddy's mouth twitched as his smile melted into shades of menace. "I wasn't exactly giving you an option, Dibsy. It's juvie hall, or working for me. You decide. Shall we say, I have connections that can put you in the slammer"—he leaned in toward Dibs, hardened his voice into a cold edge, and snapped his fingers on each word—"just (snap) like (snap) that (snap). And if you even think of squealing, juvie hall will seem like a pleasant option. Believe me Dibsy, you don't wanna' mess with me."

As Eddy sat back and waited for a response, Dibs kept his focus on the floor and shifted uncomfortably in his seat. At the mention of juvenile hall his thoughts had turned fuzzy. His palms were clammy, his tongue was stuck to the roof of his mouth, and sweat beaded across his forehead. He sat silently, not knowing how to respond to his seamy blackmailer.

Urielle heard a gutteral cackle coming from the direction of the drab hovering in the distance. She ignored its mocking tone and placed herself directly in front of her earthling. Bending down to look into his human eyes, she said, "Hey little man, don't give in to this guy's tough talk. Don't give his words energy, and you'll be able to see beyond them, to a better way."

A full thirty seconds passed while Dibs silently contemplated Eddy's supposed offer. Looking up, he decided there was no apparent way out. He was trapped. With all the optimism he could muster, he cleared his throat, forced a smile, and said to his new extortionist boss, "Sure, Eddy. It'll be great to work with you. When can I start?"

Slapping Dibs' knee, Eddy warmed up instantly. "Atta'

boy, Dibsy! I knew you'd come around. You show up at the salvage yard tonight around nine, and I'll bring donuts to celebrate your first night on the job."

Tall Eddy stood up and headed for the door, then turned around to say one more thing. "Oh, and I don't know what's gonna' happen with your little girlfriend. But if she makes it through the police interrogation, I wouldn't mention anything to her about your job. Might get you both in serious trouble, since bein' a snitch is disloyal. And we don't take kindly to that." He formed a gun shape with his right hand, pointed two fingers like a barrel at Dibs, and shot an imaginary bullet in his direction. "We'll treat you real good if you treat us good. Know what I mean?" Eddy's face filled with a crooked smile. "Get some sleep so you're fresh for tonight, kid."

As Eddy left the warehouse Intrigue flew beside him, wearing a similar slanted grin. For the drab, the only thing that could have trumped the experience would've been for Light Stealer to see how skillfully his earthling played the boy into the palm of his hand.

"Maybe someday I'll become a chief!" Panting with excitement, Intrigue pictured himself as a boss of UnderSide with a horde of peon drabs bowing down to him. The idea made him even more determined to make his human host as despicable as possible. Surely then, someone in the upper echelons would take notice and promote him to a higher rank.

While Intrigue conjured up his own personal grandeur, Urielle stilled her form and pulled near to her human. He hadn't been able to stand up against the conniving man, at least not this time. But he was a Light-Seeker and that was reason for hope. She leaned in and laid her light-hand on his head. "Don't give up, little man. Don't you ever give up, you hear?"

Dibs crumpled onto his smelly sofa, too scared to think straight. The hostile sound of Eddy's threats echoed in his mind. Everything had happened so quickly. He could only stare into space for quite some time and wonder how his life had turned into such a huge mess.

After mentally walking himself into the doldrums, Dibs got up and went outside. Needing something to sweeten his sour disposition, he decided to beg for enough money to buy one of those delicious icy, mocha caramel, whipped cream, coffee kinds of drinks.

Stuffing down the reality of his predicament, he chose to focus on the good side. *Soon I'll be eating three meals every single day.* "Can't beat that," he said bravely to himself.

Dibs strolled toward the outdoor shopping mall, where he knew he would find somebody in a good mood. In exchange for a joke or a funny comment, he'd get them to part with their unwanted pocket change. And in no time at all, that frappé drink would begin filling up the empty pit in his stomach that had formed somewhere in the middle of his conversation with Tall Eddy.

CHAPTER TEN

Shin leaped out of her seat and opened her natural eyes, too stunned to know what to do. "Holy smoke!"

"Stay there, Shin." Oscar extended a calming hand in midair, his face lit up with a smile. "Everything's all right. Just stay there."

Sitting down again, she looked away from Oscar and shut her earth eyes. She was suspended in space against a thick, soft wall. It was tinted in some incredible hue she'd never before laid eyes on—not at all like the dreary grays or blacks of Earth. And it was humungous. The membrane-like barrier stretched up and down, left and right, as far as she could see.

Shin felt herself being pulled into its gel-like substance. Almost as quickly, something pushed her through and she was standing on a hard surface on the other side.

Weird! She took inventory of her body to make sure she'd made it safely through the bizarre wall in one piece. Nothing had changed. Or had it? Glancing down at her arms, she noticed there seemed to be a new tone to her skin. Shin looked back at the membrane. Its hue was identical to the new shade on her arms, as if some of its gel had stuck to her body.

She scanned her surroundings and saw no buildings, no

terrain, no vegetation. Only a vast, flat surface in the middle of nowhere.

A bright mistiness floated lightly around her body. Shin waved her hand through its cloud-like haze. It curled around her fingers. Dipping her hand up and down, the mist repeated her exact movements. She swung her arm in a wider circle. It followed her motion and swirled in a large, graceful arc.

Glancing up from her hand, Shin startled. During the short time she'd been playing with the mist around her waist, the remainder of its substance had been rapidly expanding. *Quite* rapidly. No longer just around her body, it was billowing high and wide and deep and resembled a gigantic system of thunderhead storm clouds. Continuing to shoot upward and outward, its size increased so quickly, that by the time Shin was able to grasp what was happening, the cloud's mistiness had already taken over the whole atmosphere. Turning full circle, she could see nothing else. She was entirely surrounded.

And right away, it began to brighten. As a great flash erupted within its expanse, the cloud's once gentle glow transformed into a vivid radiance. After a second explosion of light the whole mass became a glare so blinding, Shin instinctively squinted hard and shielded her face with her hands.

At that moment she was struck with the familiarity of the whole scene. *This is the nightmare I had! It exists!* In her dreams she'd stood inside the same kind of violent light, feeling utterly exposed.

Being in such brilliance was the opposite of staying cloaked. She wanted to bail—to run away. Oscar's words popped into her mind. He'd said no one *had* to stay in this place. She could open her earth eyes and forget the whole thing. It would be easy to leave, to get away from the powerful blaze of white.

Following on the heel of those thoughts came another one. It was the sort of rare thought that rose up from somewhere deep inside the middle of desires, the type of thought that cut through confusion and distraction—not at all a normal thought for someone whose goal in life was to remain invisible. And this was her thought: *I am so tired of running.*

Ever since escaping from foster care Shin had lived like a fugitive, camouflaged in plain view, avoiding people and places, terrified of authorities, dreading danger, and scared stiff of being caught. Her life existed in round-the-clock surveillance, constant self-protection, and a never-ending vigilance.

She was like the stray dogs that frequented the trash bins at the zoo. They were too frightened to allow anyone to come close, yet she could tell they wanted to be loved, wanted desperately to find their pack. She'd seen the fear in the eyes of those nervous mutts, and she could identify with the twitching in their muscles and their readiness to run if anyone came near.

But what if the things Oscar had said about this bizarre world were true? What if there *was* a family in this place? No family in their right mind would ever like her instantly, she knew that much. But what if they didn't outright reject her? She might be able to work her way into being allowed to stay.

Though nothing made sense to her well-developed cloaking skills, a stony stubbornness set itself in Shin's gut, and she made her decision. In spite of the blinding atmosphere, she would stick it out.

In this particular instance the part of Shin's personality that was headstrong was to her benefit, since the second she looked down and caught sight of herself, a stab of fear coursed through her body. Standing in the midst of such a vigorous light, everything about her was highly visible, every flaw strikingly exposed. She was as conspicuous as a raven in a snowstorm.

Panic surged into her throat. But the possibility of being able to meet that family flooded her mind, and it was just the shot of courage she needed. *I won't run.* She set her jaw and said it out loud. "I WON'T run."

Sitting down on the surface, Shin tucked her legs underneath her, folded her arms across her chest, and closed her eyes to wait for something or someone to show up.

"Look up, Amber."

Only a few seconds passed before the voice spoke, calling her by her real name. She raised her head just enough to see the form of a man silhouetted against the light.

Leaning down, he offered his hand to pull her up.

She stood on her own strength, her head lowered and her eyes on the ground. Images of taunting hoodlums passed through her mind.

"My eyes, dear one. Here are my eyes."

He was standing in front of her. She could tell by his motions he was gesturing toward his own face.

"Find my eyes, Amber."

Anything but the eyes. Asking her to fight a wild animal was an easier proposition. On the streets, eyes turned in Shin's direction meant someone wanted to use her, or sell her for a profit, or get rid of her like food gone rotten. Or worse, they wanted to lock her up in foster care and throw away the key. Eyes were gates to a private garden. Once people looked in her eyes they had permission to walk right into her life. She wasn't sure she wanted to give this stranger access.

"They won't harm you."

She'd come this far. How could she turn back now? Shin sighed, desperately wishing for these eyes to be different. Daring with a shred of hope they *were* different, she pulled up and forced herself to look into the face of the man standing before her.

What she saw became her undoing. Suddenly her need became as palpable as the one who stood with his eyes focused on her, and it was too much for her to bear.

In Earth's realm Shin reacted by crying, which soon turned into sobbing with loud and choking wails. Oscar moved closer and placed a gentle hand on her shoulder. Her guard down, she unconsciously leaned against his side for support.

With grandfatherly comfort he pulled her to himself and held her, soothed her. "Let it all out, my dear. It's all right, just let it come." He'd been in her situation and knew how the Light Prince's fathomless love opened up hidden wells of hurt and pain, of failure and rebellion, that festered in recesses of the soul.

Shin wept for quite some time as the stranger held her gaze. His eyes washed her within, back and forth, back and forth, loosening filth and contamination. Tenderness flowed like a living, moving stream and lifted out the sediment of her shame.

Those eyes seemed to hold dreams of the future and other good things she couldn't quite recognize, because they were new and foreign to her present way of thinking. But with each passing minute the power of his fixed affection lightened her heart. Gradually the impurities fell away, incinerated by the light around her being.

Finally Shin was clean, her darkness gone.

She stood staring into his eyes. They were as deep as an ocean, and she was floating on their gentle waves of peace.

All at once he leaned over, scooped her up into his strong arms, and laughed. "Amber Grace McConnell, welcome! I'm your brother, the Light Prince. I'm so glad to finally meet you here in OtherSide!" After a long embrace he set her down again on her feet.

Shin wasn't used to being shown affection by another human being. Neither was she accustomed to anyone calling her by her real name. But even more unexpected was what the Light Prince had called himself.

"You're my *brother*?"

"I am!" The prince smiled and then motioned to the soft wall behind her. "You passed through the Crimson Wall and now you're my sister!" He positively glowed with pride.

Her face pinched with uncertainty, Shin startled herself by speaking her thoughts so openly. "But you're a prince!"

"True, and you are the newest member of our royal family."

"You're part of that family Oscar talked about? And it's *royal?*" If that was true, she'd never be allowed to join. For one thing, she hadn't been born into a genuine bloodline. She'd been born into yuck. Plus, she knew as much about palaces and royal customs as cartoon characters knew about real life.

Raising her eyebrows, she gaped at the prince person who had just shocked her by giving her a big hug. He was confident and dignity oozed from his being. She inspected her scrubby clothing and glanced back at him. *I'll never be royalty, and I'll never be part of his family.* He was clean, with those incredibly kind eyes, a great beard, curly dark hair, and some sort of a radiating aura coming out of him. *I'm not anything like him.*

The Light Prince responded to her mind as he playfully mussed the hair on her head. "Little sister, you will need to learn how to think like a princess."

There had to be a mistake. She'd never even dressed up in a princess costume. Once, a foster mom had put an old sheet over her head, cut two holes for eyes, and sent her trick-or-treating. She'd been a bedhead ghost, while everybody else in the neighborhood walked around in fancy-pants ninja outfits or fairytale princess gowns. As far as she was concerned, that pretty much described her place in life.

The prince patiently explained the facts. "You and I have the same blood now, Amber. After you came through the Crimson Wall you wondered if some of it had stuck to your body. But in reality, it isn't *on* your skin. The crimson is now part of you, forever.

Shin looked at her arm. Sure enough, it still had that same, fabulous new tone.

"Now, come and look at my arm."

She felt weird and wrinkled her nose questioningly.

"Go on, take a look at my arm." Her prince brother held out his right arm for her to observe. "What do you see?"

"Uh, a few freckles. And hair."

"Underneath."

Studying his arm more closely, she saw the same shade in his veins that was now in her own. "You have the same stuff inside!"

The prince laughed. "Exactly. My dear, you are now royalty, just like me."

Before Shin could talk herself out of being noble, the Light Prince motioned for her to follow and then turned and walked away.

As she trailed after him, she noticed the hugely intense atmosphere was gone. The gentle, glowing mist was back, slowly circling around both of them. Shin shook her head. *What was up with that spooky monster cloud?*

"Bright light is only frightening when there's something to conceal." The prince turned around and looked straight into her eyes. "Dear one, there's no need to hide. You never have to run away again."

Shin stopped and stared. She couldn't remember a time when she hadn't hidden. Beginning at the age of two, when people in her house raised their voices and then started hitting each other, she quickly learned to disappear into a bedroom closet to bury herself under piles of clothing. Like a possum, she would pretend to be dead, staying perfectly still, until the only sound left in the house was a solid rhythmic snoring. Then, and only then, she would uncloak herself and tiptoe into the kitchen to fix a bowl of cereal for dinner, or for whatever meal had gone by during her hidden time in the closet.

Ever since those days she'd worked hard to perfect the art of laying low. Of keeping out of sight. Of hiding.

He was watching her again. She lowered her eyes and tried to mask her discomfort.

Gently, he pulled her chin up until she couldn't avoid him. "You're safe now, Amber, and no matter what happens, you'll always be safe."

Shin forced a smile. Even though they'd just met, he seemed to know her inside and out. She wanted to feel secure, but it was all too new for her to trust.

He answered her thoughts. "Trust will come, don't worry. But right now, I have something to show you."

CHAPTER ELEVEN

As she turned to follow the Light Prince, Shin did a double take. "How did that get here?" A large mansion stood right before her eyes. "I'm sure that building wasn't here before!"

"Travel in this realm is different than on Earth. Here, without the use of time, we walk through light doors and move easily from one place to another." The prince walked up the steps of the huge house and onto the porch. "You and I just left the region of Hearth White, at the outer rim near the Crimson Wall. We walked through a light door, and now we're in the region called Fire's Flame, in central OtherSide."

He motioned for Shin to join him on the porch and invited her to take a seat on one of two large, overstuffed chairs. Sitting on the other chair, he gestured toward their surroundings. "Look around, little sister. Now that you've become a Lightning, this is your home as well as ours."

Shin sank down into the plump cushions, her mind still trying to wrap around crimson walls, and mega-sizing clouds, and royalty. And now he was talking about timeless travel, and being a Lightning, whatever that meant!

Her prince brother leaned in to explain. "Before, you were known as a Light-Seeker. But people with opened star-eyes are called Lightnings."

Shaking her head, Shin grinned. On the streets, except in the middle of the night when forced to wake up and take cover, she'd thoroughly enjoyed the rousing light shows put on by a good storm. Being a Lightning sounded great to her.

She ran her fingers over the pillows on her chair. They were soft, but reflected light as though made of smooth metal. And the material under her shoes was plush, yet it shone like glass. *Weird things in this place!*

The Prince's eyes twinkled. "Actually, OtherSide is the original. The things on Earth imitate our realm." He pointed to the spongy texture below their feet. "See this substance? We created moss on your planet as a natural expression of this flooring."

She gaped at him as three or four thoughts jammed into her brain at once: that OtherSide was the real deal and things on Earth were a copy, that this prince guy said he'd created the stuff on Earth, and that where they were seated looked a whole lot more pristine than anything in her ratty neighborhood.

He smiled. "It's all true. We designed your world as a reflection of OtherSide. But we don't take credit for Under-Side's mutations, or for what has been spoiled by human twistings."

Her mind was reeling with new discoveries, so the part about UnderSide and its mutations flew right past Shin. Neither did she realize the prince was always reading her thoughts. She was too absorbed, taking a long, full drink of OtherSide's luscious atmosphere.

Her eyes wandered out to the view beyond the porch, where all sorts of unfamiliar plants glistened beautifully in the breeze. But it was what danced on the horizon above the vegetation that drew Shin's attention and made her catch her breath. Vibrating and gyrating across the whole sky was an endless display of incredible tones and shades. *Holy Smoke!*

There are zillions of those things! And they're not at all like Earth's icky grays.

"They're called colors, and there *are* "zillions" of them. Compared to Earth, OtherSide's colors are endless."

Her eyes bugged out. "Earth has these?"

He nodded. "They're magnificent, aren't they?"

"Well, I don't think they exist where I live. Our sky is boring. It doesn't look anything like that." Shin shot a quick look at the Light Prince, astonished at how freely she was expressing her opinions out loud. *He sure is comfortable to be around.*

"Dear one, your star-eyes have been opened now. You'll be amazed at the colors of your planet. And for that matter," he grinned, "you, princess, have your very own color. It's a lovely tone called Amber yellow."

As her new brother pointed toward her color on the horizon, the misty substance hovering around her took on the exact same shade of yellow.

"I have one of these . . . co-lors?" She spoke the new word out loud and turned to stare at the richly hued yellow cloud circling her body. "This is mine?"

"All yours!"

Seriously? It's so pretty! She stared with awe, glad that it belonged to her. But there was a problem. She hated that name: the one her mom had chosen for her. As far as she was concerned, she was, and always would be, "Shin."

The prince looked at her, his eyes softly serious. "You shouldn't hate the name Amber. It's beautiful, and it fits you perfectly."

Shin jerked her head around. He was reading her mind, just as Oscar and Crazy Lady and Madison had done! *How in the world do you DO that?* And then it occurred to her, in one way or another he'd been reading her mind ever since they'd met.

He answered her mental question. "In this realm no one

needs to talk, because all our thoughts are fully transparent. Speech is just an option."

You can read all my crappy thoughts? she thought, and knew he would. And being comfortable with the prince got hijacked by the embarrassment of having a transparent brain.

"Don't feel bad. Here in OtherSide we love perfectly, so see-through thinking isn't threatening."

Love stuff or not, Shin wasn't happy. Having visible thoughts was worse than clipping her underwear onto a clothesline and hanging it out to dry in plain view, for the whole world to see.

"Maybe it will help you to know that on Earth, our kind of communication is less frequent, since there's far too much interference for a constant transmission."

The inexperienced princess tried not to think.

The Light Prince leaned in and said kindly, "Amber. Look at me."

She did.

"We saw you in your alleyway. We see you at the zoo and the library, and when you eat at the Hungry Appaloosa. We've known you forever and we love you."

Her eyes were wide with disbelief. She shot back defensively, "But how do you know about all those places? How did you see . . . ?" Shin's voice trailed off as her mind filled with confusion and suspicion. "How did you know . . . ?"

He looked into her frightened eyes. "We share your realm. We're all around you. Even though we're invisible to your earth eyes, we're just across the veneer that separates Earth from OtherSide. You never need to hide again."

As she pictured the prince frequenting her alleyway, reading all her thoughts and watching everything she'd ever done, Shin's brain began to overload. Hot humiliation flushed her face and a familiar pressure rose in her chest. She almost opened her earth eyes to escape from OtherSide, but just then he reached over and gently pulled her self-conscious frown toward his own face.

"If you only knew how happy you make us, you'd never worry again about being seen. We're wild about you Amber, and that will never change."

Shin was shocked. His words were full of goodness, just like Oscar's words about her. She didn't know how to carry them, not in her heart, and not in her head. That anyone could be interested in her—much less *like* her—was as believable as the moon being made of cheese.

"The Light Stealer's done that to you, dear one. One of his most detestable schemes is to persuade human beings to dislike their own names, their own colors, and even the presents we've placed in their lives."

She looked away without a clue as to who the Light Stealer was, but knowing she'd done that very thing. She had completely rejected Amber. And as for presents, Shin was positive there weren't any in her life. The only presents she got were at Christmastime, whenever stores gave away free candy canes or pens or little promotional trinkets.

"When you entered through the Crimson Wall you became part of us. You became royalty. And that means you'll need to learn to accept the treasures that belong to you."

Shin stared tensely into her lap while her strange new brother unfolded a bunch of bizarro ideas. He spoke as if his words were made of threaded gold.

Protesting weakly, she said, "I've been Shin a long time."

"Look at me."

Forcing herself to raise her head, she focused on his face.

"They're green-brown." He smiled and little creases surrounded his warm eyes.

She scrunched her face into a question.

"The colors in my eyes are called green and brown."

As Shin stared into his green-browns, a measure of safety came and filled that part of her where Amber had been silenced so long ago.

"You can choose to start accepting our gifts and to enjoy your name."

He said it like he was a true expert on the subject.

"Go ahead, you can do it."

"What?"

"Say your name."

Safety flew away again as Shin squirmed uncomfortably in her chair and considered her options. She could leave OtherSide pronto, try to speak that other name she despised, or refuse. But of course, he would get upset with her if she refused.

"Amber, I will still be perfectly happy with you if you choose not to say your name. You're safe here, dear one."

Shin shook her head. She'd never get used to someone reading her thoughts. Observing his face to see if he meant what he'd said, she saw a smile stretched across his lips. Even his eyes were smiling. Her anxious mind calmed. *If he's so sure, then I can at least try.*

"I am . . ." Water began to float up into Shin's eyeballs. Trying to say her birth name definitely pinched that silent place inside. She winced in pain.

"You're a pretty yellow Amber, and in the whole universe there's not another color like you."

His expert words weren't helping her hold back the dripping from her eyes. She wiped her cheeks.

"I'm . . ."

She stopped. The truth was, she didn't want to identify with that stupid kid who was yanked out of her family the way a dentist pulls a rotten tooth. That kid was obviously a complete misfit. An oddball. A freak. At least *Shin* had some street smarts. She wasn't always a total loser. Not like the previous weirdo version of herself, the one this prince specialist wanted to her to suddenly start liking.

"Dear one, that little girl named Amber was perfectly loveable."

That confounded transparent thinking was making it impossible for her to stay cloaked! She sniffed hard. *How difficult can this be? Just SAY it!* Getting irritated at herself for being such a wimp, it was just what she needed. With all the determination of a willful street kid she pressed sound through her lips—"I'm Amber."

All the colors on the horizon vibrated and every yellow hue became absolutely brilliant.

Light Prince touched her on the shoulder. "Brava, Amber! Well done!"

Shin still felt uncomfortable and squishy-sad on the inside, but said the name again anyway—"Amber." She glanced up and caught her new brother grinning from ear to ear and looking at her like she'd just won an Olympic medal.

"You're radiating beautifully."

Sure enough, the light cloud around her body was filled with her yellow, and it was brighter than ever.

"Holy smoke!"

The whole idea of color was simply scrumptious. It occurred to her she probably wasn't the only person with one of those things. "Hey, does Oscar have a color?"

The prince nodded and pointed to a spot of red-orange over to their left. "Oscar orange is there." Then he gestured to another, softer shade of lemony-orange. "And there's Madison orange. And straight ahead," he motioned to a color directly in front of them, "is Maggie green."

Sitting back in his chair, his expression turned to sheer delight. "We have an infinite number of hues, and each one is extremely valuable." He waited for their eyes to meet before continuing. "Even though there are countless yellows, your Amber yellow is very precious to us."

He's gotta' be confusing my color with somebody else's color. Oh, wait. This must be one of those new princess concepts.

"See? You're already starting to think royally!" He held out his hand for her to slap it, the way she did with Dibs.

Grinning, she gave the prince a palm clap.

They sat in easy silence.

"Why are colors so valuable?" In the quiet, she'd been thinking. All those colors were gorgeous, but being extremely valuable made no sense. Not for something that couldn't be held, or used, like money. As far as she could see they were just pretty.

He looked at her and the lines on his face grew serious. "Human beings value money because it gives them power to change things: their homes, their reputations, their situations. But in fact, your earth money is only worthwhile if it is an expression of *love* and *confident expectation*. These are what we prize most in OtherSide."

Shin sure understood the value of money. As a homeless person, having some made all the difference. And love, she could agree it was valuable, which was the reason there wasn't much of it on the streets. But confident expectation? That was a strange concept. Unless he'd meant to expect the worst and be confident it would happen.

From his explanation the only thing getting through to her was how cheap she felt.

"Look at your Amber yellow."

She glanced at the glowing mist around her body. She had to admit, it sure was a great color.

"It's when our *light* mingles with *your color*, that love and confident expectation can happen."

He paused.

She waited for him to say something that made sense.

"When our realm's light shines into your Amber yellow—and then you shine on another human being—your light-infused color changes that person in a way no one else can." He smiled. "And that's valuable."

His face was full of honest glow.

At the thought of being worth something in OtherSide's system of value, Shin's muscles relaxed and she felt lighter.

Almost weightless. Still, she would need some time to start seeing her own color as precious.

The Prince stood up and motioned for his sister to join him. "Come with me. There is one more color to see, a significant hue."

CHAPTER TWELVE

They took a few steps and Shin noticed the prince's mansion was no longer there. "Hey! What in the—?" Her head spun around. "Where did—?" She gawked. "Did we just—?"

"Light door. We're in the region of Morning Glow, which is in northern OtherSide."

"I never even saw the change coming!"

"Stick with me, sister, and you'll go places," he said with a laugh.

They were standing on a magnificent portico lined with great marble pillars, facing a long rectangular table. On the table was one item, a large round pottery bowl sitting in the middle as a spectacular centerpiece. With delicately carved leaves edging the entire rim, it was the loveliest piece of pottery Shin had ever seen. Made from a shimmery, silvery-white material that emitted a warm glow, the bowl and its decorative leaves sparkled with light.

She leaned forward and peeked inside.

"This is crimson." He nodded toward the beautifully hued liquid filling bowl.

"Wow." It was the most amazing color, in her opinion the best one she'd seen so far. A look of recognition spread across her face. "Hey! That's the color of the wall I squeezed through when I first came here!"

"That's why we call it the Crimson Wall. It's the way to open your star-eyes."

"But Oscar said you open our star-eyes."

"I did. Crimson is my color." His face brightened. "The Crimson Wall surrounds all of OtherSide, and everyone who comes here for the first time passes through it. But once you've come *through* it, you're always *inside* my crimson."

Light Prince turned and bowed to his little sister. "You, princess, now live in two realms simultaneously—on Earth, and also in OtherSide. You'll always be within our realm, so whenever you want to, you can easily cross through the veneer into this invisible sphere and come for a visit."

"No kidding! I live both there and here?" He was going sci-fi on her. She loved every second.

"Yep. OtherSide surrounds your whole universe and far beyond."

"Wow." This place was cooler than any of the books she'd ever read: science fiction, fantasies, mysteries, comedies, and for sure, those girly romance ones.

"You've experienced a lot today. We can finish this discussion at another time." He reached over and brushed away a strand of hair from her face. "Whenever you like, you can come here to meet me. And you'll also want to meet Father Forever and The Light, and then Original Family introductions will be complete." He playfully touched her nose with his finger. "But now it's time for you to return to Oscar and his family. They're eager to hear about your first journey to this realm."

"No!" she called out impulsively. "I like it here! I don't want to go back!"

The Light Prince gently took her face in his hands. "Sweet one, you're still an earthling. You're needed there for Dibs, and for Oscar's family, and for so many others you haven't even met. But now that your star-eyes are opened, we can be together anytime." He leaned over and kissed her forehead the way a big brother smooches his favorite kid sister. "I can't wait to see you here again. And until then, I'll be close by—just on the other side of the veneer."

And with that, Shin sensed herself coming back into the living room of the Owens family.

She opened her earth eyes and smiled up at Oscar.

He gave her a big sideways hug and almost hollered in her ear. "Welcome back, dear one! I can't wait to hear all about it!"

She shook her head and blinked a few times, wondering how long she'd been in OtherSide.

"Well, how was it?" Oscar was brimming with excitement.

"Definitely cool. I met the Light Prince!"

"Oh, that's wonderful! Just wonderful!"

Maggie and Madison Owens entered the hallway from the back yard and Oscar exploded with enthusiasm. "Shin met the Light Prince!"

"Oh, honey, that's fantastic!" Maggie pulled up a chair and sat down.

"He's amazing, isn't he?" Madison smiled widely as she plunked herself down on the sofa next to Oscar and Shin. Sighing dreamily, she said, "He's the real Prince Charming."

Glancing at the swooning girl, Shin started to mentally make fun of her.

"You know, he's the one all the fairy tales talk about."

Madison had said it as though it was the most obvious thing in the universe. Shin wasn't used to being around other girls, let alone the squeaky-clean, sappy kind. But something didn't feel right about mocking. Her thoughts wandered to the Light Prince. He would never pick on anybody. She decided she wanted to be nice.

"What else did he show you, Shin?" Madison asked.

Conversations with the prince about her OtherSide color and her birth name came to mind. But explaining what had happened over there felt uncomfortable.

"You don't have to tell us if you don't want to, dear one."

Shin looked over at Oscar. He was such a nice person. "No, it was great, I just..." she hesitated. They wouldn't make fun of her. At least, she didn't think they would.

"I have a new name."

Madison leaned closer. "You do? What is it?"

There wasn't one hint of meanness in Madison's voice. *Maybe she won't laugh at me.* Shin bit her lip and looked down at the carpet. Carefully, she said, "My real name is Amber."

"That's beautiful!"

She lifted her head. Madison was being sincere, she could see that much.

"Yeah. And I wanna' be called that from now on." Shin sat up quickly, astounded at how easily she'd spit out that announcement! But it felt right.

"Amber. It's so colorful." Mrs. Owens rolled the new name off her tongue, as if tasting a new flavor.

"It's also my color, Amber yellow." All at once, Shin-turned-Amber remembered what the Light Prince had said about Earth having color. She shot a glance around the living room and leaped off the sofa, shouting in stunned amazement. "There IS color on Earth! He was right!" Turning slowly, she stared at the pictures on the wall, the coffee table, the curtains, the rug, the vases, and everything else in the entire room.

The whole Owens family was nodding and smiling.

"Go ahead, Shin—I mean, Amber," Oscar said, "and have a look around. Your star-eyes are open now, so you'll see all the color on the planet."

Catching a glimpse of herself in the mirror on the opposite wall, Amber noticed even her hair had color. She walked over and looked at her image. Her eyes weren't gray. They were some other shade.

Oscar smiled warmly. "We all have color, dear one—our faces, our hair, our eyes. Just like the Light Prince."

"Holy smoke!" Soaking in every tone and hue, she thought to herself, *There should be a holiday just to celebrate this stuff! I wanna' learn every single one of their names.*

"I'll teach you their names," Madison said as she stood up and walked over to where Amber was standing. "Your hair and your eyes are brown."

"Brown." Amber sounded out the word. "Sort of like the Light Prince."

"Well, his eyes are more—"

"Green-brown." She finished Madison's sentence and looked at her for confirmation.

Madison smiled. "Yeah, green-brown."

Oscar looked at Amber and then caught Maggie's eye and gave her a nod. It was time to divulge their plan. "Well, Amber dear," he spoke her new name with great care, "we've talked about this as a family. And we'd like to invite you to live with us for a few days, until we can sort out a more permanent solution. Would you like that?"

That people she barely knew were inviting her to stay in their house was beyond her comprehension. Once, she'd eaten gobs of free ice cream on the hottest day of summer and had gotten sick to her stomach. Staying in the home of these nice people was a lot like that. The idea made her slightly nauseous, but it was too delicious to pass up.

Even if some of that pressure had begun to build up in her chest, Amber surprised herself again by saying, "I guess I could stay a couple of days." Before, she wouldn't have done that in a million years.

Quickly, in case they were offering out of politeness, Amber added, "If you guys are sure. I mean, I don't want to be a bother or anything."

"You're not a bother, Amber. We like you!"

At Madison's kind words Amber's cheeks flushed with warmth. She focused on the carpeting.

"And you can have some of my clothing. It'll be like

we're sisters sharing things from our closets." Madison was beaming, obviously pleased with the idea of having another girl in the house.

"That should work." Maggie eyed both girls. "You two look like you're the same size."

They took Amber on a tour of the rest of the house and finished with a room they called the guest bedroom. Except, then they changed their wording and said for the next few days, it was her bedroom.

She asked to take a shower, and they loaded her arms with all sorts of good smelling soaps, a huge, soft towel, a pair of Madison's jeans, and a T-shirt. Disappearing into the bathroom, she stayed under the hot water spray for a long time. After all that washing up in cold water sinks at public restroom facilities, she felt plain rich.

Amber stood still as the water stream massaged her face. *This is gonna' be totally weird. I can't believe I'm doing this.* Her shoulder and neck muscles tensing with fear, she closed her eyes and stuck her whole head under the water.

As the steam rose around her, several colors from that strange new world floated across her internal vision. Oscar Orange. Maggie Green. Madison Orange. Amber yellow. They were Lightnings, the word the Light Prince had used to name people who went through the Crimson Wall. She saw the prince's vivid color in her mind's eye and smiled. Even if Oscar and his family were practically strangers, she had two things in common with them. They'd been to OtherSide, and they had met the prince.

Maybe staying with them wouldn't be so frightening.

She remembered what Madison had said about "weird" being negative, but "unique" being positive. "Okay, it's gonna' be totally unique," she said to anyone who was listening. So far, this new OtherSide life was positive. Amber was almost positive she was going to like it.

CHAPTER THIRTEEN

Today was her third day at the home of the Owens family. Oscar, Maggie, and Madison were all at some sort of meeting uptown, so Amber had time to herself.

In the worst way, she wanted to get out of the house and go to the zoo, or the library, or a park. After being cooped up for three whole days she was starting to understand why penned zoo animals paced all day long in their cages. They needed to be in the wild as much as she needed to be in the open air.

The problem was, Oscar had told her not to leave the house until they sorted out her runaway status. He'd explained it was too risky, because she could run into serious trouble.

But he didn't have street smarts like she did, and besides, no police cars had been spotted around the house since that first day. *I can be back before they get home, and they don't even have to know I went out. What could it hurt?*

Amber pulled on her new white and pink sneakers. As she tied her laces she wondered where to go. She considered heading to the library so she could thank Falisha. Mr. Owens had insisted on paying for the two books left in the alleyway, which meant everything was squared away with the librarian. The whole incident had even worked out to Amber's benefit, because Oscar was able to get her a real library card. Once the housing situation was settled, she would be able to legitimately borrow books.

But the library wasn't outside and she was craving fresh air. That settled it. She would head to the zoo.

Closing the front door, Amber bounced down the steps and out into the neighborhood. She pushed down a nagging guilt that tugged at her insides the way Dibs pulled at her sleeve whenever he wanted something from her.

Rahzell followed the girl and Ahnah flew by her side. Both dazzles were on duty to keep the young Lightning out of scrapes. She was new to OtherSide and didn't quite understand she had invisible enemies who were out to make her life miserable.

After a quick ten minute run Amber was at the zoo. Happy to be in a wide-open space, she sat down on Crazy Lady and Oscar's bench and swung her feet back and forth. Over to her left the retirees were perched on other benches, their arms folded across pudgy midriffs, their mouths gabbing away. They didn't recognize her in new clothes, which was just perfect. She didn't want to be noticed.

She gazed at nature all around her, still filled with wonder at the existence of color on Earth. Madison had explained the names of the basic colors, so Amber knew the trees and bushes were green. And the sky *was* blue, as Crazy Lady had once declared so confidently: and with a big, round sun shining out in all its brilliance.

A tiger slowly strolled into view from behind a stand of trees. She grinned widely. "Holy smoke! Will you look at that! They have color too!"

Her joy was cut short as two rough hands pulled against her face and covered her eyes. Former fight-or-flight instincts took over, and in one motion she leaped up and turned to face her mugger.

"Shinny! Sorta' edgy today, aren't you?"

"Oh, man! I hate when you do that, Dibs! Coming from behind and attacking me!" Her heart was thumping wildly.

"Attacking? Aw, c'mon, I was only teasing. Don't be so uptight."

"Well, you would've done the same, you rat!"

"Nah. Girls are jumpier." Dibs giggled and jerked his arm back, expecting a punch for calling her a jumpy girl.

She swung and missed his arm and they both sat down.

He stared at her. "Look at you, new rags and sneakers an' everything! I hardly recognized you. What'd you do, score another hundred bucks from Crazy Lady?"

Amber smiled and started to answer, but Dibs kept talking.

"And anyway, where ya' been? You never came back after Eddy left the other day. At least you could'a let me know you were okay, y'know."

"Yeah. I'm sorry, I thought about getting in touch with you. But things have changed a lot and I couldn't make it over to the warehouse."

She was softer and Dibs' face filled with worry. "You okay, Shinny? Not in trouble, are you?"

"No, it's not that." How could she explain all the changes of the last three days?

"Well, you gonna' leave me in the dark? C'mon, spill the beans."

She looked at him and decided to be direct. "I've been to OtherSide."

"Say what?" With all the new developments in his own life, Dibs had forgotten all about their conversation with Oscar only a few days before, on the very bench where they sat.

"Crazy Lady and Oscar,"—she slapped the bench with her hands to jog his memory—"they said we were Light-Seekers, remember? And when our star-eyes were opened they told us we'd meet the Light Prince." In her mind she saw the prince's great, pure eyes, and her voice filled out all thick and round. "I've met the Light Prince in OtherSide, Dibs. And he's incredible. You'll love him!"

Rahzell winked at Ahnah, and Urielle spun in a jubilant circle. A lively storm of brightness surged invisibly above the bench-sitters.

Dibs released a long, low whistle. "Oh man! I thought they'd put you in a foster home or somethin' drastic!" He was clearly relieved that she was okay. "The cops didn't find you, did they?"

Once again, he totally missed her words. Amber thought it wasn't so easy, communicating these new experiences.

Then his question hit her. "WHAT cops? How did you know they came after me?"

He stared at her, his face full of confusion. Or guilt. Or both.

Amber pulled out her suspicions as a weapon of defense and quickly put the facts together. Dibs had heard Oscar telling her the James Street address while they were at the zoo. Dibs was the only person who knew exactly where she was going when she left the warehouse. Dibs gave the address to sleazy Eddy. And from there, somehow Eddy's despicable lips leaked the information to the cops.

She gripped the edge of the bench. "YOU gave me away, didn't you? The cops came to James Street because of you!" She let go of the bench, pushed him hard, and stood up. "I could have been caught, Dibs! I could've ended up in foster care!"

Gaping at her without a sound, Dibs looked like he'd been hit over the head with a two-by-four.

"You don't have anything to say, do you? I'm right! You turned me in! I thought you were my friend!" He was a toxic plague, and she had to get away from him. "Ugh! You're disgusting!"

Three dazzles swirled around at the same time, keenly

aware their atmosphere had taken a turn for the worse. Ahnah smelled the inky stench of a scared drab, but she couldn't see its form anywhere.

"There they are!" Rahzell pointed to the right, where three drabs were approaching. Though the whiff of fear was strong, not everyone in the odious cluster was so timid. "One of them comes boldly. We may be in for a fight."

The more daring drab flew to within fifteen feet of the dazzles but did not attack.

"It sure is strutting its stuff." Urielle flew next to the other dazzles, her laser-sword drawn and ready.

"What do you want?" Ahnah asked. She always got to the point.

"We have a right to the girl. Back off and let us have her." Shame, the nearest and most brazen drab, sneered darkly.

"You have no rights." Urielle's voice was even and strong.

Fear was directly behind Shame and raised his voice accusingly. "But she disobeyed!"

"The Light Prince takes responsibility for her disobedience. She belongs to him." Rahzell answered the brute decidedly, having heard deviant drab reasonings more times than he cared to count.

"She dissobeyed human Oss-car. She'ss oursss." Though in a severely weakened state from having recently been impaled by the slimmer dazzle's light-saber, Control offered his cowardly defense from a good distance behind his cronies.

Clearly, the drabs felt they had legal precedent.

Rahzell moved straight toward them. "The girl is not yours. She has passed through the crimson forever and belongs to OtherSide. YOU back off!"

All three drabs flinched at the mention of the prince's color. They knew the crimson was a game-changer in every sense of the word. But on the basis of the girl's failings, the whole lot of them refused to leave and merely retreated far enough to stay out of harm's way.

As contention filled the unseen realms, Amber's brain was turning to fried mush. A twisted jumble of emotions made it impossible to think, let alone move. Her only real friend had ratted on her. Double-crossed her. Turned her in to the cops!

Forcing herself to focus, she said rudely, "I'm going home."

"Home? You got a place to live?"

"Yeah." She smirked, happy to throw her good fortune into his homeless face. "I'm staying with Oscar's family."

"Oh." Dibs was glad for her, but he couldn't help thinking about living alone in his rundown warehouse. He opened his mouth to explain about Eddy, but stopped. In the worst way, he wanted to tell Shin he'd been forced to give the cops the James Street address. And he wanted to tell her how he'd been blackmailed into working at the chop shop. He was sure if she heard the whole story, she would understand. But he couldn't breath one word. Now that he was part of the gang, Eddy was being nice. But the guy had a mean streak that could definitely be hazardous to her health, not to mention his own. Crossing his new boss was out of the question.

He pretended enthusiasm. "Hey, that's great, Shinny! I'm glad you got a real home and that you're happy!"

"Yeah. See you," she said sharply. His voice was so fake. How had she been so blind about his lies? She turned and walked away.

A quiet, "Later, Shinny," called after her, but Amber kept moving.

Above her, Urielle nodded to Rahzell and Ahnah and followed her human as he walked away. They each returned a quick nod, their attention focused on the drabs trailing after them.

On the way home Shin was lost in troubled thought. She forgot all about her place in that other realm and could only think of traitor Dibs. The one person on the planet she'd trusted, and he betrayed her! *All that talk about getting a room together, like a real brother and sister. Some family he turned out* to be.

If things were reversed—if she had been the one being asked to give away his whereabouts—she was positive her lips would have stayed firmly zipped.

"What a lowlife," she said out loud. He didn't deserve friendship. As far as she was concerned they were no longer buddies. And for sure, he would never be her stupid brother.

People are so complicated! The ones who are supposed to be good to you end up hurting you the most. The more she thought about it, the more she wondered if Oscar and Maggie and Madison could be trusted. *They seem harmless, but I thought Dibs was harmless and look how he turned out. Why ARE they being so nice? And what if the cops show up again? If the Owens family is pushed, they might give me away, like Dibs gave me away.*

The last thought sent a shudder down her spine. She wasn't safe anymore. *I can't stay. It's too risky. Better to live on the streets than take a chance like that.*

Her mind was made up. She'd pack and leave before they got home. Take food for a day or two and hit the streets.

Invisible Shame twisted his head and leered at Rahzell from one side of a beady eye. "Look at her, she hates her friend! She's better than him. She is self-right. She sides with us. That is UnderSide behavior."

Fear flapped his wings hard and chimed in, "The child doesn't want to be with your side anymore. She separates herself. Look, she's running away again! That's proof she belongs to us."

Ahnah glanced at Rahzell. "These drabs incriminate themselves to gain access to humans."

Fear poured on more accusations. "She hasn't changed at all. She's ours!"

In the frenzy of the moment, even Control's claims grew more bold. "She'ss ourss, not yourss. The liar iss ourss, and you musst let uss have her!"

Ahnah and Rahzell held their ground. Unlike their enemies, they were privy to Father Forever's purposes. Even if the new royal family member was presently agreeing with UnderSide, and even if she had disobeyed Oscar's advice, even so, she belonged to OtherSide.

Amber arrived at the Owens' home and headed into her bedroom to gather her things together and fold up her sleeping bag. She sat on the bed and took one last look around the room that for a short time had been her own.

Was it all my imagination, what happened over there in that other place? Did I make it up? Just to be sure, she would try to go to OtherSide once more. Closing her eyes, Amber tried to see the Light Prince. But disloyal Dibs, creepy Tall Eddy, and looming cop cars crowded her thoughts.

Too tense to sit still, she got up and headed into the kitchen to grab food from the fridge. With her arms full of apples, oranges, and a few yogurts, she heard the sound of a key going into the lock of the front door.

After a few seconds Oscar, Maggie, and Madison waltzed into the house.

Madison was her usual bubbly self. "Hi Amber! We have some good news for you!"

"Oh yeah? What's up?" Amber was having a hard time putting up a front. She hoped they couldn't read her mood. Shuffling the food into her room without explaining what she was doing, she came back out to the dining room.

"Have a seat, Amber. We'd like to talk." Maggie sat down at the table and patted the chair next to her.

Amber sat. She'd leave later, when they were all busy with other things.

Conversation about future plans unfolded like a roadmap filled with treacherous switchbacks on dangerous mountain roads. Oscar and Maggie had been to the Department of Social Services that morning to ask about the requirements of becoming a foster home. And now they were cooking up some sort of idiotic scheme.

An earnestness appeared on Mrs. Owens' face that overshadowed the laugh lines around her eyes. "Amber honey, for you to remain here without informing the authorities is breaking the law, and we could be arrested for illegally harboring a runaway. But if you go into a temporary foster care situation, it will allow us the time we need to apply for our own foster home license." She brushed Amber's hair back from her face and smiled. "Then, once we're official, we'll bring you back into our home to live with us legally. You'll only need to be placed in another foster situation for about two months. But even then, once we've gotten clearance for visitation rights, we'll be able to come and see you."

Great. The timing of going back to the streets was perfect. There was no way Amber would return to that system. Period. Her mind was absolutely firm on that point.

"I've been in foster homes. I'm never going back."

They all sat in silence.

Oscar closed his eyes and breathed in deeply.

She'd seen him do that a couple of times before and knew it meant he was supposedly going to OtherSide. If that place really did exist. She wasn't sure of anything anymore.

Getting up from the table, she walked down the hall toward her room. *Why did I ever think being in this house was a good idea?*

Madison got up too, and followed Amber. "The Light Prince wants to know why you're so afraid. He said he's with you, so you don't have to worry."

Stopping abruptly, Amber faced Madison and snickered sarcastically. "Then HE should go to foster care. He'd love it. All the princes and princesses in the world go there." She went into her bedroom and slammed the door behind her.

Madison didn't even bother to knock. Opening the bedroom door, she walked in and plopped down on the bed. Amber was busy making room in her pack for the yogurts.

"Here, take my hand."

Amber shot her a look of disbelief.

"Come on, take my hand."

This is ridiculous! Sighing loudly, Amber roughly grabbed the hand extended her way.

"Now, close your eyes and remember him. Think of when you were standing in front of him, and he was looking at you."

Sitting down on the bed, Amber closed her eyes. Too bugged to sit still, she immediately opened them and glared at Madison. But then she decided to make herself try once more, and closed her eyes.

Nothing. Thirty seconds of dark silence and there was still no sign of anything. Then she saw a flicker of something passing through her internal vision, like a faint arc of light. The arc turned and came straight toward her, growing larger as it got closer. Soon the hand she was holding was no longer Madison's hand, but his. The Light Prince was flying beside her.

CHAPTER FOURTEEN

Amber and the Light Prince landed on a brightly shining grasslike turf somewhere in OtherSide.

He turned and greeted her enthusiastically. "My sister, the princess!"

I'm not a princess and I'm not your sister. I don't even know you very well. Her mood was as raggedy as the street clothing she'd once worn.

He sat and gestured for her to sit beside him. She plopped down to his right and folded her arms tightly.

"You're upset. Please tell me why." He knew the reasons, but he wanted to hear her heart.

Amber said nothing. But she was thinking that getting close to humans was about as safe as being thrown into the lion pen at the zoo.

The Light Prince waited quietly.

After a lengthy silence she uncrossed her arms and blurted out, "I don't belong! Not with Oscar's family and not with Dibs! And I don't want to go back on the streets, but I don't belong anywhere else!"

"You belong here."

She grimaced. That was as believable as a fairy tale.

"You forgot my eyes, dear one." The Light Prince turned

to face her and waited until she was willing to look at him.

He was smiling.

Breaking eye contact, Amber turned away. "I thought I could trust Dibs, but he's just like everybody else. Thanks to him, I almost got caught by the cops!" She pulled off a piece of a glossy green blade from the surface. Another segment instantly appeared to take its place.

"There are some things you don't understand about his situation."

What is that supposed to mean? Her mouth twisted into a sarcastic frown.

He leaned his head forward her to draw her eyes in his direction. "Do you think I can be trusted?"

They'd only been together once before, but somehow she knew this prince guy was the real deal. Glancing his way, she slowly nodded her answer.

"Then trust me when I say your street friend loves you like a sister."

"But he ratted on me!"

"He was forced to give your location." Now it was the prince who pulled off some bright green strands and twirled them in his hand.

Amber sat quietly as his answer slowly seeped through her state of mind. Impulsively she asked, "But who would do—?" And the answer was there. *Of course! Tall Eddy!*

She imagined Eddy threatening Dibs and making him tell all. A second image followed of throwing Eddy into the lion pen at the zoo. But before she had time to picture his demise, the prince interrupted.

"Release him, Amber. You'll feel better."

Whatever releasing was, it didn't come close to what she was seeing for Eddy.

Her thoughts soon wandered to Dibs and their last conversation at the zoo. The one where she'd vomited nasty accusations all over him. *Oh man, I am such a jerk.* She wanted to take back every word.

"You should probably release yourself, too."

Pulling another tuft of green from the surface, Amber promptly flung it away from her. "I told you I don't belong here." The way she'd treated Dibs was proof. Why had she assumed the worst about him? Her brain was a garbage dumpster. Why couldn't she be nice, like the Owens family? They always thought the best of everyone.

Who said I like their personalities more than yours?"

She startled at the prince's question, until she remembered OtherSide's transparent thinking. Still, as far as she was concerned, there was no comparison. The Owens family was a million times nicer.

"Release yourself, dear one. You're changing."

I just blew up at my only friend. Amber looked away.

"In this realm we see people through our star-eyes. As you learn to do the same, you'll throw away your measuring stick." The prince tossed aside the green strands in his hand. "Measuring and calculating aren't our way. They're traits of the Light Stealer."

She'd never considered that she measured. But other people sure did! On the streets, in restaurants, at the library, and especially in that stupid foster system—for her whole life, practically everybody had sized her up as a worthless throwaway. Except for loyal Dibs.

The Light Prince turned toward her, his eyes filled with honest kindness. "Those people weren't seeing you through their star-eyes. They couldn't see your beautiful Amber yellow."

Amber snorted at hearing her name tied with the word *beautiful.*

"Let's go for a walk." Her brother stood up and offered his hands to pull her up to his side.

She joined him reluctantly and they headed down the slope of a hill.

After walking in silence for a few hundred feet, the prince turned to her. "I'm not going anywhere, Amber. I'm staying right here, with you. And when you're on Earth I'll be as close as we are now, just on the other side of visible." He smiled calmly. "So you can learn how to be safe with people. Even if they're not perfect."

Amber stopped walking and practically shouted what was bothering her. "I don't want to go into a foster home! They're not good places to be in! I ought to know, because I've been in seven of them!" Her face contorted as she fought back tears. "If that's the only way I get to live in Oscar's family, I can't do it."

"But you've grown. You're a Lightning now and no longer that small child. You'll be amazed at your own strength." He rested his hand on her shoulder. "And I'll be right there with you. Find my eyes and everything will be all right."

He didn't understand her. "All those foster families I lived with? They only kept me for the money. They never wanted ME at all."

"Sweet one, the people in your previous experiences couldn't see your treasures. Release them. Let them go."

How did he do that? How did he orbit her world and manage to see it from a completely different perspective?

The prince pulled her chin up. Fixing his eyes on hers, he said intently, "I give you my word. Foster care will work out for your good."

He wasn't backing down. Amber stood still and quietly studied his face. It was as serious as a promise. After a lengthy consideration, she finally said, "You're telling me, IF I think about going back into that system, you'll go with me."

"Absolutely."

"And it will be different."

"Yes."

Closing her eyes, Amber tried to imagine the Light Prince trailing her invisibly through a foster home. There were dark hallways and cold bedrooms and people she didn't know, but in her mind's eye the prince was nowhere to be found.

Opening her eyes, she looked up at him and sighed. So far, her success record in the foster system had been a big fat zero. But she was older now—he was right about that. And she was a Lightning, though a very new one, which meant the prince would be just across that veneer thing.

"Way to go, princess. You're braver than you think!"

"But I didn't say I would go!" That mind reading trick of his wasn't fair.

He smiled and said nothing as they continued walking.

Amber's muscles tensed and she slowed her pace. Just one hour earlier she'd tried to find the Light Prince through her star-eyes and failed miserably. What if she got stuck like that while in the middle of foster care?

"Why couldn't I see you this morning? When I needed you, why couldn't I find OtherSide?"

He smiled his charming smile again.

"In OtherSide, interdependence is our way. We cooperate and collaborate: you and I, the Owens family, and all Lightnings. That's the way of true families."

What kind of an answer was that? As far as she could tell, it had nothing to do with her question.

"And it just so happens, I've got a great vantage point for viewing your world. Learn to trust my leading and things will go better for you."

The Light Prince sat down on a large flat boulder. Amber noticed the rock was every bit as solid as the ones on Earth. But its surface was soft to the touch and it reflected pretty tints of brown and purple.

He motioned for her to join him.

She frowned and sat down, still puzzling over what he'd said. The only *leading* she hadn't followed earlier in the day was Oscar's instruction about not going out of the house. She'd known it was a bad idea to leave, but dismissed the pangs of guilt and went anyway. And then she and Dibs ended up having that huge fight: the one where she'd acted like an idiot.

"We were interacting with you through your star-eyes this morning, before you left the house." The prince tapped his chest. "They're right in the middle of your true and noble heart. We're always communicating to you through them."

His words rolled around in her mind. *Star-eyes . . . In the middle of my true and noble heart . . . Always communicating.*

Amber gasped in recognition. "That was YOU telling me not to go outside, when I knew it was wrong!"

"That's right."

Staring into space, she contemplated his words. "But that means seeing through my star-eyes is way different than seeing through my natural eyes."

"Way different," he nodded.

"So, you knew I'd go to the zoo and have that big fight with Dibs?"

"As I said, I've got a great perspective. And people like Oscar, they've had a lot longer to practice using their star-eyes. When he told you to stay inside it was because he and I had talked together. That's collaboration and interdependence: the Owens family, you, me, and other Lightnings. We hear each other, heart-to-heart."

Amber was flabbergasted. An image of Crazy Lady popped into her mind. *When she called me a Light-Seeker, she was seeing me through her star-eyes!*

The prince nodded again in confirmation of her thought.

"And those nice words Oscar said the first day I was at his house—the ones about me becoming some kind of an ambassador—he was seeing me through his star-eyes."

"Yep. He was calling out your treasures."

It was all starting to make sense. Communication through star-eyes was a whole new, incredible kind of seeing. "So, by paying attention to that true heart thing . . ." She couldn't remember what he'd called it.

"To your true and noble heart."

"Yeah. If I pay attention to that, I can learn to see through my star-eyes?" Her voice turned her sentence into a question.

He grinned, looking immensely proud that his smart little sister was grasping a new insight. "I couldn't have said it better myself."

"Cool!" Amber grinned too.

Lying back on the flat surface of the rock to watch the sky, her self-distain faded. Above them, the endless colors of OtherSide ebbed and flowed in a dance of cosmic splendor.

After some time she sat up. She was thinking hard about foster care. Going back into the jaws of that system was still a frightening idea. But now that she understood her star-eyes were like a satellite dish for receiving OtherSide signals, being in a foster family felt a little less threatening. The prince's communications might help her survive a few months in the home of strangers, until Oscar's family could officially bring her back into their home.

She could hardly believe she was going to say it. "Since you said it'll work out good, I might try foster care. But just until I can live with the Owens family."

The prince held his hand up for a high five slap. "Wonderful!"

She whacked his outstretched hand.

"You won't be disappointed." He gave her a brotherly side hug, then stood up and faced her. "Come often, Amber. I can't wait to see you on your next visit."

Gathering from his comments it was time to go, she objected. "But I'm not ready! I like it here." Hanging out with him was a thousand times better than being anywhere on Earth.

"Yes, but the Owens family is waiting." He cocked his head. "Besides, Earth is where you learn to use your star-eyes. It's a great place to practice, don't you think?"

He was doing it again, revolving around her world with his quirky OtherSide view. But she had to admit, she was the teeniest bit eager to figure out her true and noble heart so she could learn how to use her star-eyes.

Just that quickly, Amber felt herself being lifted on the wind and blown back into her bedroom.

Madison was sitting beside her on the bed, smiling. Oscar and Maggie stood in the doorway, their faces full of concern.

She looked at them and said truthfully, "I can go to foster care if it will bring me back here to be with you."

"That's great!" Mrs. Owens walked over and pulled her up on her feet. Giving her a hug, she said, "I knew your gutsy heart would find the way, honey. We won't leave you. We're in this together."

As Amber's face pressed against Mrs. Owens' soft cotton shirt a glorious, happy presence filled the room. She pulled back from Maggie's arms, her eyes wide with awe. "The Light Prince is here! I can feel him, just like when we're together in OtherSide!"

Madison laughed. "Duh, they live on the other side of visible."

"Hey, I just used my star-eyes, didn't I?"

Grinning with pleasure, Oscar moved beside her and gave her a sideways hug. "You sure did, dear one."

"Awesome!" Holding out her palm for him to slap it, she realized he probably had no idea why her hand was extended, which made Amber giggle out loud.

She put her arm down, thrilled to discover that her star-eyes had worked for a second time while on Earth's side of the veneer. They would definitely come in handy.

Now all she had to do was get the hang of using them.

CHAPTER FIFTEEN

Police Chief Paul Monson was dead. His passing was the reason Joe Cutter, Adam Fox, and Tall Eddy were gathered behind closed doors in the basement den of Cutter's suburban home, under the guise of spending a guy's night together. Even though Joe's family was away for the evening, a baseball game played on television in the background to help mask their conversations.

"Heart attack, they say." Adam was explaining what he knew of Paul's death. "Yesterday. The funeral is Monday at eleven. For now, the acting Chief Of Police is Bill Sanderson."

"Sanderson? He's a lousy conservative, isn't he? Oh, that's just great!" Cutter leaned forward and rested his balding head in his hands. He didn't like hearing that news at all. Looking up at the others with a face full of worry, he spoke in strident tones. "The chief was the main reason we've stayed under the radar for two years. He was the shop's safety valve!"

"Don't get worked up, Joe," Adam said confidently. "Paul did successfully steer a couple of leads elsewhere. But don't forget, I'm still at the station, and I say it's safe to go on as usual. Your heist crews have been thorough about switching up routines, and that's helped to throw off any threat of bloodhounds. I haven't sensed one iota of suspicion anywhere in the precinct."

Adam put his hand on Cutter's shoulder to reassure him. "I'll do my job and keep my ears and eyes open. We'll be fine." He pointed at Eddy. "You just make sure those crews of yours don't screw up out there on the job."

Cutter shook his head. "I don't know. I don't like it. Think about all the people who, if they had a mind to, could bring this operation right out into the open." He counted off on his fingers. "Spiteful parts dealers, suspicious garage owners, nosy neighbors . . ." Without finishing his list, Joe sat back and rubbed his wrinkled forehead. "I'm telling you, anybody my garage interacts with makes me feel like we're this close to being discovered." He was holding his fingers about an inch apart. "And what about that homeless kid from the alley? She's still out there somewhere. What if she knows about us and decides to blab in order to make herself some money?"

Eddy leaned front and scowled. "For cryin' out loud Cutter, you're overreacting! Nothin's changed!"

Joe shot back, "A lot has changed, Eddy. Paul Monson is no longer a vital part of the team." He hunched forward and started wringing his hands. "Maybe you guys need to move the operation to another place."

Raising his hands in protest, Adam countered with, "Okay, since there's no immediate need to change anything, let's just maintain status quo. And in a month we can revisit this whole discussion. Guaranteed, we'll all be glad we didn't panic." He looked at Joe. "And as for the girl, we're working on her whereabouts. She's probably harmless. But don't worry, we'll bring her in." With both eyebrows raised, he directed his question Joe's way. "Does that make you feel better?"

Cutter's stubborn fear said nothing and friction clouded the air.

Eddy said with a demanding voice, "Well, Cutter, Adam asked you a question. What's your answer?"

The salvage yard owner stared, his bloodshot eyes revealing heavy fatigue. "I want out, guys. I don't sleep well at night. And during the day I'm always looking over my shoulder, wondering who's watching me. Wondering who knows something." Sitting back, he threw up his hands. "And if I ended up in prison it would just destroy my wife and daughters. I'd rather go back to running a junkyard. I know it doesn't pay as much, but at least I could enjoy life." His pleading gaze met theirs. "Please find another place for the chop shop."

Adam's jaw muscles tensed as he stood and towered over Cutter. "You leave me no choice, Joe." Putting his hand on the garage owner's shoulder, he pinched his neck muscle hard and let him feel a strong, painful pressure. "You're in this. You agreed at the beginning, and there is no backing out."

With his other hand, Adam picked up a framed photo of Cutter's family from the coffee table. "It would be a shame if something were to happen to these sweet girls of yours, just because you decided not to cooperate anymore. None of us wants to see them come into harm's way. But it's amazing how accidents seem to happen when people are no longer loyal." Releasing his grip from Cutter's shoulder, he glared. "You understand?"

Joe turned white as a sheet and sweat broke out on his bald head and face. His eyes followed the photo as Adam placed it back on the table. He stared at his family for some time and then said weakly, "Yeah. I understand. Like you said, I'll wait a month." Pasting a smile on his face, he forced himself to look at them. "I'm probably getting uptight for no reason."

With an edge to his voice Adam sat down and said, "You pushed me, Joe."

Cutter stood. "Well guys, you'll be careful, I know you will." He gave them another sad smile and picked up their empty coffee cups. "Thanks for coming."

Even with such an obvious hint, Adam didn't budge. Clearing his throat, he said, "One more thing before we go. Now that I'm taking more risk at the station, I want an increase in my cut of the profits. A ten percent increase." He looked at the others. "For all the monitoring I do and all the tips I give to clear heist locations, it's only fair. And nothing will change for either of you, since I'll just be absorbing what used to be Paul's cut. Any problem with that?"

The muscles of Eddy's neck tightened into hard lines. It was clear he resented being coerced, but he lacked the power to negotiate. Without a crooked cop the whole operation would quickly crash and burn. Forcing his voice to sound calm, he said, "No problem, Adam."

Cutter added his quiet consent, and they called it a night. Eddy left the house first, and Adam slipped out into the darkness fifteen minutes later. Cutter fell exhausted onto the sofa, not caring one bit that his favorite team was losing by three runs in the ninth inning.

CHAPTER SIXTEEN

The next morning a small band of Lightnings sat in the waiting area of The Department of Social Services. Being inside the walls of the agency wasn't exactly a walk in the park for Amber, but neither was it like previous visits when she'd hurled her lunch from sheer dread. This time Oscar, Maggie, and Madison sat by her side for support, so the fear of living in a foster home didn't entirely overtake her mind.

Still, her chest was tight, her mouth was as dry as toast, and she couldn't keep from nervously bobbing one leg up and down.

While her caseworker sat at a desk pulling up files on a computer, Amber leaned back and closed her eyes. She tried to see through her star-eyes, but the sounds of ringing phones and office machines and squeaky desk chairs filled her ears. It was impossible to focus. *Light Prince, where are you?* Supposedly he was around, but she sure wasn't sensing him. *You promised, remember? You said this whole thing would turn out okay. I hope you know what you're talking about!*

Hearing the loud creak of a desk chair, she opened her eyes in time to see the social worker get up, walk quickly into a co-worker's office, and shut the door behind her. Amber looked anxiously over at Oscar.

He was sitting next to her and patted her knee. "He's here, dear one. Even if you can't feel him, he's right here."

Amber exhaled loudly. For once, she was glad Oscar had read her thoughts. He knew just what she needed to hear. At least his star-eyes were working.

After what seemed like an elastically long twenty-minute stretch, the woman finally came out of her co-worker's office and approached their little group.

"I apologize for the delay, but Amber, when we pulled up your file on the computer it showed a recent police inquiry. And unfortunately, we won't be able to place you in a foster home until the police have been able to ask you some questions."

As if someone had pulled a plug in her head, all the blood drained from Amber's face. Before she could think or react—deny, protest, or stand up and bolt out the door—two policemen appeared from around a doorway.

She recognized the cop. He'd chased her from her alleyway on the day she lost her street home.

The caseworker introduced them. "This is Officer Adam Fox and his partner, Officer Ron Brown. They will take over for now, until we can get this all cleared up."

Adam Fox's voice was commanding. "Amber, come with us. We would like to ask you some questions."

Both Oscar and Maggie stood to go with her, but Adam held up his hand.

"We'll need to question the young lady alone." Glancing at Oscar's face, he hesitated. "Aren't you the one we talked with a few days ago? You live on James street. Is that correct?"

Oscar nodded.

"On second thought, you come with us too."

As the cops took the arms of their detainees to lead them toward the exit, Oscar glanced back at Maggie and Madison and smiled. "We'll be back, don't worry."

Maggie tried to smile back. Madison leaned against her mom and nodded bravely.

At street level, the two Lightnings were deposited into the rear of the police cruiser. Oscar turned and whispered to Amber, "Remember the Light Prince." Leaning back against the seat, he shut his eyes.

He was going to visit OtherSide.

Amber's leg started to bob. She put her hand on her bouncing knee to make it stop and tried to relax. Her thoughts were as jumpy as her muscles; there was no hope of crossing the veneer. The most she could manage was to picture her prince brother's kind face and loving eyes. It was enough to keep her from slamming her body against the car door in a last-ditch effort to escape.

In no time at all they pulled up to the station and were escorted inside, through the lobby area, and into the administration section of the building. They were led into separate rooms for questioning. Officer Brown took Oscar, while Adam Fox directed Amber into an adjoining room.

Shutting the door, Officer Fox pointed toward a folding chair at a small table in the center of the room. "Sit down, please." He walked to a padded leather chair on the opposite side of the table and sat down.

Facing her, his brow furrowed as he opened a file folder and picked up a pen to write. "Amber, you lived in the alleyway next to Cutter's Salvage Yard, is that correct?"

Sitting on her hands and staring downward, Amber mumbled into her lap. "Uh, yeah."

He ordered sharply, "Sit up and speak clearly so I can hear you."

She sat up and raised her voice. "Yeah. I did." Her leg started bobbing.

"How long did you live there?"

While Earth's atmosphere became strained with uncertainty, angry drabs gathered around the outer edges of the room and sneered threateningly. To either side of the young Lightning in the center of the room, two Watcher dazzles stood as sentries of OtherSide, their light-wings unfurled around her human body, their intense focus on making sure their earthling was cared for and protected.

As the policeman posed his second question, Amber willed her body to sit still and ordered her mind to do the same. And for some odd reason, she decided she wanted to be truthful. About everything. It just felt right to do so. *I don't need to hide anymore.* She caught her breath. That was exactly what the Light Prince had told her in OtherSide. *That thought came from him! He's speaking to me!*

Body and soul calmed, and she found herself releasing a tiny grin. Her attention returned to the room, where Officer Fox was staring at her sternly.

"I said," he repeated impatiently, "how long did you live there?"

"Uh, six and a half months. Sir." She tagged on *sir* to let him know she wasn't trying to be disrespectful.

The interrogation lasted for about an hour. Officer Fox asked questions about everything having to do with her life in the alleyway: her daily schedule, sleep patterns, whether she'd heard any odd sounds while living there, where she had obtained the found things around her sleeping bag, who came to visit her, and what kind of interactions she'd had with the salvage yard.

He was especially interested in that junkyard. Eager to find out what she knew about its daytime and nighttime activities, he pumped her with questions about the comings and goings of people and vehicles at the garage.

With all the focus on Mr. Cutter's business, Amber was beginning to think she might not be in trouble after all. Unfortunately, she didn't know very much about the salvage yard. Except that sometimes the mechanics were awfully loud at night when she was trying to sleep. She told the cop about the noise.

Figuring he would want to know about a dangerous criminal who was still on the loose, she also took the opportunity to tell him about the mugger who had attacked her in the middle of the night. He made a few notes but didn't show much interest in hearing what she had to say.

After that, the officer seemed to run out of questions.

Grabbing the paperwork where he'd been making notes, Adam Fox pushed back his padded desk chair and stood up. He was frowning at her with the same sort of disgusted look that people give their shoe right after they've stepped in something gross.

"Stay here. I'll be right back," he said, and left the room.

Returning a few minutes later, he motioned from the doorway for her to get up and follow him. "Officer Brown has finished questioning Mr. Owens. We'll take you both back to The Department of Social Services."

She got up and followed the cop.

Oscar was sitting on a bench in the hallway. "How are you, dear one?" he asked tenderly, as he stood to his feet.

Amber exhaled in relief and whispered, "I didn't get arrested!"

As they headed to the police car, she said excitedly, "Oscar, I think the Light Prince spoke to me. I think I heard his voice in my head!"

Gushing with pride, Oscar pulled Amber toward himself in a sideways hug. "That's just marvelous!"

"Yeah, I know!" She grinned, pleased that in the middle of a scary situation she'd actually seen through her star-eyes.

Back at Social Services the foursome marked waiting room time by discussing Amber and Oscar's separate police encounters. Officer Brown had gotten upset when he found out Mr. Owens housed Amber at his house without reporting her whereabouts. But in the end, since Oscar had encouraged her to voluntarily turn herself in to The Department of Social Services, the police weren't going to press charges. The cop issued a warning but let him go.

Reporting on Officer Fox's questions, Amber explained that Mr. Cutter, the junkyard owner, might be in trouble with the law. She said the reason for the sudden police interest in her life was probably to ask what she knew about his place, which wasn't very much.

Amber's caseworker interrupted the conversation to ask questions, and for the next several hours the time was filled with completing mounds of paperwork, waiting for responses to phone calls made by the agency, and making numerous trips to the snack machines downstairs.

Toward the end of the afternoon, the caseworker approached their little entourage with an announcement. "Well, Amber, your new foster parents are in the elevator on their way up to meet you. I think you'll like them very much."

Madison squeezed her hand tightly for support and Amber forced a smile. No matter what this social worker thought, she knew she would never like anyone connected to the foster care system.

"Unfortunately, Mr. Owens, since you and your daughter-in-law failed to notify our department immediately after Amber came to live with you, approval for any interaction with her while she's in foster care will need to be reviewed by a panel. That means until you've been cleared to do so, you and your family are not permitted to call her or visit her or contact her in any way. That includes texting or internet communications." The woman looked at Oscar intently. "Is that clear?"

"Yes Ma'am, I understand." Oscar glanced at Amber and smiled soberly.

"Good." The woman handed Oscar a clipboard with a form attached. "Please sign here to acknowledge that you will abide by the policies of our department."

Just as Oscar finished adding his signature and the date and handing the clipboard back, the door opened.

The caseworker walked over to meet two grown-ups and a tag-along kid that looked to be in his teens. She brought the new arrivals over to their seating area. "Amber, I would like you to meet your new foster family. This is Mr. and Mrs. Gordon and their son Jared." Turning to the Gordons, the social worker then gestured toward Amber. "And this is your new foster girl, Amber McConnell."

The Owens family stood. Amber followed their example. Sandwiched in between Oscar and her new state-assigned caretakers, she was beginning to feel out of sorts. Something in her stomach tossed and turned.

The man spoke to her.

"Hi Amber, it's great to meet you. If you prefer, you can call us John and Darlene."

She threw a couple of glances toward the strangers who had come to take her away. They were wearing jeans, and she hoped that meant they weren't stuffy people. Agewise, they appeared to be somewhere in their late thirties to early forties. Their son looked to be fourteen or fifteen.

The man was tall and thin, not thin like a junkyard dog but sleek like a leopard, as if he was a sports jock of some type. His hair was short-cropped and curly brown, and he wore the kind of black-rimmed glasses Amber had seen in magazine ads. His top was a button-down, short-sleeved office shirt. He was good-looking but not drop-dead handsome.

His wife was a couple of inches shorter than him, with straight, shoulder-length blonde hair, a pretty face with petite features, and the most milky-white teeth Amber had ever seen. She was dressed in a blue top that was long enough to cover up her wide hips. Around her neck was a cool matching wooden necklace that was as chunky as her butt.

The kid looked a lot like his dad, with a longer and messier version of the same curly brown hair, and a similar pair of stylish eyeglasses. He was also thin, but closer to the junkyard dog kind of thin, like some teenage boys look during growth spurts. Most likely, he was in one of those at the moment. His glasses were sliding halfway down his nose, and he was wearing a T-shirt with the words, "Computer Geeks Make Great Cookies" printed across the front.

Amber became aware of the man holding out his hand for a handshake. She shook it without looking at him. "Yeah, you too, nice to meet you." And immediately, so there could be no mistaking the fact that she wouldn't be staying in their home for very long, she introduced the Owens family. "And this is Oscar, Maggie, and Madison. I'm gonna' go live with them as soon as they have a foster home license and can take me back."

At Amber's announcement the Gordons exchanged surprised looks and then smiled politely.

When it was time to say goodbye, Oscar and Maggie and Madison gathered Amber into their arms and gave her a group hug.

Mrs. Owens pulled a brand new purple and white striped diary out of her purse. She handed it to Amber. "If you want to, you can write about your new life with the Gordons. And when we see each other again we'll read all about your experiences."

Amber took the book and leafed through its blank pages. It was as if she was being invited to create her own story. She loved the idea. "Thanks! I promise I'll write in it!"

After one more hug from each member of the Owens family, she picked up the suitcase they'd lent to her and tried to be brave. But as she walked toward the door, a strong case of the willies threatened to smother her brain.

The Owens family called out final goodbyes and Amber turned to wave at them. A rush of nausea hit, and she imagined dropping her suitcase and making a break for the door.

Why had she agreed to this stupid plan?

For the first time in three years, Amber was back in the system and about to move in with unfamiliar people who made money by keeping her in their home. As she walked through the double doors at the end of the hall, Amber remembered OtherSide. *Light Prince, I hope you can hear me, wherever you are. You gotta' stay close, okay?*

She called back over her shoulder, "Bye! See you soon!" as the lock on the door clicked shut.

Officially, for the umpteenth time, she was in the care of total strangers.

CHAPTER SEVENTEEN

Exiting the revolving doors on the first floor of the Social Services building, the Gordons and their new foster daughter headed toward a white SUV.

Four dazzles across the veneer floated with them, and since they hadn't all previously met, they were making introductions.

"I'm Morgan. Great to meet you," said a medium-built dazzle with dark, curly hair. He bowed toward Rahzell and then nodded Jared's way. "He's my watch."

Floating to Morgan's left was another dazzle who was slender like Ahnah but slightly broader in the shoulders. Accented with golden strands, her auburn hair was woven into a radiant braid at the back of her head. She bowed in Rahzell's direction. "And my name is Caeree. I watch the woman."

"Rahzell here." He introduced himself and returned a bow to the others. "I share the assignment of watching the girl with my compatriot Ahnah, but currently, she's catching some R and R.

The only dazzle who hadn't introduced himself cocked his head questioningly. "R and R?"

"Rest and Recreation." Rahzell was grinning. "It's a

human phrase describing what earthlings do to refresh themselves." He could tell by their expressions the others didn't quite understand, so he clarified. "Ahnah is delighting in the company of our sublime monarchy."

Everyone nodded with understanding. The greatest refreshment in all of OtherSide, the bliss of every dazzle, was to be with the Original Family.

Tall and thin with silvery, short hair, the dazzle smiled and bowed. "I'm Solm. I'm with the earth man."

"It's a pleasure to meet all of you, and I look forward to watching together." Rahzell gestured toward his earth girl. "I call her Little Streak. She runs. A lot."

Caeree laughed. "Morgan, I see you have a kindred spirit in this one."

A grin spread across Morgan's countenance. "I call the boy Fast Cookies."

Now it was Rahzell who tilted his head to wait for an explanation.

"It refers to something inside the communication boxes they call computers. But he also likes to fill himself with sweet foods from time to time, so I'm killing two drabs with one stone."

Rahzell was the only dazzle in the group to burst out laughing at Morgan's transformation of a human idiom. "Can I borrow that? I'd like to kill a few drabs with one stone!"

Morgan laughed and nodded approvingly.

Caeree and Solm looked at each other, astonished that the Original Family had just seen fit to send another jokester into their midst.

When the humans arrived at their car, the dazzles settled back into watching routines and set aside their banter for another time.

Rahzell noticed his Little Streak seemed nervous. He wanted to give her strength, so he drifted closer and laid his light-hand on her head.

John unlocked the doors, and while Amber slid into the middle seat he put her suitcase in the back.

As the stranger-boy jumped in and sat on the seat next to her, a wave of melancholy washed through her being. *I hate foster homes and I hate starting over.*

It had been a grueling day, and she hoped they wouldn't ask her a bunch of stupid questions. Especially not about her past, which seemed to be a favorite topic of nosy new foster families.

As they pulled away from the curb to take her to another unfamiliar life—to a strange neighborhood, home, and bedroom—just as she feared, they started in with all their questions. She rolled her eyes. *I knew it. This is gonna' be a drag.*

Amber gave them the briefest possible answers. And whether they took a clue from her lack of words, or they were trying their best to be good tour guides, the conversation soon changed to pointing out things of interest in the area. Some of it was interesting, like the library and the art museum and good ice cream shops. But mostly she was grateful they were doing the talking. It meant she didn't have to say a word.

After three quarters of an hour, just as dusk blanketed the horizon, John pulled into their family garage. Everyone got out of the car and followed Jared into the Gordons' bungalow.

Entering a small, cluttered kitchen, Jared took Amber's suitcase for her. "I'll put your things in your room while Mom and Dad show you around your new home."

His voice cracked into a high-pitched squeak and Amber thought, *He must be going through puberty, like Dibs.* More than once she'd teased her street friend about sounding like a honking goose.

Jared disappeared down a hallway.

John was motioning toward the room. "Well, this is the kitchen," he continued walking into the adjoining dinette area, "and here's the dining room." Moving to his right and turning the corner, he flipped on a light switch. "And, voilà, our living room."

Painted across the entire wall at the far end of the rectangular room was a skyscape of billowing white clouds shaded with hues of blue and purple. Just below the center of the image, rays of yellow sunlight poured through in large, bold brushstrokes.

The artist had placed two laughing men, one of whom looked older than the other, on top of the most magnificent fluffy cloud. Both the men were half sitting and half lying down, as though they were at the beach. Except, they were in the middle of the sky.

After learning the basic colors from Madison, artwork had taken on a new fascination for Amber. She thought this picture was as well done as anything she'd seen in library books.

"Wow, that's amazing."

"Thanks. It was fun to work on."

"You painted that?" She looked at Mr. Gordon.

"Yes."

Having never met a real, bona fide artist, she watched him with curiosity.

Jared rejoined them and changed the subject. "Hey, I bet Amber's as hungry as we are." He gave his mom a starving teenager look. "Shouldn't we order dinner?"

Darlene turned to the newest household member. "What do you feel like eating, Amber? We opted to get take-out food, because we didn't know what time we'd be coming home. And since it's your first night with us, you may choose whatever you want."

Jared pushed his glasses up on his nose. "Yeah, we want you to feel special, so it's your call."

Amber could feel her face flushing with embarrassment. Except for Dibs, she'd rarely given her opinion to anyone on Earth about anything. Opinions were in a mental category called, Things To Be Avoided, since that level of interaction meant she was uncloaked. And being called *special*: her mind definitely filtered that into the I Am Way Too Visible category.

Even though she was now a Lightning, past habits were still solidly engrained, and she was unskilled at finding her true and noble heart. Remembering her star-eyes wasn't instinctive, so it was only natural that with all the attention suddenly focused on her, old uncomfortable pressures began to surface.

Her throat constricted and her chest tightened and she was positive someone had hijacked all the oxygen from the room. Lowering her head, Amber focused on the wall-to-wall carpet beneath her feet. She rubbed its nap with one foot and desperately wished she could escape from planet Gordon.

"You can pick anything!" Jared coaxed. "Pizza, Chinese, fried chicken, burgers, or whatever you want!"

While she stood feeling as awkward as she'd felt in days, several familiar drabs floated in through the living room wall. Fear and Shame kept their distance from the nearby dazzles, but the opportunity was too good to resist. The girl child was acting like her old self, and they wanted to use circumstances to swing the advantage their way.

Shame taunted, "You should feel stupid, birdbrain! Look, they're staring at you like you have three heads!"

Just as he'd done for years, Fear began preying on the girl's skepticism. "They're just reeling you in! Don't trust their motives! Get away from these weirdoes! Protect yourself, because nobody else is going to protect you!"

Amber wasn't yet aware of the existence of drabs, but her emotions were as comfortable with their mendacity as her lungs with breathing air. She thought about making a dash for the door and disappearing into the night. Anything was easier than sleeping in the home of these strangers. For all she knew, their niceness was a front. What if they were axe murderers waiting for their next victim to fall soundly asleep in the guest room?

At the presence of drabs Rahzell moved in close to the girl. It was obvious she was upset. "Little Streak, you're a Lightning now." He glanced at the UnderSide rabble fouling her atmosphere. "These drabs? They don't hold a candle to all Light Prince has to offer. You can fight their trash-talk. Think of your prince brother. Remember your fantastic yellow color. Use your star-eyes, sweetie. They're right inside of you."

As the dazzle continued to encourage his favorite earthling, Amber decided she had to get hold of herself. *Stop it, you jerk! Don't be such an idiot!*

Normally, harsh self-talk was enough to settle her brain so she could think, but this time it wasn't working. She was seconds away from charging out of the house. *Quit it, you stupid—* As she tried another insult, OtherSide quietly snuck into her thoughts. *Light Prince, I don't know what to do. Help me!*

Soon a vague memory of him moved into the center of her mental fog. She squinted, and just that quickly the thought became a faint image. But the prince wasn't in OtherSide. He was standing beside the Gordons in their living room. The picture sharpened and she saw him watching her. He was wearing a huge smile, his arms were relaxed across his chest, and his head was nodding in the direction of her foster family as if to say, "Why are you so upset? They just want to know what you'd like to eat."

The Light Prince extended his hand and released a beam of light. It shot out from his palm and hit her right in the chest. Ricocheting off of her, the beam became an explosion of Amber yellow light that splattered everything in the living room. The carpet, the coffee table, the sofa, and walls: yellow rays even washed over the Gordons and the Light Prince.

A teeny smile accidentally crept across her lips.

Her prince brother grinned. *Isn't it beautiful?*

She shrugged. It was pretty. But she'd just acted all wimpy, and he'd seen it all. She glanced at him. Still watching her with that huge smile, he didn't seem to think any less of her for being a big baby.

He pointed at the yellow splashes of light throughout the room. *Love, and confident expectation. Remember?*

The words were vaguely familiar, but she didn't get the point.

When our light shines through your color—

Amber interrupted him. *Hey, your light's shining through my yellow!* She stopped and stared at all the brilliant yellow in the room. *Wait. This is part of the love and confident expectation thing?*

Yep.

She had to admit, something had changed. The panic was gone, she could breathe again, and she no longer wanted to escape. He was right: his light radiating through her Amber yellow had filled her with an unexpected calm.

Well, what are you waiting for? He nodded toward the Gordons.

Opening her earth eyes, Amber saw her foster family standing there looking as happy as a dog's wagging tail and waiting patiently for her decision. She wondered how long she'd been silent. "Uh, could we get pizza?"

"Certainly! What kind do you like?"

Amber told Darlene her favorite flavors and Jared grabbed the phone to place an order for two large pizzas.

They cleared several piles of paperwork from the dining room table. And before long, everyone was sitting down to the "Phhhhttt" sounds of soda cans being opened and "Mmmms" slipping through Jared's smacking lips. Digging into the pizza boxes, they all chowed down on warm, cheesy slices of Hawaiian style and pepperoni, the picks of the evening.

Toward the end of the meal Amber could no longer stifle her yawns. Darlene took a cue from her fatigue. "You've been through a lot today, so if you want to sack out early, feel free. Your bed's made up, and a there's a towel and a washcloth set out for you in your room."

"Or we could all watch a movie together!"

Judging by the eager expression on Jared's face, his preference was obvious.

Amber was tired, but it had been a long time since she'd seen any kind of entertainment. And she loved the rare opportunities she'd had to watch a good film. She liked films almost as much as she liked books. "Maybe a movie," she said.

"We've got a subscription so we can watch whatever we want. Come on, I'll show you," Jared said.

The adults sat down on the sofa in the living room while Jared explained to his new pupil how to find movie options on their flat screen TV. After discovering that Amber had hardly seen any of their family's most-liked films, he chose a comedy.

"It's one of my favorites. I know you'll love it," he said.

He was right about the movie. She did love it. As she washed her face later, Amber looked at her reflection in the bathroom mirror. *They didn't lay out any rules. Only fun for the first night.*

Plus, she'd seen the Light Prince through her star-eyes! And he *was* just on the other side of that veneer thing. "How cool is THAT?" she asked her mirror image, without expecting an answer.

Woven into the newness of seeing through her star-eyes was a thread of emotion Amber couldn't immediately identify. It was light as a feather and airy, like the brightest of days.

All at once she realized its name. Hope.

"Holy smoke," she said, and smiled at the mirror.

She'd always envied Dibs because he managed to be so positive. Her outlook on life had been the opposite: to never expect anything pleasant.

Until now.

It felt good.

She wondered why she'd freaked out over a simple choice of which takeout food to order. *That sure was weird!* Shaking her head, Amber headed into her bedroom and changed into her nightshirt. Plucking Herbie from the middle of her things, she hopped into bed. And just like she'd done with her sleeping bag while living on the streets, she yanked the covers up and tucked them tightly around her neck. Only this time it wasn't to squeeze out the cold night air. It was to do something habitual, something familiar and comfortable in a bedroom that didn't belong to her.

She remembered the diary Mrs. Owens had given her and got out of bed to pull it from her suitcase. Oscar and Maggie and Madison were the only real family she'd ever known on Earth, and she couldn't wait to see them again. But until then, Amber was glad she could jot down everything that happened. Writing to them made it feel a little bit like they were with her.

Jumping back under the covers, she picked up a pen from the nightstand and started writing details about dinner (*Hawiien, my faverite flavor of pizza!*), and the movie (*Jared picked it on TV*), and the cool painting on the wall (*Mr. Gordon did it!*). She ended with an apology (*Sorry for any words I misspelled*) and signed it at the bottom.

Amber put the pen away and slid her diary under the bed. Settling back down into the soft, warm covers, she pulled Herbie against her waist and decided not to think about anything negative: not about cops, not about being in a foster home, not about leaving the Owens family, not about her life on the streets, not about Tall Eddy forcing Dibs to rat on her, and not about the thug whose attack had started the whole chain of recent events. Thinking about those things only made her sad. The expectation of hope was a much better feeling.

CHAPTER EIGHTEEN

Turning over the next morning, Amber wondered where in the world she'd spent the night. Slowly wrestling herself to consciousness, she looked around the room. Even when she sat up nothing was recognizable. *Dark walls. What's that color? Red. Who's got red walls?*

Rubbing her eyes, she stretched as her sleepy brain finally put everything into place. *Ugh. Foster home. No wonder I didn't remember.* Lonely for something routine, Amber got dressed in yesterday's outfit, a practice from her homeless days.

She flopped back down on the bed. Searching for Herbie, she found him under the bunched up sheet and pulled him out for a reassuring cuddle. Holding him while contemplating the unfamiliar bedroom—blame it on not being a morning person, or on being in another new place, or on sheer habit, or on any number of things—Amber forgot about the hope of the previous night.

Great. I have to face strangers again. No matter how nice people were or how cool their digs, starting new relationships was unnerving. She'd already done it too many times in her twelve-year-old life. Plus, her positive experiences of family were about as developed as an amoeba.

There was a large bedroom window to her right. She

noticed it had a latch that was easy to open. In no time at all, she could crawl out, take to the streets, and be free once more.

But entertaining that idea only lasted for about thirty seconds, because into her head popped a picture of the Light Prince sprayed with Amber yellow. At the thought of her color plastered all over him, she giggled. Clearing her throat, she said, "Wherever you are, could you help me with the freakiness of relating to people I don't really want to be around?" Her morning voice cracked and the word *freakiness* came out sounding as if it were upside down.

The thought of a cup of coffee crossed her mind. It was just the motivation she needed to work up a mood pleasant enough to greet whoever was waiting to make her talk before she was fully awake. She gave Herbie a gentle toss toward her pillow and stood to open her door. Walking out of the bedroom, Amber plodded toward the kitchen to show her face.

"Good morning, Amber," John Gordon called out from another room and then got up and followed his voice to meet her. "Did you sleep well?"

"Uh huh."

He opened a kitchen cupboard. "Good! Hey, we do breakfast informally around here. Darlene's at work and Jared's still sleeping. We're all on different schedules in the morning, so it just doesn't work any other way. I hope that's okay with you." He looked at her and pointed to the boxes lined up in the cabinet. "You want cereal? Oatmeal? Eggs? Toast? Just say the word and I'll make it happen."

She pointed to the coffee maker. "Coffee."

John gave her a questioning look. "You drink coffee at your age?"

Here we go again. "Yeah. On the streets it's something warm in the morning."

His face registered understanding and he grabbed the half-empty carafe. "Is warmed up coffee okay, or do you want a new pot?"

She smiled. "Nuked is great. Thanks."

Amber was glad Mr. Gordon returned to wherever he'd come from so she could be alone. For the next half hour she sat on the sofa in the living room with her knees pulled up against her chest and her feet on the cushions, sipping a reheated cup of not-too-bad java and staring at the clouds suspended on the wall.

By the bottom of her cup she was almost fully awake. Still examining the mural, she wondered whether John could see the colors he'd painted, or if, to his eyes, they were all shades of gray. Then she thought, *But if he SAW color, that would mean his star-eyes are open!* Putting her mug down on the coffee table, she walked over to get a closer view of the images on the wall. That's when she saw an uncanny similarity.

"You've got to be kidding," she said to herself. "Seriously?"

Curiosity overcame bashfulness and Amber quietly walked to the room where John sat working at his computer. She leaned against the doorframe and waited until he rolled his chair back from his desk to give her his full attention.

"Waking up?" He smiled.

"Uh huh."

"Darlene and I are both pretty chipper first thing in the morning. But Jared's like you, he kind of eases into the day. During the school year he finds it tough to make it out of the door on time." He grinned at Amber. "So you'll fit in just great with our family."

"Yeah. I like to take it slow in the morning." Amber stared at her sneakers and scuffed at a scrap of paper laying on the floor.

"Listen, I know it'll take some time for all of us to get to know each other. And at some point we'll need to talk about how you feel, what your needs are, and all that stuff. But for now, we want to give you freedom to slowly become acquainted. We don't want to push anything. So if you have questions or if you want to talk, let us know. Okay?"

"Are you Lightnings?" Though timid, as a street-kid-turned-foster-kid, Amber was nonetheless direct.

John tilted his head and his eyes met hers. "What gave you the first clue?"

Amber couldn't believe it. This was too good to be true, like the time she'd found an unused lottery ticket on the sidewalk. She'd taken it to the nearest gas station and won ten bucks. They were Lightnings!

Rather than answering John's question, she asked another one. "The painting. Is that you and Jared? Or is it . . . him?"

"It's the Original Family."

She smacked the doorframe with her hand. "I thought that one guy looked like the Light Prince! Holy smoke!"

Her new foster dad laughed. "And that means you're a Lightning, too!"

"Yeah. But I'm real new."

"That's terrific, Amber! Just super!" John jumped out of his seat to give her a hug but at the last second, thought better of it. Instead, he held up his hand for a high five.

Grinning, she gave his hand a slap.

"How long have you been a Lightning?"

Amber counted backward to the morning in the Owens' living room when she'd first met the Light Prince. "Five days."

"We should celebrate!" He started walking toward the kitchen and turned to ask, "Do you like chocolate chip pancakes with hot fudge and whipped cream?"

"Uh, yeah!" Amber trailed after him. The truth was, she'd never had chocolate chip pancakes. But the combination of all that deliciousness was a no-brainer. It had to be scrumptious.

John opened some cupboard doors. "You can mix up the batter while I get the rest of the things ready." He pulled out the box of buckwheat pancake flour and handed it to her. "Have you ever done this before?"

"Not really." She shook her head. Cooking wasn't exactly

a street people activity.

"No problem. Here's what you do." Reading the instructions out loud, he showed her step-by-step how to proceed.

While she beat the eggs and pancake mix together, he gathered the chocolate chips and whipped cream and heated the hot fudge in the microwave.

A mess of chocolate chip pancakes later, they sat down to eat. On the table in front of them were two breakfast plates that Amber thought looked as mouthwatering as the ones she'd seen on the covers of food magazines in the grocery store.

"One more thing." John motioned for her to wait and held up a birthday candle. Striking a match, he lit the wick and stuck the candle into her pancake stack, right in front of a small mound of whipped cream.

"Happy birthday Amber!"

"But my birthday isn't until September."

"Not your earthly birthday. Your OtherSide birthday. You're in two families now."

Entirely caught off guard, Amber felt heat creeping into her chest, moving up her neck, and swirling around her head.

"Well go on, make a wish and blow it out."

Something was squeezing her brain. She blew out the flame but forgot to make a wish. *Ugh! Everything was going great until this stupid birthday candle showed up.*

Shame flew in through the garage wall and into the kitchen area, skirting a dazzle as he came.

Morgan was nearby and saw the drab sneaking in a wide circle to avoid them. "That's right. You should keep your distance. If you give me the chance, I'll skewer you faster than you can slink."

Hovering close to his earth child, Rahzell glanced at the drab. "And if he doesn't get you, I will."

But the drab knew his rights and defended himself in a sniveling sort of way. "She wants my help. She asks for me!"

The Other Side Of Visible 163

The dazzles intentionally turned toward watching their humans and ignored the lies.

As he cursed the human girl Shame crouched, ready to evade advancing dazzles at a moment's notice. "Look at yourself! You know you don't deserve to be celebrated! You're nothing but scum! A worthless piece of junk! Garbage, that's what you are!"

Solm floated toward the dining area and looked at Rahzell and Morgan. "Some day that thing will regret every despicable syllable."

Rahzell turned and nodded in agreement. "I'd like to make it regret them now. But the girl is a fighter. She's getting stronger. And by her rule, the drabs will lose their power."

John noticed the expression on Amber's face had taken a turn south. He pulled out the extinguished candle and tossed it onto his napkin. "Birthdays aren't a happy time for you?" It was more of a question than a statement.

Amber despised birthdays. She'd hated them ever since taking to the streets. But it wasn't until now, that she finally figured out why. It was all because of Sheena Becker.

Her last foster family before going homeless, the Beckers had been the final straw. Their idiotic birthday party for their real daughter was the reason Amber had slipped out of a bedroom window and escaped to live on the streets.

Sheena had turned eight years old and her parents had gone all out. They'd invited more than thirty children, hung *Happy Birthday, Princess!* signs and streamers everywhere, hired a clown who made balloon animals, prepared all kinds of games with real prizes, and bought a fancy cake shaped like a princess wearing a ball gown. Amber had never seen such a birthday celebration.

And in addition to gifts from the partygoers, Sheena's parents bought her a new bicycle. Of course, Amber was only a foster daughter and not a genuine member of the family. But a month earlier for her eighth birthday, they'd given her a card and three new undershirts. She hadn't even gotten a cake.

At her foster sister's party, she began to cry. And when her foster mom asked what was wrong, Amber timidly answered that she wanted a princess cake and a bike for her birthday too, and not just undershirts.

Mrs. Becker was incensed. "You ungrateful little girl! We feed you, buy you clothes, take you to school and help you with your homework! And all you can do is be jealous of your sister's good fortune!" She pointed an angry finger toward the kitchen. "To the basement right this minute, young lady. No more party for you."

Amber was locked in their basement whenever she was bad. Hearing she was being sent there again, she cried even harder. And that only made her foster mom madder.

Grabbing her arm, Mrs. Becker dragged her from the party into the kitchen. With eyes like daggers she glared and said through clenched teeth, "Now, stop it. Don't go making a scene just to draw all the attention to yourself. This is your sister's party, you little brat." Pointing toward the basement door, she ordered, "You get down those stairs right now," and glowered until Amber stepped inside.

The door closed, the key turned in the lock, and Amber heard Mrs. Becker's footsteps move away from the kitchen area.

She sat at the top of the grey wooden steps, crying. After an hour Amber moved to a plastic chair at the bottom of the steps. By the end of the second hour she was still sniffling a little bit, but mainly she'd stopped all the fussing. Crawling up on the workbench, she stood on her tippy toes and looked out the half-window near the ceiling. There was nothing else to do, and she wanted to see what was happening outside.

Otherwise, she sat. And sat. Until all the partygoers were gone and she could hear Mr. and Mrs. Becker cleaning up the family room. Until dinner came and went. Until everyone else was getting ready for bed.

Finally the basement door opened, and with disgust the birthday girl said, "You can come up now, brat. Dad said it's time for bed."

Slowly walking up the stairs and through the kitchen toward her bedroom, Amber felt ashamed and numb.

Her foster sister closed the basement door and ran to catch up to her. And that's when the big news came that changed everything.

"You know, the only reason you're here is because of the money we get from the foster agency for keeping you. This will never be your home and you'll never be a part of our family."

Sheena Becker smiled smugly, disappeared into her own bedroom, and slammed the door.

Amber was stunned.

From the age of five, her life had been a revolving door as she moved from one foster family to another. She'd always dreamed the next family would be the one that would give her a permanent home. But with Sheena's revelation, the picture was abundantly clear. Those families only kept her for the money. Not one of them cared about her.

That night she ran away.

Surfacing from her memories, Amber glanced at John. His eyes were closed and he was sitting quietly, his pancakes untouched. Except for a small lump that remained in the middle, his whipping cream had melted into a pool of thick milk.

"Vile girl, this man doesn't care about you! He's just like all the others. He's toxic! He'll use you. You're in danger!" Fear had smelled the girl's frailty and flown through the dining room wall to join Shame in the fray.

Control was also with them, still recuperating from his wounds and keeping a careful distance from dazzles. "Ssstupid girl. Sstop fooling yoursself! Get away from thessse people before it'ss too late!"

Amber was irked, to say the least. There was no way she would endure another fiasco like the one she'd experienced at the Becker's place. She had to know whether history was about to repeat itself. Better to discover the truth up front, before things went any farther.

"Am I only here because you get paid to keep me?"

"What?" John opened his eyes and looked at her.

It was obvious he hadn't caught the question. Anger rose up from somewhere inside and she raised her voice. "I want to know if I'm your foster kid only because the foster system pays you money! And don't lie to me!" Ready to bolt if he showed even one tracc of dishonesty, her body tensed with anticipation. She could almost taste the disgust of being exploited by another family.

Her new foster dad was silent for a few seconds. Then he leaned close and said in a gentle voice, "That's the reason you ran away, isn't it? You felt used."

That certainly wasn't what she'd expected to hear. But he hadn't answered her question, at least not directly. He wasn't going to get off the hook so easily.

"Well?" She kept her eyes on the table. "You still didn't answer my question."

Without a hint of impatience, John said, "You have a right to know, so here's the truth. The money we receive from foster care goes toward your expenses: food and clothing, any school expenses, and to offset the normal costs of having another person in the house. That includes things like paying for additional gas, electricity, and water usage.

But often, some of that money is leftover at the end of the month. And in that case, we use it to take day trips together as a family."

Amber's posture eased slightly. She leaned over and began scraping at a piece of dried food on the table.

"Does that make sense?"

She stopped picking, sat up, folded her arms across her chest, and frowned. "If I'm here that long, do I get to go with you on those day trips?"

Her new foster dad threw his arms out to his side, his eyes wide with surprise. "Of course you do, Amber! I was including you in our family. You're part of us now. You belong here as much as Darlene and Jared and I."

When he said the "B" word there was a sudden flip-flopping in Amber's stomach. She couldn't tell if that was a good or a bad sign.

"Look at me." John inclined his head to lasso her eyes and pull them into his gaze.

Reluctantly, she turned toward him and their eyes met.

"We will not use you."

She stared at his face. He seemed as honest as a baby. Amber wanted to believe he was telling the truth, but she'd been burned way too many times—and especially by other foster families—to trust his words.

"I know you've been burned way too many times, and probably by other foster families. But I promise you, in our home everyone is treated with equal honor. We're all valuable."

Amber blinked and turned away. Mr. Gordon repeated her thought, just like Crazy Lady and Oscar had done. And his words sounded exactly like something the Light Prince would say. She slouched back against her chair, a little smile pulling at the corners of her mouth.

Beyond the veneer three sullen drabs murmured and fussed. They'd flung more diatribes at the girl than archers have arrows, but that detestable glow from the other invisible atmosphere was neutralizing their mission. For the time being, they angrily gave up the fight and disappeared through the kitchen wall to wait until more advantageous circumstances presented themselves.

"Good riddance!" Morgan said.

"Forever!" Rahzell added, as the drabs flew away.

Immediately, Morgan's attention was drawn to the slow arrival of his sleepy human. Looking at the other dazzles, he gestured toward the teen. "Now there's a sight for star-eyes—Fast Cookies, my earthling. He's a marvel and a wonder. I wonder how he can ingest so much food, and I marvel that it never seems to be enough."

Rahzell laughed. "And my Little Streak is a mystery and a surprise. Her life has been a mystery to me, but the surprise is in her awakening."

Solm inspected Rahzell's appearance. "And it's obvious you couldn't be more thrilled."

Rahzell examined his own light-shine. He was glowing with exhilaration. Deep admiration spread across his face as he looked Solm's way. "The Original Family's power to recolor humans will never cease to amaze me." He pointed in the direction of Little Streak. "Seeing her become OtherSide royalty was as rewarding as watching them spin the galaxies and planets."

Morgan nudged Rahzell and nodded toward his young earthling. "Now that he's arrived, food will disappear."

Rahzell grinned and turned to watch with curiosity.

"Hey, how long have you guys been up?" Jared was shuffling out to the kitchen, yawning and stretching toward the ceiling as he walked. He stopped behind Amber's chair and scratched his mop of bedhead hair.

"Morning, Jared," his dad said.

Jared caught sight of the food. "Chocolate chip pancakes! Why didn't you wake me up?"

John grinned. "Take it easy, there's a plate of extra pancakes next to the stove. You can reheat them in the microwave."

"All right!" Jared pushed his glasses up on his nose and went to grab the remaining stack of pancakes. "Wow, Amber, we don't get to have this kind of sugar rush very often. Must be 'cause you're here."

"Do you want to explain? Or should I?"

She answered John's question by pointing at him.

"Amber's recently become a Lightning, so we're celebrating her OtherSide birthday."

"Seriously!"

Amber grinned at Jared.

"Awesome!" He walked over and held out his hand. "Félicitations!"

"Huh?" She slapped his upturned palm.

"That's French for congratulations."

"Oh."

Though she had no idea why John and Jared were making such a big deal about her OtherSide birthday, Amber realized she was no longer feeling all those awkward emotions. All the pinching stuffiness was gone. Something had changed. *Weird! But I won't complain.*

"You want to reheat your pancakes and then we'll add more whipped cream?" John was looking at her cold plate of uneaten food.

"Yeah."

"Jared, show her how to use the microwave."

"I can do it myself." Amber picked up her plate and headed into the kitchen.

"You only have to press the number one, then hit the start button," Jared said, as he pulled a plate of five steaming pancakes from the microwave and took it to the table.

Amber reheated her pancakes, grabbed the can of whipped cream, and sprayed a small white mountain on top. Setting the can back on the counter, she asked John, "You want me to reheat yours?"

He hopped up. "I can do it. Eat, before your food gets cold again."

Amber sat and watched Jared shovel in a huge bite of pancake that was loaded with whipped cream and hot fudge. She took a bite of her own. It was delish.

Her foster brother gulped down another mouthful. "So, does this mean we get birthday cake tonight?" He looked hopefully at his dad, who was returning to the table.

"Sure, why not?" John glanced at Amber. "What do you say about that?"

Twenty minutes earlier, a birthday cake would've reminded Amber of her outsider status. But this foster family wasn't excluding her. Instead, they seemed to be inviting her right into their little circle.

But before she had a chance to answer Mr. Gordon about the cake, Jared was onto his next question.

"What flavor do you like?"

"Definitely chocolate." No hesitation there.

"Yessss!" he raised his hand for a high five and they smacked hands again.

"Is a store-bought cake okay? I mean, today there's not time—"

Amber interrupted John. "Store-bought is great!" *I always wanted a store-bought birthday cake!*

"Great. I'll call it in." John finished his last bite, carried his plate to the kitchen, and put his dish in the dishwasher. He leaned over and looked at Amber. "I was thinking of a princess design for the cake. But that's probably too young for a twelve-year-old, isn't it?"

Her eyes shot practically to the moon and back, as images of Sheena Becker's princess birthday cake popped into her mind. How did he know? As though the party had been yesterday, Amber could still envision every detail of that gorgeous cake. The ballgown design had been formed with hundreds of ribbons of icing that imitated the satin material on a real princess dress. She never did get a taste of it to find out whether it was chocolate or vanilla.

Having no clue how to answer her foster dad's question, she shrugged and said nothing. Street living hadn't exactly made her an expert in popular trends. And anyway, what were twelve-year-olds supposed to like?

John momentarily closed his eyes and went somewhere else, the way Oscar sometimes did. Finally, he opened his eyes.

"Well, since you're now an official princess of OtherSide, I think a princess theme is perfect."

Warmth filled Amber's chest, but this time without the pressure. She smiled shyly. "Yeah, it's perfect." For more reasons than Mr. Gordon could know. And besides, who cared what other twelve-year-old kids wanted?

John winked at her. "I thought you might like that." He walked through the kitchen and stopped to ruffle his son's head of hair. "Hey, Jared, I've got to get back to work now. Will you please clean up the kitchen?"

Jared was licking whipped cream off his thumb. "Okay." He turned to his new foster sister. "And then, do you want me to show you my latest video game?"

"Yep. I'll help you with the kitchen."

"Cool."

While they did the dishes, a sugar high set in and Jared started telling jokes. *He's funny!* He reminded her of the main teenage character in the last sci-fi novel she'd read.

Loading another dish into the dishwasher, she took a peek around the corner at John, who was back to work in his office. *He seems nice, too.*

Amber couldn't wait to tell Oscar and Madison and Maggie that her first day of foster care wasn't a disaster. And although he already knew everything, she wanted to tell the Light Prince he was right. So far, foster care seemed to be working out. Just like he promised.

CHAPTER NINETEEN

At two o'clock in the morning, during the blackest part of night, Dibs rested his elbow on a pipe bracketed to the stuccoed wall of a city duplex. The shadowed side of the home was perfect as a lookout point for their heist.

While Julio hot-wired a car sitting in a nearby driveway, Dibs scanned up and down the block to search for movement. His jaw clenched in concentration, he was ready to warn the crew if a stranger entered the vicinity. Three minutes and twenty-five seconds into the theft he heard the engine start. Clicking the stopwatch in his hand, he hightailed it to join Robbie in the getaway car.

Jumping in beside him, Dibs shouted, "New record! Julio beat the old one by six seconds!"

"Nailed it!" Robbie hollered.

They fist-bumped, and Robbie shifted gears to speed away and join the gang at Cutter's Salvage.

Back at the shop they parked their car off to the side and entered quietly through the rear entrance.

There was a standard procedure for bringing in a stolen vehicle. First, the car's driver made a phone call to alert the work crew of his estimated time of arrival. Once certain he wasn't being followed and all was clear, the driver pulled into the salvage yard. Shop lights went out as the garage door quietly opened, and the car entered the shop's pit area. When the garage door closed again, someone was assigned lookout duty to make sure there would be no surprise visitors.

Inside, the lights were turned on, and piece by piece the mechanics tore into the vehicle's disassembly. Once parts were removed, they were inventoried and cleaned in preparation for resale to auto repair shops and body shops.

At the end of the night the new inventory was carried down to underground storage. The passageway was then locked, and the entry to the hidden storeroom was covered over with a large rubber mat and a rolling shelf.

Speed was an essential part of the chop shop routine, since stolen parts were sold for less money than regular parts. The faster a car could be dismantled, the sooner another car could be brought in, and the larger the take they all made for the night.

During his first days as part of the chop shop crew, Dibs had more or less been afraid of his own shadow. But then he noticed Tall Eddy wasn't acting all mean and threatening anymore. Instead, his new boss was treating him as though he belonged there as much as everybody else. He wasn't ready to trust the guy without question. But since Eddy was no longer acting like such a creep, Dibs found himself able to relax a little bit and concentrate on getting the hang of things as a lookout for the heists, and as a runner for the shop mechanics.

Though he still had nervous misgivings about the dishonesty of the shop, he was no longer as uptight about being forced into the deal. There were even a few flickering moments when he liked being part of the shop's gang.

At the end of this particular shift, Eddy came around to give him a handshake. "Dibsy, you're fitting in real good here." He grabbed the teen's outstretched hand and went through a series of motions that were part of his signature greeting. "You keep doin' your job and pitching in the way you've been doin', and you might even prove to me you're a real man." He reached over and squeezed Dibs' upper arm.

Dibs hardened his muscle to appear more masculine.

"Show yourself hard core, and in a couple a' weeks we might even have to give you some dead presidents."

"Hey, I wouldn't argue, that's for sure. About the dead presidents, I mean." Dibs had the sense the rest of the guys in the shop did pretty well in this lucrative business. Longing to improve his own lot in life, he couldn't wait to get paid, like the rest of them.

Poking Dibs' stomach, Eddy teased, "Looks like you're already showin' a little flab there, from the three squares I've been feeding you every day."

Dibs grinned and pulled away from his hand.

Nodding toward the side door, Tall Eddy said, "All right, Rookie, get outta' here. Go catch some Zs, and we'll see you tonight."

While Eddy walked away to start wrapping up his tools, Dibs waved to the mechanics and then said to his heist crew, "Later, Julio. See ya', Rob."

Julio grunted and Robbie waved.

Dibs walked out into the cool night air to make the trek home under the shadow of a thumbnail moon. Passing Shin's alleyway, he thought of her fear of moving around in the dark. He was glad he didn't have that kind of fear.

Feeling bad about their busted friendship, he rationalized that for now, it was safer for everyone to keep her out of the picture. But someday, when he was rolling in the dough and living in his own apartment, he hoped she'd come around and they could be friends again.

Shaking off the tension that had crept into his shoulders, Dibs started mentally planning his day. The first thing was breakfast. With the daily food money Eddy gave him, Dibs could buy his meals instead of begging. That was a good thing, now that working took up a lot of his time.

Even so, he was tired of being poor. He had no idea how long it would be until Eddy started paying him. All the other guys at the shop had their own digs. It was time he lived in a proper home too, and not in a dilapidated warehouse. He also wanted his own belongings, the kind most people have in their houses: a decent sofa, a fridge, a table and chairs, and a real bed.

While Dibs strolled toward the warehouse, an idea occurred to him. *I could beg to get cash for goods, just like I used t'beg for food!* But then he remembered he was terrible at saving money. The green stuff ran through his fingers faster than water. Still, now that he didn't have to worry about paying for his next meal, money might not be so slippery.

Oscar came to mind, the old guy at the zoo. Dibs wished he could hit him up for some bills. *He sure throws money around like he has it.* Soon he was formulating a plan to visit him. If the two of them were still on friendly terms, meaning, if the old man wasn't holding a grudge and taking Shin's side about their recent quarrel, he was going to ask him for some money.

With time to kill before the zoo opened, Dibs decided to check out that new coffee shop on King Street. If the joint was swamped with early commuters, it'd be a cinch to beg for enough cash to add to the money Eddy had given him. He wanted to splurge on an extra large caramel frappé. Just the thought of it made his mouth water, and he sped up to get there in time for the peak of morning rush hour.

CHAPTER TWENTY

Dear Oscar, Maggie, and Madison,

It's hard to beleive I've been here for almost two weeks. I wish I could talk to you on the phone. I like writing in this diary you gave me, but it will be a lot better when we are allowed to talk to each other.

This week Jared's been teaching me all about computers. I think he will become a scientist, or something like that. He sure knows lots of stuff. I like learning about it, but sometimes my brain feels as full as a blowted tick. And guess what? He showed me how to download library books! I can borrow them and read them on a computer!

I got so exsited about that, I spilled soda all over the carpet. Jared did a web search (that means you look up stuff on the computer) on "How to clean soda from a carpet." And it's easy. You only need dish soap and warm water.

I apollogized a million times. But they didn't seem to get upset. I'm sure not used to that, let me tell you.

Anyway, things are going good here. The Gordons are really nice. I found out today John's faverite ice *creme flavor is chocolite, just like me. Darlene likes rasberry. I think Jared likes all the flavors. He sure eats a lot!*

Like I said before, I know some of my spelling isn't so great. That's probably because of not being in school, ha ha ha. Guess I'll catch up when I go back in Setember. Madison, when I come back to your house, maybe you can help me improve.

So, how are you? I know you can't anser until the agency says it's o.k. But I wish you could.

Oh, BTW (Jared told me BTW is a short way to say "by the way"), I hung out with the Light Prince a couple of times this week. He is VERY cool.

I'll write again soon,
Amber

Amber finished her journal entry for the day, put her pen in the drawer of the nightstand, and tucked her diary in its hiding place under her bed. Even though it was ten o'clock at night, thanks to downing a cup of coffee after dinner, she was wide awake.

She decided to take a trip to OtherSide.

Closing her earth eyes, she felt an immediate wind at her back. Its current picked her up and carried her across the veneer. Soon she was being lowered directly onto the surface near the Crimson Wall.

Her landing was in the exact location of her first visit to OtherSide. The same fogginess circled around her waist. Catching sight of the cloud, Amber pulled her hands in against her body and froze straight. The first time she'd seen that innocent little mist, the thing had promptly supersized itself into a ginormous mass of blinding white.

She wished her prince brother would hurry up and make his appearance.

"Actually, Amber, the Light Prince won't be joining us

today." A voice spoke nearby in answer to her thought.

So as not to disturb the cloud, she turned carefully to face whoever was talking.

"Who's there?"

"I'm The Light," the voice responded.

Though she couldn't see anyone, Amber breathed a sigh of relief. Her prince brother had mentioned this royal family member during some of their earlier conversations. Now that he was around, she felt sure the cloud wouldn't do its creepy expansion trick.

Turning slowly in a circle, she searched for the person behind the voice. Not a soul was in sight.

"I'm sorry, but I don't see you."

"I'm in plain view. Just look around."

Doing as the voice suggested, she scanned the whole area a second time. There wasn't a living being anywhere, as far as she could see.

"If I may say so, life doesn't always appear in creature form. I'm *The Light* around you."

When the voice emphasized the words *the light*, Amber finally looked down at the gleaming mist.

"I'm so glad to finally make your acquaintance!" A splendid glow shimmered throughout the cloud.

Amber stared, wide-eyed. The fog was alive! And it was talking! She quickly struck her previous icicle pose. A cloud that could talk and also supersize itself to take over an atmosphere certainly wasn't on her list of Things To Get To Know In OtherSide.

"Dear one, I don't plan on supersizing myself, as you say."

She stood speechless.

"Don't be afraid. I won't harm you."

Yeah, but you don't mind frightening me to death! The thought burst into her head and she frowned. The mist was probably reading her mind.

"When you first met the Light Prince you needed my

brightness."

Since it was pointless to try and hide her thoughts, Amber knew she might as well be straightforward. Her body relaxed and she looked down at the fog. "What do you mean?"

"Here, relationship is based on being transparent and honest. You needed my great white light to let the real you meet the real prince."

"The real me."

"Yes. The broken, genuine, trusting you."

Amber could identify with being broken. But those other words, they didn't feel like her. She looked away, out beyond the cloud, into empty space.

"That first day, before you met the Light Prince, you chose to stay in my intense whiteness. You didn't run or try to escape my light. Instead, you risked being seen as you were. That, my dear, is trust." His glow increased considerably. "And now here we are, genuine you and brilliant me."

She smiled for the first time since meeting this strange new thing. No, that wasn't right; it obviously had a personality. But it—or he—wasn't in human form. Amber didn't know how to think about it: or him.

"Now, would you like to experience one of my other forms?"

Just when she'd begun to relax, he or it was throwing her a dangerous question.

"I think you'll like this expression."

I suppose it can't be any worse than a terrifying blast of white. She shrugged. "I guess."

"See, your trust IS growing."

Amber raised one eyebrow. *That sounds just like something the Light Prince would say.* The Light's answer settled her dilemma. As a member of the Original Family, HE was definitely not an *it*.

"Here we go!" He unfolded himself and grew into a spectacular luminous band of light that stretched all the way to the horizon. Sweeping her up onto his back, his beam began racing up and down and twisting left and right, like a giant roller coaster. There were no seatbelts and no handles, but each time The Light's beam flowed swiftly in any direction, he adjusted himself to cradle her body with the perfect amount of curve and tension. She sat back to enjoy the ride.

As his band of light pressed softly against her skin, Amber started to giggle. A living light wave was taking her on the most unbelievable ride of her life. They zipped wildly around the region of Hearth White, the wind blowing marvelously in her face and her skin tingling from the bubbliness of his rays. Never having been on an amusement park ride, she was positive this beat them all hands down. Soon she was laughing out loud for sheer joy.

After a few minutes of exhilarating speed and precision spins and turns, his beam of light straightened and slowed. He settled Amber back on her feet and immediately shrank down into his previous size as a smaller light cloud.

She was still giggling. "That was awesome!"

"Thank you." The Light glimmered softly. One of his favorite pastimes was teaching too-serious human beings how to play.

Looking down, Amber realized her T-shirt had gotten disheveled during the ride. While she smoothed it with her hands, The Light spoke.

"There is someone I want you to meet, Amber."

And faster than a thought, Crazy Lady stood directly in front of her.

"Hello dear one! Oh, how lovely to see you here in OtherSide! You're really HERE! Welcome, love! A thousand times, welcome!"

Amber was more than a little astonished to see her earthly begging connection standing in this strange new land. She stared at the woman, who seemed much younger now, and spoke with a clear, strong voice. A deep-blue, sparkly glow radiated from the lady's insides, almost as if she'd been hanging around The Light's cloud and some of him had leaked into her.

As Priscilla gave Amber a hearty hug, The Light sent a celebratory shower of iridescent particles into the air above them. His glitter landed softly on their heads and shoulders.

And in the way a child looks skyward to catch falling snowflakes, Priscilla raised her face toward the sparkles. After a full thirty seconds of feeling them land gently on her eyes and nose and cheeks, she sighed contentedly. "*Pure Love*—that's what I've named The Light—Pure Love thrills when humans love each other. He just cannot contain himself!"

Glitter stopped coming down, and The Light took on his previous white cloud shape and surrounded the two ladies. Amber studied this peculiar Original Family member. He was unlike anyone she had ever encountered. She wondered why Crazy Lady had called him by a different name.

The Light interrupted her musing. "Amber, most Lightnings call me by a name of their own choosing. Officially I'm known as The Light, but what name would you like to give me? He brightened and whirled around the two of them.

Where Amber had come from, people she'd met for the first time didn't usually give her the option of naming them. She looked to Crazy Lady for help.

"Dear one, as a gesture of affection, humans on Earth often create special nicknames for those they know and love." She looked adoringly at The Light. "In the same way, Pure Love is delighted when Lightnings call him by a name they've created for him."

In her old habit of putting a negative spin on people and situations, and before she could catch herself from thinking it, the name *Weirdo* popped into Amber's head. She cringed in embarrassment because of OtherSide's transparent thinking.

The Light's brightness stood still, the way two people on Earth might stop, if one of them wanted to share a deeply personal thought. With all seriousness, but without any anger or criticism, he spoke truthfully. "Don't condemn yourself, Amber. You're not the first earthling to dismiss me. It's hard for humans to think of me as part of the Original Family, because I don't present myself in a form like your own." His mist started swirling again. "And in fact, I can take on many forms."

Moving forward, he said, "Come. Let's walk together."

As the three of them strolled down the pathway, Amber kept her focus on the smooth colored pebbles beneath her shoes. Why couldn't she think nice thoughts? *Crazy Lady doesn't seem to struggle with OtherSide's see-through thinking. How does she manage to have good, transparent thoughts?* She decided to ask.

"Crazy Lady, I don't know how to stop my brain from—" Amber sucked in air and cut herself off. She'd just let fly with her not-so-nice nickname for the woman! Clapping her hand over her mouth in horror, she tried to do a verbal U-turn. "I mean . . . uh . . ." But for the life of her, she couldn't recall the woman's real name. Oscar had mentioned it once, but the nickname Crazy Lady had been stuck in her brain for so long it was cemented there, like one of those Hollywood sidewalk stars she'd read about in a book.

The Light stopped moving and said gently, "Perhaps I should introduce you." He formed himself into a sparkling curtain and swirled up behind the woman. As though presenting some sort of dignitary, he announced, "Amber, may I present to you Ambassador Priscilla Conrad."

Amber stared at her shoes so she wouldn't have to make eye contact with such an esteemed person as an ambassador: especially one she'd just dreadfully insulted. Embarrassment swelled up in her esophagus and she considered opening her earth eyes to escape from OtherSide.

"Don't be ashamed, Amber. Things of this realm always seem crazy until the first visit." Priscilla placed her hand on

Amber's shoulder to reassure her. "When you knew me on Earth your star-eyes were still profoundly closed, so naturally I seemed loony."

The Light glowed and drew closer. "What you're experiencing isn't unusual for new Lightnings. Have patience with yourself. There's a learning curve to using your star-eyes. But don't worry, I'll help you."

She couldn't face either of them. That Crazy Lady—that *Priscilla*—wouldn't be hopping mad was hard for her to believe. The adults in her previous experiences would've gone ballistic. And they would've made sure she understood how bad she'd been by dishing out a punishment: sending her to the basement, walloping her with a switch, making her sort two months of recycling cans, or some other such penalty.

The Light's essence moved closer and hugged her snugly. "Amber, in OtherSide we child-train. We never, ever punish. To help you fully develop, we give you choices." His cloud brightened and turned Amber yellow. "My dear, punishment is a thing of your past."

Out of the corner of her eye Amber noticed his mistiness had taken on her hue. It made her feel a little better and she risked glancing up at Priscilla. Speaking almost too softly to be heard, she asked, "So, you're not angry with me?"

"Come here, dear one." Priscilla drew her into a generous hug. Patting her on the back, she whispered into her ear, "Growing up in the royal family is much different than growing up in our earthly families." Standing back, the older woman gazed into Amber's eyes. "Many earthlings condemn us for making mistakes. But believe it or not, OtherSide welcomes mistakes!"

She didn't believe it.

"It's true! We learn from them. That's the reason the Original Family considers mistakes an essential ingredient of the maturing process."

Amber shook her head at what she was hearing. Sometimes the realm of OtherSide was as similar to Earth as a skyscraper was to a slug.

She watched the lady she now recognized as important. On Earth, she had decided old people were irrelevant and basically clueless. But it was becoming obvious the royal family's point of view was quite the opposite. This woman was an influential ambassador for their realm. It dawned on Amber she could probably learn a lot about life from older people like Priscilla and Oscar.

"Thank you *Priscilla,* for being patient with me." She emphasized the name to imprint it over top of the nickname that had gotten stuck in her brain.

Turning to the cloud, she said, "And thank you, The Light."

Calling him by his official name felt awkward, like calling Dibs, "The Dibs," or Oscar, "The Oscar." She sure wouldn't want to be called, "The Shin," or, "The Amber." Just the thought of it made her grin.

If they were going to hang out together, she would need to come up with a nickname. Pure Love, Priscilla's name for The Light, fit him pretty well. Except it didn't account for his turbo-charged roller coaster light-ride, or for the energy of his mega-sizing atmosphere trick.

As they continued their walk together The Light said, "Don't worry, Amber. In time you'll find your own special name for me. And whatever you choose will be perfect, because you'll be seeing me through your star-eyes."

"Thanks." It was nice that he was giving her time to think about it. She watched his light-infused cloud, and an idea zinged through her head.

"Hey, can I call you Mister Energy for now?"

Newly titled Mister Energy began to chuckle, and soon he was erupting with immense OtherSide laughter. "It's perfect!"

His joyful sound grew so exuberant, it vibrated the entire

surface and jiggled the two humans around like pebbles on a busy roadway. Being joggled by such rollicking laughter, both Priscilla and Amber began to giggle. Soon everyone was rolling around in howls of laughter, the ladies holding their stomach muscles with each deep belly laugh.

Mister Energy billowed and bubbled around them, until his chortling slowly subsided into immeasurable peace. The three of them lay still in a happy, contented pile.

What seemed like hours later, The Light drew Amber to her feet. She sighed contentedly. If only she could always be so happy.

Looking around, she noticed her older friend was gone. "Where's Priscilla?"

"She's returned to another part of OtherSide. I'd like to spend time, just the two of us, getting to know one another."

After all that laughter and incredible peace, Amber thought Mister Energy was every bit as interesting as her prince brother. And the fact that he could take on many forms was fascinating, like good sci-fi read. Being with him certainly wouldn't be boring.

Trillions of indigo light-granules crystallized as The Light formed a glittering, twirling funnel. He brought himself to the front of where Amber was standing and said, "Perhaps you'd like to have my shine inside of you."

She stared at him. "Inside me?"

"Yes. That way, we'll always be together. And I can help you be a more effective Lightning."

It meant a lot to Amber that the crimson color of the Light Prince was permanently in her veins. Whenever she was in OtherSide, she only had to look at the hue of her skin to remember she belonged in the royal family. But what if The Light super-sized himself while inside of her body? Images crossed her mind of becoming inflated, like an excited pufferfish.

"My being isn't made of your realm's matter, dear one. I'm

The Light, remember?"

Amber's eyes widened with understanding. *Oh yeah! And I'm a LIGHTning!*

As The Light's revolving funnel shot sparklers in every direction, Amber grinned. He looked like a gentle tornado in party mode. Her mind was made up. "Yeah, Mister Energy, I would like you inside of me."

His granules glowed brightly. "Good. Here I come!"

She closed her eyes to wait.

As he gathered around her, Amber felt herself being lifted off her feet. His breeze began gradually but soon grew into a gale-force wind. In no time at all, a deafening noise filled her ears and great pressure pushed against her chest.

Amber opened her eyes. Her arms and legs were flailing about and her hair was flying haphazardly every which way. At a height of more than one hundred feet above OtherSide's surface, she was completely out of control.

"Let me carry you."

Amber shouted to him above the roaring sound, "I have no choice!"

"But you do, dear one; *allow* me to support you."

Shutting her eyes once more, she intentionally leaned back into the current of his powerful whirlwind and told herself to let go.

After a few more bursts of wild energy—while she continued to be tossed to and fro—The Light's iridescent wind tunnel finally slowed down and his resounding boom slacked off. They were descending.

Opening her eyes, Amber saw she was being lowered onto OtherSide's surface. There were flowers everywhere: white tulips, purple anemones, red poppies, and countless other varieties she couldn't identify. She started to get up.

Mister Energy's voice communicated inside Amber's thoughts. *Rest, child. Stay quietly and let yourself soak in the garden's beauty.*

She lay back down in the middle of the flowers. The surface was softer than her bed and refreshingly cool. Fragrances floating in the air were sweet, like the aroma of the hot cinnamon buns sold in the bread shop near the library. She smiled. *This must be what a spa feels like.*

For a long time she lay still, until curiosity got the best of her, and she finally sat up. For as far as she could see, there were flowers and trees of every variety, color, size and shape.

Do you like this place?

"Uh, yeah! It's a million times better than the parks at home."

Welcome to the Garden Of Possibilities.

"That's a funny name."

This is where Lightnings come to dream. It's the place where possibilities are conceived.

As far as Amber was concerned, she didn't have an imaginative bone in her body. Her thoughts were as boring as gray.

Dear one, we'll learn to dream together, you and I. We have so much to discover!

She stood up and became aware she hadn't been hearing an audible voice. "Where are you?" Turning in a circle, she searched for him.

I'm in you now.

Glancing down, she saw a glowing yellow light emanating from her being. He was all lit up inside her, like the lights on a Christmas tree. "Holy smoke!" Amber stared at the sparkles in her fingers, arms, legs, feet, and throughout her body.

We'll never be separated again.

"But wait a minute!" She didn't know where to look and spoke awkwardly toward her own glowing waist. "Does that mean I'll never get to ride on your airstream again, or hang out with all the other cool versions of you?"

Instantly, vapor appeared all around her. Amber jumped in surprise and then laughed.

"I'm still in you, dear one, but then again, I'm everywhere."

She liked this new family member.

"Close your eyes."

Wondering what he was going to do, she hesitated.

"Go on, close your eyes."

Amber shut her eyes and stood still. A wash of affection grew inside her, the sort of deep, satiating love she'd thought only existed in fairy tales. Tears trickled down her cheeks as waves of his gentle kindness flowed through her whole being.

She opened her eyes. The Light's cloud still surrounded her.

With a whisper so as not to spoil the atmosphere, she asked, "Was that you, Mister Energy?"

"Mmmm-hmmm. That was my hug for you."

"Wow." Amber was fuller than a waterfall, as carefree as air. She yawned and felt a good fatigue, like the tiredness that comes at the end of a perfect day at the zoo.

"Time to return to Earth, dear one."

"No! I'm not sleepy! Honest!"

The Light was silent and stopped moving.

Amber frowned. "Okay, I am tired, but I don't want to go."

Her internal glow brightened to match the Amber yellow shine of his mist. "I'm in you, little Lightning. Remember that."

Another yawn came. She tried to stifle it and reluctantly closed her drowsy eyes. When she opened them again, she was lying on her bed at the Gordons.

She sat up quickly. "I forgot to ask you! What was that insane tornado ride all about?" Since The Light was in her now, she looked at her stomach for an answer. The glow was gone. Her body looked normal.

"Mr. Energy?" Amber heard nothing and fidgeted. "You said you'd still be here. You promised."

Silence.

She sat still. As she waited, old doubts crept into her

thinking. *Where are you?* After another minute, she lay down and pulled Herbie toward her. Disappointment blanketed her mind. *You said you'd be inside me.* She pursed her lips in frustration. *None of the stuff that happened over there meant anything, did it? Nothing's changed.* The thoughts were automatic.

But as an image of The Light's glistening whirlwind crossed her mind, she caught herself. "Wait. That's not true. I felt your love. I know I wasn't making that up." Looking around the room, Amber spoke to the invisible. "Okay, I'm pretty clueless about finding my true heart." She didn't say "true and noble heart," because of how ignoble she felt.

More silence.

In the end, she decided just to sit quietly and focus on OtherSide. Gathering her blanket around her, she closed her earth eyes. After a while her mind quieted.

The Light spoke into her thoughts. *The whirlwind was my power. The Garden Of Possibilities was my love. I give you both.*

His invisible energy swelled, and a surge of peace rolled across the room, knocking Amber back onto her bed.

"Holy smoke." Even if she couldn't see him, there was no doubt that at the moment, Mister Energy was up close and personal.

There were a thousand other questions she wanted to ask, like what having power meant. And, could she learn to see his amber glow inside of her while on Earth's side of the veneer?

But she was getting quite sleepy. She turned off the lamp by her bed. "Thanks, Mister E. You're as cool as the Light Prince." Abbreviating his name came naturally, as though they'd been friends for some time.

"Good night." She yawned and turned over onto her side.

Good night, dear one.

For the rest of the night on the other side of the veneer, Amber's yellow hue glowed brightly throughout the room. But she didn't see a thing, because she was fast asleep.

CHAPTER TWENTY-ONE

By this time, even though he was four years older than Dibs, Robbie had become a good friend. They fought on occasion, but that was mainly because they were spending five nights together each week working at a job that carried a fair amount of tension.

Relating to his crew leader was a different story. Julio could be undeniably nasty, especially while high on his meth pills. When the initial buzz of those pills faded, anyone was fair game for his violent anger.

That was one reason both Robbie and Dibs chose to sit in the back seat of the car, rather than in the passenger seat next to their mean boss. Messing around on the way to the first snatch of the evening, the boys—and even at eighteen, Robbie acted more boyish than manly—were punching each other's arms in a contest to see who would wince first.

After several blows, Julio had enough and bellowed, "You imbeciles! Lay off it, or I'll give you a pounding you won't forget! Now shut up and pay attention, both of you!"

The boys rubbed their sore arms and gave each other sympathetic glances before tossing dirty looks at their fuming driver.

As they approached their target area, Julio gruffly ordered

them to keep their brains on their jobs. They were supposed to be on the lookout for the sedan that had been chosen in an earlier scouting expedition.

Robbie saw it first. "Bull's-eye on the right, just ahead."

They drove past their mark. Robbie nudged Dibs and shot an imaginary bullet at the car. They both giggled nervously. No matter how many vehicles they'd stolen, each theft produced stress that had to be dealt with in some way. Tonight the tonic-of-choice was silliness.

"Knock it off, idiots!" Julio yelled, his eyes glaring at them from the rearview mirrow.

As they approached the stop sign half a block beyond where their prize sat waiting, he slammed on the brakes. Dibs got out and quickly disappeared into the shadows to establish a lookout post. Julio circled around and parked at the opposite end of the block. All three then made connection with each other by phone.

Once they were sure everything was quiet in the neighborhood, Julio got out of the car and headed down the sidewalk. Robbie switched to the driver's seat, where he acted as a second lookout and got ready to take off as soon as the bossman finished his hotwiring job and started the engine of the stolen vehicle.

Julio arrived next to the car and took a good look around to make certain the coast was clear. He jimmied the lock and slid inside, promptly going to work on the wires below the steering wheel.

Sentinel Dibs started his stopwatch the second Julio opened the car door, then turned to his left and slowly scanned the neighborhood in a clockwise direction. Glancing down at his stopwatch, he realized it wasn't working properly. He pressed a few buttons to quickly reset it.

Ten seconds later he looked up to see a man walking toward the car Julio was hijacking. Panic shot through his body and Dibs yelled louder than he should have into his phone, "Julio, get outta' there NOW! Somebody's comin' right at you!"

Robbie heard Dibs' warning on his phone and started his engine. Julio's head surfaced above the steering wheel just in time to see the approaching stranger reach for the handle of the car door. Opening the door, he slammed it into the man as hard as he could and took off in a sprint toward Robbie's waiting car.

In the case of a heist gone wrong, the plan was to pick up Dibs and race away to one of several hiding places, where they would then hunker down and wait. But if it was too dangerous for Robbie to circle around and pick him up, Dibs had instructions to quietly disappear into the city. And later, when the heat was off, they would all make a connection by phone and meet at another specified location before heading back to the shop.

But things don't always go according to plans.

Watching it all from his post between two buildings, Dibs squinted so his eyes could focus in the darkness. He saw the stranger regain his balance, glance in the direction of the get-away car, and bend down to pick something up off the ground. As he straightened up again the glow of a cell phone reflected from his hand.

Julio had dropped his phone! Dibs had no idea what to do, but he knew perfectly well that in the wrong person's hands, the information on that cell phone was bad news for the operation. He reacted with the only plan he could come up with on the spur of the moment.

"Help! Help me! He's after me!"

Dibs shouted as though someone were chasing him and ran straight toward the stranger. His intent was to run full steam into the man, knock him off balance, grab the phone, and then continue racing away until he was far out of sight. But just as he was about to throw his body into the stranger's side, a swift foot landed squarely on his head.

The force of the blow knocked Dibs down, and he collapsed onto the sidewalk. He tried to get up and fight, but his head was spinning and the sidewalk was dipping and bending violently, like a wild roller coaster ride.

Falling back onto the cement, he saw the man towering over him, talking to someone or something. The pain in Dibs' head kept him from being able to focus on the words. Trying once more to pick himself up, he felt a foot press into his back, hard and strong. It took his breath away.

Through the fog of a raging headache, he heard two new voices approaching. They joined the first man and formed a ring around him. When he tried to sit up again they moved in closer.

"Not so fast." A hand clenched his arm with a powerful grip.

Dibs realized he couldn't fight. Not in his condition. He lay back down. Absentmindedly, he touched the throbbing spot near his right temple. A sharp pain shot through his face. He quickly pulled his hand away. His fingers were wet with blood.

Sirens blared in the distance and gradually got louder. Soon their wailing stopped in front of the group, and the bright lights of a police car flashed through the entire block.

Desperate to escape, Dibs tried to stand. The muscle men tightened their circle and pinned him firmly to the sidewalk.

Two officers joined them and questions and answers flew back and forth. They were talking about him.

As last, a cop bent down next to him. "What's your name?"

Dibs was silent.

A hand touched his face near the throbbing spot. He pulled away.

"Looks like you've got yourself quite a bruiser." The cop gripped Dibs' arm. "Stand up."

Dibs wanted to do more than stand. He wanted to get up and run away.

The policeman pulled him up onto his feet. And before he knew what was happening, he was being read his rights, his wrists were put in handcuffs, and he was escorted into the back seat of the police cruiser.

A second police car arrived and soon Dibs was ferried away from the scene, first to receive medical attention and then to spend the rest of the night in a secure detention care facility.

The right side of his head ached where four stitches had been sown into his flesh. It was morning, and a dose of painkiller had dulled the pain enough to enable Dibs to stand questioning by two police detectives.

One was a woman with straight, shoulder-length black hair. The other was a physically fit man with closely cropped, light-colored hair and arm muscles that bulged against the sleeves of his white dress shirt.

A bandage covered the wound on Dibs' face and worry covered his mind.

The woman introduced them. "I'm Detective Johnson, and this is my colleague Detective Martin." She looked down at information in the manila file folder. "Your name is Byron James Colby, is that correct?"

"Yeah." He knew the cops would call him by the name he never used.

The detective continued matter-of-factly. "And your file indicates you were a ward of the state until three years ago, when you disappeared from the system."

"Yeah." Dibs frowned. He hated being called a ward.

"Where have you been living since then?" She looked up from the paperwork and waited.

Not wanting to disclose the location of his warehouse, he answered vaguely. "I lived on the streets."

Putting down the file she was holding, the cop rested her arms on the table and leaned toward Dibs. "Well, Byron, it appears as though you might be in a lot of trouble."

He stared silently at his lap.

"Last night we recovered a cell phone at the location where you were picked up. We're rather sure it's the link to a car theft ring we've been trying to bust for almost year." Detective Johnson raised her eyebrows. "Do you know anything about that cell phone, Byron, or about the car theft ring?"

The bump on Dibs' face throbbed as blood rose and flushed his face. He sat forward and vehemently defended himself. "I don't know nothin' about a cell phone! I was bein' chased by a drug dealer who mistook me for somebody else. That guy on the street, I ran to him for help, but he hauled off and clobbered me!" He touched his aching bruise. "Like you said, he probably thought I tried to steal his car."

"And what were you doing out at three o'clock in the morning?"

"I told you, I live on the streets. That dealer came into my space and he was high and all hot under the collar, so I got up and ran. I was scared." Dibs' eyes were big and serious. He hoped his story sounded convincing.

Detective Johnson stood up and began to pace. "Young man, you can cooperate, and maybe," she stopped pacing for emphasis and looked right at Dibs, "maybe you can get time off. Or, you can say nothing and live happily ever after in juvenile hall." Her high heels clicked on the floor as she walked. "It's your call, Byron."

Hearing the lady mention juvenile hall made Dibs' skin crawl, but he didn't move a muscle. As long as he could distance himself from that cell phone they had nothing on him to put him back in that horrible joint. He was sticking to his story.

It was Detective Martin's turn. He stood and walked around behind Dibs. "Byron. Is that what they call you on the streets?"

Dibs was relieved to change the subject. "I go by Dibs."

"Dibs? That's a nice nickname. Cheerful. Do you mind if I call you Dibs?"

Dibs shrugged.

"I wonder, Dibs, if we'll find any information on that cell phone that might implicate you in some of this illegal activity. Let's say we find a voicemail, or address information. Or texts, or phone numbers. You know, the kind of detail someone could type into their phone and think they will erase later, after they've taken care of business. Do you think there's any chance of that?"

The strapping detective came around the table and sat down across from Dibs. He didn't seem to be in a hurry, as if he could wait all day for an answer.

Dibs' head was pounding. He shifted nervously in his seat. What if there *were* things on that phone about him? A voicemail from Tall Eddy, or maybe from Cutter, where his own name had been mentioned in the conversation. Or texts. Anything was possible.

Slumping forward, he lowered his head, feeling as trapped as the day Tall Eddy had blackmailed him into working at the chop shop in the first place.

"Take your time, Dibs. We've got all day. It's good for you to consider everything. Think long and hard about where you could end up and about your own life and what's best for you."

Detective Johnson sounded calm. There was even a hint of kindness in her voice.

For the first time during their entire interchange, the possibility of being hauled back into juvenile hall was hitting him hard between the eyes. Juvie hall had been the worst experience of his entire life. The less time he spent in that joint, the better.

But what about all those threats of bodily harm Eddy had promised to dole out if he ratted on the operation? With the mean streak that guy had, he'd be in Danger with a capital D if he told all.

"Dibs, do you have anything to say to us?"

Feeling very much like a boy rather than a man, Dibs quietly said to the lady cop, "They could come and get me."

Detectives Johnson and Martin exchanged glances. It was Martin who asked, "Who, Dibs? Who could get you? The people in the theft ring?"

Dibs nodded.

"We can offer you witness protection if necessary. But remember, if these men are convicted they'll be put behind bars." Detective Martin leaned forward and looked into Dibs' faltering eyes. "Go ahead. You understand it's the right thing to do."

"Okay. I'll tell you what I know." Dibs surrendered and began to relate the story of Tall Eddy and his threat, of old man Cutter, and of the people at the shop. He told them everything he could remember about the whole operation. The hardest part was when he squealed on his friend Robbie.

Almost two hours passed before all the details were fully disclosed and all the detectives' questions had been answered. Dibs was spent physically, emotionally, and mentally.

Closing her files, Detective Johnson called for an officer to escort Dibs to the detention center.

"Byron," Detective Martin looked him in the eye, "you have been very brave today. We'll both put in a good word for you during any proceedings. And we'll tell the judge you were extremely cooperative." He held out his hand. "Good luck, young man." Surprised by the detective's gentleness, Dibs shook his hand and responded with the tiniest of smiles. "Thanks," was all he could offer before he was led out of the room, away from civilized freedom, and into the familiar world of angry kids and dangerous losers who were locked away behind bars to waste young lives and valuable years.

CHAPTER TWENTY-TWO

Darlene Gordon sat down beside Amber at the dining room table. "So, kiddo, you've been here about three weeks. How do you like it?"

Amber was two sips into her morning coffee. She wiped the sleep dirt from her eyes and set her mug on the table to consider the straightforward question being thrown at her before she was fully alert.

Her foster mom grabbed a box of granola and poured some cereal into a bowl.

"I know you wake up slowly, but I have to go to work in an hour and I wanted some time with you this morning. A girls only breakfast. No men allowed." Darlene grinned, opened a carton of almond milk, and poured the liquid over her cereal. "And I was just curious to know if you're comfortable with us. Because we're really enjoying having you in our family."

Amber felt her face flush. She'd never thought of herself as a source of enjoyment to anyone on the planet. Especially not to a whole family.

After two more swallows of coffee she cleared her throat and said the only thing that came out. "I like it here."

When nothing more was offered, Darlene said, "Is that all?"

"A lot."

Mrs. Gordon laughed. "You and Jared sure wake up slowly."

"I feel comfortable with everybody. You're all really nice." Amber thought of saying more about the fact that she was finally in a foster home where she felt liked, and maybe even loved. But she didn't want to wreck things by saying it out loud. She wasn't about to push things too far.

Her foster mother chewed thoughtfully and swallowed. "Is there anything you don't like? Anything that bugs you about being part of our family? Anything we should talk about?"

Amber wrinkled her nose. Those sure weren't the kinds of questions previous foster families would've considered asking.

"Uh, I can't think of anything." Her mind replayed the past weeks of mealtimes, movies, computer, reading, talking, riding bikes, and yard work. And sitting in a dentist chair for two hours while he repaired cavities that had formed during her three years on the streets. That part was no fun at all, but nobody with a brain would get excited about a dentist's drill.

Finally she came up with something to say. "Oh yeah. I hate okra. And fish, unless it's breaded fish sticks."

"Well, you know the policy here: everybody has to taste a few bites of each new food. And if you still don't like it after you've tried it, you don't have to eat it." Darlene smiled. "But if that's the only thing that bothers you, we're doing pretty well."

"And I like that nobody yells or gets mad. That's a lot different than I'm used to." She took a swig of coffee. "Well, at the Owens' place it was the same as here. Nobody yelled. But other than that . . ." Instead of finishing her sentence she drank more coffee.

"Some of the previous homes weren't so safe, huh?"

"No."

"In your family, or in foster homes?"

"Both. But my family was a lot worse. My mom, she drank." Amber chewed a spot on her lip and stared at her mug. Not accustomed to being so honest about her past, she wasn't sure she wanted to say more.

"And your dad?"

"He left a couple of months after I was born." A lump was forming in her throat. A cold, hard lump. She'd had enough of the conversation and stood up with her coffee cup in her hand.

"Honey, you don't have to talk about it until you're ready." Mrs. Gordon stood, gently cupped Amber's face in her hands, and pushed back a few strands of hair. Her voice was soft around the edges. "Everything in its time, dear."

Amber couldn't look into her foster mom's eyes. "Thanks." She pointed to her bedroom. "I think I'll go and read, or write, or maybe go to OtherSide."

Darlene took Amber's coffee cup, set it down on the table, and pulled her into her arms for a strong hug. "Have good day, and thank you for spending some time with me." She pulled back and added, "I think you're wonderful."

"You too." Like three flavors of ice cream scooped onto one cone, Amber's emotions were squished together in a mixture of awkwardness, sadness, and love.

Pouring another half cup of coffee from the pot, she headed into her bedroom and closed the door behind her. Thinking about her real family wasn't a favorite pastime, not to mention the fact that it was slightly nauseating. Swallowing okra was more palatable than the icky taste those people left in her mouth.

Sitting back on her bed, Amber folded her legs under her and pulled Herbie close for comfort. She needed something to do that would take her mind away from unhappy thoughts. But writing in her diary didn't interest her, and her current library book wasn't such a great read. There was the possibility of trying out the stuff Jared had taught her on the computer, but Amber quickly chalked that off the list. It was too early for that kind of concentration.

That left only one thing on her list of options. She would go and visit OtherSide. Amber put her coffee cup down and closed her earth eyes to focus her star-eyes on what lay beyond the veneer.

When beautiful green-brown eyes appeared, Amber smiled at the thought of seeing her prince brother. But as she drew closer, she became aware the pair of eyes belonged to another man, to someone she'd never met.

Just then, a moving pillar of golden light showed up to her right. It glistened with honey-colored sparkles.

"Mister Energy!" Amber recognized his unmistakable fragrance. He always smelled like a delicious blend of sweet Middle Eastern spices, similar to the aromas that hung in the air at the Newberry Street Grocery Store.

"Amber, dear! Seeing you is more satisfying than sipping a cool fruit-berry smoothie from the Garden Of Possibilities!"

At the mention of food, she wondered how eating and drinking worked in OtherSide. But before she had time to ask, The Light spoke again.

"Amber, I want you to meet someone very special."

She assumed he was speaking about the stranger standing in front of her. Like everybody else who was connected with this place, a glow radiated from his being. It was coming out of his middle and it was deep purple. His face was kind and he was good looking too, with a button nose, two dimples when he smiled, and the same greenish-brownish eyes as her prince brother. He was slim-built and approximately the same age and height as the Light Prince.

"Hello, Amber, I'm your father. I can't tell you how great it is to finally meet you!"

She gave him a curious inspection. *This is Father Forever? I thought he'd be older. And taller.*

"Amber, this isn't Father Forever. You'll meet him later,"

The Light clarified. "This is your earthly father, Edward McConnell. He asked to be introduced to you, and the time was right."

Edward McConnell's voice was steady and gentle. "I can't tell you how happy I am to meet you in this place. It was only a year ago that I became a Lightning." His smile faded to sober kindness. "I wanted to meet you and tell you how sorry I am for walking out on you when you were just a baby. I wasn't a responsible human being, much less a good father. And if I could do it all over again, I'd change everything in a heartbeat." He searched her face with his eyes. "I know I hurt you like crazy." Reaching out, he took her hand. "Please forgive me."

Amber's body had gone rigid and her brain was on fire. She couldn't break her stare at the man. As far as she was concerned she had no father. True, she knew enough about health class facts to know that along with her mother, someone had obviously created her. But that guy hadn't stuck around. In her mind he no longer existed.

She pulled her hand away. His touch was contaminating.

The man motioned to The Light but called him by another name. "Comforter has told me all about you and how brave you've been." He smiled widely. "I couldn't be prouder to be your dad."

Her stomach turned with aggravation and Amber felt queasy and lightheaded. OtherSide's surface seemed to rock and sway beneath her feet.

The Light morphed into a ribbon-like band of shimmering warmth. Wrapping around Amber's shoulders, he pulled her to himself. "Brave one, your father has met the Light Prince. He's a different man than the one who lived on Earth."

"Are you visiting here?" It was the only thing she could think of saying while heading into a mental meltdown.

Shaking his head, her father answered, "I'm no longer an

earthling. I've homecome."

Amber had no idea what *homecome* meant, but neither did she care.

"Dear one," The Light explained, "Edward has passed through the veneer permanently. He lives in OtherSide now. He's homecome, like your friend Priscilla. Though he'll always be human, he's no longer an earthling."

"So he's dead." Speaking intentionally to The Light, she ignored the creep standing nearby. She said it with disgust and added to herself, *Good. At least I'll never have to face him on Earth.*

"Oh no! Death is the pathway that leads away from OtherSide, and it's an awful, painful thing! Your father certainly hasn't died: he has homecome."

The man took a step closer. His cheeks were wet.

"I must tell you, Amber, I should have loved you every single second of your life. I should've held you and played with you and cared for all your needs. And your mother, I should have treasured her as a jewel." Edward fixed his eyes intensely on Amber's face. "As your father, I'm completely to blame." He added gravely, "Please, don't blame yourself. You're an innocent daughter."

Tears rolled down his cheeks. Not tears of pain, because pain doesn't exist in OtherSide. His were tears of compassion. And in a gesture of affection, he held his hands out toward his earthly daughter. "Please forgive me, dear one."

When Edward McConnell said *father* and *mother* and *daughter* all close together, Amber had enough. She opened her earth eyes to get away from him.

Flinging Herbie away from her, she shot off the bed and paced back and forth. Anger boiled up and pressed hard against her chest. She rammed the desk chair into the desk and stifled a scream that wanted to explode from her throat. The air in the room grew hot and suffocating. She had to escape.

Her bedroom door flew open and Amber charged toward the entryway.

John Gordon saw her. "Hey, Amber, where are you going?"

The front door opened and then slammed shut and John jumped up to find out what was wrong with his foster kid.

She was stomping down the sidewalk by the time he came outside.

"Amber!"

Rounding the corner, she increased her pace.

He trotted and called out to her again in case she decided to sprint. "Promise me one thing: promise you'll come back!"

Amber stopped in the middle of the sidewalk. Her seething insides wanted to totally blow him off. She didn't know if she planned on coming back to the house, or whether she was going to run away and never return. Right now she just had to breathe. She answered through gritted teeth. "I promise." That would get him off her case.

John Gordon wanted to give her space, but he was also concerned. Regardless of how well he thought he knew her, Amber was a foster kid. And from experience, he knew they didn't always have a grid for making good decisions while under pressure. He was scared—not for his sake, but for hers.

After a few seconds he decided to risk and trust her word. He held his hand out toward her and released a shining. It found its mark and swirled around her being, filling her space with OtherSide light and propelling her forward.

She kept walking until she reached a small park not far from the Gordons' home. The place was deserted. It was all hers, and she couldn't have been gladder to be alone. Walking over to a bench surrounded by four pine trees, she sat down.

There was no doubt about it. She was mad. In her whole life she'd never been so hot. Thinking about that man's words, she spit as hard as she could on the ground in front of her. *Dear one? Of all people, YOU have no right to call me DEAR ONE, you lousy, no good rat! You screwed up, party boy!* Amber gave the ground a solid kick. *You did your thing with my mom and moved on to your next fling, but WE got left behind in a crappy house, with crappy stuff, and a crappy life!* She felt like a lawyer building a case against a guilty suspect. *And you think saying, "Oops, sorry," is gonna' fix all that?* Her face twisted sarcastically at the thought of his pathetic apology.

Amber looked up at the sky and shook her fist in the air. She had one final, convicting piece of evidence against him. "You LEFT me with a Mom who was all boozed up! She couldn't even take care of her own kid, and you left me with HER?" It was both a question and an accusing statement. "Think about THAT, Edward McConnell! Think about all you DID and DIDN'T do!"

She had no idea whether people in OtherSide could hear her, but Amber hoped he felt horrible. Standing up, she practically shouted at the sky. "And one more thing: I am NOT your daughter! Daughters belong to people who are FATHERS! Not to morons like you, who leave their families!"

She sat. Another thing disgusted her. *And how come, when I wanted to meet the Light Prince or The Light, I ended up in front of that man? Was that some kind of prank?* To anyone who was listening across the veneer, she said, "Was that some kind of mean joke? What was that, anyway?"

Her feet scraped the dirt under the bench. Back and forth, back and forth. She sighed a huge, miserable sigh. Amber liked the Gordons, and Oscar's family, too, but why all this other stuff? *Why did all this come up now? I thought things were changing for the better!* None of it made any sense.

She sat at the park for a long time. In the end, she didn't feel much different than when she'd arrived. There was still a messy, knotted clump in her stomach. It was just sitting there, soaking in the irritation and confusion of churning digestive juices.

Her stomach gurgled. Lunch was past due and she was hungry. The easiest place to get food was at the house, but she wasn't sure she wanted to go back there and face stupid questions from probing adults.

On the other hand, the thought of returning to the streets took her breath away. Now that there was the possibility of some sort of real life ahead of her, homelessness seemed like an energy-sucking nothingness.

She looked in the direction of the Gordon home. By now, Darlene was at work and Jared was at soccer practice. That meant Mr. Gordon was the only person at home. Several times during the past weeks when she had needed to be alone, he'd given her space. Which meant she might be able to go back to the house and eat without being hassled.

Amber stood and headed back home. Ten minutes later she walked in the front door and went to the kitchen to look for something to eat.

John Gordon heard her and came out from his office as she was opening the refrigerator. "You know where all the sandwich fixings are," he pointed to the meat and cheese drawer, "and here's the bread." He handed her a loaf of organic whole wheat bread that she took and laid on the counter. "What else would you like for lunch?"

Do I look like I wanna' talk right now? Shrugging a rude non-answer, she pulled out the lunchmeats to grab a few slices of turkey.

"Mind if I join you?"

Another silent shrug. Amber glared down at her sandwich preparations as John grabbed two pieces of bread to build his own sandwich of roast beef, cheese, pickle slices, and mayo.

They sat down at the dinette table.

Five or six bites into swallowing the stiffness in the air around them, John decided to break things open. "I don't know why you're upset, but I know at some point it would be good to talk about it together. Since we're living as family."

Family. There's the stupidest word in the universe. "I'm not ready." Weird. Even though she'd only known him for a couple of weeks, she could be honest with this guy. He wasn't intimidating like some foster parents in previous homes.

"I get that. Take your time."

She gulped down her sandwich and disappeared into her bedroom. As she left, John extended his hand toward her and released another shining.

Amber sat on her bed and backed up against the crimson wall. She felt a strong urge to bawl, though that was something only sissies and cowards did. But she was alone. No one would see her, and somehow it seemed okay to have a good cry.

She grabbed her pillow, held it against her face to muffle the sound, and let out all the choking sobs that were rising from deep in her belly.

A whole hour later Amber sat forward, dazed and empty. But it wasn't a despairing kind of empty. It was more like when a hard rain comes and pounds a muddy pavement and washes the dirt away and makes things a little cleaner. The empty inside her was a little bit like that.

Questions started to surface and she had no answers. She glanced at her door. Even though her trust in adults was suddenly thinner than spring ice, John Gordon was one of the better grown-ups she'd met. He always seemed to know when she didn't want to talk, or when he shouldn't press her for more information. Plus, he had suggested they talk.

She went to his office door. "I think I could talk now. If you have time."

"Sure." He saved his current graphic design project. "Where to? Living room or dining room? Your choice."

Shrugging, she finally decided, "Living room."

They sat on two armchairs along the picture window side of the room. John was quiet, probably because he was waiting for her to say something.

She pulled her feet up on the chair and wrapped her arms around her knees. It was hard to make her mouth move.

Finally she mumbled, "What's the point of meeting my dad in OtherSide?"

"You met your father?"

"Yeah."

"Was Father Forever there with you?"

"I haven't met him yet." *Not sure I WANT to meet him either, especially if he's gonna' pull stupid tricks on me.*

"Well, I don't know. What did your dad say to you?"

Amber tried to speak, but the words got all thick in her neck and stuck there instead of coming out. She had to clear her throat several times before they budged. "He said he was sorry . . . that he . . . abandoned me." The next words were even harder to say. "He said if he could do it all over again, he would've been a good dad."

"Oh."

No one spoke.

She hugged her legs more tightly and glanced over at her foster dad. The lines of his face were tight and serious, but his eyes were soft with caring. A stab of hurt shot through her chest. The guy she'd met in OtherSide was a complete stranger. But fathers aren't supposed to be strangers.

Her face muscles twisted hard in an effort to hold back another stream of emotions pushing up from inside.

John inclined his head toward her. "Amber, look at me."

She couldn't meet his eyes.

He spoke anyway. "It's better to express what you're feeling in this safe place, with a safe person, than to keep it all stuffed inside. After all, you have every right to be upset. Your dad completely neglected you. And even if he apologized, you must hurt like crazy. Go ahead and get mad. OtherSide understands."

A choking sound escaped her lips and tears coursed down her cheeks. To hear an adult admitting her dad had been awful—and she'd always *felt* he'd been awful—was unexpected. But telling her it was okay to get peeved about it? That caught her by surprise.

She felt like laughing and crying at the same time. And she did, first one, then the other, while grabbing tissues to blow her nose.

John leaned forward and propped his elbows on his knees. "Feels good, doesn't it?"

Nodding, she wiped her nose again and grinned and sobbed in that order.

And after a few more minutes the tears subsided and she sighed and stared down at the carpet. She didn't know why, but hearing Mr. Gordon's words had made the knotted clump in her stomach get a little smaller.

"Amber. The Light knew you needed to hear an apology from your dad today. But that doesn't mean you have to do anything about it right now. Except, it might be good to tell the Original Family how you're feeling. Don't hide from them. It often takes time for us to completely release people."

There was that word again. She didn't think she could ever release that man.

They sat in more silence.

After some time, John patted her knee affectionately. "Any other questions?"

Amber couldn't think of anything else and shook her head.

"Then I'll get back to work. Let me know if you need anything or if you want to talk more. Okay?"

She nodded and John returned to his office.

Staring blankly at the clouds painted on the living room wall, Amber frowned and looked away. Life was too complicated. She didn't want to think. Picking up a magazine from the end table, she leafed through it. A photograph of two smiling, ebony orphans who were being held by an aid worker caught her attention. The article below the picture explained that the aid worker had adopted the two boys into his family.

There was that stupid word again. Family. Amber felt

totally out of sorts, but John had told her it was okay. At the moment she didn't need to be different.

She picked up the remote and flicked on the television. And for the rest of the afternoon she lost herself in children's cartoons, where the good guys always won and the bad guys always got what was coming to them.

CHAPTER TWENTY-THREE

Dibs hated incarceration. It was the opposite of everything he loved about life: the hustle and bustle of city sidewalks, soaring skyscrapers, fluttering pigeons, morning coffees, hot dogs from street vendors, and so much more. Even begging was fun when compared to being locked up behind bars.

But now, that world was off limits. He was penned in behind thick walls against his will, doomed to follow orders, go where others commanded him, and eat what was offered. With a release date that seemed as far away as old age, he'd been separated from society and tossed into a jailhouse—stuffed inside one giant, institutional can for dead meat losers like himself.

With all the depressingly negative mental choices he was making, Urielle couldn't do much to help him. A drab was approaching, and it almost seemed as if her human had invited the thing to come near and make itself at home.

Seeing the scowl on her human's face, Urielle sighed and raised her sword to tap him lightly on the crown of his head. "Hey, little friend, remember the fun we've had. Don't let this dullsville drab find a landing place. Don't give into his idiocy. Come on, laugh a little!"

But it was no use. Her young man had decided he was going to be miserable, and drabs are drawn to miserableness the way flies are drawn to molasses. Urielle was doing her best to encourage her young earthling, but with all the poor choices he was making, she was fighting a losing battle.

"Well, well, for love of fear, who in the world do we have here?" Restlessness, the drab flying near Dibs, crooned a malicious tune. "You haven't been in these cages for ages and ages and ages!" He snickered, awfully pleased with his own rhyming sensibilities. "But I see you got the hammer and now you're in the slammer." The thing tittered and tee-heed. "I think you need an alter ego: you need me, your new amigo!"

Restlessness was feeling deviously lucky to be reacquainted. He'd encountered this human here and there during recent years, and at the present time he happened to be without a person. No other drabs seemed to be claiming the boy, and by all morbid appearances the young mortal was ripe for UnderSide's influence.

Evidently he'd found himself a comfortable new home, which made him one cruelly happy drab.

Squirming and twitching as he walked, Dibs was clueless about the UnderSide lackey hovering nearby. He only knew he was antsy to be anywhere else than in that corridor.

A stoutly built guard with a buzz cut for hair and a no-nonsense attitude was accompanying him on his return trip from the infirmary. Someone in Dibs' section had tested positive for narcotics, and now every person in the entire ward had to pee into a cup for a drug test.

Not in a hurry, the officer ambled slowly toward Dibs' cell. For him this was a job, so it didn't matter how quickly or how slowly he walked. When five o'clock came around his work would be finished for the day, and he would go home to his wife and family.

Captive Dibs had no reason to rush either, but creeping along like a turtle didn't suit him. He couldn't stand the officer's nonchalant pace. The faster he went, the faster time would pass, and the faster he would get out. At least that was his current reasoning.

As they walked, Dibs' mind bounced to the circumstances that had gotten him into the whole mess. Everything led straight back to Tall Eddy. Plain and simple, the guy was bad news. He never wanted to be within a mile of that fink again.

They arrived at a barred metal door three quarters of the way down the hall on the left. The corrections officer pressed a talk button and spoke into a small mic attached to his shirt collar, which was connected by a cord to a two-way radio clipped on his belt. "This is Officer Shilton. Number twenty-three, please." After a few seconds a loud buzzer sounded, a metal lock clicked, and the door rolled back automatically. The guard motioned for his prisoner to enter. "There you go, Byron. Keep yourself out of trouble, you hear?"

Dibs stepped into the cell. Every single time Shilton escorted him back to his cell, he made the same annoying comment about staying out of trouble. It was starting to get on his nerves.

The sound of the metal door clanging shut behind him echoed down the wide corridor. After the guard left he walked over to the tiny sink next to the toilet in the far right corner. Splashing his face with cold water, he pulled his shirt up and wiped it off, lowered his shirt, and stared at the cement wall in front of him.

Seven days, eight hours, and about fifteen minutes in this place, and he still felt like crying. Though he couldn't exactly say what it was that gave him an urge to blubber uncontrollably, he had to get hold of himself. Tears were weakness. And here, weakness meant being vulnerable. Being vulnerable meant he could be the victim of a beating the next time the guards weren't around to intervene. No room for bawling in this place. He had no choice but to pull himself together.

He stared at the dull gray of the walls. This juvenile hall

wasn't as old as the other one where he'd done time, so none of the paint had peeled off. But in Dibs' opinion the walls were still ugly. Cement blocks only looked good if they were part of his warehouse digs.

His eyes shifted to three sketches of rappers taped on the wall to the right of the sink. Jamie had drawn them. Dibs had to admit, his roommate was a pretty good artist. Leaning in to take a closer look, he noticed each of the rappers' faces seemed agitated. Just the way he was feeling.

He glanced at the toilet. The lid was leaning to one side, like the tilted hat on a street rapper's head.

For the time being, he was alone. Jamie was still at the infirmary waiting for his chance to empty his bladder into a paper cup. That was okay by Dibs, since his jerk roommate hadn't spoken a word to him. Not one single word during the whole time they'd been together. He'd tried to start lots of conversations, but the guy remained as silent as stone. In fact, the only reason he knew his name was because the guards had addressed him.

Jamie had the top bunk and Dibs was on the bottom. The advantage of having the bottom bunk was being able to get up and whiz in the middle of the night without waking his cellmate. But for privacy, the top bunk was definitely the better option. Given a choice, he would've picked the upper one. But no one asked him.

Dibs sat down on his bed, sighing loudly at his own sorry situation.

This joint was only for people who had committed a real crime. He wondered what his cellmate had done, and from there his thoughts drifted to Julio and Eddy and the chop shop guys. He worried about his buddy Robbie having to do jail time.

The interrogation officer had called Dibs brave for telling all he knew. Juvie hall's residents used a different word for people who did what he'd done. They were snitches. And nobody ever admitted being one, because loyalty on the streets was as strong as death. Dibs would never breathe a word in this godforsaken place that he'd confessed to the cops or ratted out the rest of the guys in the operation.

His mind jumped to his dad, who was doing time in an adult prison. *What a crummy old man!* When had they lived together, his father had almost always been high on something. And when he wasn't high, he was moody. Dibs had learned the hard way that whenever his dad's voice got low and sharp, he needed to hide, and quick. That tone often meant a fist in his face, or a foot on his back, or a book flying toward his head.

And all those times his father had promised they'd do something together—play ball, or go to the park, or to the movies—not once did he keep his word. He was a raunchy, deadbeat dad.

Punching his pillow to force it into a usable shape, Dibs snorted in disgust and settled down to take a snooze. After half a minute, he whacked the pillow again and rolled onto his side to face the wall. His mind was racing.

The door buzzer sounded. Looking over his shoulder, he saw Mr. Potbelly Shilton standing outside the cell. Next to the guard stood his roommate.

As Jamie entered the cell, Dibs sat up and threw him a sideways glance. In typical style, his roommate treated him as if he were a ghost, blowing by him without a word. Then he climbed up onto the top bunk and settled in to his usual silent routine.

In the realm of UnderSide, a ghostlike drab trailed along after Dibs' cellmate. And when Jamie crawled up the ladder, his unseen escort hung nearby, at the edge of the mattress. Dangling his spiny legs down over the side, the creature installed himself quietly beside his speechless human.

Restlessness floated just below him, near his own earthling. With a snide snout he sang sourly into the boy's right ear, "Hootie patootie, isn't he snooty!" Piling on the self-pity, he whined toward his human and added a good amount of irritation, "Poor child, you should be riled. If I were you I'd take offense, at how he's made your life so tense!" Then, as if correcting himself, the drab shook his head. "No, with this roommate, you should be irate!"

Restlessness straightened out his form and peered proudly at the other drab. Applauding his own poetic cunning, he clacked his claws together and bowed. Then, all at once his whole demeanor changed. Like flipping a switch, he leaped toward his UnderSide crony and challenged angrily, "What are YOU looking at, you little brat?"

Isolation, the drab laying claim to Jamie, hated confrontation. The sordid truth was, he hated all interaction. Period. But if pressed, he could defend his territory to save his hide. He answered sharply, "You scoundrel, keep to your own earthling, and leave me alone."

Restlessness backed away and feigned remorse. "All right, all right, don't get so uptight! I was only making light!" Instantly, his countenance switched again and he narrowed his eyes into a horizontal line. Pointing a threatening, solitary talon at Isolation, he scowled. "But don't cause me trouble, or I'll see you pay double."

Isolation folded his leathery arms across his chest and turned away with loathing. The other drab's manic, rhyming shenanigans were too much for him. Such jittery behavior was almost as annoying as having to put up with dazzles. If only he could dispense with his irritating sidekick!

While Restlessness and Isolation quarreled invisibly, Dibs lay on his bunk and stewed, getting more and more agitated about his dumb roommate's rudeness. Why was Jamie acting like such a snob?

He was well aware the best approach for being in the bowels of The Hall was to keep his mouth shut, until the day came when he would be let out of the cage to fly again.

But there was one place where maybe that rule didn't apply. Roomies who became buddies had a much better chance at surviving juvie with their hearts still in one piece—and not ripped into shreds.

But Jamie had made things crystal clear. He had zero interest in being friends. And that bugged Dibs worse than an itchy mosquito bite.

What happened next certainly wasn't anticipated. In fact, if Dibs had thought about what was going to follow his words, he would have held his tongue. But he *didn't* think. He simply reacted out of the frustration building up in his chest.

Hopping off his bed, he stood and glared angrily at his roommate. With his hands on his waist, his voice dripped with sarcasm. "Oh Honorable Silent One, if we're gonna' be roomies for a long time, don't you think it's a good idea that we start talkin'? Or am I not good enough for Your Highness?"

Silence.

What a jerk. Dibs gritted his teeth and stared hard at Jamie, waiting for a response. Thirty seconds passed. "Look," he demanded, "I been here every morning and every evening for a week. You can't keep pretending you're the only one livin' in this box. It'll drive us both nuts!"

Jamie lay still, his hands clasped behind his head, his eyes fixed on the ceiling.

That did it. Dibs was fed up. "Fine. Go ahead. Live in your own reality. See if I care!" Grabbing his pillow, he threw it hard against the wall beside his bed and spoke out loud what he'd only thought earlier. "What a jerk!" Flopping onto his bunk, he tossed and turned and groused inwardly.

After several minutes an accusing voice from above broke the angry quiet.

"You touched my goods."

Dibs glowered and said to the bunk above him, "What are you talkin' about?"

The voice threatened through clenched teeth, "If you touch my stuff again, I will kill you!"

Dibs sat up. He was intimidated by the likes of Tall Eddy, who was older and more dangerous. But in this place he either carried his own weight with peers, or got tagged as a target. And targets had a bullseye painted on their backside that begged everybody, "Beat Me Up."

He snapped an answer to his roommate's warning. "I never touched none a' your stuff and I ain't gonna', either." Then, to make sure the kid knew he was just as tough, Dibs added, "But don't even think about messin' with MY stuff or with ME! Bein' new don't mean I'm scared a' you, or anybody else. I can take care a' myself. So BACK OFF!" He smirked. That last part was a nice touch to let Jamie know he wasn't going to be pushed around.

Faster than a circus acrobat, Dibs' roommate was down on him, grabbing his shirt at the chest and pulling him to within an inch of his own crazed eyes. He hissed, "I don't back off, pig face. And don't EVER threaten me again."

Dibs wasn't normally a fighter, but when push came to shove he could be as aggressive as anybody else. Soon the two scrappy teens were on the floor of the cell, punching each other 'til kingdom come.

By the time Officer Shilton entered the cell they were no longer fighting. Well aware of juvenile hall's zero tolerance policy on violence, Dibs had pushed his roommate across the room and was sitting on his bunk. Because of his lousy roommate's temper, the chances were pretty good he would be hauled off and locked away in solitary confinement.

Jamie was no longer throwing punches, but he looked as if he could start another round in the blink of an eye. Every muscle was wound and ready for action. His hands were balled into tight fists. Seething anger poured from his nostrils and eyes.

Officer Shilton grabbed Dibs' wild-eyed roommate,

shoved him against the wall face-first, and as quick as a magician, slapped a set of handcuffs on his wrists. Pulling sharply on the cuffs to bring Jamie to his feet, the guard commanded, "Let's go."

Dibs sat with his head in his hands, listening as the cell door opened and closed, and as the guard and Jamie walked down the hallway. He heard the ward's large electronic doors roll back and then clang shut. The sound of their footsteps soon disappeared into silence.

Warm tears rolled down his nose and a few dripped onto the floor. He sniffed quietly, wiped his wet face with his sleeve, and rubbed the spots on the floor with the bottom of his shoe so no one would know he'd been crying. Waiting to be hauled away to some padded room where they isolated dangerous inmates who did things like fight their roommates, he thought his situation couldn't be more dreadful.

He'd done time in solitary confinement during his previous stay in juvenile hall. It was the worst place in the whole world. Everyone in solitary was under twenty-four hour supervision. No magazines or books were permitted. Meals were eaten alone in the cell and there were no activities. There was nothing to do but sit and stare into silent space. And brood.

Sure enough, potbelly Shilton returned. Handcuffing Dibs, he hauled him off to Solitary, where he would stay until someone in charge decided he was no longer a threat.

Once in the confinement room, Dibs lay down on the hard mattress next to the spongy wall. A lump that hadn't been there before throbbed on his left cheek. *Ow!* It sure was a bruiser. Clasping his hands behind his head, he propped his knees up to think. And what he thought was, he'd been given the most pathetic roommate in the whole blasted hall.

Restlessness was nearby, hovering rather calmly, at least for him. His idea to instigate a fight had turned out to be atrociously effective. He chuckled to himself and chanted a little rhyme over and over again. "Oh, yes. Oh, yes! When I oppress it's a success. Oh, yes!"

Oblivious to the goings on in that world, Dibs stretched out on the bed and worried about a dark future. At last, whether out of boredom or simply wanting to escape the misery that clouded his thinking, he turned over onto his side. His eyelids grew heavy as he drifted off into uneasy sleep, tossing and turning fitfully the whole night long.

CHAPTER TWENTY-FOUR

There was an irritation inside Amber, like the time a tiny splinter had gotten under her fingernail and pressed against her skin. It sat there, not saying anything, not doing anything, but she knew things weren't right. And until that little piece of wood was removed and her nail was relieved of the force, she just wasn't herself. She was only free of the nuisance and pressure when it was finally gone.

This time the irritation wasn't under a fingernail, but in her mind. Someone was to blame. A specific someone. Edward McConnell, to be exact. He was the culprit! Meeting him and hearing his pitiful sob story had made her as eager as a three-toed sloth to visit OtherSide again. Ever since, Amber had no problem conveniently avoiding that place by filling her time with activities.

"Hey sleepyhead, whatcha' doing?"

She was struggling to jot something down in her journal for the Owens family. The Department of Social Services still hadn't cleared communications between them, and Amber was starting to feel as though Oscar and Maggie and Madison lived in China or Antarctica or some other far away place. Besides, keeping a journal was a waste of time, because when they got together in person they could easily catch up on everything.

Amber surfaced from her thoughts and answered Jared. "I wasn't sleeping, doofus, I was thinking."

"I thought I smelled something burning." With a knuckle he shoved his glasses back up his nose and plopped down beside her on the sofa.

"It wasn't my brain. It was your pants on fire." Amber elbowed his side and he grunted. She closed her journal, grateful to have a distraction. "What's up?"

"Nothing. Just hanging out."

"So, what's the book?" She eyed the volume in his hand.

"Oh this? It's my Manual Of Nobility."

"It looks old."

"Well, the book's not old, but some of the stories are."

"Can I see it?"

"Sure." Jared handed her the leatherbound, hard cover book.

Amber touched the delicate tooled design on the front, with its gold embossing. Two leather straps encircled the entire book and met in the middle of the front cover, where they were joined together by golden clasps.

"Open it." He nodded encouragingly.

She unclasped the straps and flipped it open. The inside of the front cover and its adjoining page were solid crimson, the exact same tone of the Crimson Wall surrounding OtherSide.

It's the prince's color," she said admiringly.

"Wait a minute. It shouldn't be still."

She glanced at her foster brother's pinched eyebrows. "What do you mean?"

Jared frowned and rubbed his hand across the motionless pages. "This book is the Original Family's creative story. Each page should be alive." He pointed at the book. "And especially this crimson. On this side of the veneer, his crimson is always a shining. I mean, usually the whole book is one big shining."

Normally, learning new stuff about OtherSide was a

major rush for Amber. But in her present personal funk all she could think was, *he's talking gobbledygook*. She'd found the word *gobbledygook* on an author's web page. It perfectly described how his words were hitting her.

"Are you okay?"

He was looking at her cockeyed.

"Yeah. I'm fine. I just didn't get what you were saying."

"About the book?"

"About anything."

He pointed to the crimson. "Okay, so you know this should be a shining."

Irritation flared up. "No. I didn't know that." She hated when people assumed she knew stuff. "What's a shining, anyway?"

Jared gawked. "Nobody's told you about them?"

She shook her head.

"Shinings are when The Light is released into Earth's atmosphere."

The pinch of his eyebrows was gone, and eager eyes stared back at her.

"Every Lightning can, you know."

His gobbledygook was really getting annoying. "What are you talking about?"

"Every Lightning can release The Light's shinings. Here, hold out your hand like this." He extended his arm to demonstrate, his hand in a vertical position.

Amber imitated his motions.

"Now, think of a friend of yours."

Dibs' name popped into her head.

"Did you think of someone?"

She nodded.

"Okay, now ask The Light to release a shining to your friend."

"I don't want to." She dropped her hand.

Jared pushed his glasses up again and quietly studied her.

"You're touchy today."

"SO?"

"Why? What's wrong?"

Amber moved away from him and raised her voice. "Didn't you ever have a bad day? Or are you always Mr. Perfect?"

"Ouch." He grimaced but said nothing else, and silence clouded the room.

Handing the book back to Jared, she got up and walked away.

"That's it?"

"What?" She turned and glared at him.

"You're doing it again. That thing where you just get up and leave and pretend there's nothing wrong."

"What do you want me to do, Mr. Perfect?" Her voice was sharp.

He shrugged. "Well, I thought for starters we could treat each other with respect."

She headed toward her bedroom. He was acting so smug!

"Okay," he called after her, "be that way."

I will. She closed her bedroom door hard. Sitting down at her desk, Amber grabbed a book and opened it to her bookmark.

There was a knock on her door but she ignored it.

"Amber, come on. Every time we argue, you blow me off. Can't we talk through stuff?"

Finding her place on the page, she started reading.

After a minute or so of quiet, he said through the door, "When you wanna' talk, let me know."

Amber heard him walk away. Her eyes stared mindlessly at the words, until she slammed the book shut and tossed it onto the desk. Leaning back, she folded her arms across her chest. Everything he'd said was whirling around in her head, especially his suggestion to talk through stuff. She smirked. *On the streets, that idea would last five seconds.*

Glancing up, she looked at the picture hanging on the

wall in front of her desk. John had painted an OtherSide landscape just for her, to remind her of the colors of that realm. He'd painted every imaginable hue along the horizon. But the main background was her color: Amber yellow.

That place. Why is it so hard to ignore?

Sitting forward, Amber absentmindedly grabbed a pencil on the desk and rolled it back and forth. She felt trapped. If she didn't sort things out with Jared, she'd be miserable. But what if OtherSide came up in their discussion? He might find out she'd been avoiding the place.

Before OtherSide, none of these stupid "talk-through-it" issues had existed. Before becoming a Lightning. Before discovering her Amber yellow color. Before the Light Prince's interdependence concept. While she had still been Shin, if a conversation bothered her, she just walked away.

Amber's chest rose and fell with a sigh. *Now what do I do?*

As soon as her mind had asked the question, she knew the answer. Her body tensed with worry. She picked up the pencil and nervously tapped the desk with the eraser end. After a few minutes she tossed it onto the desk and forced herself to get up and walk out of her room.

Jared was in the dining room. "Hey." She stared anxiously at the floor.

He looked up from his laptop. "Hey."

Amber scuffed at a scratch in the linoleum. "Sorry."

Closing his computer, he pushed it aside and leaned his elbows on the tabletop. "So, do you wanna' talk?"

Even though she felt totally weird, Amber nodded and sat down at the table across from him.

"I'm sorry I called you touchy."

With her eyes on the table, she said, "I was touchy."

"Still, I should've been nicer. And yes, sometimes I have bad days."

She kept her eyes focused downward. "I'm sorry I called you Mr. Perfect."

"Am I that much of a perfectionist?"

His voice was sincere, not angry or defensive. Since Amber didn't know how to answer him without hurting his feelings, she said nothing.

"Ouch."

He knew perfectly well what her silence meant. "That's not necessarily a bad thing," she said quickly. "Lots of people are . . . precise."

"Precise."

"Yeah. You know, exact."

He pushed on his glasses. "I'll work on not being a perfectionist. Until I've perfected it." A smile snuck into one side of his mouth.

For the first time during the conversation Amber made eye contact. He was grinning. Majorly relieved he wasn't mad at her, she grinned back.

"Friends?" He held out his fist for a fist bump.

She met his fist with her own.

"So, why's your day been such a bummer?"

Of course, her foster brother was a perfectionist, so he wouldn't forget their previous conversation. She shrugged and looked away.

"Do you wanna' talk about it?"

No, I don't! Amber thought automatically. But if she got mad and left, she'd just have to face him later. It was hard to stay cloaked around him, which was annoying.

They were both quiet, until Amber spoke hesitantly. "I think Mister Energy—I mean, I think The Light—is mad at me."

He leaned in. "Cool name! Is that what you call him?"

"Yeah. For now. It fits his superpowerness."

"Dad and I call him *Wild One*. Because of how unpredictable he can be."

"No kidding." She snorted sarcastically. It was The Light who had unpredictably introduced her to that horrible man.

"But he's only wild in the best sense of the word."

Still stinging from the uninvited face-to-face encounter with that creep of a human, she didn't respond.

"Anyway, The Light never gets mad at anybody. So he can't be mad at you."

Amber glanced up to see if her foster brother was being serious. Just then her mind flashed back to one of her previous discussions with Mister E. "Punishment, my dear, is a thing of your past," he'd said to her.

Maybe it wasn't Mister E. who was miffed.

Slowly leaning back on her chair, she crossed her arms and sat still. Jared was probably watching her, waiting for her to say something. Old habits of wanting to be invisible pressed into her thoughts. She searched for a way to avoid the rest of the conversation.

"Hey."

She looked up. Her foster brother's hair was a curly mess that stuck out in several directions. He sure wasn't a perfectionist when it came to his his looks.

"The Light is definitely not upset at you."

She bit her lip and uncrossed her arms. "I might be the one who's mad."

"Did you tell him?"

Amber shook her head guiltily.

"Why not?"

"It's a long story."

"You should talk to him honestly."

Her jaw tightened with aggravation. Jared wasn't just a perfectionist. He was bossy, too.

"I mean, I don't want to tell you what to do or anything. It's just—" Without finishing his sentence he stopped and closed his eyes.

He was going to OtherSide. Amber's face and neck flushed with embarrassment. *He's probably gonna' complain about me.*

Shame slipped into the room and began to flap toward his earth girl. But just as he was about to regurgitate his usual rubbish, a dazzle appeared from out of nowhere. Utterly surprised by its stealth arrival, the drab screamed an obscene string of words, shot straight up, and zoomed away like a falling star in reverse.

"And stay out!" Ahnah called after the drab. She chuckled, grateful for all the creative approaches to watching she'd learned from Rahzell. Including sneaking up on drabs. Laying her light-hand on the girl, she said, "Peace, little Lightning. This is only child-training. The Original Family is in love with you."

Jared opened his eyes, pushed his laptop to the side, and went into the living room to grab his Manual Of Nobility. Returning, he put the book on the table between them and sat down. Opening it to the inside cover pages lined with crimson, he asked softly, "Amber, can I get real with you?"

She didn't like the question and only managed a reluctant shrug. He must have taken it for a "Yes," since he kept talking.

"This book is a portal between OtherSide's realm and Earth's realm. But when we block the flow, the manual looks normal, like any other book. That's why we only see pigment on paper right now."

"Are you saying it's my fault?" There was a sharp edge to her question.

"Nobody's being blamed. It's just that, when we close ourselves off to the Original Family, OtherSide can't be released. We can clog the portal."

His blunt truth was like terrible tasting medicine: good for her, but hard to swallow. She stood to leave.

"Amber, please don't blow me off again."

He was staring.

Her emotions were all tangled up in a tug-of-war. At last, she turned and slumped back down into her chair.

"Just tell The Light what's bugging you. I mean, he already

knows it anyway."

Amber lowered her eyes. *Oh, man. I am such a lowlife.* How could she have forgotten? For the past week, while she was ignoring the Original Family, they'd been just across the veneer. And now they were in the room somewhere, hearing every bit of their entire conversation. Even more humiliating, The Light was supposedly *in* her, though at the moment she couldn't imagine how that could be the case.

Glancing over at Jared, Amber saw his eyes were firmly shut again, which meant he was somewhere in OtherSide. She closed her own eyes. If she talked to The Light, like Jared had suggested, what in the world would she say?

Stumbling into an awkward conversation in her mind, Amber started with, *Mister Energy, I don't understand.* But she wasn't able to go any farther. Admitting her own negative feelings to others was almost as frightening as having a rat run right across her legs. It had only happened once, but a rat's a rat, after all, and her encounter with that one varmint had been enough to make her sleep all hunched up on the landing of the nearby fire escape for a whole week.

This time, though, there was no fire escape. She knew she couldn't run or hide, because the Original Family was just on the other side of that stupid veneer thing. They were in her stupid room and in the whole stupid house. They were stupid everywhere.

There was only one way through.

She took in a deep breath and let it out. *Oh boy.* Closing her eyes, she turned her focus to OtherSide. A couple of quiet minutes passed before her thoughts became less muddled, and words began to flow again. *I'll be honest. I don't get why you allowed Edward McConnell to come and talk to me. I mean, what difference does it make that he apologized? It's too late to change anything now. The damage is already done—and I have four years in foster care to prove it!*

Her cheeks were wet. She wiped a sleeve across her face

and glanced over at Jared. He was still in OtherSide.

Irritation and sadness turned her mouth into a frown as she closed her eyes again. *I hate what that man did to Mom and me.* She really did detest how he'd ruined their lives.

Not knowing what else to add, she sat still, until one more thing came to mind. Though she'd been upset at The Light, he wasn't to blame. It wasn't his fault. But voicing those words meant becoming even more vulnerable.

Facing OtherSide's transparent thinking was tons more challenging than living an invisible life! Yet, if she ever wanted to hang out in OtherSide again, she had to continue. Another sigh escaped her lips and she said ashamedly, *I know it's not your fault. You didn't do anything wrong. I just got mad. I'm sorry I avoided you, Mister Energy.*

A familiar, spicy aroma emanated from the pages of the book and began to fill the room.

Jared and Amber opened their eyes and said simultaneously, "Wild One!" "Mister Energy!"

She sat front and exhaled what amounted to a small windstorm. *So he's not mad at me!*

Her foster brother looked over and said gently, "Not even for a nanosecond."

Amber grinned. Jared had caught her thought with his star-eyes.

All at once, a beam of light shot up from the crimson and washed her with a reddish glow.

Her eyes got as round as red Mars. "Holy smoke!" She rubbed her hand over the surface of the pages. As the ray of light hit her fingers, a calm settled into her whole being.

"You got shined!"

The warmth of The Light was soothing, not just on her skin but also on her mind, like a soul shower. "Seriously? This is a shining?"

His nod was full of enthusiasm. "So, you wanna' turn the page and go for more cool stuff?"

Leaning in so The Light would bathe her whole head, she said, "No, I like this shining! It's my first one."

Jared laughed. "You've already had lots of shinings. You just didn't realize it, because on this side of the veneer, they're mostly invisible." He glanced at her shyly. "Like, ever since you came to live here, I've been releasing shinings to you. I didn't want you to be weirded out in a new foster home."

Amber's mouth hung open in amazement while she swallowed that bit of news.

"And Mom and Dad have also been sending you shinings."

There was more gaping while her true and noble heart started to do a happy dance around the room. They genuinely cared about her!

"By the way, thanks for talking through stuff with me."

She shot Jared a questioning glance. "Is that what we just did?"

"Yeah. Way to go." He held up his hand for a high five.

Smacking his open palm, it occurred to Amber that though it wasn't all that comfortable, in the end the idea of talking through stuff had turned out well.

"Ready for the next page?"

"In a minute!" She gave him a don't-rush-me eyeful and for the second time, stuck her head into The Light's glorious reddish shaft of light.

Jared sat back and laughed.

It was her first visible shining! But she could tell he was itching to share more of the book with her, and he was probably right. After all, if the blank crimson pages at the beginning of the book were giving off The Light's incredible atmosphere, what kind of stuff would happen in the story pages?

CHAPTER TWENTY-FIVE

Jared and Amber had moved into the living room and were sitting on the sofa, watching the Manual Of Nobility come to life. Mister E. was saturating a watercolor painting of OtherSide's royal mansion. The entire design swirled and danced with activity.

Flying in and out of the royal residence were luminous beings Amber had never seen during her trips across the veneer.

"Dazzles."

Jared said the word almost reverently. She stared at the celestial creatures. Magnificently formed of light, each one had unique characteristics. But they all had one thing in common: apart from the Original Family, they were undeniably the purest beings she'd ever laid eyes on.

"Dazzles?" She looked at Jared for an explanation.

His head flew up in surprise. "You haven't heard about dazzles?"

She shook her head.

"They're awesome!" He turned to face her, folded one leg up onto the sofa, and dangled the other leg over the edge to touch the floor. "Dazzles are made of OtherSide's light, and they're all around us. And get this! All of us have a dazzle. You have a dazzle assigned to you."

"No way!"

"Yep."

Even though she knew they were invisible in Earth's realm, Amber unconsciously scanned the living room for one of those dazzles. "What do they do?"

"Lots. They pour on the strength, get us out of trouble, load our atmosphere with OtherSide, and all kinds of stuff. Oh, and they fight drabs."

Immediately, a parade of memories marched through her mind where it sure seemed like nobody had gotten her out of trouble. She wondered what they'd been doing in those situations.

Amber glanced down at the book's living painting and saw two dazzles fly out of the front doors of the prince's mansion. They stopped to talk to each other, and what she saw next made her heart pound with nervous excitement. Their attention turned upward and they stared at the Manual Of Nobility. Peering through its pages into Earth's realm, the dazzles gazed directly into her eyes!

Their faces were so clear and fresh and filled with fiery light that when their eyes met hers, Amber got the shivers. Her knees started shaking, her stomach did a somersault, and her whole body went limp. But she couldn't pull her eyes away—they were mesmerizing!

Everything about them was formed from light, even their clothing. The taller one had a radiating face like a fairytale hero and glistening, shoulder-length hair. He wore a light-shirt under glowing bib overalls, and gleaming boots. All buff and burnished bronze, he looked a little like a cosmic carpenter.

As he held Amber's gaze the dazzle smiled widely. She could've sworn he even winked at her!

The other dazzle standing next to him was also well-built, but more ruddy. With lustrous curly hair, his light-clothing resembled a man's T-shirt and jeans. Around his wrists were wide, metallic-like bands that blazed vibrantly. On his feet were shoes that gave off a similar brilliant glow. His lips were turned upward in a smile, and he appeared as jovial as the first dazzle.

While she and Jared watched, the two dazzles unfurled their wings and lifted off the surface of OtherSide. Even the fastest vehicles on Earth require acceleration to reach full speed, but that wasn't the case with these two spectacular beings. As soon as they were airborne their speed was instant. They flew straight toward the manual and at such a velocity, Amber instinctively jerked her head back to avoid a collision. Blasting right through the pages of the book, the dazzles shot into the Gordons' living room.

An invisible wave hit Amber and Jared and they flew back against the sofa.

"Whoa!"

"Holy smoke!"

Of course, when they entered into the Gordons' home, Rahzell, the carpenter-like dazzle, and Morgan, the jeans-and-T-shirt dazzle, were no longer visible. But having come directly from the prince's mansion, their beings were charged with tremendous power, and a surge of energy surrounded them. The surge filled Earth's air molecules with such force, that for at least ten minutes the humans were enveloped in OtherSide's buoyancy, the way swimmers float in water. Then slowly, like awakening from a dream, they came to their senses.

"Wow." Amber turned and looked at Jared.

"Double wow."

In a hushed voice she said, "Any clue where they are in the room?

Jared shrugged. "Maybe they're chasing drabs."

Amber rolled her eyes. She didn't want to hear about those spooky things, but he kept bringing up the subject.

"Okay, I give up. What's up with these drab creatures?"

For the next half hour Jared brought his foster sister up to speed about the Light Stealer and all his nefarious drabs, about UnderSide, and about their mission to remove all light, color, and goodness from the cosmos. She listened squeamishly, not being one who liked books with sad endings, or seeing anything suffer, or watching scary movies. Hearing about all the horrible things drabs did certainly wasn't her idea of a good time.

She closed the Manual Of Nobility and stood up. "After all that, I need a snack. Something sweet."

Jared laughed. "But I didn't get to the good part!"

"With those monsters there isn't a good part, is there?"

"Sure there is. The best part is, we win."

Amber walked into the kitchen and opened the fridge to look for sugary things.

Jared followed her and grabbed an apple from the fruit bowl on the counter.

"Doesn't your mom ever buy junk food?"

"Sure." Opening a cupboard door behind him, he grabbed a bag of mini-ginger snaps and handed them to her. "Here. This is the closest you'll get to sweet, unless you want to spray it with whipping cream. Oh, and I think there's still some chocolate sauce left."

Amber took the bag of cookies and closed the refrigerator door. Ginger snaps weren't her favorite, but with a cup of java for dunking they would work. Grabbing the carafe of leftover coffee, she poured half a cup, put it in the microwave, and shoved a cookie in her mouth. Chewing and swallowing, she said, "Not bad. So, are these health food?"

Finishing a bite of apple, he said, "Sort of. Cane juice instead of white sugar, and organic, non-GMO whole wheat flour instead of bleached white flour."

"Could be worse." She chomped another bite. Actually, they were pretty good.

The bell on the microwave dinged. As Amber pulled out her coffee cup she got the idea to squirt it with a gob of whipped cream. Shooting half a cup's worth on top of her coffee, she put the can away and sat down at the dinette.

Jared sat across from her, grinning as she spooned fluffy whipped cream into her mouth.

"What?"

"You're funny."

"Hey, things get invented this way. Somebody gets hungry and they figure out a way to get their sugar fix, and bam! A new snack is created." She slurped another spoonful of cream-coffee. "If you can't beat 'em, join 'em."

"Nah. I don't drink coffee."

Amber smiled and imagined the possibilities. "Pizza coffee with whipped cheese. You ought to like that."

He made a face. "Uh, keep working on those inventions. I think you're on a roll."

She stuffed three mini-ginger snaps into her mouth and took a sip from the mug. A white line formed on her lip.

"Good one!" Jared pointed at her cream mustache.

She mumbled through her mouthful, "You're juth jealouth 'cauth you can't grow one of theeth yet."

"Touché."

Her foster brother rubbed the peach fuzz on his chin, looking slightly chagrined.

"I can't help I'm still changing from boyhood to manhood."

Feeling bad for making him self-conscious, she swallowed and grabbed a napkin to wipe her face. "Sorry."

"No problem. We were just having fun."

"Anyway, what did you mean, we win?"

Jared looked confused until he was able to shift gears back to their earlier conversation. "Oh. I meant we win over the drabs. After the Light Prince died, we became royalty. And all those drabs lost their rights of harassing us."

Amber's jaw almost dropped right onto the table. A horrified look crossed her face and she panicked.

"The Light Prince DIED?"

"How else do you think he made the Crimson Wall?"

"What?"

"That's his blood."

"Ewww! You can't be serious!"

"As a heart attack."

"But I squished through that thing! And he was inside, waiting for me!" To Amber, the idea of being all bloodied by OtherSide's outer wall was repulsive. She glanced at her arms. In OtherSide, his gorgeous crimson shone beautifully in her veins. But honestly, blood?

Jared could see his foster sister was grossed out. He leaned over and gave her hand a friendly punch.

"Hey."

She looked his way.

"His crimson in your veins is why you're a color now. Otherwise you'd still be a dull, dead gray."

"But what's up with the blood?"

Finishing his apple, Jared set aside the core, grabbed a napkin to wipe his sticky fingers, and leaned forward to explain.

"So, the Original Family is perfectly royal, right? And everything in OtherSide is totally pristine."

"Yeah." To Amber, that much was obvious.

"Well the thing is, we earthlings used to be exactly like them, all pristine and bright with royal colors." Jared's face turned serious. "But we bailed on our connection to the Original Family. We ran away. And that's when we began to turn gray and lose our colors."

All the talk of death and blood was bringing Amber's grumpiness back in full force. She chafed at the runaway example and shot him a prickly look. "You still haven't told me what the deal is on the whole blood thing."

"Okay, let's say you're the royal family. What are you gonna' do? You've got to keep your lineage pure—no contamination whatsoever—or the whole kingdom would turn gray. And when that happens," he snapped his fingers, "everything is compromised."

"Will you get to the point? I mean, would you just *tell* me?" She said it brusquely. He was treating her as if she had no brain.

Jared stopped and stared at her. His jaw tightened with frustration. Blowing off steam, he pushed back on his chair. "What's with you, Amber? It's not always easy to explain things about their realm. They do things way differently than we do." Clamping his mouth shut, he glared down at the table.

Amber stared downward too, her lips pressing together in self-disgust. She'd just been incredibly rude to her foster brother. After a short silence she said softly, "I'm sorry. I don't know why I got so upset."

Jared nudged his sliding glasses but said nothing.

"So, go on," she said encouragingly.

He glanced her way. She showed him a conciliatory smile.

Carefully, he said, "I don't want to bore you."

She gave him a wider smile so he would see she wasn't going to bite his head off. "I promise, I'm all ears."

Jared studied the sides of her face and returned a small smile. "I thought they looked larger."

Grinning, she motioned for him to continue.

"You're not gonna' spaz out on me?"

Amber lowered her head. "Sorry I yelled."

Jared sat front again and the lines on his face relaxed. Taking a big breath, he started in where the conversation had previously ground to a halt. "Okay, here's the deal. When we earthlings lost our colors, it broke the hearts of the Original Family members. We'd lost our star-eyes and our colors, but THEY had lost US."

Jared's eyes grew wider. "And that was when they set in

motion a brilliant plan to recolor us and make us pristine again. The Original Family sent the Light Prince here to our planet, as a fully-colored earthling, with one hundred percent royal blood."

Sitting back, Amber's foster brother threw up his hands as though he were revealing a profound science discovery that would forever change the way things were done.

"And he died. Such a stroke of genius! They substituted the Light Prince's untainted blood for our tainted blood!"

Amber's mind was turning around Jared's words like a wobbly, spinning child's toy. "But he's not dead! I know, because I visit him in OtherSide!"

"Exactly. The Light Prince didn't stay dead. He was the first earthling to enter OtherSide, the first human being to homecome. He went there and painted the town red, so to speak, covering all of OtherSide with his crimson. And now, every human who passes through the Crimson Wall gets untainted and recolored. All their gray is totally wiped out, their star-eyes are opened, and they rejoin the royal family."

She gawked at him as if he were some anomaly from the zoo, her mouth hanging open like a small cave. After a full minute of contemplation she asked, "But why would they do that? It's so extreme!"

"I know, right? It's outrageous!"

Like wet morning dew is laden with water, the air around them grew thick again with the atmosphere of OtherSide. Neither one said anything until Amber answered her own question.

"It was so *we* could be their family."

He nodded.

She understood it was true, but that kind of affection was heavy with worth and wasn't to be taken lightly.

Jared broke her quiet reflection. "And now that we're royal, we can tell those drabs to take a hike. We win."

"We win what?" She squinted, unable to follow his train

of thought.

"The Original Family is in charge of everything, right?" She nodded.

"So, when we go through the Crimson Wall, we become part of the royal family. We're brought into their bloodline. Which means, by their mandate, we can take charge and tell those drabs to get lost."

All the dazzles in the vicinity beamed. Ahnah, Rahzell, Morgan, and even Solm, who had drifted closer to listen, were engrossed in what was playing out in the human conversation.

"Little Streak is on the move!" Rahzell's light-shine swelled in supernova style as he lifted up and spun around, creating a golden funnel of light.

Ahnah was right there, twirling with him. "And it won't be long until she is one formidable earthling!"

Solm glanced at Morgan. "By their reactions, you would think our friends were just reassigned to the Prince's mansion."

Morgan grinned. "Watching an earthling take on her authentic form is quite an honor."

"Indeed," Solm said. "As is collaborating with the Original Family in any renovation process."

Slowing his speed, Rahzell came to a standstill next to Ahnah. They glanced at each other, their smiles matching the brightness around them.

Jared and Amber felt a third wave of invisible energy swirl around the living room.

Awestruck, Amber suddenly wanted to be alone. Her respect for her prince brother had just gone through the roof and was heading into outer space, passing the moon, and continuing upward toward the sun.

"Hey, Jared. I'll see you later." She stood up.

Catching a glimpse of her star-struck face, any remaining irritation Jared had felt toward his foster sister melted away. In its place was a bond he'd never experienced with any other kid they'd kept in their home.

"Take the Manual Of Nobility with you, if you want. I've got another one."

"Are you serious?"

"As a heart attack."

"Cool! Thanks."

Picking up the manual, Amber slipped into her room to think about dazzles and drabs, about blood and royalty, and most of all, about the incredibleness of her amazing prince brother.

CHAPTER TWENTY-SIX

At first when he'd gotten released from that silent padded room, Dibs had pinched himself to make sure he wasn't dreaming. But when he found out *why* he got out of solitary so soon, he wanted to pinch his chump roommate.

In this particular juvie hall there was a blasted program that rehabilitated problem residents by giving them janitor duty. For a whole month. Which meant that every afternoon during break time, while his entire ward got to play basketball outside, Dibs and his chump roommate would be stuck inside cleaning toilets, mopping floors, washing windows, and cleaning up muck in a bucketload of other idiotic jobs.

He was fed up with Jamie. It was all his fault they were walking on either side of Potbelly Shilton, being escorted to the dumb custodian's office.

In the unseen realms, Isolation was quite satisfied with the present situation. Settling down quietly on his human's back, he wrapped his arms and legs and clawed feet around the boy's torso. He was roguishly happy and gave a drab's rendering of a smile, which, on a human face would've been called a rude, rumpled snoot. As long as his earthling was miserable, he was doing his job. And so far, things were shaping up perfectly gloomily.

"Hey, hey, hey, what do you say? You don't get to go out and play. You've got to stay in and clean today!" Restlessness sat on his own human's shoulders and snickered at his clever choice of words. "Too bad. So sad. You've been had." He chortled and then dug a claw into the flesh of the boy in order to adjust his position and make himself more comfortable.

Dibs felt a sudden charley horse in his shoulder muscle. He grabbed it with his hand and gave it a quick massage. After a few good rubs, it seemed to be gone.

But the real reason he no longer felt cramping was that Restlessness had stopped clawing his body. The drab had caught sight of the imposing dazzle ahead of him and skedaddled faster than cockroaches scatter at the flip of a light switch. Isolation had also cleared out, since neither one of them wanted to be anywhere near such a large and daunting foe.

While the drabs sped away, the boys and their guard arrived at the custodian's office. Officer Shilton directed the teens to enter through the door. He hung back and parked himself near the entrance.

Dibs hoped a particular person wasn't going to be a jerk and cause trouble. He certainly wasn't planning to get himself thrown back into solitary. So if his roomie behaved himself they might eventually be able to play sports instead of hanging around with some broom-sweeping, chaw-chewing janitor.

He scoped out the custodian's office. Just as he suspected, the place wasn't like one of those plush, New York skyscraper offices. It was only a dumb old oversized closet with a little desk in the corner, a workbench, a couple of large sweepers, and a few mop buckets. Shelves full of neatly arranged supplies lined the walls. In the middle of the L-shaped room hung a lonely light bulb.

Looking left and then right, Dibs saw nothing of interest in the whole place, which only confirmed his hunch had been right. The next month was going to be as much fun as a bad case of the flu.

The broom-sweeping janitor walked into his office-that-was-really-a-closet and stood directly in front of them underneath the bare bulb. An ebony man of considerable height, he had short, tightly curled white hair that wrapped around the sides of his otherwise bald head. Dibs noticed with some surprise he wasn't gnawing on a chaw of any sort. And though he was pretty sure the custodian was old enough to be a grandpa, he seemed to be in rather good shape. Most likely that was due to all the physical work required in his job.

Behind the ebony man and invisible to the humans, stood Gaelig. The drabs had been right to fear this impressive dazzle. He was so tall, his head and shoulders rose up through the ceiling and extended into the second floor of the hall. His chest was broader than the chests of two strapping human weightlifters standing side by side. His arms were as round as sizeable tree branches, and his legs as well-built as small pillars.

With fiery-green eyes and a chiseled countenance, the dazzle's appearance always had the same effect on drabs: when they saw him they fled away in trepidation.

Presently, Gaelig was observing the two young male earthlings who faced him. Smiling and relaxed, he watched as his human, an ambassador of OtherSide, made introductions.

Putting on his reading glasses to look at some official paper in his hand, the ebony custodian took them off again. Towering above the two teens with his tall frame, he asked, "Which one of you is Jamie Ferguson?"

Of course, stubborn Jamie said nothing at all.

"Well, one of you has to be him. Says so right here." He lifted the paper in their direction. "Speak up, boy."

Dibs couldn't stand the kid's silence and pointed at his roommate. "He's Jamie." What he thought was, *He's Jerkface Jamie,* but he only said, "He's Jamie," because adding the word *jerkface* would've led to a brawl and landed him right back in solitary confinement.

Jerkface Jamie stared at the wall behind the janitor and stood still, like a statue made from rock, his muscles in tense knots. Dibs thought he *was* stone, as hard as he was acting.

The custodian gestured to Jaime's chest and said, "Sugar, boy, you've got some anger in there, that's for sure." And then he mumbled something that sounded like having to work out some kinks.

"Well, never mind, it's a pleasure to meet you, Jamie."

The man smiled and Dibs snickered under his breath. He never would've used the words *pleasure* and *Jamie* in the same sentence.

"And you, boy."

Dibs felt himself being studied.

"You must be Byron Colby."

"Yeah." He knew the janitor's paper would list his birth name and not his street name.

"Well, Byron, believe it or not, it is also my pleasure to meet you."

Dibs didn't believe him. He wondered when the man's sarcastic niceness would turn into a lecture about how they were the dregs of society, and maybe a month of lowlife janitor work would teach them not to be so scummy. He wanted in the worst way to be somewhere else.

"And I am Mr. Clarence Jones. You may call me either Mr. Jones or Clarence, it doesn't make a difference to me." He set the official paper down on the workbench. "Now, boys, for the next month consider yourselves recruited for an important mission here at the Roland P. Emerson Juvenile Hall."

Jamie snorted and jerked his head away from the man in complete disgust.

Dibs didn't let on that he agreed with Jamie on this one. He didn't mind work and even enjoyed it in the right circumstances. But cleaning toilets and all sorts of cruddy stuff instead of having fun during free time, that didn't seem like an important mission no matter how much this guy blew smoke and crowed about his own significance.

While officer Shilton leaned against the doorframe and cleaned the dirt from under his fingernails, the janitor kept talking as if he'd never seen Jamie's sharp reaction. "The thing is, boys, everything the three of us will do during these days is to be done with excellence."

Dibs imagined cleaning the same thing gazillions of times because this man wanted excellence. *Excellence, schmexcellence. This is punishment.*

"I know you think this is punishment, being here with me to clean toilets and floors and such. And I know you're giving up free time to be here."

Mr. Jones squared his shoulders and his face got serious.

"But I promise you, when our time together is through you'll wish you could stay on in this assignment."

Dibs knew that wasn't going to happen and Jamie's twitching fists showed he thought the same.

"And one more thing. Officer Shilton, he and I have an understanding. If you boys cooperate with me, he'll just be an observer. While you're here we can have some good times together. Isn't that right, Mr. Shilton?"

"Yessir, Mr. Jones. You are in charge of these young men. As long as there's no trouble."

Ten minutes later the threesome, plus lurking Potbelly Shilton, stood at the end of a long hallway beside three mops, two mop buckets filled with hot water, and a custodian's cart with clean rags and other things they needed for the rest of their two hours of work. As Mr. Jones picked up a mop, Jamie leaned against the wall and defiantly crossed his arms over his chest.

"Now I know you've both probably mopped a floor before, am I right?" He didn't wait for an answer. "Well, allow me to show you how to wash a floor so it's clean when you're done, and you can feel proud to admit it was your work." The janitor stuck his mop in the soapy water, squished it in the ringer to get out excess water, and gave the floor six ordered and careful swipes. Then he did the same mop bucket process all over again and continued with several more strokes before standing to lean on the handle.

"See how it's done, with each pass of the mop overlapping the last one? You'll notice I pulled it toward me so my footprints wouldn't mark up the wet part of the floor. And I rinsed my mop every six or seven strokes to keep the floor evenly clean. Now you try. And take your time. We're not in a hurry."

Dibs sighed. The janitor had to be a mad scientist in disguise. And his sinister plot was to take over Earth by hoarding all its dirt, which would make him very rich when he sold it back to farmers and baseball teams.

Clarence Jones handed him a mop and instructed him to roll one bucket down to the other end of the hall. Jamie was to start where they were standing. The two would meet in the middle, where the janitor went to watch and wait.

Dibs suddenly felt cooped up. He wanted the sky overhead and room to breathe—to be out there, begging for money to buy a cold, sugary frappé. He imagined getting a fiver from that old man at the park and maybe even having enough money to get a big cookie with his drink.

By the time he finished swabbing his side of the hallway, Jamie had already been finished for two minutes and was holding up the wall again with his backside, his arms folded in protest, and his eyes burning a hole in the newly mopped floor.

"Now, boys, let's walk to where the floor's already dried and you tell me what you see." Mr. Jones headed toward one end of the cleaning job and motioned for Dibs to follow him. "Jamie, you too," he gestured toward statue-boy with his hand.

Jamie pried his butt free from the wall, his attitude dragging him down and making it hard to catch up with the janitor and Dibs.

"What do you think?" The custodian was looking down at the dried floor as if he really wanted their opinion.

Dibs said nothing. He was tired of being the only one to talk. And he wanted no part of any evil scheme to steal the world's dirt.

"Sugar, boys, speak up. What do you think of the floor? Does it make you feel proud?"

He couldn't believe this man was making such a big deal about the hallway. He used to neaten up his warehouse all the time when it looked a little sloppy. But good grief, he'd mopped up most of the crud and that was good enough, especially since the whole thing would just get dirty again as soon as people walked on it.

After Jamie said his predictable nothing, Dibs finally muttered what he really thought. "It's just a floor."

He would've said, "It's just a dumb old floor, for cryin' out loud," but he didn't want Shilton to threaten him, and he didn't want more time added to a punishment period that already felt like it was borrowing from eternity.

"It's where you walk."

Well, that was obvious. *So what?*

"You boys think too little of yourselves or you'd care about where you walk. Put your things down. We're going to talk."

The janitor-gone-mad showed them an alcove. They deposited everything there and followed him inside juvie hall's cafeteria.

Dibs would've given anything for that frappé drink.

While Shilton perched himself at the entrance doors, Mr. Jones directed the boys to sit on plastic chairs at a long lunch table.

The custodian sat down across from them and leaned front, resting his arms on the table. His face was intense. "Byron. Let's start with you. And Jamie, think about what I'm going to ask him because I'll be asking you the same questions in just a minute." He eyed Dibs. "Byron, who are you?"

To Dibs, the man's honesty and his serious expression felt about as comfortable as liking a girl but getting tongue-tied in her presence and wanting to disappear. He shifted uncomfortably in his chair and decided to be funny. Standing quickly, he saluted as though he were in the army. "Sir! I am Byron James Colby! Sir!" Dropping his salute, he glanced at Shilton, who was giving him the evil eye. He sat down and looked at his roommate, hoping they could share a smirk together. But Jamie was slumped in his chair with his eyes boring a hole in the floor again.

"Byron."

The custodian's dark eyes gazed at Dibs. He seemed unimpressed by his comic efforts.

"Who are you?"

Annoyed, Dibs looked back at Mr. Jones. "I'm Dibs."

The custodian had evidently been around juvenile hall long enough to ask, "Your nickname?"

Dibs nodded.

"Well, Dibs, what is it about you that makes you worthwhile?"

This was crazy talk. Why should a janitor interrogate him? Dibs stood up and rolled his eyes. "Can we get back to work now?"

"No. Sit down. I want to know what you see in yourself that is worthwhile."

Dibs sat. *I can hotwire a car, whatta' you think of that, Mr. Clean?* He almost said it out loud.

"It's not a trick question. Think."

Dibs pressed his lips tight together. If Jamie could get away with silence, he could too. He folded his arms across his chest and slouched like his roommate.

"You've both got dreams in you."

The man was pointing to their chests.

"You don't even know they're inside, but if you allow

yourselves to think about the possibilities, you might get your heads above the walls of this place. You might get beyond fighting on the streets, to find a real future out there."

Mr. Jones asked the same, "Who are you?" and, "What's your worth?" questions to Jamie—whose only sign that he hadn't gone deaf during the last ten minutes was that he looked away several times when he was being addressed.

Then the grandpa-janitor-mad-scientist started into this lecture kind of talk that wasn't at all what Dibs expected to hear on the first day of a month-long punishment.

"First, let me tell you who you are not, boys. You are not bad human beings. You are not stupid. You are not evil. You are not throw-aways of society." He leaned toward them for emphasis. "And don't let anyone try to pin these lies on you. I can tell you're both smart, interesting, creative, and fun. I know you've made a mistake or two—we all have—but you're good boys, and you *deserve honor*." He emphasized the last two words.

"And that's why you do a good job with your work. You clean for the sake of other boys like yourselves who deserve the same honor and worth. They need to know they're not riffraff, but princes." Clarence Jones stood. "You are cleaning floors where princes walk. Boys, I want you to begin to see yourselves differently. And it starts here, today." He waved for them to follow him. "For now, we've got work to finish."

As they re-mopped the same hallway under Mr. Jones' watchful supervision, Dibs' thoughts jumped around like popcorn in hot oil. He couldn't think of one person in juvie hall who acted royal, unless you counted the royal pains who bullied everybody.

As for his own worth, the chop shop guys had liked his hustle and that made him feel worthwhile. He knew he could also charm little old ladies when he begged. And he could steal stuff from the grocery store without getting caught.

The Other Side Of Visible

When he was hungry, those skills were worthwhile.

But none of that would count to Mr. Jones. Most likely, there wasn't very much about his life the janitor would consider worthwhile. That was probably the whole point of all those things he'd said in the cafeteria—to point out there wasn't anything of worth.

Even so, his insides were churning and he couldn't forget that one comment about dreaming. At his warehouse he'd often fallen asleep by imagining what it would be like to be rich and have a nice house. And someday, he saw himself marrying and having kids. He liked the idea of dreaming.

Still, the only reason Dibs did well on floor duty was because he knew if the job wasn't done right his new boss would only make him do it all over again. And he didn't want to be there forever. Mr. Jones probably thought he'd reformed him, but it would take more than a snazzy speech to change his mind. And the man wasn't fooling him either, with his get-rich-quick scam of stealing dirt.

Finished with their work for the day, the teens and the custodian walked back to the janitor closet under the eagle eyes of Officer Shilton. Clarence Jones thanked them for a job well done. And while the guard looked the other way, he handed them some of his wife's homemade chocolate chip cookies, which they took readily.

While they munched, the janitor gave them a homework assignment. "Boys, for tomorrow I want you to answer another question for me." Clarence paused to change subjects. "And by the way, for the next thirty days we'll have a lot of time to talk. I don't like boring work, and if we don't converse about good things the time will drag on like a sweltering summer day." The custodian rubbed his forehead. "Now, where was I?" He thought for a second. "Oh, yes. Here's your question for tomorrow: if you could do anything with your life, what would you do? Let's say money is no issue and schooling is no issue. You can do anything you choose. What would it be?"

Clarence offered them each another cookie. As Dibs took it, he had the opinion that the janitor should be a professor at some other kind of institution.

"And don't think you can't do great things."

Lowering his voice, the professor bent over until his face was level with theirs. He gazed at them as if he were divulging a great, new solvent formula. "Nobody can stop you two from dreaming, and dreaming is an important step to believing in yourselves."

Several minutes later Mr. Jones gave them back to the jurisdiction of Officer Shilton. As the guard led them away from the janitor's office a shining hit each boy squarely in the back, and immediately spread all over their insides.

Clarence E. Jones, ambassador of OtherSide, was entirely grateful he'd chosen this particular part-time job following his retirement from teaching. Working with troubled juveniles was comparable to mining treasure out of bedrock. On the surface they seemed like plain old worthless stone. But underneath there was usually a valuable vein of some sort just waiting to be discovered. And in his opinion, he'd just struck gold.

The boys' trek through juvenile hall's maze of gates and corridors ended back in the fourth ward, at cell number twenty-three. The barred door clicked open and Shilton said his usual, "There you go, young men. You keep yourselves out of trouble, you hear?"

Brushing off the guard's tiresome comment, Dibs stepped inside the cell and immediately flopped onto his bunk. In the worst way, he wanted to ask Jamie what he thought about the mad scientist. But they still hadn't said a word to each other, and he was leery of causing another explosion. In the end, he decided to keep his thoughts to himself.

Wondering what to do next, he clasped his hands behind his head, propped one leg up on the other, and tried to think about something other than life in juvenile hall. The Hungry

Appaloosa floated into his mind's eye, which led to thinking of Shin. He genuinely missed her. Though he was sad their last encounter had ended in a fight, he sincerely hoped she was enjoying her new life. Thanks to old man Oscar, at least she had a home now.

Pulling his hands front to rub his face, Dibs frowned. He could feel himself heading straight into a dismal comparison of his own disgusting circumstances with Shin's happiness. There was no point in staying in that train of thought.

He remembered the question the custodian had asked them to consider. Since there was nothing more worthwhile to think about, Dibs decided it couldn't hurt to at least give the janitor-professor's question a shot.

Staring above him at the underbelly of his roommate's mattress, he pictured himself with loads of money and some kind of real education. Soon ideas about a pretend future were flying through his imagination. *I'd be a jet pilot. Or a racecar driver. Or a mountain climber.* One thing was certain. He could never be stuck in some high-rise office as a businessman or an accountant. *I could buy a yacht and sail around the world.*

After a while he settled on his favorite idea. He'd be an explorer. All those other countries and places he'd heard about: he'd go sightseeing and eat exotic foods and sleep in fancy hotels that had marble floors. And he'd make important discoveries. Maybe he would find a new mineral deposit or rediscover a jungle animal that researchers had determined was extinct. Exploring was important, but he also needed to make a difference.

Dibs rolled over. His punishment with the janitor felt less dreadful. Maybe the guy wasn't nutso after all. *If Jamie's gonna' ignore me, bein' with Mr. Jones might not be so bad. He likes to talk.*

He looked at the wall next to his bunk. A former occupant had scratched a swear word into the paint, and it made him giggle. *May as well make the best of it. I don't get frappés in this joint, but there's nothin' wrong with homemade cookies, that's for sure.*

All that thinking was making him hungry. When the blare of the dinner bell sounded, Dibs jumped off his bunk and stood eagerly at the barred door to wait for roll call and the mealtime lineup. Their door unlocked and he fell into place with the rest of the ward's chow line.

Though he couldn't have said what made him do it, as he passed by the watchful stare of Officer Shilton, Dibs flashed him a small, hopeful smile.

During the second and third afternoons of janitor duty, Mr. Jones explained they were under a deadline to complete a special cleaning job in the gym using a rented wax machine. As a result, there was no time sit down and talk about the dreaming question. Then it was the weekend and Clarence didn't work weekends, so they weren't together again until he returned on Monday.

By then, especially since dumb Jamie still hadn't spoken a word, Dibs was busting to tell the janitor about being an explorer. He'd been locked in their silent cell every evening and was itching in a big way for some conversation.

On Monday during break time they sat in the cafeteria, Mr. Jones on one side of the table as before, and Jamie and Dibs on the opposite side. Officer Shilton was once again holding up the doorframe of the entryway with his leaning potbelly.

When the janitor asked what they'd dreamed about, Dibs answered immediately.

After hearing his idea, Clarence Jones said, "An explorer? That's great, Dibs. Where would you go first?"

The explorer knew his first stop. "The desert dunes of Morocco." While in school during a foster care stint, Dibs had been impressed with their immense size and stark beauty. He imagined riding a camel over them, battling a ferocious sandstorm, and finding an oasis just before almost dying of thirst. Since most of the kids in juvie probably had no idea they even existed, he was proud he knew about those dunes.

"So, Dibs, you're going to need some cash in order to go there. Once you get out of juvenile hall, how are you going to prepare for the life of an explorer?"

Dibs gawked at the janitor-professor. "But you told us to dream like we were rich! You didn't say nothin' about needin' money!"

"That's right. I wanted you to find the big dream inside of you. But you know dreams can happen, don't you? And in order to see them come true, you've got to start somewhere. So what could you do to make it happen?"

Mr. Jones' question was sillier than putty. Dibs hadn't given a bit of thought about how to follow his dream, because dreams weren't real. They were just daydreams. Except the dream about saving money and getting an apartment. That had been a true dream.

"What if you *could* be an explorer, Dibs? What if the dream could become reality?" Clarence leaned back to include Jamie in the discussion. "What I mean is, you can set goals for your lives and one step at a time, pursue them. Dreams can come true if you plan and work ahead three, five, ten, or even fifteen years."

Dibs didn't see any way to be an explorer. Not to Africa. Not to Morocco.

"How about learning journalism, or photography, or archeology, Dibs? Or studying some other skill that will pay you to explore. What do you think?"

Dibs shrugged like quiet Jamie always shrugged. "I don't got a clue, Mr. Jones. I never thought about me bein' a photographer or nothin'." He liked taking pictures but he'd never owned a camera. Certainly not one with special lenses and all that professional stuff real photographers carry around. And though he'd heard of archeology, he had no idea what those guys did, other than scraping dirt off of important rocks.

"I'll tell you what," the custodian said, "tonight, dream about how you could make it happen. You dreamed about exploring, now think and dream a little deeper."

While the three human beings returned to work, Olyim, the Watcher for the silent boy, moved next to his earthling. Rather than seething and fuming just beneath the surface, his boy was fairly calm, an unusual state of mind for him. Thanks to the ambassador's shinings, the pesky drab that normally hung around was nowhere to be found. The foul thing would return, he knew that much by experience. But to his great delight, he also knew the child would receive more shinings. As long as his earthling had breath, the royal family would never stop pursuing him.

Urielle sidled up next to Olyim, nudged his wing, and pointed at the ambassador. "As far as I'm concerned, that man can hang around our humans until the end of time." Fluttering up and down, she shook herself from pure joy. "It's been a while since I've been around this much of The Light's energy on Earth!" She giggled and flexed her wings upward and outward until they were completely unfurled, then flapped them hard back and forth. "Oh, that feels terrific."

Olyim, who had been lost in thought, turned to look at her. "It's wonderful, isn't it?"

"Fabulous!" With a burst of energy, Urielle spun herself in a happy circle.

Smiling at his friend's spirited response, Olyim expounded on his previous comment. "The royal family takes an earthling's poor choices and masterfully weaves them into a sterling plan." His eyes sparkled with pleasure. "I wonder how long ago Their Majesties envisioned the conscription of our young humans into this ambassador's service."

"Best thing that ever happened to them!"

Gaelig threw his head back and laughed out loud. "Urielle, you have a marvelous way of succinctly communicating joy."

Olyim folded his arms across his chest and nodded his agreement toward Gaelig. "I will say, she is the epitome of exuberance."

Urielle was still fluttering up and down as the two young humans began to follow the uniformed man back to the room where they slept.

Flying to stay alongside their young earthlings, Urielle and Olyim bowed toward Gaelig.

"See you later," Urielle called back to him.

"Until the next time, my friends." Gaelig bowed in return.

While they hovered beside their earthlings for the remainder of that earth day, Olyim and Urielle formed their own dreams for the boys. Dreams that crossed the veneer into OtherSide. Dreams that satisfied every good desire held in the hearts of the Original Family. Dreams that far exceeded anything the young humans presently had capacity to dream for themselves.

CHAPTER TWENTY-SEVEN

After discovering how the Light Prince recolored humankind using his very own crimson, Amber was eager to go and see him. But the possibility of meeting Edward McConnell in OtherSide—that man who had ruined her life—had her feeling jittery. Their first meeting had given her quite a jolt, and the thought of encountering him again was enough to make her jaw cramp with worry.

She fidgeted, took a sip of coffee, and set her mug back down on the nightstand. *Okay, if he does show up, I don't have to stay. I can come back here and he'll be gone.* That idea was enough to satisfy. With a way of escape she could risk trying.

Leaning back against the crimson wall next to her bed, Amber felt the soothing warmth of its shining on her spine. She shut her eyes and soon found herself resting against a different wall across the veneer.

The OtherSide wall was soft and supple and covered with a silky white material. Its most extraordinary quality was its movement. Expanding and contracting in a slow, regular rhythm, it almost seemed as if it was alive.

Amber craned her neck to look straight up. The wall towered above her as far as her squinting eyes could see. Matching its soaring height, its width stretched out to her left and right and continued outward beyond her view toward both horizons. Immense didn't begin to describe the wall's size.

She ran a hand over the surface of the floor beneath her. Like the wall, it was made from a pliable smoothness and also continued forever in every direction.

Leaning back, her jaw muscles relaxed. The wall was soothing, just like her bedroom wall at the Gordons' home. *Sure feels great.*

She sat up and scanned her surroundings, breathing a sigh of relief. *Good. No sign of that man.*

The scent of Mister Energy's fragrance hit her nostrils. She spun around to find him and watched as a glowing fireball hurtled toward her and came to rest by her side. He resembled a giant torch, but his blaze wasn't hot.

"Hello, dear one!" The Light's voice spoke from the middle of his flaming orb. "I'm thrilled to see you again!"

She tensed. Being with Mister E. was a blast. But he was the one who had introduced her to that man, so it was hard not to be concerned about what was coming her way. She was tempted to open her earth eyes and leave OtherSide.

"Hiding won't help, Amber. It never does. But in case you're wondering, Edward McConnell won't be coming."

She exhaled in relief.

"His time with you accomplished its goal."

Amber shot him a look. *What on earth did that mean?*

"On Earth, meeting your father may not have seemed important," he answered literally, "but here in OtherSide it was incredibly significant."

With all her guts, she wished thoughts couldn't be read in this place.

"My dear." His ball of fiery light moved against her and expanded to hover over her and engulf her. "You're safe here."

With Mister Energy's orange glow surrounding her, Amber's mind calmed. Her muscles began to relax and she leaned back against the soft wall.

"May Light Prince join you?"

"Uh, yeahhhhh!" She bolted straight up again to look around for him.

In a flash he was there, inside Mister Energy's flame, giving her one of his brotherly hugs. "Princess! What's new?" He grinned.

She stood back and stared at him.

He waited for her to speak.

"You were a human."

"Yep, it's true. I'm still a human."

"But you're the Light Prince."

"That too," he nodded.

She peered into his green-browns. "Thank you for recoloring me with your crimson. I had no idea."

"You're welcome."

Amber stood still and gazed. He *did* sort of resemble a fairytale Prince Charming, just as Madison Owens had once declared so adoringly.

He gestured to The Light's presence all around. "What do you think of our ambience?"

"I like him! He's all comfy."

"Would you like to dance?"

The prince's eyes sparkled with a quizzical expression, as though he were inviting her to explore a new planet with him. She thought he was as loopy as the rings around Saturn.

"Dance? Me?"

He nodded. "You're growing up, sis, and soon boys on Earth will be asking you to dance."

Amber didn't want to think about that yucky idea.

"Oh, I see! Dancing is yucky, is it?"

The prince laughed and picked Amber up off her feet. He swirled her around and back and forth, and after a few minutes, placed her carefully back on her feet. "Now that wasn't so bad, was it?"

Out of breath and giggling, Amber wondered if this was what being a child felt like. She'd grown up at such a young age, most of her own childhood had gotten skipped over. With wide-eyes she said, "Do it again!"

After more twirling the prince set her down again on the surface.

She leaned back against the living wall and slid down to a sitting position. Turning her head to look around, she said, "Mister Energy sparkles like a disco ball."

Her comment sent the prince and The Light into a round of laughter while they imagined Mister Energy as a disco ball that released shinings to unsuspecting partygoers.

"Now, that is a stellar concept, princess!" Still chuckling, the prince took a seat beside his young sister. Leaning back against the plush wall, he rolled his head and smiled in her direction. "You're becoming more yourself, Amber." He pointed toward The Light. "We both see you growing more and more lovely."

Amber blushed. No one on Earth had ever called her lovely.

Matter-of-factly, the prince asked, "Would you like to become even more you?"

She threw him a puzzled glance.

"Sometimes we don't even realize we've gotten cloudy." Her brother smiled. "I'll be glad to bring you more sunshine."

She definitely wanted to be more herself, but there was a seriousness to his offer that made her sweat glands perk up. Looking into his eyes for reassurance, she saw his incredible confidence and relaxed. He would take care of her.

"Okay," she said, "I like sunshine."

As Mister E.'s luminescent atmosphere grew to three or four times its original brightness, The Light Prince stood, pulled her up onto her feet, and spoke gently. "Amber, you're being held back." He pointed to her waist.

Following his gesture with her eyes, she glanced down

at her own midriff. In the light of Mister Energy's increased glow she could see a thick black rope encircling her waist. Stretching out and away from her body, its end disappeared somewhere beyond the horizon.

"How did this thing get here?" She tried to wriggle free but the rope held firmly.

"You've had it for a long time."

A rope around the waist—and an ugly one, at that—didn't seem like OtherSide behavior. Amber's face flushed, her sweat glands reported back on duty, and she got hot with embarrassment. Lowering her eyes away from the prince, she pretended to examine the cord more carefully. The mortifying lasso was made of hundreds of individual strands that had been woven together. If the blamed rope had been around her waist for a long time, why was it only showing up now?

"You're finally in a safe place, Amber. The time was right for this to be revealed."

His answer to her mental question didn't change the fact that she was wearing a hideous noose, a twisted fashion statement that proved once again she was a total loser.

She spoke almost too quietly to be heard. "How do I get it off?"

With his hand the prince pulled her chin up until their eyes met. He didn't seem the least bit unsettled by her predicament. "Dear one, each fibrous strand was created by something negative you've said or thought about yourself. You grew up blaming yourself, and you needed to know the truth. That's why you met your earthly father."

Figures he'd have something to do with this. What a selfish coward! Cringing as soon as the thoughts whizzed through her mind, she looked away. "I'm sorry." Oh how she wanted her thoughts to be hidden! She'd just mentally assassinated another Lightning in front of the Light Prince. Why couldn't she be nice? Like Darlene Gordon. Now there was a nice person. Why hadn't she been born as someone like her?

She was doing it again. Measuring and calculating. Comparing herself. Like she wasn't supposed to. *Oh, I am such an idio—* Amber cut it short. More bad thoughts about herself. They just came. Without even trying, her mind automatically went to negative thoughts.

The Light Prince held out his arm to her like he did whenever he wanted to go for a stroll.

Now? With me?

"Go on, take my arm."

Forcing herself to put her arm in his, she walked by his side.

"You know, getting upset at yourself will only make things worse."

That was easy for him to say. He didn't have a black cable tied around his waist that screamed, "Sleazebag."

He stopped and faced her. "Look at me."

Amber managed to pull her head up but immediately lowered it. She couldn't hold his gaze. "It's not working!" She hated the stupid rope and wanted it gone. "And anyway, why do all my thoughts have to be lit up like a neon sign that the whole universe can read? It's so unfair!" Might as well spit it out. He already knew every stinking thing flying through her brain.

"Amber, no one in OtherSide is judging you. In fact, your journey is going marvelously well."

Pulling her arm away from the Light Prince, she backed off and insisted, "I told you, it's NOT working!"

He turned in her direction. "But we're not finished."

"Ugh!" Stomping her foot, Amber looked down at the rope and then shouted, "I'll never be nice and kind and good like you! Of all people, you should know I'm a terrible Lightning!" She withdrew even farther from him. "Can't you see who I am? I'm spoiled goods! I'm street trash!"

She turned and ran away, choking and stumbling as tears blinded her eyes.

The Light Prince chased after her, caught her by the shoulders, and swung her around to face him. The Light's fire flared to brilliance and reflected in his eyes. Hot with fervor to defend her dignity, he said, "Amber Grace." Wiping the tears from her cheeks, he cupped her face in his confident hands. "You are no longer that person."

She couldn't look at him.

"When you entered through the Crimson Wall you were joined to a new, royal bloodline. And no one, not even you dear one, has the right to declare you unfit for your position as an heir to the thrones of this realm."

He pulled out a cloth for her tears and handed it to her. "Furthermore, hear me: you *were* orphaned on Earth, but not any more. That orphan is dead. She died coming through the Crimson Wall."

Hearing about that dead orphan made Amber cry all the harder.

He pulled her to his chest and held her shaking body until her muscles calmed and the throbbing stopped.

With each stroke of his gentle hand against her hair, Amber's hateful mind quieted. After several minutes she managed to look up at him.

"So, why am I still wearing this stupid rope? If I'm—" she stopped short of calling herself royalty.

"Because you're only beginning to learn how to rule in the courts of OtherSide."

"But I don't feel—I mean, that orphan doesn't feel dead."

"Of course she still feels alive. Drabs keep telling you that you're an orphan, and you agree with them."

His words stung, mainly because Amber didn't want to hear that drabs could be involved in her life. Truth being told, she was plain scared. As a master of avoiding confrontation with humans, she certainly wasn't thrilled with the idea of facing things as frightening as drabs.

"Of course you're scared," he answered her thoughts.

"They've trained you to be afraid of them."

She gawked at him. "*They* trained *me*?"

He nodded. "Remember Mr. Cutter's dog at the junkyard?"

"Yeah!" She frowned emphatically. On more than one occasion that nasty Pit Bull's ferocious snarling had almost given her a heart attack. In her book of horrible creatures it was rated at the top of the list, right next to rats.

"It made you nervous."

"Scared the life out of me!"

"But wasn't it on a chain?" Having been in her alleyway, the Light Prince knew the answer, but he was making a point.

"Uh huh." Amber wrinkled her nose and wondered where this conversation was headed.

"So all that barking and growling wasn't really harming you."

"Well no, but . . ." She didn't know what else to say.

"That's what the drabs do to you. They snarl and tell you you're an orphan, and because you were an orphan you believe what they say. And it makes you afraid, and you want to run and hide away in your alleyway cave."

Like when the sun first peeks through the clouds on a rainy day, a little bit of OtherSide's light seeped through the cracks of Amber's faulty thinking.

"But what if you owned the salvage yard?"

"I'd get rid of that stupid dog!" She didn't even have to think about that answer.

He looked around at The Light's fiery red atmosphere and held out his arms as if the problem were solved. "Princess of OtherSide, if you're willing, we can get rid of those drabs!"

For her whole life Amber had believed she was the dirt on the bottom of the world's shoes. And whenever people wanted to, they could easily walk all over her. Taking charge of anything, even a junkyard, didn't feel like her personality. Not in the least little bit.

"It'll help if we deal with this rope."

He was pointing at the ugly noose.

Ten minutes earlier, Amber would've been too consumed with self-loathing to hear one word of the Light Prince's ever-living honesty. But everything he was saying made sense. And seeing Mister Energy's fire reflecting in his eyes, and hearing his strong words of promise—these things made her willing to listen.

Still, a thumb can get sore if it's whacked with a hammer, and Edward McConnell's rejections were that hammer on her sore brain.

"Tell me what to do," she said frankly.

"Release him. And release yourself, and you will become more you."

Release him. John Gordon used those same words about her earthly dad.

"But how?"

"With your will, and with your words. Tell him."

Looking down at the surface of OtherSide, Amber scuffed back and forth with her sneaker and considered how to release that man. She knew the first thing that needed to go was the grudge she'd held against him for her entire life.

Quite sensibly, she sighed and said, "Edward McConnell, I release you."

Shrugging, she waited for something to happen. At that moment the black cord around her waist shook itself into a looser sort of bowed shape.

Amber was amazed her words had that kind of power. She stood taller, and in a stronger tone of voice said, "Edward McConnell, I release you one hundred percent."

Images came to mind of her penniless mom and their ramshackle apartment, and she felt both sad and mad. Forcing herself to continue, she spit out, "I release you for leaving us." Moisture welled up in her eyes. She tried unsuccessfully to blink it back, and water rolled down her face. The thoughts kept coming. "I release you for how alone I felt. And how poor we were. And how it made me feel that you didn't want me. And for how much time I spent in foster care. And for how you messed up my life." The tears were coming faster.

The Light's fire glowed brightly in the eyes of the Light Prince. He pulled her close.

There was a splitting sound. Amber wiped her snotty nose with the cloth the prince had given her. Pulling back from him, she looked down. The rope around her waist had begun to fray. The tiny fibers were starting to disintegrate right before her eyes.

"I release you from having to pay for what you did." She breathed it out softly. Somehow she knew it was time to stop punishing him in her mind. "And from having to pay for what you didn't do." She had to let go of his absence, too.

"Brava, Amber. Brava!" Her prince brother was next to her, his voice spurring her on.

She glanced at him. Unable to come up with other stuff to release Edward McConnell from, she said, "I can't think of anything else."

He nodded. "And now the rejections, dear one. All those negative things you've believed about yourself. You weren't to blame."

Amber scrunched up her face to fight back more tears. She'd always assumed she was the reason her dad hadn't stuck around. She'd been too little. Or too ugly. Or too stupid. Too demanding. Too boring. Too awkward. Too girlish. Too boyish. Or any of a thousand other reasons.

Because if he'd liked her, he would've stayed. She glanced at the prince questioningly. *Wouldn't he?*

"It wasn't your fault."

Amber bit her lip hard in order to knock some sense into the lachrymal glands feeding her eyes. How did they manage to make so many tears, anyway?

"Release yourself from the rejections. You'll much feel

better. I promise."

Slowly, she began a conversation in her head with the Edward McConnell who had ditched her as a child and made her feel like she was nothing more than a lowdown scumbag. *Edward McConnell, I am NOT bad. I am NOT trash.*

"Say it out loud, princess. Let your words sing out who you are."

After more lip biting she got hold of her self enough to be able to push sound past the lump that had formed in her esophagus. "I'm not worthless." But that was all she could get out before her lachrymal glands started up again like there was no tomorrow.

"You can do this."

Choking on a sigh, she tried again with a quivering voice. "I'm not ugly. I'm not a hopeless loser." Tears and snot mingled together and ran down her face. She used the prince's cloth to remove it.

So far, his promise of feeling better didn't seem to be working.

"You're doing great, honey. Now speak out who you *are*."

Pictures of who she *was* filled her mind: a dirty, homeless throwaway with filthy clothing, grimy fingernails, and ratty hair. The stench of rank body odor filled her senses like a memory gone sour.

She pushed it all away and made herself say something. "I am . . ." Her lips fought hard against the words. "I'm—" *You stupid idiot! Just spit it out!*

"Amber. Look at me."

She found his face.

For quite some time, the Light Prince held her gaze until she stopped crying, because she knew again how he saw her.

"I am a real . . . princess."

There! She said it out loud.

"Don't stop."

Once more she looked into his eyes. "I am your princess

The Other Side Of Visible

sister." The thought of it made her want to giggle.

Suddenly, there was a flood of memories of all the times when she'd given her own meals to little, hungry kids on the streets. And during a weeklong downpour she'd searched and searched for a plastic tarp so an elderly homeless lady wouldn't constantly be soaked. And while in foster care, she'd protected quite a few younger foster kids from nasty school bullies.

She wasn't an entirely horrible person after all! *Sometimes I act bad and sometimes I think bad things—* Interrupting her own thoughts, Amber stopped and stared pensively at the prince.

His face was serenely fervent. "That's right, dear one. You've been tremendously unkind to yourself. In fact, you've bullied yourself."

Her mind argued as she looked down and away. She wasn't anything like the street punks who used to throw things at her, spit on her, and shout mean words her way. And then she saw it. Hadn't she just called herself a stupid idiot? Only one of the choice names she used for herself on a regular basis, it proved his point.

"Well done, princess! Seeing how you've treated yourself is a crucial step toward becoming authentic you."

Her shoulders rose and then sank again as she released a large sigh. "I have a true and noble—" Voicing it felt like such a lie!

"Go on." He nodded for her to continue.

She latched onto his eyes and held fast with her gaze, until she could speak the words. "I am a royal princess of OtherSide with a true and noble heart."

All at once, there was a loud cracking sound and a bright flash exploded around her. The thick black cord snapped free from her waist and instantly recoiled outward, its loose ends disappearing somewhere toward the Crimson Wall.

Amber started to fall over backward from the force of its

release, but the Light Prince caught her in his confident arms. Regaining her balance, she stood to her feet. And the next thoughts in her head were something like: *I need a REAL father! I want a father!*

Faster than toast pops up from a toaster, another man stood next to the Light Prince within Mister E.'s glow. He was older than her prince brother but younger than someone Oscar's age. In fact, Amber thought he seemed both young and old at the same time.

Three or four inches taller than the Light Prince, he had a regal nose and cheekbones, a close-cropped white beard, and snowy white hair that virtually glowed next to his bright countenance. His eyes, though, were by far his most stunning feature. They were crystal blue, clear as a cloudless day, and carried the universe in their sparkle. They were jewels enhancing a rich king's crown. Amber knew these had to be the original star-eyes from which all human star-eyes were formed.

She wouldn't have guessed anyone else other than the Light Prince and Mister E. could make her feel so completely safe. But then again, if she had one wonderful OtherSide brother, why couldn't she have two?

The man smiled and the laugh lines around his sapphire blue pools deepened. He took her hand in his, bent over to kiss it in the way kings of old used to do, and then stood to introduce himself. Tears of joy brimmed over and ran down his cheeks as he said, "Amber Grace. Love of my heart! I am your Father Forever!" And with that, he only needed to say one more word. "Come." Gathering her into his arms, he held her close against the light in his heart. "My white dove," he spoke softly and caressed her as the Light Prince had done so many times.

Her princess cheeks were next to the silky white warmth of his shirt. At first, since they'd just met, she didn't know whether to hug him back. But after a few seconds of adoring, wholehearted affection, all her inhibitions melted. Amber squeezed her arms tight around his waist.

Smiling from ear to ear, she felt The Light's warm, liquid gold filling up her insides. *I have a father! A real father!*

And this time she didn't care one bit that her thoughts were known.

CHAPTER TWENTY-EIGHT

At the beginning of the second week of janitor duty Jamie stopped being an arm-crossing wall-leaner, and he started listening to Clarence's daily cafeteria table time questions about life. He still only ever shrugged his shoulders for answers, but his gaze rose from floor level to the tabletop. And once in a while, he actually looked Mr. Jones directly in the eyes.

During that same time, Dibs decided what he wanted to do while exploring. He would make videos and report on things that needed changing in the world. If he could help poor people get proper housing, services, and necessary supplies by telling their stories, gallivanting all over the world would be fun—and, it would make a real difference.

Soon after Mr. Jones set them to planning now for their futures, the janitor-professor announced a change of subject matter. Just like that, he was jumping ship on the "What would you do?" question to float another topic during their talks.

Dibs was slightly perturbed. Because unless he could find a way to hide in somebody's suitcase, he still didn't know how to get to those dunes in Morocco, where all his big adventures were going to begin.

But when the janitor brought up the next subject, he decided going to Africa could wait.

"So, young men. Our next discussion question is this: what does it mean to be a man? Think about it, and we'll talk together tomorrow."

Dibs desperately wanted to know the answer to Clarence's question, since no one in his life had ever explained to him how he was supposed to live. At one point, he'd thought Tall Eddy might help him. But in the end, that good-for-nothing turned out to be as bad as his own dad.

His old man had done drugs and crimes, and he'd even carelessly killed a guy while being high. Dibs knew that kind of stuff was as far away from manhood as juvie hall was from the Sahara Desert.

At age fourteen, he was on his way through puberty with some tiny beard growth and a voice that cracked from bottom to top whenever it felt like it. And honestly, becoming an adult scared Dibs more than nightmares. He couldn't control nightmares and he couldn't stop getting older. They both just happened. If he could just know ahead of time how to be a man, he figured he might survive growing up.

Lobbing a piece of wadded up scrap paper at the trash can under the sink, Dibs settled back onto his bunk to come up with examples of manhood. But after a few minutes of hard concentration, he'd only thought of actions that weren't manly. Like, one time he backed down from a fight when some moron had called him "Chicken." That felt unmanly. Stealing was another thing that was unmanly, though, on the streets swiping food from time to time to keep from starving couldn't be helped. Neither was cheating manly.

He jotted down a few more thoughts in the notebook the custodian had given to him. But after rereading them, Dibs decided they were all dumb ideas. Closing the journal, he slipped it under his pillow for safekeeping. Discovering manhood would have to wait until tomorrow, when they would be together with Mr. Jones.

The old custodian was smart, a lot wiser than Dibs had judged him to be at their first meeting in the janitor's closet. And just like Clarence had promised, he was sort of dreading the day their janitor assignment would end, and he could once again use his free time to play sports. Being outside was a great idea, but never in his whole life had he talked about the stuff Mr. Jones brought up for discussion. The cafeteria table sessions were as good as cold frappés. Maybe they were even better, because they didn't give him sugar headaches.

Dibs looked around the cell. He was glad Jamie was elsewhere finishing up some sort of art project. Since his roommate was still sealed up like an Egyptian tomb, he preferred being alone. It was boring, but at least he didn't have to put up with the silence of a dead mummy.

Restlessly, Dibs turned over on his side and faced out toward the wall where his roommate's sketches were hanging. *I wonder if Pretzel Boy does rap.* He'd given him that nickname because of how often he stubbornly folded his arms across his chest to resemble the crossed parts of a pretzel. Jamie wasn't looking so twisted these days, and he wasn't sucking air or spitting in disgust anymore when Mr. Jones said certain things. But the name was still stuck in Dibs' head.

At the thought of his silent roomie trying to bust a rapper move, he grinned and rolled over onto his back. Something slipped off the top bunk and landed on the floor. He lifted his head to see what it was. There, right next to his bed, laid Jamie's journal. Pretzel Boy's Don't-Touch-My-Stuff-Or-I'll Kill-You book was in plain view. The pages were lying open to a drawing and a series of notations.

Dibs didn't even have to do anything. It was facing him, just waiting for his eyes to latch hold and begin reading. Leaning forward, he felt a tinge of guilt and then a touch of fear. Lately his roommate hadn't seemed as threatening. But push might come to shove, so to speak, if Dibs took a peek at the book and somehow Jamie discovered he'd touched his things.

After considering that reality for a few seconds boredom won out. Dibs picked the journal up off the floor and sat back to read. He was an explorer about to unseal an ancient crypt and take his first peek inside.

Across the top of the page was written:

If I could do anything with my life, what would I do?

Below the question was a sketch of someone at a desk in a cubicle. Around the cubicle were lots of other identical cubicles. There had to be fifty of them filling a large room.

Dibs looked closer. *Hey, that looks like Jamie!* He studied the hair and physique of the person sitting in the nearest cubicle. It was the spitting image of his roommate.

The title underneath the drawing was: *First Step*.

Continuing to scan down the page, Dibs saw a heading with a list underneath.

FIFTEEN YEAR PLAN:
#1. Do research while in juvenile hall. Find grants, loans, etc., on the Internet. Look for ways to pay for my education.
#2. Get out of this joint.
#3. Ask Uncle Joe about living with them, away from Dad and Mom, for now.
#4. Talk to Uncle Joe about my job idea.
#5. Apply for grants or loans.
#6. Get a job in evenings and go to school by day. Graduate.
#7. Get job in accounting. Work on C.P.A. license.
#8. Get C.P.A. license. Pay off loans (if no grants).

#9. Find partner for firm—scrutinize their character.
#10. Create accounting firm with partner.
#11. Build client base.
#12. Buy house for my folks and me.

Dibs looked up from the page. He was stunned. Shaking his head, he said out loud to nobody in particular, "All this time, Pretzel Boy's been actin' on Mr. Jones' advice!" He snickered. "But ACCOUNTING? You gotta' be kiddin'."

Still grinning, he looked back at the page. Sitting behind a desk and messing with math figures was about as fun to Dibs as eating paper. In his opinion, all that pencil pushing was definitely tasteless and not his idea of an amazing future.

Even so, he was impressed that Jamie had written out a fifteen-year plan. Wondering what *scrutinize* meant, he turned the page. Equations and figures were scribbled randomly all over the next page, evidence that his roommate had been trying to solve a math problem. At the bottom, printed with capital letters in front of a large number were the words:

TOTAL DOWN PAYMENT FOR A HOUSE:

The scribbled figure was: $50,000.00.

Dibs heard what had become a familiar sound by now. The large metal door at the end of the hallway was opening. Most likely, Officer Shilton was returning with his roommate.

He leaped off his bed and looked up at Jamie's bunk. *Where do I put it?* Not knowing how the journal had been positioned before it tumbled onto the floor, he didn't want to arouse suspicions by leaving it in an open position if it had been closed, or vice versa. As footsteps got closer and louder, Dibs decided the journal should be closed. Quickly placing it in the spot he guessed it fell from, he allowed it to hang over the edge of the bed, but not so much that it would fall again.

Just before Potbelly Shilton and Jamie arrived in front of the cell door, Dibs sat down on his bunk. He grabbed his own journal, zeroed in on its pages, and tried to look like he was thinking hard.

Pretzel Boy entered the cell with his usual zipped up lips. He climbed the ladder to the top bunk, and for at least a minute there wasn't a peep from up above. Not a movement, not a sigh, not one sound. Dibs held his breath and imagined Jamie suspiciously examining every inch of all his puny possessions to make sure they hadn't been fingered.

The springs above him squeaked a well-known rhythm as Jamie lay down on his mattress. Dibs exhaled a low, quiet breath. He'd gotten away with opening the tomb and looting its hidden treasure! Lying back on his bunk, he decided all his exploring was making him tired. He rolled over and closed his eyes to join his mummified roommate in taking a short nap before afternoon janitor duty.

CHAPTER TWENTY-NINE

Amber loved going with her foster dad on his daily jog. It was their special time to be together, just the two of them. For the first few days her whole body had ached and complained about being put to the test. But after a month of running by his side, she was fit and entirely able to keep up with John's longer stride.

They were climbing the Locust Street hill, the toughest part of their regular running route. John looked over at Amber and through a rhythm of inhaling and exhaling said, "When you start school this fall, maybe you should consider joining the cross-country team or the track team."

"Really?" she answered between breathy puffs.

"Really. You're good. I've been a runner for most of my life, and it only took you a few weeks to match my pace."

Grinning shyly, Amber increased her stride and ran ahead. She still felt uncomfortable whenever compliments came her way.

He sped up to stay with her. "Just an idea. You can think about it."

"Okay."

As they crested the hill and rounded the corner at the park to head toward home, John's cell phone rang. "Sorry,

Amber." He stopped and unzipped the pocket on his sports shirt to pull out his phone.

"That's okay." She stopped to wait for him. He had mentioned he was expecting a particular client to call, so the interruption didn't bother her.

"Hello?" John listened for a few seconds and a look of recognition crossed his face. "Oh, hi! How are you?" He glanced at Amber. "Yes, she's right here beside me. It's been great to have her in our family. We've loved every minute!"

Amber tilted her head, curious about who was on the other end of the line.

"What's his name again?" John ran his hand through his hair. "Dibs. That's right."

Who knows Dibs that also knows the Gordo— Amber stopped, and her heart practically leaped into her throat. *Oscar!* It had to be him! She smiled knowingly at John, feeling both happy and strange. Living with the Owens family had been so long ago, it seemed like wisps of a forgotten dream.

"I'll let the two of you catch up." John listened again, then nodded. "Here she is." He handed his cell phone to Amber. "It's Mr. Owens. He'd like to talk to you. And before you hang up, I'd like to talk to him again. Okay?"

She nodded and took the phone while they continued walking down the sidewalk.

"Hello?"

"Hi dear one! It's Oscar!"

"Hi!"

"Well, it took a lot longer than we expected, but we've finally gotten clearance with Social Services. It's terrific to be able to call! How are you?

"I'm good!"

"We have certainly missed you."

"I've missed you too," Amber said self-consciously. With her free hand she began twisting the bottom edge of her T-shirt into a knot.

"I have some good news for you."

"You do?"

"Yes I do. Maggie and Madison and I are almost a foster family. After two more classes it'll be official."

"That's great!" She heard his jolly chuckle on the other end of the line and spun several more turns into the knot on her shirt.

"And in no time at all you'll be able to come and live with us!"

"Wow! That's great!" Amber said again, not knowing what else to say. The knot was as large as it was going to get. She stopped twirling and heaviness settled into her stomach.

"Oh, and I should tell you, soon after you left, your friend Dibs came almost every day to visit me at the zoo. He's a good young man. I think he gained a few pounds from all those breakfasts he was eating." Oscar's laugh traveled through the phone line.

"Yeah. He's nice." With regret, she remembered her fight with Dibs. He was a good friend and she missed him. She wondered how he was doing now, and wished they could hang out together for an afternoon.

"I haven't seen him for a few weeks, though. Perhaps he's found another way to take care of himself."

Oscar's comment brought Amber back to the present. "He told me he might look for a job."

"Is that so?"

She released the T-shirt knot from her fingers. "Uh huh. He and I talked about the idea."

"Hmmm." There was a short pause and Oscar changed subjects. "But, Amber, you haven't told me how you've been during these last weeks. Are you enjoying your time with the Gordons?"

Bashful Amber suddenly had lots to say. "Oh, I love it! They're awesome people!" She looked up and grinned at John. "And guess what?"

"What?"

"They're Lightnings!"

"Fantastic!"

"Yeah, I know! And Jared's showing me how to use the computer, and we've been watching movies right off of the internet, and Darlene is teaching me about eating more good food and less sugar, and Mr. Gordon and I go jogging." She shot a shy smile John's way. "He says I'm good at running."

"Sounds like they're a delightful family."

"They are!"

"Good for you, Amber. Good for you. I'm so happy for you!"

The line grew quiet. Amber played with the loosened knot on her T-shirt.

Oscar broke the silence. "I spoke with Mr. Gordon and asked him if we could make plans to come for a visit. What do you think about that idea?"

"I'd like that!" She tried to sound convincing. "Do you wanna' talk to him now?"

"Well . . . certainly. Unless there's more you'd like to talk about."

"Okay, so I'll see you soon!" Unable to come up with anything else to say, Amber pretended not to hear Oscar's last comment.

"All right, dear one. Delightful to talk to you."

"You too. Here he is. Bye!" She handed the phone to John. "Mr. Owens wants to talk to you."

"Great. Thanks, honey."

While her current foster dad and her future foster dad made plans, Amber walked numbly, staring at the trees and bushes and houses that had become part of *her* neighborhood.

After a minute or two of additional conversation with Oscar, John disconnected and put his phone away. "That was quite a surprise."

"Sure was." She forced a smile.

A leaf fell in front of John's face, and without thinking he reached out and caught it.

"Here. This is for you." He offered her the leaf and she took it.

"Thanks. I always wanted one of these. I'll put it under my pillow tonight, to keep it safe."

"And the leaf fairy will come and give you fifty cents."

"Huh?"

Seeing Amber's confused expression, John asked, "Never heard of the tooth fairy?"

She screwed up her eyes and looked at him like he was nuts.

"When you lose a tooth you put it under your pillow, and the tooth fairy comes and leaves something good in its place. Usually it's money."

"So, is this an OtherSide thing?"

"No. It's a fairy tale thing," John smiled.

"Oh, I get it." The tooth fairy was obviously one of those normal childhood details she'd missed.

They walked in silence. Amber absentmindedly twirled the leaf while mentally replaying her conversation with Oscar. She glanced up at John and sighed.

Reaching the front door of the house, John pulled out his keys. "Are you excited about seeing Oscar and his family again?"

Without thinking, Amber nodded and shrugged her shoulders at the same time.

He stopped and faced her. "Is that a yes-no, or a no-yes?"

"I don't know," she grinned. Truth being told, the only thing she did know was that she liked the Gordons. A lot. In fact, she was more comfortable with them than she'd ever been with Dibs, the one friend she'd known longer than anybody else. But she liked Oscar and Maggie and Madison too, and didn't want to hurt their feelings.

"C'mon. Have a seat." John sat on the front stoop and

motioned for her to join him.

She sat down.

"So, what's up? What are you feeling?"

That was the problem. Everything inside was all mixed up. She shrugged again.

"Try putting it into words, okay? I'm having trouble reading the shrugs."

"Can't you just do that OtherSide mind-reading thing?" she asked jokingly.

John laughed. "Transparent thinking?"

"Uh huh."

"Wild One's not telling me anything. I guess that means he wants you to tell me."

Amber twirled the leaf in her hand. She was afraid to say anything.

"Don't be afraid."

"You just did it."

"What?"

"Read my mind."

He smiled. "Honey, it's not hard to see that you're scared to say what you're thinking. Go ahead."

After a few seconds she said, "I like living here."

She hoped he would get what she meant. But he looked at her as if she'd only offered him the cherry on a sundae, and nothing else.

"And, well, I don't even know if you guys want me to stay ..." He was watching her, chewing on her cherry and waiting for more. Almost apologetically, she said in a quiet voice, "I feel at home when I'm with your family." Her gut churned and she spun the leaf harder. "But Oscar went to all that trouble to get a foster license, and they're gonna' be really mad if I don't live with them." She threw the leaf on the sidewalk and started bobbing one foot up and down.

"How do you know they'll be mad?"

She stopped bobbing and said loudly, "Because they did

all that work for me, that's why! And if I don't show up they'll get torqued!"

"So you would go and live with them just so they don't get mad at you?"

She looked at him like he'd spewed that cherry all over her.

"What do you want, Amber?"

She knew that answer. "I don't want to hurt them."

"That's it?"

More spewing.

At last, she said it. "I want to stay here with you and Darlene and Jared."

"Well. Then it's settled. The rest is details."

"But all that work they did!"

"I think we need to chase some drabs."

Hearing John's comment, several light-beings across the veneer whooped and hollered a rowdy cheer, at least for dazzles.

Amber gawked at John. Why was he bringing up drabs now?

"What are you afraid of?" he asked.

These hard questions never came up in conversations on the streets. Because whenever Amber had felt afraid, she'd escaped to her street cave, or to Africa, or to some other safe place. That had always taken care of the problem. Sort of. Except, sooner or later the pressure in her stomach showed up again. Which made her life even more laborious. She learned that word *laborious* at the library.

She began to feel edgy and wanted to leave: to go and hide in her bedroom. And on the way in, as a protest against John's nosiness, she'd slam the door.

But then Amber thought of what the Light Prince had told her—that she wanted to hide because she believed what those scary junkyard drabs were saying to her. Wherever they were. If they even existed.

"Don't lissten to thiss ssstupid man! He'ss harasssing you! He'ss jusst a bully! A usser! Get away from him!"

"You jerk, look at the mess you've made! And it's your fault! You're such a selfish sleazebag!"

Control and Shame had flown close by and were disgorging an onslaught of accusations. But at the moment it was Fear who had the upper hand.

"Run! It hurts too much! Get away from here! This is too painful! Go and hide! Cloak yourself!

Amber stomped on the leaf with her foot, trying to decide what to do. These emotions sure felt like they belonged to her and not to some barking drab. That familiar tightness was filling her chest, her head was aching, and the weight in her gut was as hefty as ever. She was desperate to avoid the whole conversation.

John silently released a shining in her direction. "Honey, is it time to face that fear? I can help you."

Her head was down and she was peeved. *I'll face YOU, jerk, if you don't soon shut up.*

Amber turned away from John. How could she think such a terrible thought? Of all the adults on the planet, he and Darlene were her favorites.

Hoping he hadn't done that transparent thinking thing, she glanced guiltily in his direction. His eyes were closed, and he looked as if he was somewhere far away.

And she knew where, which was even more embarrassing. After all those talks with Light Prince about being a princess, she should know better.

Ahnah faced the girl. Bringing her wings forward, she enclosed her in a light-cocoon. "Shhhhhh. Peace, child."

Rahzell stood behind Amber, his light-hands on her shoulders, his face glowing intensely. "Come on, Little Streak. You've fought for others. Now turn and fight for yourself."

John's eyes were still closed and he had a smile on his face. "He's here, dear one. The Light Prince is here, on the other side of the veneer."

Great, she thought sarcastically, *and he's been watching me turn from a princess into a toad.*

"He's cheering for you." Her foster dad opened his eyes.

Blast! Couldn't John just leave her alone?

"Amber."

She could feel his gaze was trained on her. As a small protest, for a few seconds she ignored him. Still, he was right. Even if she didn't want to admit it, she was paralyzed by the thought of telling the Owens family the truth. But no one in earlier years had ever been so honest in pointing out her fear.

"Let me help you, okay? This is important."

In a round about way Amber gave in to her foster dad. Snapping with irritation, she said, "I don't want to tell Oscar the truth because he'll yell at me!"

"Let's ask the Light Prince about that."

Huffing angrily, Amber shut her eyes. Her mind was racing.

"Shhhhhh."

Hearing John's quiet voice, she let out a huge sigh. *How in the world am I supposed to find my star-eyes?*

"They're in your true and noble heart."

I don't HAVE a noble heart. My heart's— Amber stopped. John had seen her thoughts. She tried to focus on OtherSide. *Light Prince. Help me find my stupid true and noble heart. Show me where to find my star-eyes.*

After a full minute of silence, Amber's mind quieted enough so that through her mental fog she could see a dim impression of her prince brother. He was hunkered down on the sidewalk in front of her, gazing into her star-eyes and smiling peacefully.

They will leave, dear one, but it's you who must command them.

Amber heard his words in her mind. He was obviously referring to the drabs. But she didn't understand how to "command" them. Feeling overwhelmed, she lowered her head. *I don't know what to do.*

Don't be afraid. Let John help you. The Light has already given you his power. Now would be a good time to use it.

Catching the prince's smile out of the corner of her star-eyes, Amber's frown leveled out. The least she could do was cooperate. *Okay.*

I'm proud of you, princess! He cocked his head in John's direction. *Go ahead, you can do this.*

Amber opened her eyes and said, "The Light Prince says I should let you help me."

"I'd love to, honey. So, tell me, what emotions are you feeling?"

That pressure was still pushing on her stomach, but she wasn't sure what that meant, so she just shrugged.

"Are you peaceful, afraid, sad? Angry, happy, confused?"

She thought about how awful the Owens family would feel if they found out she didn't want to live at their place. "I feel so guilty, because Oscar and Maggie have done all that work. If I don't live with them, the classes they took will be a total waste, and it'll be my fault."

"Anything else?"

With a toe, she smashed the leaf harder against the sidewalk and tried to figure out her stupid emotions so she could give John a stupid answer. "Everything feels totally out of control right now. Like, I could so easily get up and run away."

"What do you think the Light Prince or Wild One would do in your situation?"

She threw her hands into the air and yelled. "How am I supposed to know?" Her eyes shot angry darts aimlessly into the air and her voice was full of sarcasm. "I suppose the Light Prince would sit down and talk to the Owens family, and somehow they'd all see his point of view. And in the end, everybody would live happily ever after."

"Not bad!" John smiled.

He was ignoring her irritation, which made her even more irritated. "But I'm not the Light Prince! They'll just get mad at me!"

"Okay, let's imagine."

"What." She rolled her eyes and tightened her lips into a sharp line.

"Imagine that across the veneer, those negative feelings, like fear, and shame, and control, are actually creatures. And these creatures are constantly harassing you."

Amber's eyes started bugging out as images of invisible creatures filled her head. And they sure didn't look anything like dazzles.

"Now, there are also dazzles on the other side of the veneer, so you don't need to be afraid of those creatures."

He was probably transparent thinking again, but this time she was glad. The dazzles she'd seen flying through the pages of the Manual Of Nobility were incredibly powerful. His reminder kept her from freaking out.

"And those creatures—"he paused to look directly in her eyes,"—those *drabs* keep telling you Oscar won't listen to you, because you're just a nobody." His voice was kind, but urgent. "Honey, the drabs are saying you're just a stupid orphan. But as a princess, you get to tell them to stop bothering you, and to go away."

"ME? But the Light Prince said you would help me."

John nodded. "And I will, but they're hanging around because you gave them permission to stay."

Amber's right leg started bobbing again. This whole scenario was getting more absurd by the second.

"They won't leave until you tell them to go."

Everything John was telling her sounded ridiculous. She stood up.

"That's a drab, Amber. It wants you to walk away so it can continue bullying you."

She felt like screaming. Frustrated with all her crazy

emotions and with all the aggravating things John was saying, Amber got downright annoyed. Sitting back down, she said angrily, "Oh, all right! The thing that wants me to be afraid and to escape, get away from me! The drab that's telling me to take control and run, just get out of here!"

"By the crimson in your veins."

Looking over at John, she practically shouted, "By the crimson in my veins!"

They both sat quietly for a few seconds.

"How are you feeling?"

"Mad!"

He grinned. "Well in this case, that's okay. Now do you see the possibility of how it could work to talk to Oscar?"

She gave him a sideways glance and shook her head. That idea still seemed way too frightening.

"So, you tell that fear and shame to shove off, okay? They want you to feel helpless. But you tell them. They *will* leave." John motioned for her to continue.

All this talking to air she was doing was flat out foolish. But Amber had to admit, she did feel a little better. "The drab that wants me to feel ashamed about talking to Oscar, and that wants me to go crazy with fear—" she interrupted herself, as into her mind flashed images of the times the Light Prince had told her she was a princess. That did it. She had enough. "By the crimson in my princess veins, you be quiet and get out of here! NOW!"

All the dazzles on the other side of the veneer beamed as they watched three whining drabs turn and fly away from the human child. Two of those dazzles were virtually bursting with light-filled enthusiasm. "WAY TO GO, Little Streak!" Rahzell exploded in a mini-storm of light energy and zipped around wildly in a large circle.

"At last! She DID it!" Ahnah wasn't normally as demonstrative as her partner, but in this instance she simply could not contain herself. Shooting off in the opposite direction from Rahzell, she zoomed in and out of his light stream, until their two trails combined to form a large glowing ring that resembled the crown of a royal princess.

After some time they slowed down and came to a standstill. As he'd seen Amber do so many times, Rahzell held up his light-hand for a high five slap. Ahnah grinned and playfully swirled her light-hand to meet his.

Amber sat forward, propped her elbows on her knees, and released a huge sigh.

"That wasn't so hard, was it?"

She made a face. "Well, it was kind of weird."

"To your earth eyes it is weird, but through star-eyes it's all very real." John picked up his keys from where he'd laid them on the stoop. "And I'm guessing you feel more of OtherSide now. Am I right?"

Amber sat still to pay attention to her star-eyes. "I think so. At least, I don't feel so afraid."

"That means those drabs have gone. The atmosphere has changed."

She sat back and stared at him. "You mean if the drabs scram it's easier to connect with OtherSide?"

"You got it."

A smile filled her face. "Cool!"

"So, should I call Oscar and invite his family for a visit?"

There was a habit inside Amber that wanted to immediately dodge the idea. She closed her eyes and focused on OtherSide until peace came. Opening her eyes, she said, "If you help me, I can tell them."

"Of course we'll help you." He stood and held out his hand to pull her up on her feet.

Amber put her hand in his and jumped up. "Thanks." She wiped the sidewalk dirt from her running shorts. "I feel better." *Almost normal.* She always wanted to be normal.

"I'm so proud of you, honey. What you did was awesome."

Amber blushed. For as many times as John had told her

how proud he was, she was still getting used to hearing it.

He unlocked the door and pushed it open, motioning for her to go in first. "After you, princess."

His regal foster kid entered, and John followed, closing the door behind them and going into his office to check the family calendar. Picking up the phone, he began making plans for a decidedly important meeting with the Owens family.

CHAPTER THIRTY

His two charges sat across from the janitor, both of them slouching in their chairs and squirming while he quietly contemplated their progress. The talkative one was making good headway by joining in on their discussions with all the interest of a true Light-Seeker. In time, he expected the boy would be just fine.

On the other hand, Jamie Ferguson was still sealed up tighter than a fifty-five gallon drum, and Clarence had no idea how to pry the lid open so what was inside could come out. He hoped the quiet one was a Light-Seeker too, but so far nothing had broken through the boy's steeled exterior. They were already past the halfway mark of the teens' month-long assignment with him. He'd seen other kids come and go unchanged, and he didn't want that to happen again.

Above them and from some distance away in the realm of UnderSide, two drabs fussed and fumed about the goings-on near their earthlings. The relationship between Restlessness and Isolation had never been amicable, but there was one thing about which they both happened to agree. Thanks to one appallingly large dazzle and its human ambassador, their lives had become wholly miserable. There was a disgusting radiance being released around their earthlings, and it was creating atrocious pressure. As a result, circumstances for the two drabs were such that they now felt perpetually threatened and harassed.

Desperate times called for desperate measures. They had no choice but to work together. A plan needed to be put in place quickly, before their current projects were utterly ruined. Failure was not an option, since word of defeat always got back to the Light Stealer. And he had no problem punishing losers with outright pain, something akin to excruciating shocks that continued for days on end.

Neither drab wanted to think about those consequences.

Uncharacteristically, it was Isolation who spoke first. "Simple," he said, "we have to remove our humans from their exposure to the ruinous source of that other realm's power."

Restlessness scowled. "You dunce, it's extraordinarily clear that we MUST interfere. But where and when and how are what we need to know right now!"

"Fine. I was going to make a suggestion. But if you're going to be such a dolt, then forget it." Isolation flapped his wings and flew away through the cafeteria wall.

His cohort snapped loudly, "Go ahead, leave it all up to me. But I'll tell UnderSide you turned to flee!"

In a dark flicker of motion, Isolation was back. "You wouldn't dare."

"Why wouldn't I?"

For a moment the two drabs glared at each other, snout to snout and eyeballs to eyeballs. At last, Isolation quietly grunted his opinion. "I suggest we stir up our humans to fight one another again. It's the only way they will be removed from the present danger of that loathsome brightness."

As though he'd come up with the very idea himself, Restlessness said, "Without question, that's exactly my suggestion."

Immediately, the two drabs began wrangling over how to make their humans attack each other. Isolation was insisting they wait to instigate an altercation until they were nowhere near that hideously big dazzle. But true to his name, Restlessness wanted to start right away.

Not being able to agree on a plan of action, Restlessness said something had to be done and took matters into his own claws. Keeping his beady eyes on the movements of the enormous dazzle, he flew in closer to his human to wait for an opportune moment to strike.

On Earth, Dibs was leaning in and waving his hand in front of the custodian's face. "Mr. Jones, are you okay?"

"I'm fine, Dibs, just fine." Clarence surfaced from his thoughts and sat up straight.

"Good, 'cause you seemed kinda' spacey there for a minute. I thought maybe you were havin' a stroke or somethin'." Dibs sat back and caught his roommate stealing a concerned glance at the janitor. "Hey, Mr. Jones, you even got Jamie worried! He was starin' right at you for once, and not at the table, or the floor."

Instantly, Jamie lowered his eyes, folded his arms tightly across his chest, and withdrew deep into his private little world.

For some reason, seeing Pretzel Boy's reaction made Dibs' skin crawl. That Jamie went away somewhere inside of himself for the millionth time was maddening, like the time chiggers burrowed under his flesh and built a nest. The scratching had almost driven him crazy. His roommate's rudeness was having the same effect.

Aggravation tightened his throat and his words came out sounding harsh. "Jamie, I'm sick a' you actin' like you're the only one who matters! If somebody says somethin' you don't like, you fold those dumb arms a' yours and start mopin' around." Dibs pushed back from the table and stood up. Blood pumped hard in his veins and his face flushed. "You think nobody else has any feelings except poor little you. Well, we're not invisible y'know! I mean, what are you afraid of, huh

Jamie?" He jammed his hands into his pockets and snapped out a final accusation. "You're such a coward! I dunno' why I ever thought for one second that we could be friends!"

Turning away from them to think, Dibs bumped right into Officer Shilton's potbelly.

The custodian said to the guard, "Officer Shilton. Give me some slack."

"Mr. Jones." Shilton looked at him with eyes that could've spontaneously combusted, they were so intense. "We must maintain order at all times."

Clarence nodded. "I couldn't agree more, sir. I'm only asking for the opportunity to help these young men find a new way of communicating to each other."

The guard hesitated, then backed off to give the janitor space. But just in case, he faced the threesome, planted his hands on his hips, and set his glare to watch every move.

"Sit down, Dibs."

When Clarence spoke, Dibs turned back and took his seat. He sure felt like leaving, but unless he wanted to end up back in solitary, that was out of the question.

Still, he wasn't finished with his silent roommate. He turned to Jamie and asked sharply, "Did you ever think that maybe people don't like you because you're so mean to them? And one more thing; how are you gonna' train to be an accountant if you never talk? How are you gonna' save fifty thousand bucks to buy a house unless you speak to people?"

Until that moment, Jamie had only twitched slightly during all Dibs' rantings. But after the last two questions, he shot up onto his feet, grabbed him by the front of his shirt and pulled him out of his seat. His eyes were full of rage. "You were in my stuff!"

"Yeah, well, what are you gonna' do about it, Pretzel Boy?"

Dibs shoved his roommate hard to get him off his chest, just as Jamie took a swing at his head with a fist.

The punch missed its target and landed in thin air. And

before the angry teen could pull his arm back to strike again, Clarence Jones stepped into the fray.

He may have been in his late sixties, but the custodian was as fit as a fiddle. Jumping up on top of that table and over to the other side as fast as somebody trying to avert World War Three, he placed his long arms and tall body between them as a buffer zone.

"He took my stuff! I'll kill him!" Jamie reached hotly toward Dibs again, but a large ebony hand grabbed his shirt and picked him up by the chest.

Lifting him off his feet, Clarence pulled him in close, until he was only an inch or two from his face.

Clutching a canister of pepper spray, Officer Shilton stood right behind the janitor and yelled, "Mr. Jones, I will handle this! Step back!"

Without looking away from Jamie's eyes, Clarence Jones answered the guard quite emphatically, "Give me one more minute!"

Shilton stayed put and spoke to the janitor's back. "You've got ONE minute for the situation to change drastically."

Clarence's stare into Jamie's eyes had metal-melting strength. "Nobody is going to kill anybody around here. Do you hear me?"

Jamie looked away, but his body stopped fighting and he hung limply, suspended by the custodian's grip.

Lowering the boy slowly until his feet touched the floor, Mr. Jones continued. "Now. I'm going to let go of you and I expect you to sit down in your chair without incident. Is that understood?" There was no response. "I *said*, do you understand?"

Jamie nodded reluctantly.

Slowly, Mr. Jones released him.

Doing as he was instructed, Jamie sank into his seat and folded his arms. Glowering and surly, his smoldering eyes began their normal pattern of burning a hole in the floor.

Dibs was positive Jamie's actions had been enough to earn them both another turn in solitary confinement. He was not happy, to say the least.

A very tense Officer Shilton stood directly behind the teens, ready to intervene.

Clarence pulled out a chair from under the table and plunked himself down between the two angry teens. "Now. We are going to talk through this whole matter. Because that's what MEN do. Men do not resort to fighting every time somebody crosses them. Men do not threaten with words or with fists. Men talk and work through their differences. They listen to the other person. Men honor one another by their actions and by their words." Clarence was as serious as he'd ever been. "You boys have learned to defend your honor by hauling off and cracking somebody's head open whenever they insult you or disrespect you. I'm here to tell you that is wrong, and we're going to unlearn that behavior together. We're going to learn true respect and honor, especially in conflict."

He turned to Dibs. "Did you touch Jamie's things?"

"It fell off his bunk onto the floor!"

"I only asked whether you touched his things."

Dibs sat back and looked at the janitor like he was completely missing the point. The question was entirely unjust in light of Jamie's glaring faults.

Clarence waited.

"It was already open when it landed."

"That's not what I asked."

"Yes! I touched his stuff, for cryin' out loud! I only read a page and a half, but if he hadn't—"

Jamie started to his feet and both adults in the room moved to stop him.

"NO, Jamie." Clarence grabbed his shoulder and pushed him back down into his molded plastic chair. The boy calmed enough to sit still.

Officer Shilton, who had taken several steps forward, moved back again to wait.

Turning to Dibs, Clarence said, "Please apologize to Jamie."

"Come *on*, Mr. Jones, he's been a total jer—"

"Real men admit when they did something wrong. And they don't blame. They release."

Dibs couldn't believe what he was hearing. This was sissy girl talk. Nothing in him wanted to cooperate one iota. He glared at Clarence. The man wasn't backing down. Finally, he spat out, "Jamie, I'm *sorry* I touched your dumb journal."

Clarence wasn't impressed. "I don't believe you're sincere, Dibs. Try again."

Silence.

"Sugar, boy, you have no idea what Jamie might be feeling at this moment. You violated his right to privacy, gawked at his deep inner world like it was as cheap as a penny, and did it all behind his back. Now, how is he ever going to trust you as a roommate if you don't apologize like a man, and mean it?"

Dibs was stunned. That was exactly what his dad had done to him. One time when he was nine years old, his little brother Joey had come into his room and smashed his model airplane. Out of frustration, he'd punched the kid in the arm.

When his drugged up dad found out about it, he got steamed, pulled off his belt, and whipped Dibs' bottom until the blood ran. Never punished Joey at all. Never even listened to Dibs' side of the story. Wouldn't hear how he told Joey to stop at least three times. Or that he chased his little brother out of his room twice, which was the reason he finally gave the little brat a good smack.

But his dad always favored his little brother. And he cared more about getting high than he cared about either of them.

Dibs looked up from his thoughts at the ebony man he'd admired so much. "I thought you were different. But you're just like everybody else."

The Other Side Of Visible

"We're waiting, Dibs," was all Clarence said.

"Why do I always have to be the one to take the rap? Jamie's been a jerk for weeks, and you want me to apologize for one little thing!"

"We're not finished. I haven't addressed Jamie yet, but I will get to him."

After at least a full minute of silence, Dibs said sullenly, "I shouldn't a' read in your journal, it's true." He was willing to admit that much.

But the fact that his roommate was acting like a modern day hermit in a cave they both had to share was frustrating. He said exactly what he thought about such chumpy rudeness. "Jamie, what's up with you bein' so stuck-up? Why do you pretend I don't even exist? I'm not a ghost and I'm not a monster, y'know! In case you're blind, I'm a human being, just like you."

The custodian was amazed at Dibs' honesty, even if the boy hadn't quite grasped how reading someone else's private journal was devious behavior.

Dibs had one more thing to say to Pretzel Boy. "An' what are you tryin' to hide, anyway? I think it's great that you're smart an' you wanna' be an accountant. I just don't get why it all has t' be such a secret."

His head down, his muscles trembling, Jamie was silent. The custodian hoped he wasn't about to erupt again with another explosion. Just in case, he was ready.

They sat in the stillness of the empty cafeteria, Dibs staring into space with a furrowed brow, Jamie with his arms folded and his eyes lowered, and Ambassador Jones needing a few moments to quietly discern. Officer Shilton was parked behind their seats waiting uneasily for something to happen.

Dibs felt worse than he had in a long time. *All this talk of dreams and manhood and of things bein' different. But nothin's changed. It's all a big joke.* He felt like punching someone.

After some time, it was the one they least expected who

broke the silence.

"I'm sorry." Jamie sat back, unfolded his arms, and glanced at Dibs briefly before looking at the floor again.

Dibs wanted to say a big, "So what?" to his roommate, but he kept his mouth shut. This was the first time Jamie had said anything that wasn't a threat.

"I never got to keep my own stuff."

Another sentence from Pretzel Boy.

Clarence hoped the lid on the boy's fifty-five gallon drum was about to be pried off.

"It all got taken away." Jamie started to fold his arms again but changed his mind. Awkwardly, he searched for another place to rest his hands. Eventually they landed palm down on top of his thighs. After a few more seconds he said another sentence, more than he'd spoken in weeks. "I'm sorry I got so mean."

Of course, no one in the room except Jamie Ferguson knew of his former losses. They'd never met his nasty Uncle Jack, who lived with his family while he was growing up. The man had tormented him by swiping or crushing everything he valued as a boy.

Uncle Jack used people. He used Jamie's hard working parents. He used gullible co-workers. He used women. And he especially used other people's money for his gambling habit.

He used Jamie too, and often spitefully. When Jamie was given birthday presents, somehow they disappeared. Things of little value, like his toy cars, were mysteriously stomped on, or broken. His cell phone went missing, and some of his computer gear unexplainably vanished.

Jamie's parents were exasperated by their son's carelessness, but even more so with his capacity to lie straight to their faces. Whenever he claimed not to know how something had gotten busted or lost, Uncle Jack always managed to find some undeniable evidence that verified to his mom and dad he was fibbing.

Of course, his parents believed Jack's stories—after all, he was the adult—and grew more and more disappointed each time their son stubbornly insisted he was innocent.

Three years back, Jamie finally caught Uncle Jack in his bedroom, sliding his camera into a jeans pocket. When Jamie asked what was going on, Uncle Jack gave him the thrashing of his life with a threat: "You breathe a word of this to your parents and I'll kill you!" By the look in Uncle Jack's eyes, Jamie understood he just might keep his promise. And from that time on, he learned to shut his mouth and hide every single possession that mattered to him, or risk losing it to Jack's sticky fingers.

After that, whenever his parents accused him, Jamie defiantly crossed his arms and gave them the silent treatment. At school he began to steal other kids' things for himself, just like his uncle. And just like Jack's "I'll kill you," he used threats of harm for keeping himself safe, and keeping others away from his stuff.

Until now.

"Thank you, Jamie, for apologizing. I'm mighty proud of you, son." Clarence put a hand on his shoulder and smiled, purposely downplaying the fact that for the first time since they'd met, the teen was speaking.

He turned and looked at Dibs. "And I'm proud of you too, young man."

But Dibs didn't hear Clarence. Because, in spite of the fact that he was still irked at his roommate, he couldn't help thinking about what Jamie had said. Especially the part about everything being taken away. Tall Eddy had done that to him. Blackmailed him and deceived him. And when all was said and done, Eddy was the reason he got locked up again. He lost everything because of that backstabbing, slithering snake.

Shifting in his seat, Dibs cleared his throat. "Jamie, I been lied to and I been double-crossed, and I don't wanna' be like that." Now he was the one who did the eye-glance-floor-stare routine. "I'm sorry I looked at your journal." He wasn't sure what else to say, except maybe, "I won't do it again. I promise."

As quiet crept into the cafeteria and permeated the atmosphere, the custodian gazed at each boy. When he spoke, his pupils were filled with wholehearted earnestness, his voice thick and passionate. "You're figuring out two of the fundamental principles of life: honor, and forgiveness." He leaned back, and a smile replaced some of his seriousness. "Sugar, boys, if you learn to listen to each other and apologize instead of fighting to solve your disagreements, you'll be on the way to manhood."

Eyeing Dibs and then Jamie, he said, "Now I know what I'm about to say is going to seem strange. But I promise, it's for your own good." Pausing, he looked into the face of each teen. "I'm asking you to let go of the hard feelings you've been carrying against one another." He pointed to the guard standing behind them. "If you're willing to do that, to give up those offenses you've both toted around like you owned them—and if you're ready to shake hands and put aside all that anger—well, I think maybe even Officer Shilton might be satisfied that it's going to be safe to let you return to your cell."

Dibs stood up, since by nature, he was the more outgoing of the two boys. Plus, getting out of solitary confinement after being in a fight in juvie hall was a small miracle he was keen to accept.

Jamie followed his example and also got to his feet.

But they were both self-conscious and stood with their hands in their pockets and their eyes on the floor, unsure about what should happen next.

"Well, go on. You can do it," Clarence said as he nodded. "Look each other in the eye and let go of all that resentment. And shake on it as a mark of good faith."

This kind of behavior was certainly a new concept to both

boys, but Dibs was eager to try anything that could make a friend out of his roommate. He held out his hand, looked at his roommate, and spoke awkwardly. "Hey Jamie, I'm good if you are."

Managing to look him in the eyes, Jamie shook Dibs' hand. "Yeah. I'm good."

Dibs was pretty sure the expression on his roommate's face meant Jamie was as eager as he was for a change. Right then and there he decided to do what Clarence had asked. Concentrating, he imagined letting go of all the anger he had held against Jamie. It wasn't long before he could feel it seeping out of his bones, draining down his body, and falling away onto the floor. He stared genuinely at his roommate and his chest expanded with goodwill. "New start, okay?"

Jamie's face softened and he nodded. After a few seconds he grew serious again, pulled back, and threw a questioning look Dibs' way. "Yo. What's your name?"

Dibs stared speechlessly.

"We're starting over. Get it?" A tiny smile crossed Jamie's lips.

Flashing a grin, Dibs pointed at his roommate. "Aw, you got me, Jamie!" He glanced at Mr. Jones, who was looking prouder than a male peacock about something. Most likely it was the fact that instead of clobbering each other, he and his roommate had shaken hands and were finally starting to get along.

Of course, he was thrilled Jamie wasn't stone silent anymore. To celebrate, he decided no matter how many times his roommate folded his arms across his chest, he was no longer going to call him Pretzel Boy.

As they sat down in their seats again, all around them was an invisible glow coming from the absence of dark drabs, and from shinings, and from dazzles. And from the gleaming joy of the Original Family members, who were immensely grateful for Ambassador Jones' willingness to get his hands dirty for the good of the greater family.

Clarence stood and looked at the security guard, who by this time had put away his canister of pepper spray. "Officer Shilton, I do believe these young men are learning to get along just fine. Do you agree that we can send them back to their cell?"

Several creases formed on the guard's forehead while he silently considered Mr. Jones' question.

Dibs held his breath. Nervous sweat beaded up on his face while he waited to find out whether he'd be doing more time in Solitary.

Finally Potbelly Shilton looked up from his hard thinking. "Mr. Jones, for as long as I've been shuttling teenagers back and forth to janitor duty, your ability to repair the irreparable has never ceased to amaze me." He nodded and continued, "As far as I'm concerned, everything here is in working order."

Clarence returned a grateful smile. "Thank you."

Dibs started breathing again. Officer Shilton wasn't making sense. Not once during his assignment to janitor duty had he seen Mr. Jones repair even one machine. But since the guard had a little smile on his face, he decided his answer meant nobody would have to do time in solitary confinement.

Clarence motioned for the teens to stand. "Well young men, our table time has gone a little long. We'd better get busy or I'll be here all night finishing up."

They stood and followed him to the cart of cleaning supplies. He handed each one a mop and directed them to begin where they'd left off before the break.

He knew they wouldn't complete the day's workload before quitting time. But even though he'd need to stay later to wrap up their jobs, Clarence didn't mind one bit. To tell the truth, he was so happy about what had just occurred, he wouldn't have traded it for all the clean floors and windows in the city.

CHAPTER THIRTY-ONE

Amber was desperate to talk to Father Forever. In a few days Oscar, Maggie, and Madison were coming for a visit. With John's help she was supposed to tell them she wanted to stay with the Gordons instead of moving back to their house.

Her foster dad called it *facing her fears*. She called it fighting not to turn tail and run.

Father Forever had promised to be in the room with her, one reason she was willing to follow through with the whole cockamamie idea. But there was a second reason propelling her forward. Whenever she thought of leaving the Gordons, an ache would start to throb in her chest that hurt far worse than thawing fingers or an infected tooth. Out of all the times Amber had left one foster home to start over in a new placement, this was the first time letting go of a family felt as though it might make a permanent tear somewhere inside of her.

Even so, attempting this new fear-facing stuff had her feeling nervous. It was true, the Gordons were teaching her to send away those drab critters whenever they came back to try and fill her head with their notions. But it was still hard to imagine a meeting with the Owens family where everyone would leave happy. She was counting solely on John Gordon's promise that no tempers would fly and no one would stomp off in a huff.

That was why she had to talk to Father Forever. He would help her sort it all out and give her the shot of confidence she needed. He always seemed to know exactly how to encourage her, one of the many reasons she loved being with him.

Sitting in OtherSide, Amber leaned back against the familiar warmth of the wall behind her. She had landed at this exact spot on several previous visits across the veneer. The pliable floor and the slowly moving soft wall were as enormous as ever, still extending endlessly above and beyond her view. Closing her eyes, she smiled and sighed peacefully. *This wall feels just like a shining.* Its gently contracting and expanding rhythm calmed her apprehension. Her body relaxed and her mind stopped envisioning flying tempers.

After a longer than usual wait, Amber looked around. Why was no one showing up to meet her? One of the Original Family members had always come to be with her at every arrival in OtherSide. But this time she'd sat alone for at least ten minutes.

Slightly impatient, she began to stand up, when a deep roar exploded above her head. Its sound was so loud and sudden, she jumped in fright, lost her balance, and stumbled backward into the soft wall. Both the floor and the wall began to shake violently. Already off balance, and with nothing to grab onto except the silky material covering the wall's surface, Amber clutched it with both hands and held on for dear life.

Wrenching and jerking motions tossed her about like a bungee jumper swinging wildly on the end of a rope. "HELP!" she shouted to anyone who might hear. But there was no response, and she continued to be flung back and forth and every which way.

Though in reality the thunderous quaking lasted only

a minute or two, Amber thought it would never end. The jolting and jarring slowly subsided into a smoother rocking sensation, and the rumblings lost intensity. Growing faster in rhythm and higher in tone, the noise also lessened, sounding less like the cracking of a fierce storm and more like the laughter of a giant towering above her in the sky.

Amber glanced up and saw what appeared to be the top of the wall shrinking down toward her at breakneck speed. The same thing was happening to the soft floor; out at the horizon she could see the floor's end catapulting in her direction.

In the next split second, all of the shaking stopped, the sound disappeared into contagious laughter, and as though she were tumbling into the arms of a rescuer, Amber fell directly into Father Forever's lap.

"Amber! It's great to see you!" He was laughing so hard he had to catch his breath between chuckles. Wrapping his strong arms around his daughter, he gave her a hearty embrace.

She held onto him for dear life.

Embracing her for as long as she needed his comfort, he asked through lingering chuckles, "How's my little dove today?"

After what she'd just experienced, his little dove was hardly cooing.

Finally, Father Forever pried her gripping hands from his arms and gently deposited her in front of him on the surface. He bent over to look directly into her troubled face and waited.

Glancing down to make sure she was still in one piece, Amber noticed the floor surface of OtherSide was normal. No more soft material. She wondered where the wall and the odd floor had gone. But before she had time to ask, Father Forever drew her chin up so her eyes could meet his crystal blues.

"You wanted a shot of confidence for your meeting with the Owens family."

"Yeah." But what did that have to do with the thunderous shaking she'd just survived?

"Today when you first arrived in OtherSide you were leaning against my chest and sitting on my lap."

Watching his lips, she waited for something else to come out that made sense.

He stood upright. "Look at my shirt, dear one. Touch its silky white material."

Her fingers ran over the soft fabric of his shirtsleeve. "So, what does this have to do with the floor and the wal . . ." In her mind, Amber saw an image of the wall's supple texture and its warm, smooth motion. She withdrew her hand and backed away. "Th . . . the wall and the floor were YOU? They were YOU?"

He smiled. "They were!"

"But how . . . that's impossible!"

"Not if you allow your star-eyes to see it."

Gawking at the one she had called father, Amber took another step backward.

"Why are you frightened?"

She stared.

"I'm yours, Amber. I'll always be your father. That hasn't changed."

"But that was *you*? I mean, they went on forever!"

"Exactly. Shouldn't you feel more secure, knowing I'm bigger and stronger and more capable than you realized?"

She didn't answer the father she thought she knew.

"Come." He extended his hand for her to join him. "Let's go to the Emerald Pool."

Hesitantly, she put her hand in his and turned to walk alongside.

Instantly, a glittering pool lay before them.

Amber stared at her new surroundings. They'd gone

through another light door, and again, she'd missed seeing it.

Her father grinned and ruffled her hair. "Someday your star-eyes will be able to detect them."

As they walked toward the water she let go of his hand. Feeling self-conscious, Amber avoided his eyes and focused instead on the beautiful water in front of them. It was becoming obvious there was a lot more to her OtherSide family than she'd realized.

With the exception of the grassy area where they stood and a beautiful waterfall at the far end, the water was hedged in by luscious, dark green vegetation. There was something else she couldn't put her finger on—something different about the water. Something odd. She studied the pool's flickering sparkles.

Was she imagining it?

"What you're seeing is real." Father Forever said, nodding to affirm her thoughts.

Holy smoke! On Earth, she'd seen the sun reflecting off of the city lakes to create a bright, shimmering effect on the surface. But this water was being illuminated from within. Coming from somewhere inside, its light source was shooting brilliant beams upward, until they burst out onto the top.

True to its name, twinkling greens danced across the pool and caused it to glisten like a precious jewel.

Amber wanted to ask Father Forever to explain the strange phenomenon. But since she was still feeling quite awkward about his hugeness, she kept her head down and said nothing.

She knelt and put her hand in the water. Its iridescent qualities formed a miniature rainbow on her skin that sparkled green, yellow, blue, orange, and purple. *Whoa! Would you look at that!* She pulled her hand out of the water. Her skin was dry. Not a drop of water remained. Sticking her hand back under the surface, the colors reappeared, and a relaxing massage began to press against her hand. *What a great pond!*

"Would you like to go for a swim?" Her father was crouching to her right, swirling his hand through the water.

She glanced shyly in his direction and then looked away. "Me? Now?"

"Sure. Why not?"

"Well, uh, I don't have a swimming suit."

"You don't need one. You'll be dry as soon as you step out of the pool."

Amber shook her head at the funny realities of OtherSide. She thought about the fact that she didn't swim very well. Gazing out over the pool, she said, "Nah. I love the water, but I don't think I ought to. I can hardly swim."

"Don't worry, dear one. The pool will help you."

Another peculiar concept. A small grin crept across Amber's lips. Still dodging her father's eyes, she said, "You mean, like I couldn't possibly drown?"

"Exactly. The water is Mister Energy, as you've named The Light."

"No kidding!" She looked at Father Forever. "Why didn't you say so before?" Jumping up, Amber waded into the pool wearing shoes, jeans, shirt, and all. She stopped when the water level reached her waist. The pool's temperature was perfect for a swim.

Her father laughed and waded in to join her.

Incredible! She moved her hands through the water and stared at the colors on her skin.

In the worst way she wanted to tell Mister Energy how weird she felt about her gigantic father. But of course, transparent thinking ruined privacy.

"Little dove, you don't need to hide from me."

Amber's face flushed.

Pushing the water in a large arc with his hand, Father Forever playfully splashed his daughter with a colorful wave. After a second deluge came pouring over her head, Amber splashed him back and they began a small-scale water battle.

Their fun ended in a truce and they waded to the waterfall at the end of the pond. Standing underneath its stream, they let it pour over their upturned faces.

Her discomfort was fading and Amber decided to be bluntly honest. Stepping out of the waterfall to talk more easily, she said, "I was scared out of my wits with all that thunder and earthquake stuff." She glanced his way. "I know you said it was you, so it wasn't an earthquake. Or whatever they're called here."

Father Forever stepped forward and stood next to her. "Were you harmed?"

"Well no, but . . ." No more words came.

"I had you in my lap for the entire ride."

Amber automatically thought to herself, *Yeah, but I didn't know that, did I?* She looked down and waited for his mind-reading response to her angry thought.

"I brought you here so The Light's Emerald Pool could heal your untrust. In time, as you feel more secure in my fathering, a ride like that will be fun. And as for what you called thunder, that was my laughter on a larger scale."

Another bolt of OtherSide revelation traveled through his words and into her brain. How massive was he?

Father Forever said nothing and the sound of the gurgling cascade filled the air.

After a few seconds of reflection, she protested. "But I was terrified!" Amber wanted him to feel at least a little bad about how frightened she'd been because of his vigorous laughter and his turbulent shaking.

He bent down and picked up a flower floating in The Light's water. Handing it to her, he said, "You were in my great big arms, Amber. There was no need to be frightened."

"Okay. So, you were there." She sighed and squeezed her eyes shut, trying to imagine what the bungee-jumping ride would've felt like, had she known she was safe in Father Forever's lap. Envisioning the shaking wall and floor as his body and the booming sound as his voice, she tried to picture herself in the middle of his enormous arms. And finally, she saw her body falling securely into his laughing embrace.

Wild One, the name John and Jared Gordon had given to The Light, fit everybody in the Original Family. They were anything but tame.

"Little dove. Now do you think I'm big enough to love both you and the Owens family, and for that matter, every other Lightning?"

Her eyes grew as round as the pebbles below her feet. "All at the same time?"

He chuckled and nodded. "Simultaneously."

Amber hadn't even considered how many Lightnings he might spend time with at any given moment. "Holy smoke! You mean you're big enough to hang out with all of us at once?"

"Every single Lightning."

That was impossible to fathom.

"These realities only make sense when you see them through your star-eyes. Your earthling thoughts can't hold them."

She sure agreed with him on that point. It was all mind-blowing.

"Let's go and float on the water." Father Forever gestured toward the center of the pool, and without waiting for her response, he waded farther out and lay down.

Following after him, Amber was soon lying on the water, being weightlessly supported by The Light. She felt his effervescent waters massaging her tense muscles. Closing her eyes, she tried to relax, but her mind was spinning.

Rest, child. Let yourself go. I'll support you.

Hearing Mister Energy's kind words through her star-eyes, Amber intentionally lay back on his watery strength. A sense of safety slowly seeped into her being.

Until a worried thought zig-zagged through her brain

and she yanked her head up from the water.

"I'm still here." Father Forever spoke serenely from where he was floating.

"Oh." She closed her eyes and in a few minutes, opened them again to make sure he hadn't disappeared.

"I'm not going anywhere, dear one."

"But, how do you . . . ?" The young Lightning couldn't form her question into words. As far as she could tell they were alone, and Father Forever seemed to be fully present. Yet according to his explanation, he was also with other Lightnings at that very moment. The idea made no sense.

He answered her thoughts. "It's precisely because I'm so vast that I can be with other Lightnings at the same time I'm with you." He raised his head and caught her eyes watching him. "I'm big enough to take care of you, Amber."

Standing to his feet, his irises flashed azure blue. "You don't need to worry. I won't leave you as fathers on Earth have done. I will love you for the rest of your life." He held out his arms and invited her into his embrace.

She stood and waded into his hug.

The longer he held her, the less her earthling mind needed to figure it all out. After some time, she pulled back to study her father and wondered if he loved her as much as he loved the other Lightnings.

"Yes. I do."

There was no point in keeping her questions to herself. Amber blurted out, "Do you love me as much as you love the Light Prince?" She wanted it to be true, but she was pretty certain no one else could be as special to Father Forever as the Light Prince and Mister Energy. After all, they were Original Family members, and in the same way foster kids get added into real families on Earth, she was an add-in to their family.

"Look at me."

Her eyes met his, and affection washed over her. None of it was missing.

"Yes, Amber Grace McConnell, I love you every bit as much as I love the Light Prince and The Light." He cupped her cheeks in his sturdy hands. "Dear one, in our family there are no favorites."

Boy, I gotta' come back to this place again. The untrust in her brain needed some serious soaking in Mister E.'s healing waters.

"Uh huh." Father Forever agreed.

She leaned against his chest and whispered into his silky white shirt, "You are big enough to take care of me. And the Owens family."

"Thank you. Hearing you say that is music to my ears."

"I don't know how it'll work out, but if you go with me—"

He interrupted her. "I *will* go with you." Pulling back, he caught her eyes again and said, "All of the Original Family will be there, just on the other side of the veneer."

"Then I can tell Oscar the truth."

Agreeing wholeheartedly, he held her close. "Of course you can, princess! Of course you can."

CHAPTER THIRTY-TWO

During the final week of the Plastic Chair Club, as Dibs had nicknamed their daily cafeteria talks, Mr. Jones laid out a lot of new ideas about manhood that neither teen had ever before heard. For example, according to the janitor-professor, when a mean punk called you a name like "Chicken," it *wasn't* manly to punch his lights out. Supposedly, a real man either walked away or said something sincerely nice back to the jerk.

Clarence said other things that were also foreign to their thinking: that honor meant every person should be treated with dignity, and that every single human being was valuable. He told them even if someone didn't act honorably, a real man gave back honor anyway.

Dibs wasn't so sure about that, especially where Tall Eddy was concerned. He told Mr. Jones about that snake. And fortunately, the custodian agreed that if Eddy showed up, it wouldn't be dishonoring for Dibs to leave A.S.A.P. Clarence called it "Setting Boundaries," which he explained was a way of honoring yourself and valuing yourself enough to get away from people who are bad or dangerous.

Relieved to learn about that boundary concept, Dibs made a point to remember it so he could practice it in the future.

The janitor told them Eddy was still valuable as a human being, but he'd chosen to listen to the wrong side. He told Dibs and Jamie to hang around people who were listening to the right side.

On the last day of the Plastic Chair Club, Clarence quietly obtained permission to throw a little party. His wife had sent along her homemade chocolate chip cookies and a tub of vanilla ice cream, and the three of them sat and formed cookie sandwiches. Even Potbelly Shilton smiled as he chowed down on the ice cream sandwich they'd made for him.

Dibs thought Mrs. Jones' cookies were the best ones this side of Timbuktu, even if he wasn't positive where that was located compared to juvie hall. If forced to choose between a frappé and her cookies, he might've actually picked the cookies. At the moment, he was just glad he didn't have to make such a difficult decision.

As they sat chomping cookies and licking ice cream, Dibs couldn't help thinking Clarence was treating them quite honorably. For more reasons than he could count, he was sorry to see their month of janitor duty come to an end. The older and wiser custodian was a true example of a man. And in his opinion, one month of man training wasn't nearly enough. He didn't feel ready to be on his own.

As it turned out, his roommate felt the same way. Ever since the day the two of them had apologized and shaken hands, they were fast becoming friends. Each evening after dinner they sat in their cell and tossed ideas back and forth from Clarence's daily talks. Jamie still had trouble with words, so at first it was mostly Dibs who did the talking. But then they came up with a terrific solution.

The solution was that Jamie found his voice: not his vocal cords, but his way of communicating. He also talked a little, but whenever he got stuck with words, which happened quite often, he pulled out his sketchpad and expressed his thoughts in picture form. Of course Dibs loved that, since figuring out the meaning of his roommate's depictions was sort of like a game. He interpreted each drawing until he got a nod of agreement that he'd correctly understood.

They both loved having a buddy on the inside, someone else who wanted a different approach to life. It seemed most of the hall's other detainees were more interested in figuring out how to cheat the system, or in bragging about their lives on the outside of the hall, or in arguing and complaining.

They finished their ice cream sandwiches and Dibs nodded to his roommate, which was their previously planned signal. The night before, they'd spent their cell time writing a rap for the janitor. Well, his roommate had written most of it, but Dibs had helped enough to feel excited about presenting it to Mr. Jones. Incredibly, as if someone had opened up a dam and let the water flow for a short time, tongue-tied Jamie easily pulled phrases and rhymes out of thin air.

With prodding, Jamie was even willing to perform the rap. And that suited Dibs just fine. Even though he'd stopped calling his roommate Pretzel Boy, he was as curious as an explorer to see how such a quiet kid could possibly turn himself into a rapper and say all those words.

Nodding at Dibs to show he'd caught the signal, Jamie stood and pulled out a piece of paper. "We wrote a rap, Mr. Jones. For you."

Clarence looked surprised. Smiling politely, he glanced at Officer Shilton. In juvenile hall, gang language and swearing were expressly forbidden. The janitor was concerned for the sake of the boys that their gift wouldn't get them into trouble.

Jamie must have seen the worry all over the custodian's face, because he looked directly at Potbelly Shilton and said, "We made sure all the words are okay."

Shilton nodded and Clarence relaxed and sat back to listen. He was quite pleased the young men had taken the trouble to write something in the first place and just as pleased they'd followed all the rules. "Well thank you, boys! Go ahead, Jamie."

By all appearances, Jamie choked. He stopped moving and stared at the paper and thirty seconds passed.

Dibs sat forward, feeling nervous for his roommate. "Hey Jamie, I know you can do it."

Like flicking a switch, his roommate began to sway his hips back and forth. Then his chest, shoulders, and head started bopping up and down. And with a low, singsong voice he began to rap in time to the rhythm of his movements:

"Mr. Jones, Mr. Jones, we gonna' kick a flow
On manhood and what the hood ain't nevah know
You teachin' us to live like we haven't had a clue
Showin' us wordup on what's tried and what's true
On the real, you said honor and respecting one another
Ain't throwin' it down like we forget we got a mother
And since we didn't have a dad, you taught us forgiveness
Gave the lowdown on life, so we can live our bigness
Flippin' the script on what the verdict is
Nothin' seems like it is when it comes to show biz
So we givin' up the front: the hard, the mean, the tough
You the one who taught us, bein' us is enough
You the man who fix our busted dreams with a suture
You the father figure, you give us hope for the future."

As the young earthling shared his artistic expression with the other two humans, Urielle's wings pulsated to the beat, and she giggled with laughter. When the boy grew quiet again she was still shivering with glee. "Well, I didn't understand most of what he just said, but I sure do like the energy that got stirred up while he was saying it. I LOVE IT!"

And much to the amusement of Olyim and Gaelig, she started shaking her plump light-body back and forth in an attempt to imitate the human boy's physical movements. "What are you looking at?" She swayed and playfully eyed her laughing friends.

They were exchanging humorous glances, first in her direction and then with each other.

"Well now, come on," she said to Olyim, "you can do it too."

He chuckled and shook his head. "Thanks, but I think I'll pass."

"What about you, Gaelig?"

"Urielle, I do believe you're on to something." And just for fun, Gaelig started moving his feet back and forth in time with the rhythm of her movements.

After a few more giggles, Urielle slowed her dancing to take a look around them. "Isn't it great how the boy's positive creativity made the whole atmosphere throb with light?"

All three dazzles noticed their light-shines were gleaming.

Olyim said wistfully, "If human beings understood that their creativity has the potential to release shinings from our realm, they might take it more seriously."

Gaelig answered with another thought. "And if they realized their dark imaginings invite UnderSide, they might reconsider what they create."

"At least for the present, we have no drabs." Urielle placed her light-hands on her hips and added, "They don't have the audacity to come into this brilliance!"

Glancing at the earthlings, Gaelig noted the ambassador was quite emotional. He tilted his head toward the man and said to the others, "The boys' artistic gift was received."

"That was a fine present," Clarence said quietly as he sat forward in his chair.

Dibs was grinning widely. "Hey, Jamie, that was phat! You sounded just like a real rapper!" He turned to Mr. Jones to get his opinion of Jamie's performance and saw moisture swelling up in the custodian's eyeballs.

"I'm proud of both of you. Thank you very much."

Mr. Jones wiped the corner of his right eye, which only confirmed Dibs' suspicions that he was indeed crying.

Jamie had transformed back into a mild version of Pretzel Boy. With a tiny smile on his face, he held the paper down at his side and eyed the floor.

Dibs stood up next to his roommate. He also had something to say. "Mr. Jones—" a sudden gob of nerves stuck in his windpipe, and he cleared his throat. "Ahem." When he tried again, his voice cracked. "Huhnnh, ahem." On the third try, all the phlegm cleared out and he said, "I always wanted t'know how to grow up, and you been showin' me that. Before you, I never had nobody to help me." Now it was his eyes that were getting moist. He quickly took a sleeve and wiped the water away before it had a chance to slop down onto his cheeks.

All at once, Dibs felt his guts twisting and his face contorting. He fought hard to hold back a wall of tears pushing against the back of his eyelids, like a personal tsunami. But no matter how much he scrunched his cheeks and squinted and pinched his lips, all his efforts were hopeless. A full on choking sound erupted, and he stood there sobbing in front of his roommate, the janitor, and the guard.

Clarence hurdled the table with the same vigor he'd shown a week earlier, when he'd leaped across to keep the boys from thrashing each other. He wrapped his strong arms around Dibs and pulled him into his chest.

"Son, you are a great young man. I couldn't be more thrilled to know you. Go ahead and cry. Real men aren't afraid of a few tears."

That bit of news only made Dibs blubber all the harder into the soft shirt of the man he admired more than anyone he'd ever met.

Clarence pulled a clean handkerchief from his pocket and slipped it into his hand. After another minute or so, Dibs pulled himself together. "Thank you," he said quietly, and stood in a daze.

Looking over at the other teen, Clarence saw by his red eyes that he was also fighting tears. "Come here, Jamie." He held out his arms, but Jamie stood still, like the statue-boy of past weeks.

The custodian walked over, placed his hands on Jamie's shoulders, and stared into his face. "You have grown more in four weeks than I've seen anyone grow. In such a short time you've opened yourself up and let other people into your world. You're becoming a true son and I'm mighty proud of you!" Clarence pulled him into the same kind of fatherly embrace he'd given Dibs.

At first Jamie stood stiff, his arms at his sides. Then slowly and awkwardly, he began to wrap his arms around the tall ebony man. And finally he hugged him enthusiastically in return. Mumbling quietly into Clarence's shirt, he said, "I need you."

The custodian pulled back so he could look into the teen's face. "Thank you, Jamie. You need a father, and I am honored to be here for you."

Then Clarence took the opportunity to introduce an idea that he had planned to spring on them before the end of the day. He turned so he could talk to both of them at the same time. "It just so happens that I lead a group of teens. We meet once a week in the cafeteria. And now that your disciplinary restrictions are coming to an end, you two will be able to join us. That is, if you're interested."

Dibs looked at Jamie, then at Clarence. "What do you do there?"

Oh, we discuss things very much like what we've been talking about during the last month: manhood, honor, respect, setting goals for the future, how to prepare to be a good husband. That sort of thing, and more."

Dibs couldn't believe what he was hearing. "You're tellin'

me you got a group besides us that talks about the stuff we been talkin' about? Here in juvie hall?"

"Yessir, we do." Clarence gazed straight into Dibs' eyes. "And Light-Seekers are especially welcomed."

Dibs leaped into the air. "ALL RIGHT! Count me IN!" He whooped and hollered and pumped his fists in the air and jumped up and down. Then suddenly, he stopped and stood still and blinked thoughtfully up at the custodian. "Hey, how did you know I been called a Light-Seeker before?"

Mr. Jones grinned. "Just an educated guess, Dibs." He turned to include the quieter teen. "You too, Jamie. We'll be glad to have both of you."

"You in, Jamie?" Dibs leaped around enthusiastically and jerked his head toward his roomie.

Jamie's eyes were quarter-sized from watching his roommate's over-the-top reactions. He laughed and said to Dibs, "You're crazy!" And to Clarence he added, "Yeah, I'm in."

Celebrating the fact that his training in manhood would continue beyond the present, Dibs did one more round of whoops and hollers, until Officer Shilton told him to quiet down. He settled himself and asked Clarence an important question. "Hey, do you have food at those meetings?"

Mr. Jones laughed out loud and shook his head. "Sorry, Dibs. It's against regulations. Mrs. Jones' cookies are a special exception. And remember, they aren't to be bragged about with the others in the hall."

"Well, that's okay. It'll just be awesome to continue the Plastic Chair Club! Yeah!" Dibs shouted, and then remembered he was supposed to tone it down. "Sorry, Mr. Shilton," he said in a more normal voice.

The guard tried unsuccessfully to stifle a smile and shook his head at such exuberance.

Clarence decided it was time to corral the boys' boundless energies toward work. "Well, we'd best get to cleaning again." And with that, ambassador Jones and his two Light-Seekers picked up their rags and cans of dust polish and charged out of the cafeteria toward the hall's classroom wing. As they walked, the ambassador quietly released a shining to each of the teens.

For the remainder of the afternoon Dibs and Jamie worked willingly, their stomachs filled with goodies and their hearts filled with hope that the rest of their stay in juvie hall wasn't going to be so bad after all.

CHAPTER THIRTY-THREE

Amber sat at the dinner table pushing the green balls on her plate with a fork. Stabbing the smallest one, she glanced nervously at Oscar. The Owens family had come for dinner, and he was sitting across from her at the table, quietly talking to John Gordon.

After everyone was finished eating she was supposed to make her big announcement. But they were all taking their good old, sweet time. How long did it take to eat, for crying out loud?

Even if Brussels sprouts did taste kind of buttery—and not at all like dirty socks, as she'd first thought they would—with all those Lepidoptera flitting around in her stomach, Amber couldn't imagine stuffing one more bite of food down her gullet. She learned that word *Lepidoptera* from reading a sign outside the Butterfly House at the zoo.

Laying down her fork with its impaled sprout, she glanced at the people sitting around the table. The Gordon and Owens families were preoccupied with gabbing away to each other, which meant she could be incognito. She learned that word *incognito* in a sci-fi novel about an alien spy.

Sighing, Amber closed her earth eyes and tried to find her star-eyes. *Father Forever, where are you?* She waited.

Silence. *Light Prince? Mister Energy?* More silence. *Okay, I know you're here somewhere, even if I'm too uptight to see you right now.* She imagined herself sitting in Father Forever's lap. In his gargantuan lap. And soon, warmth crept into her chest that was soft, and full of comfortableness. She made up that word *comfortableness*. It was the only way to describe some things in OtherSide.

"Oh! Amber, I have some good news about Dibs!"

Oscar's voice pulled her back into the room and she opened her eyes. "You do?" The butterflies in her stomach were resting quietly now.

"Yes! Last Saturday I went to a reunion at the high school where I taught Social Studies for thirty years. My old friend Clarence Jones was there and oh, it was good to see him again." He wiped his mouth with his napkin, put it back on his lap, and leaned forward to look at Amber. "Clarence is a Lightning who taught geography in the classroom next to mine. We made for an interesting pair." Chuckling, he waved his hands in the air as he talked. "When Clarence retired from teaching he took on a part-time job. And you'll never guess where it is!" Pausing briefly as if anyone would venture a guess, when no one did, Mr. Owens continued. "He's the janitor at Emerson Juvenile Hall, the detention center for teens on the north end of the city. And Clarence has become friends with our very own Dibs!" Leaning back against his chair, Oscar looked quite pleased.

Maybe it was because they hadn't spoken directly with Clarence and didn't know about all the good things that were happening in Dibs' life, but whatever the reason, the other persons seated around the table didn't share Oscar's exuberance.

"You mean to say Dibs is in juvenile hall?"

John asked as if he was making sure he'd heard correctly.

Oscar's smile faded into a straight line at the gravity of being incarcerated. "Yes, and it appears as though he'll be there for two whole years, unless he can get time off for good behavior."

Jared, Madison and Amber all gasped at the same time. Madison said what they were all thinking. "Two *years*?"

That was practically a lifetime!

"Do you know why he's there?" Darlene asked.

Oscar shook his head. "Clarence couldn't tell me why. But he reassured me, no matter what has happened in the past, Dibs is going to be just fine." Mr. Owens' mustache twitched happily as he threw his hands up into the air again and announced in momentous tones, "Because Dibs is now a Lightning!"

"Dibs?" Amber was stunned.

Oscar's green irises sparkled with OtherSide light. "Yes, dear one, your street friend has been through the Crimson Wall."

Amber sat back in hushed awe. How Dibs happened to end up in the particular juvenile hall where Clarence worked, and how Clarence happened to be a Lightning, and how he happened to know Oscar, and how Dibs, her only friend from the streets was now a Lightning; well, the news was almost too fabulous to hold in her twelve-year-old heart. She began to feel weightless, as though the butterflies in her stomach had spread their wings and taken flight. And now they were lifting her up and carrying her along on a breeze of wonder.

Mister E. was there. His comfortableness filled her being with blissful satisfaction. She knew he'd played a big part in Dibs and her both becoming Lightnings.

That was when the name popped into her head. For weeks she'd been pondering ideas for Mister Energy's permanent name, rolling them off her tongue and sounding them out each time they came. But nothing had fit, until now.

Holy smoke! That's it! You're the biggest, hottest, most powerful light in the universe, and beyond! You're HolyFire!

Something fizzy whirled around inside of Amber. She

figured it was HolyFire approving of his new name. He made her feel so good, if she hadn't caught John staring at her with a funny look on his face, she may not have given the Big Announcement another thought for the rest of the day. But when their eyes met, something made her mindful of the fact that she still had to tell Oscar, Maggie and Madison she didn't want to live with them.

Remembering the Big Announcement made the fizzies stop immediately and caused those stupid Lepidoptera to take a crashing dive toward the bottom of her gut. All that wonder promptly turned into the old wanderlust, and suddenly she wanted to run and hide in her bedroom.

Mister E., I mean, HolyFire, help me!

Not wanting to give herself even a nanosecond to chicken out, she sat up and forced herself to blurt out rather loudly, "Uh, everybody, I have something to say." The room got quiet. She made herself keep talking. "It's about my foster care—"

"Wait! Honey, if it's okay, I'd like to speak first."

She looked over at John. Why was he cutting off her Big Announcement?

"When I'm finished, you'll understand why I interrupted."

There was a funny grin smeared across his face.

"Amber, you know Oscar and I have been calling back and forth on the phone for the last few days."

"Uh huh."

"Well, the Owens family is already aware that you want to live here as our foster daughter."

"You KNOW?" Amber gaped at Oscar, Maggie, and Madison.

Three heads simultaneously nodded her way.

She shot John and Darlene a confused look. *Why didn't you TELL me?*

John said apologetically, "Honey, it probably won't make much sense to you, but I was hoping to have some other things set in place before we all had dinner together today.

That's one reason I had to tell Oscar."

He was right about one thing. It made no sense.

Darlene grinned proudly. "But just being willing to talk to them shows you've already conquered your fear. You won, Amber!"

The blood returned to Amber's brain. Her nerves stopped tingling, and all the butterflies in her gut flew the coop. Exhaling in relief, a dry patch in her throat made her cough. She thought it was probably caused by a leftover butterfly wing that had stuck to her esophagus on the way out.

She glanced in the direction of Oscar and Maggie. "Boy, after all those foster classes you took so I could live with you, I sure thought you'd be mad!"

Oscar eyed his family and smiled. "When we heard what John had to say, the three of us sat down and talked about it. And we think staying here with the Gordons is perfect for you."

John stood up and came around the end of the table, that goofy smile still stretching his face sideways. Darlene got up and moved next to him. Plastered across her face was a silly grin that looked just like the one he was wearing. Jared jumped up and stood beside his mom, hiding something behind his back and flashing a teenage version of his parents' kooky expressions.

Amber thought they were acting *quite* strangely.

Nudging his glasses with a knuckle, Jared promptly produced a pink T-shirt from behind him and held it up for her to see. The words "I'M A GORDON" were printed in dark blue across the front of the shirt.

"Here, this is for you."

Blushing, Amber took the T-shirt and grinned back at them. "So this is why you guys were giving me strange looks." She held the shirt up to her body. "Thanks. I like it!" Even if she was technically their foster kid, the Gordons sure had nice ways of making her feel included.

John's smile turned serious and he cleared his throat like he was starting some sort of important speech.

"Amber, we've loved having you as part of our family—"

Jared interrupted him. "So what we'd like to say is this—" he stopped and motioned for his mom to complete his sentence.

Amber made a face. *They are definitely acting weird.* She noticed water beginning to float around Darlene's eyeballs.

Finally, her foster mom finished where Jared had left off. "Amber, we want to adopt you!"

"That is," John was quick to add, "if you want to become part of our family, we'd love to adopt you. I've put in a call to your caseworker to explore the idea. Of course we'll have to check on your birth mom's rights and go through the proper channels of the legal system. But it's all dependent on what you want. There's no rush for a decision, so take your time and think about it."

When she heard Darlene and John both say the word "adopt," a wave of emotions welled up in Amber's stomach and surged into the places where the butterflies had flown. The wave washed upward and billowed around her pounding heart, swelled into her throat, and sounded like the ocean as it sloshed higher into her ears. Finally, its breakers crested over her mind, and her head began swimming, and her brain blew a fuse.

"Honey?" Darlene was kneeling, looking intently into her foster daughter's face. "Amber? Are you okay?"

The water level was blurring her vision, and Amber's voice was as tight as the locks of a canal. She managed a nod to her foster mom before burying her face in her hands.

Darlene moved closer. "So you *like* the idea of being adopted?"

Her head nodded harder as tears coursed down Amber's cheeks and ran through her fingers.

Darlene stood, pulled her foster daughter to her feet, and

hugged her hard.

Amber squeezed back with all her might: more vigorously than she'd ever hugged anyone on Earth in her entire life.

John's cell phone rang. Normally, he ignored incoming calls during family times and let them go to voicemail. But it was Yvonne Williams, Amber's caseworker. Her timing couldn't have been more perfect. Walking eagerly into his office, he shut the door and pressed the answer icon on his phone. "Hi Yvonne! Thanks for calling me back."

The voice on the other end of the line said, "Hello John. How is Amber?"

"She's doing just great. In fact, never better." He didn't bother mentioning to her that Amber was currently shedding a bucket of happy tears because of his family's version of a big announcement. "So, you got my message about wanting to adopt Amber?"

"Yes, I did. And you're wondering how to proceed."

"Exactly."

"Well, since Amber's whereabouts were unknown during her time on the streets, her birth mother's parental rights were never terminated. The first step would be to file a request in court for termination of those rights. Since Ms. McConnell hasn't responded to any inquiries, and neither has she come to any of Amber's weekly parental visits—and because no other relatives have come forward to claim Amber—I may be able to include that request in the next scheduled review of Amber's case."

"Great. That review is coming up, isn't it?"

"Let me take a look at your file and I'll tell you the date."

John flipped to the calendar app on his computer and answered his own question. "It's on Wednesday, the ninth."

"Yes, that's right. At two o'clock, in courtroom number five."

"Perfect." John ran the fingers of his free hand through his hair. "And once those rights are terminated, we can begin filling out the mountain of paperwork for Amber's adoption, right?"

Yvonne Williams laughed. "You know the system well."

John grinned and added an off-the-cuff remark. "Since the birth mother's been a complete no-show, won't the hearing to terminate her rights basically be a formality?"

For a few moments there was silence, and then Yvonne Williams answered, "I'll be honest with you John, we've seen every scenario, with every possible outcome. But let me add that, assuming there are no changes during the next two weeks, I see no reason for any surprises concerning Amber's case."

Silence filled the airwaves while John's brain filtered through what he was hearing.

"Now, don't start worrying. As Amber's caseworker, I'll certainly do my part by giving the judge a strong recommendation on your behalf. Your family has done wonders for her."

"Thank you." John released an involuntary sigh.

"Do you have any more questions?"

"I don't think so."

"Then, I'll see you soon."

"Okay, thanks again, Yvonne."

"You're welcome. Good bye."

"Bye." John disconnected and sank down into his office chair to reflect for a minute on the phone call. He would've preferred a less ambiguous answer to his question about the termination of parental rights. But Yvonne had said, barring any legal surprises, in as early as two weeks they might be able to begin adoption proceedings. That was good news.

John's chest filled with grateful warmth as he stood to rejoin the others. Before he opened the door, he paused and breathed his thanks to everyone across the veneer.

Darlene, Jared, and the entire Owens family were gathered around Amber. Her face was radiant. Even though her eyes were red and blotchy from crying, she didn't seem to care.

"Dear one," Oscar was saying to her, "I would love if you would consider me your grandpa."

"And I'll be your Aunt Maggie," Mrs. Owens added, her voice fighting to climb over a lump.

Madison pushed past the Gordons, grabbed Amber around the waist, and squeezed enthusiastically. "And you and I can go to the mall together!"

Amber laughed and cried and laughed some more. She wanted to remember this moment forever. It was rich and full and complete, like standing under the waterfall at the Emerald Pool and letting the water pour down over all of her. Not only did she have a real family, she had an extended family, with honest-to-goodness relatives. The kind she could grow up with and visit on special days and holidays.

The invisible atmosphere swelled with an unearthly glow.

"The Original Family is here! I can feel them!" She turned around in a circle to try and find them through her star-eyes.

"Of course they're here. They're celebrating as much as we are!"

Jared's words were as true as crimson. The Original Family *was* celebrating. Father Forever and the Light Prince were right in the middle of all the human hugging. And HolyFire was filling the room with a glistening explosion of Amber yellow.

Rahzell and Ahnah and a passel of dazzles were also celebrating. They shimmered and shouted and shot about in a glorious display of light and speed and cheering. They reveled, because they understood the view of the royal family, which was high and wide and encompassed all things past, present, and future. The young princess was safe. And her days of distinction were only beginning.

Aware that OtherSide was swirling everywhere, Amber looked around. Moved with an intense desire to belong to these people, to live with them and spend her life with them, she felt for the first time what it meant to be in love. "I have the best family in the whole world!" A surge of unseen energy made her laugh and she corrected herself. "I have the best *families* in *both* worlds!"

And deep in the center of her true and noble heart, Amber knew she'd finally found home.

GLOSSARY OF TERMS
USED IN THE OTHER REALMS

Ambassador: a Lightning who has spent much time visiting with the Original Family in OtherSide. As a result, they have highly developed star-eyes.

Color: a.) the unique OtherSide tone given to an earthling. **b.)** a substance Light Stealer hates and wants to remove from Earth. **c.)** one or a combination of components comprised of hue, saturation, and brightness. **d.)** constituents of light that can be separated into differing bands of hues on a spectrum.

Crimson: the OtherSide color of the Light Prince. When found on Earth, crimson is a shining.

Crimson Wall: formed from the Light Prince's crimson, it is the large outer wall surrounding OtherSide, through which every Light-Seeker passes in order to have their star-eyes opened.

Dazzle: powerful beings created from OtherSide light, who serve the royal family of that realm. When serving in Earth's realm, dazzles can also be called Watchers.

Drabs: beings composed of UnderSide darkness, who exist and operate in that realm. Underlings of the Light Stealer.

Emerald Pool: an iridescent body of water made of The Light. Located in OtherSide's region of Morning Glow, it contains healing properties.

Fire's Flame: the region of central OtherSide, and home of the royal family's mansion.

Garden Of Possibilities: a.) a large garden with an endless variety of OtherSide vegetation, including trees, shrubs, herbs, grasses, ferns, mosses and flowers. It is located in southwest OtherSide. **b.)** where Lightnings go to dream and imagine.

Hearth White: the region of the outer rim of OtherSide.

Homecome: a Lightning's final and permanent crossing of the veneer into OtherSide.

Laser-sword: a weapon similar in shape to an earth sword but made of OtherSide light. Used by dazzles. Also called a light-saber.

Light Door: a portal through which one steps as a means of timeless travel in the realm of OtherSide.

Lightnings: a.) an all-encompassing name to describe earthling members of OtherSide's royal family. **b.)** what Light-Seekers become when they pass through the Crimson Wall. **c.)** On Earth, lightning is a release of electricity between a cloud and land, or within a cloud, and occurring with a bright flash and/or thunder.

Light-Seeker: an earthling who is looking for more than the ordinary gray life but has not yet been through the Crimson Wall.

Light Stealer: chief of UnderSide. Hater of light and color.

Mansion of the Royal Family: the home of OtherSide's greater royal family, located in the region of Fire's Flame, in central OtherSide.

Manual Of Nobility: a large, often leatherbound, animated book using OtherSide colors and language to tell the story of the Original Family and their love for the greater royal family. Serves as a portal through which The Light may be experienced on Earth.

Morning Glow: the region of north central OtherSide.

OtherSide: the royal realm of the Original Family. Invisible to earth eyes, it encompasses Earth, Earth's universe, and far beyond. It is entirely separate from the realm of UnderSide.

Original Family: the indigenous royal kin of OtherSide. The family is comprised of Father Forever, the Light Prince, and The Light.

Recolor: the restoration of a human being's true OtherSide tone, effected by the opening of their star-eyes as they pass through the Crimson Wall. Recoloring enables earthlings to perceive color on Earth.

Royal Family of OtherSide: comprised of OtherSide's ruling Original Family and all Lightnings of their bloodline appointed as royal family members and given royal status and authority.

Shining: a release of The Light into Earth's realm.

Star-eyes: OtherSide eyesight. A human's star-eyes are located in the center of their true and noble heart.

Transparent Thinking: communication within the realm of OtherSide that occurs without the use of spoken words, by perceiving, thinking, seeing, sensing, feeling or hearing.

Treasures: royal presents unique to each individual that are placed inside their true and noble heart at the time of their conception, in order to be opened at a later time.

True And Noble Heart: where star-eyes are located in a human being. The place within an earthling that holds memory of their OtherSide color and OtherSide treasures.

UnderSide: a.) the lightless realm ruled by the Light Stealer. Invisible to human beings, UnderSide includes the realm of Earth and Earth's atmosphere, but is entirely independent of OtherSide. **b.)** where drabs exist.

Veneer: the unseen divider separating Earth's visible realm from the invisible realms.

Watcher/Watching: the assignments and/or actions of dazzles in Earth's realm, including protecting, strengthening, encouraging, and helping human beings.

ABOUT THE AUTHOR

The Other Side Of Visible is a story about two young people orphaned through life's circumstances, who each carry in their heart the dream of a better life.

Janet Keller Richards understands what it's like to have the heart of an orphan, even while growing up in the middle of a committed earthly family. It was her orphan heart that led her to striving in order to feel loved and accepted. But pushing relentlessly to gain the approval of God and others is tiring. Her striving slowly turned to fatigue, which eventually led to exhaustion.

Thankfully, kind and wise counselors (who are part of the real invisible royal family) led her through a journey of healing for her orphan heart. Slowly, self-hatred turned to self-acceptance. Rejection began to fall away. Her ability to receive love increased. And her friendship with the Original Family became more real.

Her journey has given her some important insights. That bravery is admitting our need and taking action to pursue cleansing and healing of our hurts and wounds. That courage is not giving up until we experience true healing, recognizing that much of the process is gradual, rather than instantaneous. That Father Forever rewards us for our bravery and courage. And that joy is: discovering who we are in the eyes of the real Original Family, knowing our purpose on Earth, and walking through life in vital friendship with the real Original Family.

To all the brave and courageous ones, I cheer for you, and so does the Original Family!

A SECOND NOVEL AND A STUDY GUIDE

A storyline has been growing for **another imaginative fiction novel** filled with exciting adventures, unexpected challenges, and new discoveries on Earth and in OtherSide. Like *The Other Side Of Visible* it promises to be creative, chock-full of fun, and a source of encouragement for readers of all ages.

Also being considered is **a study guide** to explore the spiritual realities hidden within the story of *The Other Side Of Visible*. With an interactive style, the guide will use allegorical concepts from the book as a springboard to search for exciting discoveries in the Bible. Here are a few possibilities for topics of discussion:

"How can I spend time with the Original Family?"
"If I'm OtherSide royalty, how do I live like it on Earth?"
"How can I learn to use my star-eyes?"
"But I don't *want* to think about drabs!"
"Can I release shinings on Earth?"
"Do I have an OtherSide color?"
"Light doors, and other supernatural phenomena in the Bible."

Sign up on the author's website to receive email updates:
www.janetkellerrichards.com

GRATEFUL THANKS

There are many wonderful people who were an incredibly important part of the process of this book. To all the spiritual mentors and teachers who have sown into my life priceless gifts of relentless love and patient wisdom, thank you! A special thanks to Dawna De Silva and Teresa Liebscher, and to Chester and Betsy Kylstra, for much wisdom on how to help heal hearts.

Thanks to these friends and fellow writers who took the time to read rough drafts and give great editing feedback: *Lisa Betz, Soleil, Ellie, Araunah, Elijah, Liran,* and *Joash Boll, Lynne Burkholder, Michele Chynoweth, Dawna De Silva, Rebecca Hazelton, Cathie* and *Chloe Kearsley, Joan Lavery, Angela Leigh, Carole Nicolas, Sue Orth, Cathy Poole, Alana Smith, Matt* and *Megan Steinruck,* and *Marian Yoder* (huge apologies if I missed someone's name).

Thanks to *Bill (William) Beck, Jr.,* for terrific advice on crowdfunding, marketing, and publishing. Thank you to graphic artist *Mark Nicolas,* to website whiz *Matt Steinruck,* and to publisher *Bill Beck Jr.,* for taking time to create multiple book cover ideas. And again, thanks to *Matt Steinruck* of Big Picture Studio, for creating an awesome website!

Laurie Parke, thanks for your expertise on certain true-to-life aspects of the story. And to these teens and their parents, who helped in portraying the book's characters through photos and video segments, thank you: *Ella* and *Serge Lehman, Darien* and *Sandra Good,* and *Hopelynn* and *Diane Hauser.*

Last, but not least, merci-grazie-thanks to my husband *Rusty Richards,* who listened graciously as I read aloud each newly written portion of the manuscript. As always, your large doses of love and encouragement are a Godsend!

THANKS TO THESE CONTRIBUTORS

There is another group of people I want to thank. Many friends and family members gave to an Indiegogo crowdfunding campaign to raise funds for the first printing of *The Other Side Of Visible*. Whether great or small, whether anonymous or known, every single donation is greatly appreciated. Books can change lives. My heartfelt thanks to each of you—whether your name is printed here or not—for making a difference!

For those of you who gave to the Indiegogo campaign at the Double Decker level or above, one of your fun rewards was the promise of mentioning you by name as a contributor to the printing of this book. Thanks for your kind, Double-Decker-Plus generosity!

Craig Beck
Jeff & Sylvia Beck
Kevin & Soleil Boll
Bruce & Joan Boydell
Hope Carpenter
Valerie Claxton
Larry Cox, Jr.
Darrell & Twila Eberly
John & Ann Gibbel
Doug & Dina Hamilton
Don & Jean Hoover
Lloyd & Elaine Hoover
Carl & Becky Hudson
Kevin & Lesley Hurst
Brent & Bonita Keener
Dorothy Keller
Jeffrey Keller
Barry & Julia Knabb
Mark & Ferne Kraybill
Marsha Lauck
Serge & Angie Lehman
Elwood & Nancy Martin
Ruth Morris
Frank & Becky Noviello
Jeff & Sue Orth
Stephen & Lisa Pidcock
Paule Pobloske
John & Bonnie Reilly
Dwayne & Susan Shank
Alana Smith
Jim & Char Snyder
Jean Stephenson
Ben and Mary Ann Stoltzfus
Tonya Weiler
Chris & Holly Wert
David & Priscilla Williams
Keith & Marian Yoder
Albert & Janet Zehr
Henry & Lydia Zook

AMBER'S HOPE

It's time for every human being to know they are loveable, and to know God is the One doing the loving. Some portrayals of God are true. Unfortunately, many are not. God is often blamed for bad things that happen, or he is presented as an indifferent religious being who only wants to be worshipped. Or worse, he's seen as an angry, ruling tyrant.

The Other Side Of Visible has presented God as deeply loving, as eternally dedicated to human beings, and as passionate about walking with us in devoted friendship. In an era when hopelessness and godlessness have permeated much of our culture, this book shouts a different message. It speaks directly to the hearts of its readers with an engaging portrayal of God's good nature.

If this book has touched you in some way, it can also touch others with the same warmhearted encouragement. For people who already know God, *The Other Side Of Visible* provides a fresh perspective filled with hope. For those who have not yet recognized His work in their lives, this book holds out an invitation from God to enter into relationship with Him.

If the message of this book has stirred your heart, we invite you to pass it on. Here are some ways you can impact the world around you, by doing just that:

Word of mouth is still the best idea. Tell your friends and family, the neighborhood grocer, your peers, and others, what you loved about this book.

Give this book as a gift to friends, family, acquaintances, coworkers, and even strangers. Books can give a fresh perspective and open people up to a new way of thinking.

Donate copies of this book to prisons, halfway houses, homeless shelters, churches, youth groups, agencies, and anywhere hope is needed.

Social Media: if you have a Facebook Page, Twitter or Instagram accounts, a website, or if you're a blogger, consider recommending the book and sharing information/photos from the "Sharing Toolkit" found on the author's website at www.janetkellerrichards.com. Presenting quality descriptions and images of *The Other Side Of Visible* via your social media outlets creates exposure and interest with people you know personally, as well as in the wider sphere of your social media followers. You can also share your impressions on internet forums or via Facebook live, or through other video sites.

"Like" the author's Facebook page (Janet Keller Richards), or search using this username: @othersideofvisible. Share the author's Facebook Page and her username on your own Facebook Page, and tell your friends why you loved the book.

Other media expressions: if you've got a connection to a radio station, suggest they interview the author. Or, call your favorite radio show host and share your thoughts about the book—media people care about what their listeners think. Do you have connections to news outlets? Consider writing a review for your local newspaper, or for your favorite magazines, or for work or school websites and newsletters.

If you purchased your copy of this book on Amazon, consider writing a review of the book. The more reader reviews, the more exposure Amazon will give to this book, which will enable more people to discover and encounter the life within its pages.

If you own a business, consider displaying this book on your counter and making it available for sale.

For more information, or to be kept up to date on future creative works, sign up for occasional email communications via the author's website at:
www.janetkellerrichards.com

Thank you for sharing Amber's hope!

WHAT OTHERS ARE SAYING ABOUT
THE OTHER SIDE OF VISIBLE:

"As a leader of the International Sozo Ministry, I enjoyed seeing how Janet's insights in *The Other Side Of Visible* shed light on the unseen realm. Ephesians tells us, "We fight not against flesh and blood but against the rulers, authorities, powers of this dark world, and spiritual forces of evil in heavenly realms." Many believers have forgotten this truth. *The Other Side Of Visible* is a fresh blend of a Frank Peretti novel and *The Shack*. It does a great job of revealing the invisible realities around us, and will enable families to openly talk about what they internally hear, feel, and are responding to. Way to go, Janet!"

—*Dawna De Silva, Founder & Co-leader of Bethel Sozo International; Author, Atmospheres 101; Shifting Atmospheres Lecturer*

"Janet Keller Richards has woven together a heart-wrenching yet delightful inspirational story about the plight of two homeless young people who must choose between their dark but familiar lives on the streets and finding a better way. Anyone who believes in God, angels, and miracles will be thrilled with this mystical fantasy!"

—*Michele Chynoweth, Award-Winning Author of "The Faithful One," "The Peace Maker" & "The Runaway Prophet"*

"Janet Richards is a highly articulate writer who brings characters to life. Her imagination is boundless. The Other Side Of Visible is a page-turner you won't be able to put down. You will be entertained, engrossed and encouraged from cover to cover."

—*Mark Nicolas, graphic designer, artist, husband, father, & grandfather*

"We read The Other Side Of Visible as a family and experienced the Kingdom of heaven together! Through the story's allegorical images, abstract spiritual concepts were transformed into experiential understanding. Our relationships were deepened as we took the journey together. It was definitely one of the highlights of our family's spiritual walk!"

—*Soleil Boll, wife, & mother of five wonderful children*